Sacrificial Sins

Book 2,
The Sins Volumes

Fiction by

Mary Elizabeth Gaines

Mary Gaines Books

Sacrificial Sins

© 2018 by Mary Elizabeth Gaines

Published by Mary Gaines Books

First Printing August, 2018

Printed in the United States of America

All rights reserved. No part of this publication may be reproduced, stored in a retrieval system, or transmitted in any form or by any means (i.e, electronic, photocopy, recording or otherwise) without the written permission of the copyright owner/author.

Library of Congress Control Number: 2018905285

Mary Elizabeth Gaines, 1950 –

Sacrificial Sins

Book 2, The Sins Volumes

Mary Elizabeth Gaines

ISBN 978-1-7320026-4-7   Paperback Edition

ISBN 978-1-7320026-5-4   E-book Edition

This is a work of fiction. Names, characters, places, and incidents either are the product of the author's imagination or are used fictitiously, and any resemblance to actual persons, living or dead, events or crimes is entirely coincidental.

Cover Art and Design by Chuck Creasy

Sacrificial Sins

This book is dedicated to my dear Mother,

Loretta Butler Crosslin

(1922 - 2010)

"All that I am or ever hope to be, I owe to my angel mother."

— Abraham Lincoln

I am thankful for the many blessings bestowed

Upon me by God, Our Heavenly Father.

This book would never have been written without

His spiritual guidance and inspiration.

— Mary Elizabeth Gaines

Sacrificial Sins

OTHER BOOKS BY

Mary Elizabeth Gaines

Buried Sins

(Book 1, The Sins Volumes)

A Standalone Mystery Novel Available Now

Twin Sins

(Book 3, The Sins Volumes)

Sequel to "Sacrificial Sins"

Coming Winter 2018

PROLOGUE

It was definitely true what people said. When you're about to die, your life flashes before your eyes like a fast-forward movie playing inside your head.

He wasn't terrified as he always thought he would be. Instead, he felt peaceful. Not at first, of course, when he realized what was about to happen. But now that his mind had settled, he accepted the fact that death was inevitable. He embraced it.

As your life's blood drips from your veins, at first you think, *This can't be happening to me. It only happens to people in movies—or bad people in real life.* Then you come to realize that eventually it happens to everybody. Maybe not in the same way, but death takes you when it's your time. It can come at any moment, and you'd better be ready.

His mind had already forgotten the intense pain that had come first. Now all he felt was the warm, steady trickle of liquid life as it collected in scarlet pools beneath him. His eyes were closing involuntarily, and he thought maybe it was time to give in to everlasting sleep.

But then he saw her face. A quick jolt back to consciousness made him smile—she probably couldn't tell, since his facial muscles didn't move. But deep inside, he was happy to see her. He wished he had the strength to tell her that she was in danger, but his mouth wouldn't work. He hoped she could read his fading mind; if she could, she would know that she had meant everything to him. He wished he could kiss her one last time and show her that his love was still strong, even now. But alas, it wasn't going to happen. This was no movie.

He closed his eyes and prayed silently that God would protect her, the love of his life.

Realizing he had only a few more seconds left to breathe the earthly air, he succumbed to the comfort of impending death. His last thoughts were of the kiss they had shared only a few hours before. He let himself go as he remembered the look in her eyes when their lips had first met, and then again as they pulled away from each other.

Those eyes—those beautiful, sad eyes—he would never look into them again.

And then, there was light... .

CHAPTER 1

Friday, November 11, 1994 — Thursday, December 1, 1994

He gently laid the stethoscope on his wife's bulging stomach and listened for the baby's heartbeat. Smiling, he could tell that the baby was not in distress. The delivery should be easy for both the baby and the mother.

Douglas Brantley, the prospective father, was a registered nurse with fifteen years' experience with various local hospitals, including a five-year assignment in the maternity ward of the largest hospital in Knoxville, Tennessee. His background in obstetrics gave him the confidence he needed to convince his wife that he could deliver their baby with as much expertise as any high-priced obstetrician in the area. He had the experience and the skills, but he had more than that. He was in love with this soon-to-be mother and the baby she carried.

His wife was easily swayed and quickly convinced that Doug should be the first to see and touch their newborn baby. A home delivery was their plan; and from all indications, today, November 11th, was the day.

Stella Brantley had been in labor for almost seven hours, but she didn't call her husband at work until the pains were four to five minutes apart. By the time Doug arrived at their Lenoir City home, her contractions were only two minutes apart. Stella had dilated to eight centimeters.

"Stella, baby, are you sure you can handle natural childbirth?" the concerned husband asked. "It's not too late to get you to a hospital if you'd rather get an epidural. We'll do this however you want. I just want you to be comfortable, but you have to decide now." His eyes were misty from anxiety, happiness, and an overwhelming sense of love for his wife and unborn child.

"Doug, it's okay," the meek wife answered. "Just guide me through what I need to do so our baby can be born safe and sound."

Oh Lord, please help us through this, she silently prayed while she held back tears of pain and fear.

"Stella, this is gonna be a cinch, darling. When it's all over, you'll be wondering why you were so anxious about bringing this little baby into the world." Doug was trying hard to help Stella stay calm. He thought it had been working until another sharp contraction hit her.

Within 45 minutes of harder and faster contractions, Stella was ready to deliver her infant. Doug handled himself like a first-rate obstetrician. The delivery went smoothly. There were no complications. The baby appeared to be perfectly healthy without visible abnormalities.

He presented the screaming baby to his wife, and they cut the umbilical cord together. Doug cleaned the baby, suctioned all the proper areas, and laid his healthy newborn son in a bassinet next to his exhausted wife's bed. Also sitting at the foot of the bassinet was a 15 inch bear with "Teddy" embroidered on a white bib around its neck.

The new mother rested her head on her elbow, peering over the side of the bassinet to watch the wriggling infant adapt to his new surroundings. She imagined her future toddler dragging around this new fuzzy bear who was watching over him even now. She also thought "Teddy" sounded like a fitting name for her son.

* * * * * *

The Brantleys of Lenoir City, Tennessee, were doing well by the week after Edward Theodore Brantley was born. Teddy seemed to limit his crying to times when he was uncomfortable. As soon as his diaper was changed, he was quiet and happy again. He ate on a regular schedule, so he wasn't allowed to stay grumpy from hunger. He was absolutely no trouble at all

to his parents. He slept through the night, waking up after seven hours for his next changing and feeding. Teddy was precious.

Doug had carefully filed all the legal paperwork to register little Teddy's home birth, expecting the original birth certificate to be mailed from Nashville within two to five weeks. Meanwhile, Doug had gone back to his job at the government facility in Roane County in the employee infirmary. Stella was going to return to substitute teaching after the baby turned six weeks old. Everything was progressing at a normal pace, and milestones were being met without concern.

But then came the morning of November 21st when little Teddy wouldn't rouse from his sleep. Stella found him lying on his back in a pool of vomit, apparently having choked on milk and spit-up.

She called Doug at work, telling him he had to come home because the baby was in trouble. By the time he arrived, the baby had already turned blue. He tried CPR, but to no avail.

He gave the hysterical Stella a hefty dose of her prescribed pain medication, telling her not to worry because the baby would be fine. He said Stella needed to rest, assuring her he would take care of little Teddy while she slept for a while. Stella, still in shock, did as she was told.

* * * * * *

Doug cleaned Teddy and dressed him in a warm outfit, complete with cap and gloves. Bundling the cold baby in a crib blanket, he carefully placed him back in the bed.

With Stella now soundly asleep, Doug went to his garage to retrieve a shovel, then trekked into the wooded property adjoining his back yard. He found a spot near a leafless oak tree where he began to dig a small grave in the frozen winter ground. Afterwards, he came back inside the house and picked up the tiny bundled corpse.

He walked slowly back to the burial site, clutching his dead son to his chest as he sobbed louder with each step.

"Lord, forgive me for what I am about to do. Please accept this child in your waiting arms. He deserves to be an angel. And please forgive us for our sins," the grieving father prayed as he laid the baby in the shallow grave. He covered the infant with another layer of blankets before pitching the cold dirt atop the tiny bundle.

When he finished, he scattered leaves across the fresh grave. The heartbroken father marked the burial site with stones laid in the shape of a cross. He collapsed to his knees and shed the mournful tears of a wounded soul.

* * * * * *

On December 1, 1994—ten days after the Brantleys lost their newborn son to SIDS—another pregnant wife was making her way to the New York University (NYU)-Winthrop Hospital in Mineola, New York. Her driver was determined to take her to the closest hospital from her home, even though her neurologist husband practiced at the New York Presbyterian Hospital in Manhattan.

Their house on Long Island was miles closer to the hospital in Mineola. Their driver was panicking, knowing that babies ready for birth would make their appearance whether in a hospital or in the backseat of a car. Cathy Giordano was expecting twins, and she wasn't comfortable enough to risk the long car ride to Manhattan, either. Cathy agreed with her driver on going to the closer hospital. She called her husband, Lorenzo, and asked him to meet her at NYU Winthrop.

Cathy's mother had already arrived from Nashville, planning to stay as long as needed to take care of the Giordano's one-year old daughter, Sophia. The proud grandmother and toddler waved at Cathy as the

vehicle accelerated out of the circle driveway heading west to the nearest hospital.

* * * * * *

The female staff at New York Presbyterian Hospital thought Dr. Lorenzo Giordano should have been a Hollywood actor or perhaps a model for Armani. The classic lines of his face—combined with his olive complexion, dark hair and deep blue eyes—only added to his mystique and allure. On countless public occasions, he was often mistaken for a movie star.

He was a regular at the gym on weekday mornings and an avid runner. As a result, his custom made clothing fit him almost too perfectly. Admiring women thought that Catherine Parker had married well above her standing, and certainly above her own level of beauty. Some ladies often remarked that it was "sad when a woman's husband was prettier than she was."

Lorenzo would have gladly given up his good looks and wealthy doctor's lifestyle to be rid of a situation that had planted itself in his life during the past two years. His cousin, Tony Caprio, was a "made man" in a local crime family, and he had occasionally coerced Lorenzo into situations where a closed-mouthed doctor was needed to attend a wounded comrade. Extravagant payments for these services made Lorenzo believe he now had an unbreakable, long-term commitment to his cousin's crime family. He was becoming their go-to doctor even though he never intended to assume that risk or long-term responsibility.

During this two-year period, he had also accumulated a significant gambling debt to the same crime family. The debt had grown to such a hefty sum that Lorenzo couldn't timely scrape enough money together without finding a supplementary loan source. His cousin offered to back him with the needed cash, but demanded repayment in thirty days at 25% interest.

When Lorenzo arrived at his office on the day the twins were born, he immediately called his cousin to request an extension on the approaching payment date. His cousin Tony was not happy about the delay, which made Lorenzo more than a little nervous about his continued welfare and his family's safety.

Tony told Lorenzo they would have to talk about the payment terms over dinner that night. They made their plans and thirty minutes after they hung up, Lorenzo was notified that Cathy was on her way to the hospital in Mineola. Lorenzo's mind was in a dark and distant place as he travelled to NYU Winthrop that day to join his wife and meet their newborn twin sons.

* * * * *

When Lorenzo approached the fathers' waiting room at NYU Winthrop, he was met by the delivery nurse coming from the opposite direction. "Doctor Giordano, you and your wife are the parents of two beautiful babies. You have twins! Fraternal twin boys! They are both healthy and are in the nursery getting all their measurements taken. They're getting cleaned up to meet their father. If you'd like to follow me, I can show you the nursery window where you can get a quick peek at them before you go see your wife. Mrs. Giordano is doing very well, by the way."

As an afterthought, the nurse made another comment. "Oh, and there's a birthmark on the lower center back of one of the boys. It's quite unusual and looks like a little red diamond."

Lorenzo Giordano smiled, thinking of his own similar birthmark. Whichever baby got the "Giordano mark" would certainly grow up to do great things.

Dr. Giordano was still somewhat stunned as he followed the nurse toward the nursery area. He never expected the babies to arrive so quickly. He thought for sure Cathy would go through hours and hours of labor,

probably lasting throughout the night. Regardless, he was glad that the hard part was over for Cathy. Now he could get back to work without this distraction. Cathy and the boys would be in good hands at NYU Winthrop.

The nurse and new father arrived at the open nursery window, but Lorenzo only glanced at his crying baby boys. His mind was filled with concern about his secret gambling debt deadline he had failed to timely meet. Even the brief vision of his newborn twins wasn't enough to lift his spirits and allay his worry.

* * * * * *

Stella Brantley was in such a continued state of shock and confusion that her husband felt obligated to get more and more sedation medication for Stella to help her get through the tragedy. Gratefully, he took it from whoever handed it to him – usually friends from hospitals who knew she had a baby but was still in pain from the delivery. If that wasn't bad enough, as a last resort Doug stole valium from his workplace inventory when no other sources could produce. He never divulged to anyone that the baby had died. He told his co-workers and friends that Stella was suffering from severe postpartum depression, but the baby was progressing well.

He kept Stella sedated even when he knew he shouldn't, because he couldn't bear to face her true grief. He couldn't bear to face his own, either. Instead, he encouraged Stella to hold the Teddy Bear that was wrapped in the baby's blankets since that seemed to keep her content.

Soon the befuddled Stella began to think of the bear as her own son, alive and well. She would rock the bundle in her arms for hours, often singing lullabies and trying to feed "Teddy" with an empty bottle. When she laid it in the crib, she would sit by the bedside and rub "Teddy's" back with her hand. She always positioned the surrogate Teddy on its stomach for some

reason, but she couldn't remember why. Whenever she left the crib side, she would turn on the music box mobile to entertain the bundled "baby."

As long as Doug could keep supplying Stella with strong drugs and encouraging her to accept the substituted bear as her newborn, he believed he could eventually ease her back into reality. He didn't exactly know how to make it happen yet, but he planned to find a way. He became more desperate with each passing day.

* * * * *

Before he left his office for the day, Lorenzo Giordano called his wife at the hospital to ensure she was still doing well and to check on the babies' status. He told Cathy that he had an unavoidable business dinner that evening and requested that Cathy get some uninterrupted rest while she could. He promised her he would be by to see her first thing the next morning.

With that out of the way, Lorenzo drove to West 53rd Street to meet his cousin Tony at Patsy's Italian Restaurant. Tony was a regular there, having a favorite table reserved in the back corner.

When Lorenzo arrived, Tony was perusing the wall of framed pictures of actors and aristocracy. He spied Lorenzo as he came through the door.

"Enzo, my friend, my cousin! Congratulations on the birth of your sons, may God Almighty protect them. I think this night calls for a celebration!" Tony looked over his shoulder and barked, "Sal, a bottle of your best champagne for Dr. Giordano and me, eh? How about it, Enzo?" Tony wrapped his arm around the back of his much taller cousin.

"What are you gonna name the little tykes, huh? Maybe Little Lorenzo or Antonio, eh?" Lorenzo made no move to answer, but hesitantly smiled. Tony laughed loudly while Lorenzo struggled to keep his emotions in check.

"Hey," Tony said as he slapped Lorenzo on the shoulder, "We'll talk about that later. Come, Enzo. Sit here at my table. What a great night, huh?" Cousin Tony seemed to be in a good mood, despite the dreadful reason for the meeting, but Lorenzo was still unable to relax.

As the two men took their seats in the far corner of the restaurant, Sal arrived with the champagne Tony had ordered for the celebration. Tony approved the taste, and both men were served the finest bubbly that money could buy, at least at Patsy's.

Tony, always in control, ordered dinner for them both.

Lorenzo cleared his throat, trying awkwardly to delay their financial conversation with more talk of the new babies. "Tony, I never thought I would be the father of a son; twin sons, at that. It's going to be amazing trying to figure out their distinct personalities and seeing what kind of trouble they get into. I'll get to watch firsthand all the things I've always wondered about. Do they think alike? Do they get the same vibes and know when the other is in trouble? I've wondered what it would be like to experience this phenomenon. I suppose Cathy and I will find out for ourselves, now."

Tony took a bite of his salad, washed it down with champagne, and then cleared his throat. He looked his cousin Lorenzo straight in the eyes and said without flinching, "Well, Enzo, that's just it. You might like what I offer you better than living that suburban dream with twins." He didn't comment further and stuffed more salad into his mouth followed by a piece of bread.

Lorenzo was confused; a tight knot in his stomach was trying to rebel. His anxiety was heightened, probably—at least in part—due to dousing it with champagne before eating. "I don't understand, Tony. What are you trying to say? That you want me to take a job somewhere away from the kids?" Lorenzo inquired.

"Did I say that you had to move somewhere? You don't listen. I said I could offer you something better than you trying to figure out the twin-thing in the suburbs. Geez, you don't listen good." Tony was getting peeved.

"All right, start at the beginning and explain it to me, Tony. I'm all ears." Lorenzo stared straight into Tony's eyes awaiting his thorough explanation.

"Look, here's the deal. You owe over $1,000,000 to the Viper, right?" Tony began.

"It's $1,500,000, to be exact. I can only come up with half by the due date this week. If I could have another month, it would be doable. Everything I have is on paper, and it takes a while to convert those assets to cash." Lorenzo was sweating heavily, not certain where the conversation was going.

Tony continued, "Well, the Viper is willing to forgive the $750,000 shortage if you will do something for him. Something a little more personal, perhaps?" Tony smiled as he shoved a toothpick into the corner of his mouth.

Lorenzo looked straight at Tony and shook his head vigorously. "I am not killing anyone, under any circumstances." He took a huge gulp of champagne.

Tony started laughing again, acting as though Lorenzo had just told the funniest story he'd ever heard. "God, so you're a comedian, now. Why would *we* want *you* to do murder? That's crazy! You'd get caught trying to pull off something like that. You don't have the balls to do something so gutsy." Tony kept laughing.

"Well, for God's sake, what is it you want from me?" Lorenzo blurted out.

"Well, for starters, how about a newborn baby boy? You keep one, we get one. Fair is fair, and your debt is clean. No boogie men following you around to break your fragile surgeon's fingers or hurt your precious little family." Tony couldn't have been any plainer.

"I can't do that. I CAN'T DO IT! Do you know what you're asking? How could I possibly do that? Why would the Viper want a baby, anyway? Why *my* baby?" Lorenzo was having trouble thinking clearly now that the full offer was on the table.

Tony answered simply, "Hey, he don't tell and I don't ask. But I hear it has to do with the black market and how people pay a premium for healthy babies to adopt. They don't get hurt or nothing. It's not sex slavery or nothing like that. It's just people who want to have a baby so bad they pay the highest price to get 'em. I swear nothing bad will happen to your baby. He'll get a good home with good parents. At least that's what the Viper says. Oh, and he needs the baby by the weekend. Short notice, I know."

"And what if I don't agree with this arrangement?" Lorenzo asked through gritted teeth.

Tony smiled, closed his eyes for a long second, and then looked into Lorenzo's eyes. "My dear cousin, you do *not* want to find out. It might mean the end of your lucrative career when your hands or brain don't ever function right again,...or it could mean your dear wife might have an accident from which she may never fully recover, ...or maybe one of your children will be kidnapped by someone else anyway. No matter what, you'll still owe $1,500,000 to one nasty motherfucker who will want to collect anything and everything from you until he's bled you dry. Get the picture now, Enzo?"

Lorenzo stood up, threw his napkin down on his uneaten salad and walked toward the restaurant's front door. He turned to look at his

cousin one last time, and with hate-filled eyes, reluctantly nodded his agreement with the horrible plan. He was trapped and had no other way to keep his family safe.

"Dear God! Damn Tony. Damn the Viper. Damn all those people who are trying to force me to do this reprehensible thing. And damn me for being such a fool in the first place."

* * * * *

Lorenzo went home and walked straight into his young daughter's bedroom. He kissed the toddler's forehead, being careful not to wake her. He then moved to the adjoining room where he peered into the newly remodeled nursery. His eyes locked on the twin cribs and the duplicate sets of blankets, mobiles, and nursery supplies.

He wondered how he was going to make one of the boys disappear without involving the police. He wondered how he could live with the resultant guilt that would haunt him forever. He wondered if he could even make it happen within the two day deadline. He wondered if he would allow himself go through with it.

CHAPTER 2

Friday, December 2, 1994 — Sunday, December 4, 1994

Doug Brantley left his workplace on Friday afternoon, happy that the business week had finally ended, but not looking forward to spending the next two full days with his delusional wife. It had been shy of two weeks since the baby had passed, and Stella had remained in a state of drug-induced fantasy the whole time. Doug was running out of medication for Stella. He knew that sooner or later, they were both going to have to face a sobering reality.

He had already pushed his limit at the dispensary, taking a few pills here and a few pills there, hoping that the year-end drug inventory count wouldn't be off by much. He wanted somehow to replace the stolen drugs before then; but, if he couldn't find a new source for Stella, how could he find one to cover the drugs he had already pocketed?

Doug's desperation was affecting his work in a negative way. Assuming that his mind was on his wife's bout of postpartum depression, his co-workers tried to cover for his trivial mistakes. No one suspected that Doug's problems ran much deeper than his wife's unfortunate post-delivery mental state. Maintaining a pleasant work façade was placing an untold stress on him. He was barely making it through the week without breaking down and confessing the truth to anyone who would listen.

* * * * * *

At the same moment Doug was leaving his work station, Dr. Lorenzo Giordano's private phone line rang in his medical practice office.

The caller spoke quickly. "It's all set for Sunday night. Be at this phone number Sunday afternoon at three o'clock for the details." The line went dead. Lorenzo didn't recognize the messenger's voice, but he could tell the call was made from a payphone near a busy street.

He gathered his things, then turned off the overhead light in his office. He made his way out of the medical building and toward the Long Island Railroad for his nightly commute. With Cathy and the babies still in the hospital, he had no idea what kind of abduction plan could be executed under those circumstances. Cathy and the twins probably wouldn't be released from the hospital until Sunday morning, if his guess was right.

In his heart Lorenzo still hoped the Viper was playing some kind of sick joke on him or somehow testing his loyalty. Lorenzo prayed that the Viper would change his mind and demand the cash instead of the newborn baby.

* * * * * *

When Doug got home from work, he found Stella asleep on the couch with the muted television on. The portable baby bassinet was pulled up close to the couch, allowing Stella to keep careful watch over the bundled bear she believed to be her baby. Doug purposely made very little noise as he navigated through the front part of the house to the bedroom to change out of his work clothes.

He stood before a chest of drawers that held much of his clothing. In one narrow top drawer, Doug had saved old cards and letters from friends and family members sent throughout the years. An envelope corner stuck out of the side of the drawer and caught his eye. He pulled open the drawer

and surveyed its contents. He dug through the jumbled papers until he found one particular letter, written almost fifteen years before, promising Doug help if he ever needed it. He took the letter out of its small envelope, read it again, and laid it on top of the chest for easy retrieval. He smiled a genuine smile for the first time in nearly two weeks.

Stella didn't rouse when he came back through the living room to make his way to the kitchen. She snored loudly, sleeping deeply. Doug was thankful for her slumber, knowing that it would give him a reprieve from having to converse with her for a while.

He started making grilled cheese sandwiches and tomato soup for their dinner. By the time the food was ready, it was apparent that Stella was out for the night. Doug ate his meal silently, wrapped up Stella's portion to save for later, then helped Stella get into bed for the evening.

She whispered, "Where's Teddy?" as she rolled her head from side to side on the pillow. Doug gave her the bundled bear which she clutched closely to her bosom. She drifted off to sleep again, leaving Doug alone in his distress.

* * * * * *

"Honey, are you still asleep?" Doug whispered softly toward his wife's shadowy body in the dark bedroom. No response. She had been asleep for over two hours and made no signs of stirring. He moved into the room and tiptoed toward the chest of drawers.

After taking the letter from the top of the chest, Doug backed out of the bedroom and into the hallway. He entered the guest bathroom and shut the door, locked it, and read the short message again:

Sacrificial Sins

Doug

   11/1/79

I know it was hard for you to do what you did for me last night, and only a true friend would have handled it the way you did. You are a genuine friend and I will never forget it. No matter what you need, I'll be there for you. I am in your debt forever. Count on it.

John

Remembering the circumstances that prompted the letter to be written required some memory jogging, but it all came back to Doug in vivid detail.

During the years Doug attended nursing school, the only other male in his classes was John Sanderson. Naturally, the two guys struck up a friendship which lasted throughout the school terms and beyond. However, their friendship bond was forever sealed during an off-campus Halloween Party in 1979.

Doug had lost a significant amount of sleep trying to cram for important exams that he had completed during the previous two days. When the tests were over and he was no longer driven by adrenalin, his body rebelled. Doug wanted nothing more than to crash for days in his own bed. John had been sitting for the same tests; but in contrast to Doug, he appeared energized and mentally sharp.

John coerced Doug into attending the nurses' annual Halloween party, promising Doug that he would introduce him to some of the girls Doug had been too shy to approach. Doug reluctantly went along, thinking he could sneak out early to get his needed rest.

At the party, John introduced Doug to a red-haired student nurse. Afterwards, John disappeared into the crowd. Feeling socially awkward

with having only school in common, Doug tried to keep the conversation going but could feel the girl's attention drifting away. She tried to ask him about his outside activities and hobbies, but he clammed up. He was too embarrassed to tell her that he liked to hunt squirrels and rabbits in the country. When he offered nothing else to converse about, the student nurse said, "Excuse me," and went off in another direction. Doug was left alone, scanning the room for John's familiar face.

"Help! Help!" a loud and panicky voice screamed from the hallway. "Help him! Help him!"

Doug raced down the narrow corridor to find his buddy, John, lying in a pool of his own vomit. John was having difficulty breathing. Doug cleared most of the crowd from the hallway and went to work on John. He asked for a rundown of the minutes before John fell. The few people who had been near him overheard John say he was going to wash down his last upper with some liquor. He got the pill and the first shot down, then got strangled on his second bourbon shot and started throwing up. Then his eyes rolled back, and he collapsed on the floor.

Someone in the back of the room said, "I'm calling an ambulance."

Doug screamed, "NO! IT'S UNDER CONTROL! Don't call anyone yet!"

Time stood still for everyone, as no one moved an inch. Doug pulled back John's eyelids enough to examine his pupils. By now, John was taking shallow breaths. Doug picked up John's legs and dragged him into the bathroom, shutting the door behind them in an effort to keep all the gawkers in the hall.

Doug put a fully-clothed John under a cold shower, then slapped his friend's face hard enough to cause John to try focusing his now half-opened eyes. Then he proceeded to stick a toothbrush far enough down John's throat to induce regurgitation of what remained of the undigested liquor and drug.

Eventually John became alert enough to walk out of the bathroom on his own. Within hours, he was sober enough to realize what a life-altering mistake he had almost made. John later told Doug he was forever indebted to him for saving his life and keeping the embarrassing incident out of a police report or hospital record. John knew his future might have been permanently derailed—or quashed— if Doug hadn't taken control of the situation and handled it the way he did.

Years later, John abandoned his nursing career in exchange for a step higher on the medical profession ladder. He became a Physician's Assistant, taking a position within the Department of Energy (DOE) complex at Brookhaven National Laboratory in New York. He always hoped to someday become an M.D., but time was slipping away from him, and he was losing enthusiasm.

* * * * * *

Doug didn't know how far John would be able to go to help him in his current situation, but maybe he could provide him with some judicious and unbiased advice. He was the only person Doug believed he could trust with the truth about Teddy and Stella.

After several failed attempts through directory assistance, Doug finally placed a call to a John Robert Sanderson in Hicksville, New York. The call went to an answering machine after four rings, but the voice on the taped greeting sounded like that of Doug's friend.

"Hey, man. This is Doug Brantley, your old nursing school buddy from way back. If you are the John Sanderson I'm trying to reach, give me a call. I need some advice from someone I trust, and you are that guy. My number is 615-555-4556. Hope you're well, and I'm looking forward to getting your call real soon. Thanks, man."

Doug hung up the phone but continued to stare at it, willing it to ring. Without interruption, he sat alone in his living room by the light of the muted television until he fell asleep for the night on the couch.

* * * * * *

Early Saturday afternoon, the doctors at NYU Winthrop allowed Cathy and her healthy newborn twins to be released to go home. As Lorenzo picked the three up in his Range Rover, Cathy noticed that two perfectly matched baby seats were secured in the back. She was pleased that Lorenzo had the forethought to mount the necessary baby seats to the car's backseat hooks. She smiled at her husband in whom—at the moment at least—she saw no faults. He was going to be a great father to the boys, just like he was to Sophia.

* * * * * *

Sunday morning was a beautiful day in The Town of Oyster Bay. Cathy and Lorenzo stood on their patio overlooking their private backyard gardens. They had their arms wrapped around each other's waists, with Cathy's head leaning on Lorenzo's shoulder.

"So what are our plans for today, Dr. G?" Cathy said in a whispery voice.

"I need to go in to the office for a while. I have an operation scheduled for tomorrow morning. With all the running with the babies, I ran out of time before leaving Friday." Lorenzo was doing his best to find an excuse to be away from home during the afternoon and evening hours.

"Well, I may just go to a movie if Mother will keep all three babies. But, you know what? That's not a good idea. I guess I'll just stay here and watch a little television or read something. I'll figure it out. Don't worry," she remarked.

"Well, I'm not going anywhere until after lunch, so we may as well make the best of our time," smiled Lorenzo.

"Oh no, you don't, mister. Not this soon. The bedroom is off-limits for a while. But we can choose names for our little boys. The hospital was upset that we hadn't decided yet," said Cathy.

"I've already come up with the names. The strong one—the one with the family birthmark—will be Francesco Lorenzo Giordano III. The other one will be Enrico Salvatore Giordano. How does that suit you, Cathy?" Lorenzo asked, holding his breath.

"Ah, um… Enrico Salvatore? Where did that come from?" Cathy questioned.

"Great-great-grandfathers or something. They're all family names. Come on, honey. We can call Francesco "Frankie" and Enrico can be called "Ricky" or whatever nickname you like. What do you say, Cathy?" Lorenzo pleaded.

"Does it mean that much to you to name them with old family names?" Cathy wanted to know.

"It does, my love. It does. They are my sons. I never thought we would have sons to carry on the Giordano name."

Cathy smiled and threw her arms around her husband's neck. She kissed him on the cheek and whispered in his ear, "Then I approve of the formal names if I can give them my own nicknames."

"Deal." Lorenzo squeezed Cathy tighter, nuzzled her neck, and then kissed her on the mouth. "And now the deal is sealed with a kiss," Lorenzo grinned.

A stray tear trickled down the side of his face. Cathy wiped his cheek with her soft hand, thinking how sentimental her stoic husband had become

about the babies. When Lorenzo took Cathy's tear-stained hand and kissed it, he realized the next few hours were all that remained of little Enrico Salvatore's life as a Giordano.

* * * * * *

By Sunday afternoon, Doug still had not received a call from his friend John. He wondered if he had reached the wrong person's answering machine on Friday night. He tried to remember what he said when he left the voice message. He thought he had provided a call back number, but now his doubts were clouding his memory. He was no longer sure.

Doug planned to try directory assistance once more before Sunday afternoon was over, hoping to zero in on the correct John Sanderson. If he didn't reach John today, he would try to reach him tomorrow at his workplace, the Brookhaven National Laboratory (BNL) medical department. That would be an easy call to make from Doug's own government facility medical office.

Stella had slept off and on through the day Saturday and was stumbling around in a fog when she was awake. Sunday wasn't starting out any better. Doug's heart was broken, knowing he had transformed this beautiful vivacious woman into a zombie-like creature—or more like an over-drugged inhabitant of a psychiatric mental ward—by regularly feeding her hefty dosages of anti-anxiety and sedative medications, not to mention the painkiller narcotics.

Guilt was hitting him hard, and he felt helpless to change anything until he could get a grip on a viable plan. So far, he still had no idea how to get himself and Stella back into a normal state. He knew before long the substitute bear was going to have to go. He couldn't let her keep up that fantasy much longer. But that would bring on the grief and the heartbreak she had yet to feel. An endless cycle of crying and mourning

and counseling would be on the horizon for them both. He didn't want to think about it right now. He was taking things one day at a time.

* * * * *

When the phone finally rang at 3:00 p.m., Doug was startled and almost knocked over a glass of iced tea as he reached toward the receiver to answer the call. He heard his friend John on the other end of the line, and relief flooded Doug's body at the sound of John's welcoming voice.

"Doug, you old son-of-a-gun, how ya been? It's been so long—too long—since I heard from you. How are you anyway? How's Stella?" John gushed with questions.

Doug hesitated a moment, then gave his friend an update of the past few weeks. "We were great in early November, with Stella's pregnancy progressing so well. The baby was born here at our house, and I delivered him. It was a boy, and he was such a good baby."

John interrupted his friend, "What do you mean 'was?' Did something happen, Doug?"

Doug couldn't hold it in any longer. He broke down into muffled sobs; John could barely understand what Doug was saying. Eventually Doug regained his composure, managing to explain exactly what he and Stella had been going through since the baby died.

"Geez, man. I can't believe all this has happened. What are you going to do? You can't keep Stella drugged forever. And before long there will be people wanting to visit the baby. In fact, I'm surprised that hasn't happened yet. Do you think you should go talk to the police or the hospital personnel to report the baby's death?" John wasn't sure he knew how to handle such a legal/emotional issue like the one Doug described, not to mention the stolen drugs from Doug's workplace.

"John, I thought maybe we could talk and figure out the best route to take. I don't have anybody else to talk to that I trust. As each day passes, this mess gets bigger. I gotta have some sound advice soon or I'm going to be the one that really goes crazy." Doug started to sob again.

"Okay, man. Let's look at this logically. You have several problems. The first problem is you lost a baby and didn't tell anyone, plus you buried it and didn't tell anyone. Your second problem is your wife thinks a teddy bear is her baby because you've drugged her so much she doesn't know any better. And the third problem is you stole some drugs from work to help out your wife." John was spot-on in his simple synopsis.

Doug nodded and said, "Yeah. That's all true. No matter what I come up with, it just seems like having another baby would solve everything – except the missing drugs. Another baby is the obvious answer."

"Doug, babies take a long time to develop, you know. If you think you're gonna impregnate Stella while she's on all these drugs, then run her back through the maternity ward in nine months, that's a stupid idea. You have to solve this problem here and now."

By now, John was shaking his head in amazement on the other end of the phone. He paced in circles while he tried to think. "The way I see it—if that were even a viable solution—you'd need a newborn and you'd need it fast. I can't tell you how to get a newborn fast, just that I agree that another baby would solve all your problems but the drug one. I imagine that problem would be much easier to fix so let's not concentrate on that—you still have some time to work on that one," John stated.

"Can I buy a baby somewhere?" a half-joking but desperate Doug said. "Is there such a thing as a baby black market?"

John was stunned that Doug would ask such a thing. "They have black markets for anything and everything, I guess. But that doesn't mean you

can easily find them or afford what they offer if you do locate them." They sat in silence for another few seconds.

Then Doug asked John the one question that hit the nail on the head for them both: "What would you do if you were in my situation? How would you help your wife?"

John didn't hesitate to answer, "I'd probably try to steal a baby for her." They both sat silently holding the phone receivers to their ears.

After a few minutes, John started talking again. "But Doug, you can't do that, you know. That's wrong. And that's an insane idea, anyway. You just can't kidnap some baby. That's illegal."

Doug came back with a quick response, "And you think secretly burying a baby in the back yard and stealing drugs from the government is LEGAL? I think I've already travelled that road before, so what's one more crime?"

John was quiet again, letting his mind take in all the information and outrageous comments he had heard during the entire conversation. He could hear Doug softly sniffing on the other end of the phone, causing a tremendous sense of sorrow to overtake him. He wanted to help his friend, but he truly didn't have any idea about how to go about it.

"Listen, Doug. Let me think on this overnight. I'll call you at work tomorrow—I can find your number through the Federal Directory. And for God's sake, you stay calm. Don't do anything rash. Let me see if I can find out some things. There may be other ways to make your wish come true. I'll call you before the end of the work day. Act naturally, and let me look into it for you, okay? I promise I won't divulge anything you've told me. And I'll act like I'm doing a research project or something, all right? Can you hold on a little bit longer, Doug?"

Doug squeezed his eyes shut as his tears rolled off his face and onto his shirt. "Yeah. I can make it at least one more day, John. Thank you."

"Welcome. I'll do whatever I can for you, buddy. You know that." John's mellow voice could hardly be heard by the weeping Doug.

As he hung up the phone, Doug tried to relax and think positively, hoping that everything would work out for the best. He heard Stella in the living room bumping into furniture. *One day at a time*, he told himself. *Let's get Stella comfortable and back to sleep. There's always hope for tomorrow.*

CHAPTER 3

Sunday, December 4, 1994

Lorenzo entered the physicians' medical building promptly at 2:45 p.m. on Sunday afternoon, and hurriedly proceeded to the bank of elevators situated beyond the expansive lobby. He punched the backlit elevator button, commanding the lift to deliver him to his third floor place of business.

Once inside the massive double doors of the suite, he bypassed the office reception area, walking directly to the staff break room. He took a short juice glass from the shelf above the coffee station, then briskly walked down the back hallway to his locked office.

F. LORENZO GIORDANO II, M. D.,

NEUROSURGEON

The large gold leaf lettering screamed his name on the frosted glass pane that covered almost the entire heavy door. Usually, the sight of his high priced office door gave his ego a boost, reminding him of the many years of hard work it took to get there. However, today he was ashamed of himself for being so much less of a man than he thought he'd ever be. He was a coward and a liar, and he was about to accommodate the very man who wanted to rip his family apart. In agreeing to the horrendous plan, he had turned himself into scum—a sniveling coward who would voluntarily fling his son into an unknown future with God knows who, just to save his own selfish hide.

Lorenzo reached in his credenza to withdraw a bottle of single malt scotch. He poured himself half a glass, expecting to need a heavy drink to get through the phone call scheduled ten minutes hence. He gulped half of it down, saving the last half for after the call.

The phone rang just as Lorenzo opened his desk drawer and located a fresh notepad and pen. He reached for the phone; he leaned back in his chair, rubbing his eyes as if he were trying to wake up from a bad dream.

"You have two tickets to a Broadway show in your car's front seat. Go home, get your wife, and take her to dinner and the show. Don't come home before 11:00 p.m. If you have a preference, put a blue ribbon or some other noticeable indicator on the baby you want to keep. If not, we'll take whichever one we can get to the fastest." The phone went dead.

Lorenzo swallowed hard. The Viper was actually going through with the appalling plan. If Lorenzo tried to stop it, he would end up dead or maimed; the rest of the family would never be safe. Based on Tony's veiled threat, the baby would be kidnapped at some future point anyway—with or without Lorenzo's assistance.

Lorenzo drained the rest of the scotch from the glass and poured another helping. He contemplated alternative choices he could propose to the Viper, but soon realized there were none.

Still sitting behind his desk, Lorenzo reluctantly telephoned Cathy. He instructed her to get ready for a celebratory dinner, including an evening on the town. He told her he thought his beautiful wife deserved a special indulgence considering all she had been through lately. Lorenzo asked her to be ready to leave the house by 7:00 p.m. at the latest.

Cathy was reluctant at first, concerned that her Mother might not be comfortable taking care of two infants and a toddler with no help.

Lorenzo convinced Cathy that the babies would be asleep most of the time, and Sophia would be in bed by 8:30 p.m.

Hesitantly, Cathy agreed to go; however, she would have preferred staying home, allowing herself to recover rather than rushing back into the New York social scene.

Apparently Lorenzo, the great and powerful neurosurgeon, isn't concerned that the babies are only three days old. He must have forgotten that a new mother needs rest and time to heal after the trauma of childbirth. Lorenzo never thinks of anyone but himself, Cathy thought.

She also wondered why her husband would even consider having an evening "on the town" the night before a scheduled surgery. That thought kept nagging at her while she went through the process of choosing her evening clothing and accessories. She tried pushing the question from her mind, but it kept reemerging.

* * * * * *

John Sanderson stared at the wall for several minutes after hanging up the phone with Doug. Remembering their past together, he never pegged Doug as being the kind of person who would get himself into this kind of situation. Even before John's Halloween "incident," Doug was the procedure junkie of the two men: he always chose to strictly follow rules and obey authority. As far as John knew, Doug never even got a traffic ticket.

Now divorced, John had no current significant other through whom he could channel his thoughts or emotions. His ex-wife, Caroline, hadn't wanted children, so there were no lingering family attachments with her. The couple had split ties, going their separate ways with mutual respect and no financial issues. For that, John was thankful. However, he did miss having a warm, soft female body to snuggle up against at night. As for Caroline herself, he still had feelings for her, but he denied how deep

those feelings still ran. At least he was allowed to keep custody of their lovable beagle, Lucas, who would never ignore him or argue with him over insignificant details.

His solitude did provide him with a perfect venue for pondering problems, hypothetical situations, and emergent issues. This new event in Doug's life was something John wouldn't wish on anyone, especially not a friend. However, John knew he wasn't experienced enough to provide quality counsel to Doug for such a catastrophic and complex legal issue. Being the private person that he had become, he couldn't think of any trustworthy sources he could immediately turn to for advice.

But John excelled in research techniques; and fortunately, he was employed at a facility with an expansive library chocked full of resources. On a late Sunday afternoon, the library would be relatively empty by the time he grabbed something to eat and drove the hour's commute to BNL. For now, he had defined his first tactic in a yet unclear overall strategy to help Doug and Stella. He grabbed his facility badge, clipping it on his belt loop. After assuring Lucas he would be back soon, John left his Hicksville, New York, home to start his quest for potential solutions.

* * * * * *

As the curtain was opening on *"The Glass Menagerie,"* Cathy Giordano began to feel an uneasiness that she couldn't control. She squeezed Lorenzo's hand in an attempt to settle the butterflies that were fluttering in her stomach.

"Lorenzo, I feel a little funny. Do you think we could leave?" Cathy whispered as she leaned her head toward her husband's ear.

Lorenzo heard his wife, but pretended that he didn't. He glanced at her and smiled, squeezing her hand back, and then turned his head toward center stage.

"Lorenzo, didn't you hear me? Can we leave please? I feel strange. I need to go. We can see this play another time," she asked in a louder voice.

"You're just a little jittery because you left the babies at home. Come on, Cathy. Try to relax. We both need this time away from the house," her charming husband replied as he winked at her, once again turning his head back to the action on the stage.

Cathy tried to settle herself more comfortably in her seat, but to no avail. She was nervous and anxious, but she didn't think it was solely because she had left her children at home with her mother. This feeling was more of an internal alarm, or a red flag signal that something was not right.

She eased herself out of her seat, attempting to slide past the couple seated immediately to her left. As she made her way to the lobby doors, she felt Lorenzo's hand on her shoulder trying to slow her down. She lingered in the wide theater aisle when she stopped to let him catch up to her. When he was a pace behind, she hurried toward the double doors leaving him in her wake.

When they were both on the lobby side of the theater doors, Lorenzo was walking briskly beside his wife. "Cathy, wait. What is it, honey? Why can't you enjoy your night out?" Lorenzo asked her as she turned to look at him.

"I don't know. Something feels wrong. I need to call Mother," she said as she turned toward the bank of pay phones in the lobby alcove.

Lorenzo tried to catch her arm again as she turned, but she was too fast for him. She started digging for coins in her evening purse before she made it to a phone.

Lorenzo glanced at his watch, noting that the time was 9:35 p.m., much too early to start making their way home. He couldn't think quickly

enough to keep Cathy from making the call, so he tensely stood behind her as she dialed the number to their house.

"Mom? Is everything all right? I had a sinking feeling, and wondered if it had to do with the babies or ...   I know, Mom. I'm sorry. ….. Okay, you too. Love you." Cathy hung up the phone and looked embarrassingly toward her anxious husband.

With a sigh of relief, Cathy relayed the conversation to Lorenzo. "Mom said all is well. The children are all asleep, sleeping soundly. She said we should have a good time, and I should stop worrying about the children. They're in good hands."

Lorenzo smiled, kissed his wife on the cheek, and took her arm. He led her back to their seats. They stayed through the entire performance.

* * * * *

Genevieve Parker shook her head as she hung up the phone with her daughter. *Cathy was always a worrier*, she thought as she raised her tea cup, taking a tiny sip of the lemony lukewarm liquid. She laid her head back in the overstuffed chair, kicked off her slippers, and propped her bare feet on the matching ottoman. She thought about turning on the television to catch the news, but she was fearful the noise might rouse the children. Instead, she picked up the latest issue of "*Redbook*" magazine and thumbed through the pages of the Christmas edition.

Within ten minutes, she began to feel drowsy. Reading at night always did that to her. *I must really be getting old if a recipe can put me to sleep*, she thought as she laid down the magazine and started to rise from the chair.

A crash from the kitchen startled her into alertness. Before she was out of the chair, a masked man with what looked to be a shotgun emerged from

the kitchen doorway. He pointed the gun directly at her and motioned with the gun barrel for her to sit back down.

"I don't have much money, but you can take what I have. My purse is in the chair in my bedroom. Take it, take it all. Please …" Genevieve pleaded with the intruder.

 A second man emerged from behind the gunman, dressed all in black like his partner. He, too, wielded a long barreled gun and wore a mask. Neither man said a word, but they nodded in code to each other.

The second man approached the trembling woman, pulling a switchblade from his pocket. He theatrically sprung it open, waving it in the air for effect. When he moved the shiny blade close to Genevieve's face, her eyes followed its path closely. Her eyes crossed momentarily as she tried to inch back from the knife that now rested on the side of her nose.

"Please! Please! Don't do this! What do you want? I'll cooperate, just tell me what you want!" the whimpering woman pleaded.

 With his other hand, the menacing intruder pulled duct tape from his pocket, tearing off a long strip. He pulled a thick paper napkin out from under her tea cup. The intruder roughly stuffed it in Genevieve's mouth, securing the tape across her wrinkled, lipstick stained lips. She groaned and tried to scream, but the sound was muffled. Her captor slapped her hard across the cheek before covering her eyes with another piece of long tape.

 After her eyes were completely covered, both men removed their masks. The first intruder moved toward the nursery while the second continued to deal with the terrified woman.

The sniveling Genevieve tried to scream again, but another harder strike to her face shut her up. She urinated in her seat, causing the second captor to back away for a moment, audibly sighing with disgust.

He grabbed her hands as she tried to fight him from her chair, but his strength overtook her in seconds. He wrapped duct tape around her coupled wrists. Next he grabbed her ankles. He efficiently locked her ankles together, and then he wrapped the tape tightly enough to hamper her circulation.

The first intruder came back down the hall carrying a bundle in a white blanket. Protruding from the blanket was a tiny head covered by a blue nursery cap. Again, they nodded to each other and proceeded to make their silent getaway.

Genevieve Parker sat scared and blindfolded in the urine-soaked chair waiting for help to arrive. She had heard nothing uttered from the intruders' mouths before or after they bound her with tape, only the crash from the kitchen. She assumed that was a glass pane in the back door, but she wasn't certain.

She prayed the children were not disturbed or hurt during this dreadful ordeal. She knew that anything of value taken from the house would mean nothing to the Giordanos as long as their children weren't hurt. Surely Cathy and Lorenzo would be home soon to rescue them all. She prayed for time to pass quickly, but her prayers weren't answered.

*** * * * ***

From outward appearances, Vincenzo "the Viper" DeLuca fit the image of an intelligent, successful businessman who loved his family more than he loved his own life. He looked much younger than his 56 years, and attributed his youthful appearance to kale juice, organic foods, and regular saunas. He detested cigarettes, preferring to hold an unlit pipe in his mouth. He often was featured on the "New York's Best-Dressed" list, and was always perfectly outfitted no matter the occasion.

To anyone who casually knew him, he was a generous and kind-hearted gentleman with a penchant for the finer things in life. His inner circle

would describe him as the devil incarnate, fearful of nothing and capable of striking fatal vengeance like the Viper for which he was nicknamed.

Tony Caprio, one of the DeLuca family's captains, was one member of the inner circle who was a favorite of the Viper. Tony had brought in his cousin, the doctor, and that in itself was a major victory for the Viper. Every family needs their own private doctor on occasion, and this one was a surgeon, to boot.

The Viper now had hooks in the doctor for a significant amount of money—albeit through rigged gambling—but the outcome was a coup for the DeLuca family. His daughter, Juliana, had tried for years to have a baby with her no-good, blank shooting husband. Now the doctor was going to be the voluntary "baby" donor. Literally.

The cousin brought in the doctor, the doctor brings in the baby, now Juliana was going to be mother to his DeLuca grandson. It was a win-win for everyone, except maybe for the poor doctor's wife. The new baby was going to get the best of everything. Hell, the ungrateful doctor's wife should be thanking HIM, Vincenzo DeLuca. It's not like he took her only baby, for heaven's sake. She'd get over it, he figured.

Time heals everything, except maybe a fatal bullet wound to the head, he chuckled as he gently chewed on the end of his pipe.

* * * * * *

When Lorenzo and Cathy pulled into their circular driveway, they could see the lights were still on in the large family room. Lorenzo's hands were slightly trembling as he opened the car door for Cathy.

"Mother must have fallen asleep in the big chair again," Cathy mused as she approached the double front doors. Lorenzo turned the deadbolt with his key, and then pushed open the door for Cathy to precede him into the foyer.

"Mom? We're back." Cathy laid her evening purse on the entry table as she casually walked toward the family room doorway.

"OH MY GOD! MOM! LORENZO, GET IN HERE!" Cathy screamed as she ran toward her bound-up Mother. Cathy ripped the tape from across her mother's mouth. "Mom, are you hurt? Who did this?"

Genevieve started crying as the tape was unpeeled from her eyes. "Men, two men. With guns. Except for where they hit my face, I'm all right. But they terrified me. I don't know what they might have taken from the house. They never said a word. Oh Cathy, I'm so sorry," her mother sobbed.

Cathy turned abruptly and ran down the hallway toward the children's rooms. She rushed into Sophia's room only to find the child sleeping soundly in her canopy bed. Then Cathy sprinted toward the nursery, stopping in her tracks at the doorway.

"AAAAHHHHHHHHHHHRRRRRRRROOOOHNNNOOOOOOO!" she screamed, uttering an unintelligible concoction of words and sounds.

Lorenzo rushed to Cathy's side and turned on the nursery's overhead light. Cathy grabbed the baby who was asleep in the crib on the right. The left crib was empty. She clutched the solitary baby tightly to her breast, not allowing Lorenzo to touch him, and continued wailing in her newly developed language.

Lorenzo hastily moved to the side of the empty crib, looked down, and moved the many blankets around as if the baby could be hiding beneath them. His stunned look could have easily been interpreted as innocence.

Lorenzo slowly slid to the floor next to the empty crib; he sank his face into the blue and white quilt that had been draped across the side of the baby bed. His guttural sobs were muffled by the soft fabric which also served as a blotter for his genuine tears of remorse. Cathy sat in the floor

beside him clutching the remaining twin baby to her chest. The two devastated parents held each other and wept.

Cathy cried over the abduction of their baby.

Lorenzo cried over the abduction of the wrong baby.

CHAPTER 4

Sunday, December 4, 1994

At the BNL library, John Sanderson had looked in every publication he could think of to try to find some way to help his friend, Doug Brantley. He had even gathered law books, reading any sections referencing unreported deaths or graves found in unsanctioned burial grounds. He was out of research options. He didn't know what he was going to tell Doug when he contacted him the next day. John never expected to find any instructions on how to illegally buy a baby through the black market. He knew that was not a valid alternative any smart person would take.

By 10:00 p.m., he had put away all the books he could. John placed the remainder in rolling carts for the librarians to sort appropriately when they returned to work the next morning. He put on his down jacket and headed for the door, bracing for the frigid December weather that was about to hit him in the face.

His car revved up on the first try. His reluctant wipers pushed off the accumulated layer of thin ice that now looked like a dirty Slurpee on the edges of his windshield. He wrapped his gloved hands around the steering wheel and moved cautiously through the parking lot. Soon he would be headed home on Highway 495 where the roads were salted and much less treacherous than the back roads he usually travelled.

* * * * * *

The black van careened around a curve, headed toward the entrance of a deserted school parking lot in Syosset. The vehicle pulled into a space next to an idling black Lincoln limousine. The darkened back window rolled down when the van's driver came around to speak to the limo occupant.

"Is it done?" the gentleman in the car inquired.

"Yes, boss. We have the baby with us." The van driver turned, snapped his fingers, and the side van door started to slide open. Sitting inside was another man holding an infant with a blue nursery cap on its head wrapped tightly in a white blanket. The infant was sleeping quietly, sucking on a dark blue pacifier which had been a gift from the hospital.

"Good work," he said, motioning for the van door to close again. "Now get him to the meeting spot off 495. You know who to look for," he said as he rolled up the tinted window.

The driver nodded his head and moved around the van, getting in the driver's seat once again. He left ahead of the limousine, which was still idling in place when the van was well out of sight.

"Take me home, please. I want to be there when my daughter and grandson make their entrance," he instructed the driver.

The car moved carefully through the freshly fallen layer of snow. They headed for the largest mansion in Southampton, which overflowed with expensive artifacts and unique furnishings. But to The Viper, it was the emptiest place in the world.

* * * * * *

The small gray Mercedes-Benz sedan was parked next to a lamp pole in the parking lot of a church near Hicksville. Sunday's late services had ended over an hour before, so no other vehicles were around except the closed-up church buses.

Juliana DeLuca Moretti and her husband Diego waited patiently in the empty lot for delivery of what her Father said would be a life-changing gift. They were given no hints, and hadn't been able to guess anything that could possibly have such an impact on their lives. Diego blew it off as "probably a new car or something like that, or maybe a big vacation to Italy, eh?" But Juliana knew her father would be giving her something like that for a birthday gift or a Christmas gift or a special occasion gift. "Life-changing" never described any gifts he had bought her before in her entire life.

Down the street, they saw the headlights of a vehicle that was turning into the church parking lot. The black van parked next to them and the driver got out. Juliana rolled down her window.

"Mrs. Moretti, your Father sends his love and best wishes for your happiness for the rest of your life. He hopes you will remember him when you make a name choice."

With that said, the van door opened, revealing a baby in the arms of another one of her father's crew. He handed the baby to the standing van driver, who passed the bundle through the open car window to Juliana. The men hastily drove away before Juliana noticed they were gone.

"Diego!" she squealed. "He gave us a baby! Oh my God, how did my father do this? Oh my goodness, he's a sweet little fellow! And so handsome!" she exclaimed with delight. She ran her finger over the

infant's forehead, down to his nose, and across his rosebud lips. Her heart pounded.

As the new baby boy started to squirm and get grumpy, the two new "parents" looked at each other in wonderment. They wanted to go to Juliana's father's home to thank him properly for the wonderful surprise, but they needed to attend to the child's immediate needs first. He smelled slightly of ammonia from his heavy wet diaper.

They made a quick stop at a convenience store trying to find diapers and formula, but those items weren't the kinds of products such stores kept in stock. They soon found an open supermarket that carried the supplies they needed. While Juliana waited with the baby in the warm sedan, Diego was able to purchase enough disposable diapers and bottled formula for the night.

They changed the infant as he lay on his blanket in the back seat of the car. They kept the car heater running full blast so the child wouldn't be uncomfortable. Then Juliana tried to feed him the lukewarm formula, but he resisted and cried. "Maybe I'm not doing it right," she worried. "Here, you try," she pouted as she handed the baby to Diego. As he held the infant close to his chest, the baby latched on to the bottle's nipple and eagerly began to suckle.

When Diego saw the disappointed look on his wife's face, he remarked, "Hey, I had baby brothers and sisters. I got experience. They just gotta feel like you won't drop 'em, because they don't want to fall out of your arms. They wanna feel secure, you know?"

Juliana smiled as she watched the baby drain the bottle of formula. She took the baby from Diego's arms and rested his tiny head over her left shoulder. She began to softly pat his back waiting for the big burp of air. It came out loudly, and both new parents laughed in amazement.

44

They were now ready to go see Vincenzo DeLuca, the proud grandfather of this gift from heaven. Juliana and Diego wanted to learn what they could about the baby's background. They knew better than to ask her father too many questions, but Juliana believed she knew where he'd draw the line.

* * * * * *

The Giordano house was swarming with policemen within thirty minutes of the parents' arrival and the crime's discovery. There had been repeated interviews with both Lorenzo and Cathy, but the most interviewed person on the premises was Cathy's mother, the assault victim.

Cathy's mother had accepted medical treatment from the paramedics who arrived on the scene, and was diagnosed with a broken nose. She was lucky that the extent of her injuries were such that her looks weren't scarred for life. A broken nose was considered a lucky outcome considering what could have happened to her. She was very fortunate that she hadn't been tortured or killed.

Yellow crime scene tape was draped over the whole inside of the house from the back kitchen door to the nursery. Pathways were roped off outside the house, too. Neighbors were asked if they noticed anything peculiar happening at the Giordano's house, but none were aware of anything out of the ordinary.

The policemen were trying their best to help the Giordanos, but in Cathy's mind they weren't moving fast enough. They should be out on the roads looking in every car window they passed or setting up road blocks, or ANYTHING useful instead of standing around their house. She didn't understand, and she loudly made her concerns known. Lorenzo took her inside the house and asked her to try to calm down. He offered to give her a sedative to help her if she wanted it.

Cathy thought Lorenzo was acting too calm in the harrowing situation. She was beginning to think he didn't care about their stolen baby. Her thoughts were running the gambit from fear to anger and back again.

Lorenzo came back outside after getting Cathy settled. Within a couple of minutes, a young patrolman approached him with a notepad in his hand.

"Dr. Giordano, sir?" the patrolman asked as Lorenzo nodded. "I have a message to relay to you, sir, from someone we both admire."

Lorenzo looked questioningly at the young cop. "Yes? What's the message?" he asked.

"The package arrived undamaged. Your debt is now clear." The young patrolman turned around, joining his counterparts in reviewing the crime scene evidence.

Lorenzo knew at that moment that there would be no active investigation to find his missing son. Tonight was just busy work to make Cathy and the neighbors think something was being done. This case would be buried somewhere, never to be resurrected. His boy would be someone else's boy in a few days – maybe he already was.

But the abducted infant boy carried the "Giordano mark" on his lower back. Secretly, Lorenzo hoped his son would someday come home to him and reclaim his rightful place in the family. He wanted the Giordano blood to boil and spill all the DeLuca blood that could be drawn. Lorenzo never wanted to see the Viper again as long as he lived.

* * * * * *

John Sanderson was tired and frustrated after spending so many hours in the BNL library. His research had yielded nothing to help his friend, providing no path to follow to get Doug out of the trouble he was already in. John was mentally rehearsing the discouraging conversation he would

have with Doug the next day, explaining how his research led to a dead end. He would suggest that Doug turn himself in to the local authorities. John would urge Doug to get Stella the professional help she needed to simultaneously cope with her baby's death and her withdrawal from the drugs.

He drove silently, leaving the radio off while he moved west on Highway 495 toward his home in Hicksville. The freshly fallen layer of fluffy wet snow made for somewhat hazardous driving conditions, but John was a good and careful driver. He felt no apprehension over traveling the snowy road; instead, his concern was centered solely around his inability to solve his friend's problems.

It was almost 11:00 p.m. when John spotted the exit ramp to Hicksville. He turned on his blinker, moving carefully to the far right lane to take the exit. Within thirty minutes, he should be soundly asleep in his own bed, Lucas by his side, awaiting the alarm clock's 5:00 a.m. signal that another trip to BNL was on the horizon.

* * * * * *

Diego Moretti drove the Mercedes out of the grocery store parking lot with an ecstatic wife who was holding a content baby in her arms. That was a vision he had given up on seeing in real life. He kept glancing at Juliana, watching her peripherally as she cooed trying to make the baby smile. The child wanted to go back to sleep, but Juliana was persistent.

"Diego, I think he smiled at me. Look at him. Isn't he the sweetest thing?" the thrilled Juliana commented, not expecting an answer from her husband.

He glanced again toward his wife and the baby, attempting to hold back a chuckle. Even though he was amused at Juliana's awe of the infant, he now realized she had no idea how to care for anyone but herself. As an only child of wealthy parents, her life had not included exposure to infants

or care giving. It was clear to Diego that the everyday responsibilities for this child might be falling more heavily on his shoulders than hers.

"Juliana, a newborn doesn't really know how to smile yet. It was probably just gas," he remarked. He looked at her with a grin.

"Don't make fun of me, Diego. I have a lot to learn, I know. But I'll learn it all and be the best Mother this child could have." Juliana beamed with exhilaration.

Diego saw the signs for Highway 495 ahead. Glancing again at his wife, he reached out and touched her cheek. When he looked up again, the highway ramp was in front of him, causing him to abruptly turn to make it onto the ramp. The Mercedes took the turn smoothly, staying steady on the road even with the imperfect road conditions.

Suddenly, everything went dark.

After the sound of the crash, the baby's soft cry was the only noise that could be heard.

* * * * * *

John Sanderson was so focused on the road ahead, it was an easy maneuver for him to avoid the gray car that was coming the wrong way on the ramp. He saw it make the turn, oblivious to John's car headed straight for it. When the errant driver realized there was a vehicle in its path, he swerved the car toward the metal guard rail. Thankfully, there was no embankment or concrete abutment in the path of the out-of-control sedan.

John stopped his car a few feet from the wrecked sedan, running toward the vehicle. He immediately saw the car's front end damage was severe enough that the car wouldn't be drivable. He looked into the sedan and saw two adults strapped in their seat belts and apparently unconscious.

He could see the female passenger's chest rise and fall with steady breaths, and the male driver had blood running down his face. The blood source appeared to be a deep cut on the man's forehead— a wound that would normally produce a significant amount of blood, making it appear more serious than it actually was. John reached out with his gloved hand and checked the driver for a pulse. He found one. He quickly surmised that the two adults would recover fully, and probably only needed first aid.

But then he heard it.

A whimpering sound came from the back seat. He tried to open the sedan's rear door, but it was jammed shut. He leaned far over the driver, peering between the front seats above the console. He was shocked to see a tiny bundle trying desperately to shove his fist in his mouth.

"A miracle. God has led me to a miracle." John momentarily couldn't comprehend what he was seeing.

John stretched as far as he could over the driver and retrieved the baby from the back seat. From the way the baby was positioned, John figured the female passenger had been holding the child, but the force of the impact hurled the baby backwards from her arms.

He did a cursory examination of the child to check for obvious broken bones or bleeding, but his assessment couldn't be confirmed on the side of the road. Instead, he rewrapped the baby in its loose blanket and hurried off to his own car. He would take the baby home. He'd figure out his next moves from there.

CHAPTER 5

Sunday, December 4, 1994

She was basking in the laziness of a much needed vacation as she swam in knee-deep water off the shores of Honolulu. Tiny fish were nibbling at her toes as she leisurely glided through the cobalt-colored water. The sun briefly sneaked behind a cloud, providing a cool breeze to her face when she lifted it for air.

Suddenly, she spied a giant crab-like monster only a short distance from her feet. She feverishly tried to kick away from the hazardous pinching creature. Even though she kicked and thrust her legs with all her might, she made no forward progress. The pinch she felt on her toes caused her to jerk and thrust her foot with force as she tried to call for help from the now invisible shore.

"Dammit, Caroline! Can't you hear your phone? Wake up and answer it, for God's sake," her brother said as he tightly squeezed the toes on her right foot. Mike Lewis stood at the foot of his sister's bed in pajamas, hair amuck, and patience in short supply.

He shook her foot again to ensure she was rousing from her sleep. "Caroline, answer your fucking phone!" he said as she subconsciously booted her foot hard against his thigh.

Caroline opened her eyes to find her brother pointing to her bedside private-line phone, still blasting an irritating noise. Her brother grunted as he threw his arms in the air in frustration and then turned to stomp back to his own bedroom.

The sleepy Caroline grabbed her pinched toes with her left hand, reaching for the phone with her right. "This better be good. Who is this?" she snapped into the receiver.

"I'm sorry, Caroline, but this is an emergency. Can you come over here? I really need you," her ex-husband begged. He sounded desperate.

"You jerk, I can't believe you're trying to make a booty call to me, of all people. What the hell is wrong with you? Are you drunk? Call a cab," Caroline barked through gritted teeth. She slammed down the phone receiver and tried to bury her head deep in her pillow to reattach herself to sleep.

Within seconds, the phone was ringing again. Caroline made a guttural moan as she quickly reached for the phone, trying not to give her irritable brother another opportunity to chastise her.

"John, leave me alone. I'm trying to sleep. Call me tomorrow if it's that important..."

"Caroline, shut up and listen for a minute," John interrupted. "I stopped at a wreck on the highway tonight. I have a very tiny baby in my arms, and I don't know what to do. Please come over here now."

Caroline became instantly alert. "Where are you, John? Where's the accident? I'll come and get you. Are you all right?" Caroline was now wide awake as she started making her way up from her bed. She pulled a nearby sweatshirt off the bedside floor as she waited for John's response.

"I'm at the house. Please hurry," John begged.

Caroline stopped moving and sat erect. "What the hell, John? What are you doing at home with a baby taken from a wreck? Where's its mother? This doesn't make sense," a bewildered Caroline asked.

"Please, just get in the car and come over here. I'll explain when you get here. Don't say anything to your brother or anybody else. Just come." John hung up the phone and the line went dead as Caroline waited for more details from her ex-husband. She held the phone to her ear for a few more seconds before it occurred to her that John had already hung up.

* * * * * *

The phone call that Vincenzo DeLuca received the night of December 4th was not the one he was expecting. He thought perhaps his precious Juliana would make an impromptu phone call to sing his praises and thank him profusely for the miracle baby that was delivered to her that evening. He visibly smiled when he pictured her face of adoration and the joyful tears she would shed for her father's greatest act of kindness. She would want to know if he was still up and awake, and if they could bring the baby by to meet his grandfather. Of course, he would graciously invite them to visit regardless of the late hour. He pictured all this vividly and joyously.

However, he was not prepared to hear from the police that his daughter had been in an automobile accident and had been taken to NYU Winthrop along with her worthless husband. The couple suffered only cuts and bruises, but would otherwise be fine. Their car, however, wasn't in a condition to be driven from the scene.

What the officer didn't say was whether or not there was an infant with them.

Vincenzo had already received a report from his men that the baby had been successfully handed over to Juliana and Diego near Hicksville. The baby had to have been in the car with them when the accident occurred. Knowing his son-in-law, he probably did something stupid while driving in the fresh snow. The idiot had shit for brains.

Waiting was the hard part. Vincenzo knew better than to panic and go to the hospital. If they got wind of his arrival, the news media would be up in his face asking questions that he might not want to answer. Plus, if there was any hint of a recently kidnapped baby being recovered from the scene, he couldn't afford to be the primary suspect or linked to the crime in any way. He had no choice but to wait to hear from Juliana herself to find out exactly what happened with the baby.

He considered sending one of his "guys" to the accident scene or to locate and inspect the towed car, but he was hesitant. Something seemed off-kilter, somehow. His gut was telling him not to move too quickly, and usually his instincts were right.

Vincenzo arose from his easy chair in the den, laid down his favorite pipe on the side table, and made his way toward his wife's bedroom. As he reached the door, he could already hear the rhythmic beeping of the monitors hooked all over her body. He entered the room, and the attending nurse smiled at him. She silently moved from her bedside seat to make room for Vincenzo to approach his wife.

Vincenzo gave his unresponsive wife his nightly kiss on her forehead. It wouldn't disturb her. Since she took the terrible fall down the long stairway two years before, nothing had disturbed her. Vincenzo had seen to that—it had all been arranged weeks prior to her "accident."

* * * * * *

Caroline Lewis Sanderson parked her Volkswagen Beetle in the same spot where she used to park when she was a resident of the house as Mrs. John Sanderson. Since their divorce, she only came by when she picked up Lucas, their beloved beagle, for occasional visits. Even then, she didn't enter the house because John always brought Lucas to the door to meet

her. She had no idea what the inside of the house would be like after all this time of living apart. Remembering how sloppy her then-husband John had been around the house, she figured his solo housekeeping efforts were minimal at best.

John opened the front door when he heard Caroline's car pull in the driveway. As she hurried up the sidewalk and mounted the porch steps, he unexpectedly reached for her when she came close enough to embrace. He grabbed her and held her tightly, while she mentally struggled with what could have happened to put John in this "needy" mood. It was so unlike him. They let go of each other, and John led the way into the small house.

He said nothing as he passed through the living room area and turned left into what was once the bedroom they shared as man and wife. Caroline followed closely behind, gasping when she saw a rectangular laundry basket perched in the center of the bed.

She walked around John to get a closer look at what appeared to be a newborn baby wearing a white onesie with a blue nursery cap on his head. He was asleep on top of thick padding made of soft towels, with other towels wrapped around him. He had no blanket of his own, but it didn't seem to matter. The baby was content to suck his thumb while he slept soundly in his makeshift bedding.

Caroline examined the child without disturbing his slumber. She pulled back the towels to inspect the shape of his body, the tiny fingers that were beautiful and long, and the shape of his head. He was a handsome baby boy, but he was so small. This baby couldn't be more than a week old, if that. She looked at her ex-husband, motioning for him to follow her out of the room.

Once they were in the kitchen, John sat down at the table and stared at his ex-wife. He appeared to be shell-shocked—unable to say anything—hoping Caroline would read his mind like he once thought she could.

Caroline, expecting John to start blurting out the chain of events that lead to the situation, realized that he was still trying to wrap his mind around the predicament. She put on a pot of coffee so that they would have enough caffeine in their systems to endure what might be a lengthy conversation. They sat silently waiting for the coffee to brew.

When they had their coffee before them, Caroline took a sip and started the conversation. "How did you get this baby? Start from the beginning." She stared intently at John, trying to will him to talk.

"It's either going to sound like I'm crazy or that I have been appointed by God to answer a prayer. You decide for yourself," John answered in a monotone voice.

Caroline shook her head. John hadn't lost his touch for theatrics. "Just tell the damn story, and let me go home to bed," Caroline snapped, tired of waiting for answers.

John cleared his throat and began with the phone call he received from his long-time friend, Doug Brantley. He explained all the details that Doug had provided to him about his wife's pregnancy, the baby boy's unexpected death, and how his wife, Stella, had been pumped full of opiods and valium since the discovery of the deceased infant. John further told her the situation Doug had gotten himself into by pocketing some of the drugs from the infirmary where he worked. He rounded off the story by explaining how Doug had called him for help, even though neither of them knew how John could really help him and Stella.

"So did you steal this baby, John?" Caroline inquired with a hint of disbelief in her voice.

"Yes... I mean no... well literally I guess I did. But it was coincidental and certainly unplanned. The car came down the exit ramp the wrong way and almost hit me. It swerved and hit a guardrail. The parents were knocked out. I got out of my car to check on them. They weren't seriously hurt, as far as I could tell, and then I heard whimpering coming from behind them. I leaned across the driver and saw this baby on the back seat. I backed it out of the car, but I had to reach way over the driver whose head was bleeding from a superficial cut. The baby seemed fine at the scene, but I needed to be able to examine him more closely so I brought him home. There was nobody out on the road at that time, and I didn't know what else to do. But I think this baby is meant for Doug and Stella. I know it in my heart. I'm going to take the baby to them." John took a gulp of hot coffee and closed his eyes.

Caroline didn't know how to react. She knew what John did was wrong, but she didn't understand why he would risk his career and his freedom to kidnap a baby for someone he knew so many years ago. She wanted more information. She wanted a reason not to disclose this matter to the police.

John reached across the table to take her hand. "The people in the car didn't know the first thing about babies. I know this. I feel this. The baby didn't have a secure car seat, first off. Who in their right minds would travel in snow with a baby without a car seat or some kind of safety restraint? They either didn't know or they didn't care. Either way, that's a strike against them. They aren't fit parents in my book, based on that alone if nothing else."

Caroline started to mention that John had done the exact same thing when he took the baby from the accident scene and drove to his home. She decided to let that comment go for the moment, waiting for John to continue talking.

57

"The car was a Mercedes. Thank God for that. Any other car might have caused more serious injuries, but those things are built like tanks. So they must have some money, but again they don't know how to safeguard a baby. They probably have had things just handed to them all their lives and are selfish young people. Who knows? All I know is that baby could have been injured very badly or even killed. They don't deserve this child."

Caroline studied John as if she were about to dissect him in a laboratory. She planned to try using basic common sense with him, but she realized he was in no mood to listen or to be swayed by reason. Everything was too fresh in his mind. She believed by the next morning, John would come to his senses and do the right thing. She thought he needed time to think through everything he had told her. Perhaps she did, too.

"Okay. What provisions do you have for the baby for the night? Do you have diapers? Formula? Anything?" Caroline asked.

"There was a small pack of disposable diapers in a grocery bag next to the baby on the back seat, and the bag had some empty bottles and some dry formula. Enough for tonight, but not enough for much longer," John answered.

"So what do you want me to do to help?" Caroline really didn't want to know the answer.

"Would you stay here with us tonight to help me with him? You can go home early tomorrow, or you can stay as long as you want, but I need your help tonight. I'm lost." John looked pitifully at his ex-wife.

"All right. Tonight only. But I have to be at the office by 9:00 a.m. at the latest. Are you going to take a day off to get this straightened out, or what?" Caroline wanted to know.

"I'll have to take off tomorrow, but after that I don't know. We'll have to see what happens, I guess."

Reminded of work, John reached subconsciously at his belt where he always clipped his BNL facility badge. He felt nothing, then looked down at his empty belt loop from which it usually hung.

"My badge is missing. It's not on my belt. Do you see it around here anywhere?" John said anxiously as his eyes scanned the room. He retraced his steps inside the house, but there was no badge to be found.

He took a flashlight outside and looked on the ground leading to and from his house and car. Next, he inspected the inside of the car from the driver's side door. He had lost his badge somewhere between the facility and home. He would have to report it as lost or stolen when he returned to work at BNL.

In John's mind, that was the least of his worries.

CHAPTER 6

Sunday, December 4, 1994 — Monday, December 5, 1994

Cathy Giordano had been sedated as soon as the last policemen left the Giordano house. Lorenzo had administered the dosage to his wife, and he anticipated she would sleep restfully throughout the night. Genevieve, Cathy's mother, had her own medication she called her "nerve pills." She had been self-medicating even while the policemen were working the crime scene. By 1:00 a.m., Lorenzo found himself solely in charge of a newborn, a toddler, and two sedated women.

Lorenzo had no expectation of sleeping that night. He knew the baby would be waking soon for refreshed diapers and a feeding. He hoped attending to those activities would be quiet enough that one-year-old Sophia wouldn't be aroused from her slumber.

Considering the amount of medication his wife and mother-in-law had ingested, he was certain their sleep would not be interrupted at all. In fact, he didn't expect either of them to awaken until nearly noon the next day. By then, he would have arranged for a nanny to help out until Cathy was strong enough—mentally and physically—to take over.

So much was going to depend on how the Viper controlled the backlash from the crime. Lorenzo just had to play dumb about who could have possibly committed the abduction. He would be required to simultaneously play the part of the grieving but strong father. He believed he could do it if he didn't let his emotions go rogue. He was still pissed that the men took the baby with the Giordano mark instead of the other baby. He had expected big plans for that special boy.

*　*　*　*　*

By 2:30 a.m., Juliana and Diego Moretti were standing outside the hospital's discharge area doors waiting for a taxi.

"The hospital called your dad, Juliana. Why isn't there a car here waiting? Or better yet, why isn't he here? I thought he'd have to come to personally check on his princess daughter. We haven't heard anything from him," a mystified Diego wondered aloud.

"He has a reason. We'll ask him when we go over there. I'm sure it had to do with security or something," a nervous Juliana responded.

"What I'm worried about is what are we going to tell him about losing the baby? He's going to be so damn pissed he might get violent. And when that man goes ballistic, I don't want to be anywhere near him," Diego said as he shook his head.

Juliana took Diego's hand in hers and said, "I'll handle Papa. You just keep your fat mouth shut, and let me do all the talking." Diego looked down at his shoes.

An empty cab stopped beside them as they stood on the sidewalk, and the two scrambled into the taxi's back seat. They rode in silence for what seemed like forever from Mineola to Southampton, each wondering what the Viper might already know and what his reaction would be when he heard the baby had mysteriously vanished from their care.

Juliana fervently mumbled prayers as soon as the taxi pulled up in front of the DeLuca estate. She stood holding Diego's arm for several minutes before she had the nerve to take the steps that would lead her to the massive leaded glass and mahogany wood doors—and to the unpredictable man behind them.

* * * * * *

John Sanderson checked to see if Caroline had fallen asleep yet. He stuck his head in the master bedroom door to find Caroline reclining and lightly snoring as she lay on the bed next to the laundry basket. As Caroline and the baby both slept, John noticed she had one hand grasping the side of the basket, possibly making sure the basket was still there and stable. John wasn't sure what she was doing, only that it appeared to be a protective, maternal action.

He tiptoed back to the kitchen and looked at his watch. It was already almost 3:00 a.m. He wrestled with the idea of waiting a couple of hours before calling Doug and telling him about the baby. On the other hand, the sooner he called the more time Doug would have to prepare for an impromptu road trip. He decided not to wait.

He quietly removed the receiver from the wall phone hanging in the kitchen, stretching the long cord and walking as far away from the master bedroom area as possible. He dialed Doug's number in Lenoir City, Tennessee, and to his surprise Doug answered on the first ring.

"Hello, this is Doug," he said, sounding very much awake at the late hour.

"Doug, it's John. I don't have time to explain it all to you right now, but I have a solution for your problem."

Doug didn't respond for a moment. "You can help? How?"

John tried to talk quietly so as not to alert Caroline. He whispered, "You need to meet me tomorrow in Harrisonburg, Virginia at 1:00 p.m. or as close to that as you can make it. You'll be on Interstate 81 by that time, and you should take the exit to Highway 33, which is East Market Street. There's a Waffle House there, and that's where we'll meet. Should take you about six hours of driving, so be prepared to be away from Stella for a while. Work it out however you have to, but be there."

Doug rubbed his sleepy eyes and responded, "Hold on, man. You want me to travel six hours to Virginia and six hours back in one day? For what?"

"For me to hand over your new infant son." John offered no more detail that that, even though he knew Doug was scrambling to make sense out of the conversation.

"Wait. Wait. You have a baby for me and Stella? How ..."

John interrupted, "Don't worry about how right now. Just make sure you have a car seat, plenty of diapers, and formula-filled bottles for the little man. He'll probably sleep most of the way home."

Doug was astonished that he heard from John so quickly, and he was flabbergasted that John was offering an immediate solution to his predicament. "I'll have to call in at work and make sure Stella sleeps most of the time I'm away. I've got a lot to do ..."

"Which is exactly why I'm calling you now. Get it done, and get on the road. This is a touchy situation, and we need to do this as soon as possible. So meet me at 1:00 p.m. in Harrisonburg, Virginia, and I'll explain it all to you then. I gotta go now, but be at the Waffle House on East Market Street. I'll find you." John hung up the phone just as he heard the baby start whimpering from the adjacent bedroom.

The next noise he heard was Caroline making "shush" sounds trying to soothe the baby back to sleep. When the baby started all-out crying, John rushed in the bedroom to help Caroline with the feeding and changing of the infant. John didn't inform Caroline of his call to Doug, and apparently she didn't hear him talking on the phone. That was good luck, because he didn't intend to tell Caroline that he and the baby were taking a long road trip in a few hours. He would wait until Caroline was asleep again, and then he and the new little "Teddy Brantley" would be cruising to Virginia in Caroline's Volkswagen Beetle. He didn't want to use his own car in case

someone saw it on the exit ramp when he rescued the baby from the wreckage. Caroline's car would be the better vehicle for this trip.

* * * * * *

Juliana and Diego Moretti sat frozen like praying statues with their heads bowed and hands clasped in their laps. The loveseat they were occupying was adjacent to the favorite chair of a seething Vincenzo DeLuca. As he, too, sat motionless, he unconsciously bit the end of his favorite pipe. When he realized what he was doing, he launched the pipe across the room barely missing a valuable Faberge egg that had been his comatose wife's favorite collection piece. Juliana's body jerked with fear at her father's outburst, but she never raised her head to acknowledge the action. Diego didn't dare look at his fuming father-in-law.

Vincenzo arose from the oxblood leather chair, then calmly walked across the room to retrieve his precious pipe. As he turned, he stared at the two fearful figures perched stiffly on the loveseat.

"Tell me again how you **LOST MY GRANDSON**, you bumbling idiots! For the love of God, I hand you a miracle, and you let it slip right out of your incompetent hands in less than an hour! You don't DESERVE to have a child! You don't even know how to keep up with a baby during a few miles' drive! God knows what would have happened to that boy if you actually tried to raise him for a lifetime. You disappoint me, Juliana, and if your mother was aware of this mess, you'd disappoint her, too. Jesus, Mary, and Joseph, what's wrong with you?" Vincenzo paced back and forth in front of his captive audience. Getting no response from his daughter or her worthless husband, Vincenzo once again took his seat in the leather chair.

Tears rolled down Juliana's cheeks making a pool on her clasped hands still resting in her lap. Finally, she worked up the nerve to look at her father. "Papa, we were so thrilled! He was beautiful, and we loved him

the minute we saw him. We were excited, and the baby was smiling. I don't know what happened, I really don't. We even stopped to get diapers and formula. We fed him, Papa. It was so wonderful! I've never felt like that before.

"Then the snow started flurrying heavier, and it was hard to see to drive. We took what we thought was the entrance ramp to the highway. We were on our way here to see you. We saw headlights and swerved. Then there was nothing. Honest to God, that's what happened." Juliana wiped her dripping nose with the back of her left hand. She paused briefly.

"We were knocked unconscious, and the next thing we know we're in the back of an ambulance. I was afraid to ask about the baby at the hospital until I talked to you first. I didn't know where he came from. I didn't want to get you in trouble, but my heart ached for the baby, and I was so scared for him. When the hospital released us, they never mentioned the baby. I was afraid he was dead, but I couldn't ask. I've been so terrified and worried.

"Papa, please help us. Please find out if he's alive and if he is, help us get the baby back. Then you can place the blame wherever you want to lay it. But I just need to know if he's all right. I really need to know. I need that baby, Papa. Please. I'm his mother now."

Juliana pleaded with her father. "I promise you I'll be the best mother you ever saw, and I'll never let that baby out of my sight again. Please, Papa." Her tears now came in gushing sobs, prompting Diego to finally relax his rigid body enough to wrap his arm around Juliana's stooped shoulders for comfort.

Vincenzo remained silent. Finally, he said in an authoritative voice, "Go home now. Let me think. I need to make some calls." Without another word, Juliana stood, approached her father, and kissed him on the cheek.

"I love you, Papa," she quietly whispered in his ear while smearing her freshly shed tears on his cheek.

Clasping Diego's arm, Juliana quietly led her husband out of the room. Moments later, Vincenzo heard the sound of the massive front doors being opened and closed.

* * * * * *

By 5:00 a.m. on Monday, December 5th, a teal blue Volkswagen beetle backed out of the driveway of John Sanderson's home in Hicksville, New York. The vehicle was nondescript, with the exception of an overstuffed laundry basket securely strapped into the front passenger seat. It appeared to be a heaping basket of towels at first glance, but a closer look revealed a bundle of joy—with a blue cap on his head—sleeping peacefully as the car made its way down the neighborhood streets.

In the cramped back seat was a grocery bag filled with a few diapers and a bottle of freshly made formula, as well as water and unmixed formula powder for future feedings. John had plenty of nursery supplies for another six hours or so, and he planned to make no stops other than the required convenience breaks for the baby.

John left a sleeping Caroline an explanatory note, but without too much detail. In it he wrote:

> Caroline, I'm on the road now, taking care of the delivery I explained last night. Please take care of Lucas until I get back. Make yourself at home. Lucas likes it here, so I hope you decide to stay here with him. My car keys are on the kitchen counter. Thanks for your help and the use of

your car, even if it was involuntary on your part. I'll bring it back in one piece. Ha!   Love,

John

And so the journey began for the newly named baby, Teddy Brantley, in search of new parents for the third time in five days.

CHAPTER 7

Monday, December 5, 1994

Doug Brantley was too pumped with adrenaline to be sleepy. He had been driving since 5:30 a.m., and was focused only on the mission at hand. Five hours before, he had left his sleeping wife curled up in bed with her substitute teddy bear baby. He had placed a fresh glass of water on her bedside table with an envelope leaning against it. Inside the envelope was a note informing her that he had to go out of town for the day on "important business," but would be back in time to give her a late dinner.

Also on the bedside table, Doug had left Stella three doses of medicine in separate envelopes, each with the time for dosage scribbled on the front. A bowl of fruit and two wrapped peanut butter sandwiches were left on a tray on his empty side of the bed.

In the short time he had to prepare for his departure, he tried to cover all the bases he could think of for Stella's daytime welfare and comfort. What he couldn't provide her with was a way to reach him in case of emergency, and he prayed she wouldn't need to do that during the twelve or thirteen hours he would be away. He would try to call her during the day just in case.

* * * * * *

Surprisingly, John Sanderson's journey from New York to Virginia was going smoothly. He had anticipated several stops along the way, but the baby had not been fussy. Concerned that the infant was too quiet, he had stopped after three hours of traveling to make sure the baby was all right.

He had to wake the baby from a sound sleep to rouse him to eat, and the newborn ate heartily.

The baby's diaper was wet, but he didn't seem to mind. After feeding and changing, the newborn cooed and wriggled himself back to sleep within a few minutes of John's getting the vehicle back on the road. John was amazed at how content the baby was in his newly found, strange environment. With the trip going this well, it was surely blessed by God.

* * * * *

The Waffle House in Harrisonburg, Virginia, wasn't as crowded as Doug had expected. As he pulled into the parking lot a few minutes past 1:00 p.m., he only saw four cars. Three had Virginia license plates and one little blue VW Beetle had New York plates. The occupant was still in the driver's seat, and the motor was running as evidenced by the white-gray exhaust smoke emitted from its rear.

Doug pulled into the empty parking space next to the blue VW, glancing through the passenger window in an attempt to identify the driver. He recognized his friend immediately, and John smiled broadly.

The two men exited their vehicles and bear-hugged their hellos. Fifteen years had passed since they had locked eyes, yet it seemed like only yesterday. John was the first to break the embrace.

"I want you to meet Teddy Brantley," John said to a visibly emotional Doug.

John opened the VW passenger door of the small car, exposing a rectangular white laundry basket holding what appeared to be a load of laundry.

"Whaaatt....," Doug disappointedly began, but his question was interrupted when a tiny hand emerged from the midst of the laundry in an upward wave. The timing was so perfect that the wave looked as though it was intentional.

"Oh my God! What do we have here?" an exuberant Doug asked as he bent over the passenger seat to get a good look at his new son. "He even looks like Teddy did. He's beautiful!" Doug withdrew from his leaning position over the basket and slowly knelt on the pavement at the open car door. He rested his left arm on the side of the basket and buried his head in the crook of his elbow and openly wept. John placed his hand on Doug's back and cried, too.

* * * * * *

Caroline woke around 8:30 a.m., realizing at once that she was alone. There was no laundry basket "bassinet" beside her on the sheets. Only silence inhabited the chilly house with her and Lucas. She scooted off the bed and peered out the door toward the kitchen. No John. She looked throughout the small house, finding no one.

She went straight to the bathroom and circled back to the kitchen. She intended to reheat leftover coffee from the night before, thinking a good strong dose of caffeine would compensate for her lack of good rest.

On the counter she spied John's car keys atop a handwritten note. "Son of a bitch. I should've known," she said aloud to no one after reading John's words. "Can't do anything about it now, though, Caroline. Might as well get moving."

While still looking directly at the note, she made her sentiments clear. "John, you're an inconsiderate asshole," she declared to the empty house, then hurried out the door toward John's car.

She had to go back to her brother's place to change clothes. *No shower today for Caroline*, she thought. And of course, she'd be late to work once again. So far, the attorneys for whom she did paralegal work had been gracious about her frequent tardiness; but, she knew their patience was running thin. *"Crap, crap, crap,"* she thought to herself as she hurriedly backed out of the slick driveway.

* * * * *

Tony Caprio's orders were clear. He was to show up unexpectedly at Lorenzo Giordano's house by 7:30 a.m. under the pretense of offering assistance with the kidnapping issues. Of course, this was only for the family's benefit since Lorenzo knew exactly what had happened to his son. However, the Viper was adamant about what he expected Tony to learn: did the good doctor somehow steal his son back?

Tony had to play his cards carefully here. If the doctor wasn't aware that the Viper lost the baby, all sorts of hell would be unleashed by Lorenzo toward the Viper— and toward cousin Tony. If Lorenzo *did* know the current status, then the Giordanos had the baby or had him back home hidden somewhere. It was going to be a touchy conversation that would require finesse.

* * * * *

The Viper had ordered his crew to tow the Moretti's wrecked Mercedes to one of the family's many chop shops. The Viper demanded that the car be inspected from top to bottom, and he wanted all contents in the car removed and delivered to his Southampton home before 10:00 a.m.

As he waited, his wife's nurse appeared in the doorway of the family den where Vincenzo stood staring out the garden doors.

"Sir?" she quietly said.

Vincenzo acknowledged her presence by turning toward her and raising his eyebrows.

"We will soon need more medication, feeding tube nourishment, and sanitary supplies for Mrs. DeLuca. Would you like me to inform the doctor, or would you like someone else to handle it?" she asked meekly.

Vincenzo tried to hide his disgust at the mention of his wife's vegetative condition. Lucinda couldn't even handle toilet responsibilities or feed herself, for God's sake. But of course, Vincenzo knew that it was his fault that she was in the state she was in. He wanted to be a merciful and kind husband, but it wasn't in his heart. When she threatened to leave him for someone else after forty years of marriage, any loving feelings he had harbored for her turned to pure hatred.

"Order another two weeks' supply. I want to check to see if we can get a better deal somewhere else before we invest another fortune through her quack doctor," he barked, turning back to the view of his landscaped grounds through the doors.

The nurse exited without further comment.

* * * * * *

Mike Lewis stood at his back door drinking his morning coffee, looking out at his neighbor's heap of garbage piled only yards away from his own driveway. He had considered going over to talk about it, but the surly husband and trashy-looking wife didn't appear to be very approachable.

While he pondered alternatives to the rising garbage dilemma, he saw John's car approaching the house. It pulled in his driveway, coming to a screeching halt next to Mike's own Jeep Cherokee. His sister Caroline got out of the car and trotted toward the back door.

"You two lovebirds kiss and make up?" Mike smirked and took another sip of coffee from his mug.

"No, asshole. Far from it. I don't have time to explain now, I'm late for work. But could you go back over to John's and feed Lucas? I forgot in the rush. John had to go out of town today and won't be back 'til late. I'm in charge of the dog."

She rushed past her brother to the spare bedroom where she had been "temporarily" staying since her two-year old divorce. Over her head, Caroline shouted, "Oh, and can I use your car? John's is almost out of gas, and I don't have time to stop. I'm already late."

Mike shook his head. It was always something with Caroline... Can I use your car? Can I have this last beer? Can I eat your food? Marriage hadn't changed her, and divorce sure didn't help.

"Whatever, Caroline. I'm at your disposal, as usual," he grinned as he cocked his head in her direction. It didn't make any difference if he agreed or not, she'd do whatever she wanted to do.

Within minutes, she sped past him in a blur, grabbing his car keys off the hook mounted on the side of the kitchen cabinet.

"Bye and thanks. Don't forget about Lucas. Love you." And she was gone.

* * * * * *

There was still crime scene tape all around the outside of the Giordano house. Tony pulled his Cadillac as close to the door as possible to bypass streamers of yellow and black ribbon.

The door bell rang with deep reverberating tones, making Tony think about "waking the dead." He shivered as a chill passed down his spine,

but he recovered in time to see the door open and an unshaven, disheveled Lorenzo standing in his bathrobe in the open doorway.

"Tony, this isn't a good time. You should know that. Go away." Lorenzo started to shut the door, but Tony stuck his foot across the threshold, blocking the action.

"Enzo, please. I won't take but a minute of your time. The Viper sent me over to check on you. You know, make sure you're holding up all right. I gotta go back and tell him something, so talk to me and make it easy for both of us." Tony begged.

Lorenzo reluctantly opened the door wider, making room for Tony to enter the foyer. Neither man uttered a sound. He led his cousin to the kitchen. Lorenzo took two mugs from the cupboard, filling each with steaming hot coffee. Lorenzo gave a mug to Tony, and sat down across from him at the kitchen island.

"So, Enzo, is it safe to talk in here?" Tony whispered across the narrow surface.

"Yeah. The women are still sedated, and Sophia won't be up for another hour at least. I already fed the baby so he's good for a while, too. Miss Elmore, the new nanny, will be here at nine o'clock to take over with the children." Lorenzo stared into his coffee. It was evident that he was about to become emotional.

"So, Enzo. I hear the wife's old lady was roughed up some. Is she gonna be all right? It wasn't too bad, was it?" Tony feigned concern.

Lorenzo gave Tony a blank stare. "They roughed her up and broke her nose. That was needless violence, Tony. She'll be all right, though. She can get another facelift out of it and look even more plastic. I just hope it doesn't affect her mentally. She's crazy enough already."

"And the baby?" Tony asked.

Lorenzo shot Tony an angry look. "You mean the *wrong* baby that's asleep in the other room? God, what do you mean, 'and the baby?' You know damn well about the baby. You should be telling *me* about the baby, you cocksucker!" Lorenzo was about to lose control of his temper. He could feel it boiling up inside. Tony was just a reminder of the disgusting evil he had surrounded himself with during the past couple of years.

Tony looked confused. "No, Enzo. I don't know nothing about a *wrong* baby. *The* baby. The one that's still here? Is he doing okay? Jeez, don't blame me for this mess."

Tony felt uncomfortable, but wanted to be able to say for certain that the kidnapped baby hadn't been brought back to this house. "Enzo, can I just take a peek at the baby? I just want to look at him. Maybe he'll know some day that I'm his crazy cousin from your mother's side, eh?" Tony asked as genuinely as he could.

Lorenzo bit his tongue, but knew Tony was only following instructions from the Viper.

"I need to look in on him anyway. Just don't make any noise and wake up Sophia. Don't wake Ricky up, either." Lorenzo dropped the infant's name as naturally as if he had always planned to name his first son "Ricky." Tony didn't comment on the name selection, but wondered if the other baby had already been named, as well.

* * * * * *

Lorenzo allowed Tony to hold Ricky for a moment, then took the baby and laid him back down in his crib. The two men gravitated toward the vacant baby bed. Standing over the empty baby's crib was heartbreaking, even to Tony. Lorenzo stifled tears and wiped his misty eyes. The two men solemnly left the nursery and went back to the kitchen.

Tony tried to put his arm around Lorenzo's shoulder to comfort him, but Lorenzo shrugged it off. Instead, he turned toward Tony with fiery eyes. "You tell that sick bastard that I never want to see or hear from him again. Never. And he better make sure my son is taken care of and wants for nothing. If I ever find out differently, I'll kill the old bastard myself. You take that message back to the motherfucker for me, eh Tony?" Lorenzo spit out his cousin's name as if it was poison.

Tony nodded his response, leaving Lorenzo heartbroken and sobbing in the middle of the kitchen.

* * * * * *

Fifteen minutes before the imposed deadline, the doorbell rang at the Southampton home of Vincenzo "the Viper" DeLuca. Two men were ushered into the den, bringing with them several small boxes of personal effects taken from Diego Moretti's wrecked car.

Without direction from the Viper, one man laid a clean plastic sheet on a large area of the floor. The second man began taking items from the boxes, lining them up in perfect rows for Vincenzo's perusal. When the boxes were empty, the workers stood back while the Viper scanned each row of items.

The Viper carefully selected an item and put it in his pocket. He then instructed the men to box up the remaining items once more and deliver them to his daughter's penthouse address in Manhattan. The men were in and out of the Viper's home in less than fifteen minutes. It only took Vincenzo one minute to spy what he thought could solve the mystery of the missing child.

Vincenzo picked up his phone and placed a call to a contact he had developed at the Brookhaven National Laboratory. As the phone was ringing, Vincenzo took the item from his pocket and rubbed his thumb across the top of the slick surface. He studied the picture of the man

whose face took up most of the passport-sized picture on the BNL facility badge.

In less than five more minutes, he knew he would have the full name, address, and other demographic information about this person.

In another hour, the bastard "J Sanderson" would be dead.

CHAPTER 8

Monday, December 5, 1994

John sat in a rear booth in the Waffle House sipping the last of his coffee. He had just finished his "covered and smothered" meal that he'd ordered as soon as Doug left with the baby. John drank a few gulps of water before picking up his ticket, throwing down a five dollar tip on the table. He slowly made his way to the cash register.

"How was your meal, hon?" a tired-looking young woman asked as she rang up his total.

"Real good, thanks," he replied blandly as she handed him his change. He turned and started to leave, but abruptly turned back around. He caught the server's attention again by asking, "What kind of food can I order to bag up and take on the road with me? I'm not planning to stop for awhile, and I figure I'll get hungry again in a few hours."

The young lady thought for a moment and replied, "How about maybe a piece of pie, hon? Or I can throw in some biscuits instead, if you'd like that better. I don't think cold waffles and eggs sound too good." She smiled at John.

"Well, why don't I just order a big piece of that apple pie and a sausage biscuit? Can you fix that up for me?" John smiled.

"Sure, hon. I'll even throw in plastic forks and extra napkins. Want some bottled juice with that to-go order?"

John nodded, and the server scurried off to bag up his food. If his return trip went as smoothly as the morning's journey, he figured he would make it home before 7:00 p.m.

* * * * * *

Doug Brantley thought the trip home from Virginia would take forever. Each mile marker on Interstate 81 seemed to be farther and farther apart.

It had been over four hours since he'd talked to Stella from the Waffle House pay phone. She was groggy but otherwise fine. Stella reported that she had taken her medicine on schedule and ate part of the peanut butter sandwich that had been left on the tray. She wasn't in the mood to chat; she just wanted to get some more rest and snuggle with her "Teddy."

A contented baby – the newly resurrected Teddy Brantley — was now strapped in an appropriate, rear-facing car seat. He was riding in style in the latest Eddie Bauer model, and he was buckled securely in the passenger side back seat. John had adjusted his rearview mirror to catch occasional glimpses of the baby's moving arms and feet.

Doug was surprised that John hadn't wanted to talk about the new Teddy's background. The most John said was that the parents "gave him up" and weren't really the kind of parents who "could take proper care of an infant." It sounded as though the baby was unwanted, and Doug didn't want to prompt John to change his mind by pressing for more information. Doug let it be. John promised to have a long phone conversation with him in the near future. That was good enough for Doug. He could wait for answers.

Before Doug and the baby left John behind in Harrisonburg, John suggested that Doug use the deceased baby's birth certificate to establish a medical relationship with a new pediatrician. Reminding Doug that the new baby was so tiny, John cautioned him to wait a while before seeing

the doctor. "Let the baby get a little growth on him before you try to pass him off as being weeks older than he really is," John warned.

Doug promised to follow John's instructions. He swore he would raise the child as his own, never revealing the circumstances of the baby's substitution to another soul—not even Stella. The "new" Teddy Brantley would now be a living stand-in for the baby who perished weeks before.

Doug was confident that Stella could be quickly weaned from the induced fugue state of involuntary drug use. He planned to request additional time off from work to administer her reduced withdrawal dosages while concurrently devoting his attention to caring for the new baby. He would allow Stella to cuddle the teddy bear for as long as she wanted, but he would constantly remind her that she needed to be alert enough to care for their infant. Perhaps during the withdrawal period she would conclude that she had been "too sick," to care for her baby's needs. When she was strong enough, he hoped she would think the past few weeks had been a bad postpartum nightmare.

With the new baby in tow, the one unresolved issue for Doug was the missing drugs at work. However, unbeknownst to Doug at the time they parted, John had covered that problem, too. In the bottom of the bag containing baby supplies was a bottle of Valium, the very drug he had taken from work for Stella's daily use. The milligrams were the same. It had been prescribed to "Caroline Sanderson" several months before, and the bottle was almost full of the prescribed 60 pills. The bottle contained more than enough to cover the shortage he had pocketed over the past three weeks.

The plan was falling rapidly into place. Doug, like his friend John, also believed the recent coincidental events were the products of "a life-altering miracle." God had surely answered his prayers.

* * * * * *

Working the erratic schedule of an Emergency Medical Technician (EMT), Mike Lewis had three full days off before he had to report back to work. Precious days of personal time were perfect for running errands and catching up on laundry—at whatever pace Mike chose to do them. However, on December 5th he realized his free time would have to include taking care of Caroline's busy work.

Mike wasn't in a hurry to fulfill his promise to feed Lucas, his nephew-dog. Caroline hadn't taken the time to explain why he was appointed for this rescue mission, and he certainly was never a fan of his ex-brother-in-law, John. What he was about to do was for the benefit of his only sister because she asked—no, because she commanded. He chuckled to himself as he realized that he, like John, had always been a sucker when it came to Caroline's wishes.

After making a few business stops and paying a visit to the bank, Mike made his way to the Sanderson house and slowly pulled in the driveway. As he exited John's car, he noticed the neighborhood seemed unusually still and quiet. Brushing the thought aside, Mike walked up the driveway toward the house.

The back door—which was really on the side of the house—was ajar; however, Mike didn't notice this until he mistakenly tried to use the wrong key to unlock the door. With the first slight push, the door moved inward enough to prompt Mike to grin. *What is it with you, Caroline? Were you running too late to lock the friggin' door? Geez, girl.* Mike pushed the door open and entered the kitchen.

"Lucas? Lucas, come here, boy. Gotta get you fed." Mike listened for the sound of paws scampering on the linoleum, but there was none.

"Lucas, you asleep, boy? Where are you?" Mike walked slowly toward the living room. As he crossed the living room threshold, he was startled to

see two dark-clothed men waiting silently. One husky muscle man was sitting on the couch, and a smaller built man sat with his legs crossed in a side chair. There were no weapons in view.

"My God," a startled Mike said. "Who are you?"

The man on the couch responded gruffly, "Where's the baby? Tell us what we want to know and everything will be good here, capisci?

A confused and terrified Mike looked back and forth between the two men and then stuttered, "P-P-lease. I-I don't know what you're talking about. P-Please...I don't understand ..."

The big man on the couch shook his head in disappointment. He glanced at the smaller man in the chair, then shrugged his shoulders. The smaller man said nothing but nodded from the side chair.

The muscle man stood up and started to amble across the room toward his prey. Mike began to slowly retreat, but the big man grabbed Mike's collar as he tried to turn and escape. When Mike was jerked backwards, he lost his footing and sank to the floor, crashing the back of his head against the hard surface. Stunned and momentarily disoriented, he tried to rise but a heavy foot pushed him back down.

"The baby ... we were talking about the baby." The shorter man was talking now, bent forward from the waist and staring directly into Mike's eyes. "Now, once more. Where's the baby? We know you took him. We just want him back. Start talking now and save yourself from a long and painful afternoon of agony," Tony said.

Mike started to cry as he lay trapped on the floor. "I swear to you, I-I-I don't know what you're talking about. C-C-Caroline told me to ..."

"Caroline Sanderson?" Tony asked. Mike could only nod his head.

"You do every stupid thing your wife tells you? I guess she wanted a baby real bad, eh?" Tony asked. He stood straight up and motioned for the big man to do his job.

Mike attempted to clarify, "N-No, No. You don't understand! Caroline's my ..."

The shot rang out, but the silencer on the pistol muffled the noise. The two intruders stood there over the now faceless victim as the muscle man holstered his weapon.

A frustrated Tony exclaimed, "Geez, Carlo! Why'd you go and do that? Huh? I didn't want him dead yet. Now the bastard *can't* talk!"

"Sorry, boss. I thought you signaled that you wanted him dead, you know? No witnesses? He was looking right at us the whole time." Carlo looked at his hands like a little boy who had just been scolded by his mother.

Tony sighed deeply, then barked orders to his subordinate partner. "Go in the bedroom and get that dog's carcass outta there. You can throw it outside in the back yard for all I care. Just cover it up with something so it's not in plain sight."

Tony continued his instructions. "Then come back in here and drag this dead cocksucker to the bathroom. Put him in the tub and shut the door behind you. Leave him there to rot. Make sure you get rid of all this blood in here, too. I don't want to have to walk around it no more."

Knowing his place within the chain of command, Carlo nodded and immediately went into bedroom to follow Tony's orders.

Tony walked slowly across the living room before he finished his orders. We'll be camping out here for the rest of the day, or until this Caroline bitch brings home that baby."

Tony reached the side chair, sat down slowly, and then crossed his short legs. He stared off in the distance while he mentally replayed the past fifteen minutes.

He was glad John Sanderson swallowed the end of a pistol, but he knew Carlo should have waited a few more minutes to see if the bastard would have talked some more. It didn't matter now. He found out enough.

Tony's thoughts ran logically for once. *The wife was involved—he as much as said so. I should have known a man wouldn't be taking a baby for himself. The bitch must have been nagging him about having one. Bad luck for him that he picked the wrong baby.*

His next intimate interview would be with Caroline Sanderson. *She'd better have that baby with her, or have some good answers. Otherwise, she'd be eating the end of a pistol, too.*

But, her grand finale wouldn't come until after Tony had a chance to inflict her with a little bodily damage of his own. Tony smiled as he rested his head against the fake suede padding of the chair back. He was imagining his afternoon escapade with Caroline, complete with bondage nudity, sex and violence.

* * * * *

Caroline took a late lunch to offset her tardiness that morning. She left her office at 2:00 p.m., wondering if she should pick up a pizza to share with her brother. She felt badly about running in and out of his house so quickly, not even explaining what had happened the night before. On top of that, she'd left him with the responsibility of feeding her dog. She forced him to drive John's car, too, and it needed gas.

Poor Mike deserved some extra gratitude and attention. She would get the biggest pepperoni, sausage, onion, olive and extra cheese pizza she

could find on her route home. She was sure he had plenty of beer in the fridge, so only one stop ought to do it.

She was proud of herself for thinking about Mike first. He had always felt like he was in second place when it came to Caroline, and she had always been aware of it. During their childhood, she never tried to make him feel any differently, either. Now that they were older, Caroline often forgot about Mike until she needed something from him. *But isn't that the way siblings treat each other?* Seemed like a normal routine in Caroline's eyes, even now.

She got the large pizza and travelled swiftly to Mike's house. The car wasn't in the driveway and the house looked still. Caroline didn't stop the car's engine as she surveyed the house; instead, she stayed on the road. She was going to John's house to check on Lucas. If Mike hadn't fed Lucas like he promised, she would personally make him regret his poor memory.

When she rounded the corner on Briarwood Street, she was relieved to see John's car parked at the house. Of course, that meant Mike had driven it over to attend to Lucas.

Playing musical cars was confusing to Caroline. Here she was in Mike's car. Mike was here in John's car. John was who-knows-where in her car. Seemed more like a shell game to her. She pulled in the drive and turned off the motor.

Without thinking, she automatically reached in her purse to dig out her keychain with the house's back/side door key attached. She suddenly remembered that her keys were with John. She would have to knock to get in.

Expecting the large pizza box and full bag of bread sticks to be tough to balance going up the steps, she left the key in the ignition and her purse on the seat. Caroline planned to return momentarily to retrieve both.

Facing the house's side door from the top step, she juggled the large box and bag, giving herself an unencumbered knuckle to rap on the kitchen door's window pane. She peeped through the glass but saw no one approaching from inside. She knocked again, but harder. Frustrated, she turned the knob and the door latch released. She pushed the door open with the edge of the pizza box and took short steps to enter the kitchen.

I don't hear Lucas. Maybe Mike has taken him out for a walk. How sweet of him to do that for me. She quickly grabbed two plates from the cabinet and silverware from the drawer. She found paper napkins displayed in an ornate crystal napkin holder one of her aunts had given her and John as a wedding gift. It looked strangely out of place in the bachelor's undecorated kitchen. *I should have taken that with me. It came from my side of the family anyway.*

Caroline approached the back door again to look out the window panes. She strained to see as far around the house as possible, trying to get a glimpse of her brother with the dog. No luck. She stepped out on the top step, and suddenly her attention was drawn to John's parked car.

She slowly moved toward it, spying a tiny corner of something white caught in the front passenger's side door. She opened the car door, discovering that a white baby blanket had somehow worked its way out from under the seat or from behind the seat—she wasn't sure from where it had emerged. She picked it up and was about to go back in the house.

 A peripheral glance toward the rear of the house caused her to stop in her tracks. For a second, she would have sworn she saw Lucas' nose peeking from under a piece of old blanket near the rear house corner. Was he hiding? Was it even Lucas? Whatever it was, she couldn't get a good look at it without walking further up the driveway.

She stood there holding the white baby blanket, wondering what was coming over her. Suddenly, she felt as though her skin would crawl off her body. She involuntarily shivered, feeling the onset of "fight or flight." Her gut instinct told her to choose "flight."

Instead of listening to her inner alarm, she slowly moved closer to the rear edge of the house. What she saw made her cup her hand over her mouth in an awkward attempt to stifle a scream. A lifeless Lucas was lying under a blood-soaked blanket; only part of his muzzle was showing. She could see a horizontal line of red blood saturating the blanket—so much blood—his head must have been nearly severed from his body.

In her panic, she thought she heard movement from inside the house. Her instinct was to rush in and slap the holy hell out of her brother for not taking care of Lucas—for letting him die on his watch. But common sense was trying to barge its way into Caroline's thought process.

Mike would never hurt anyone or anything, especially Lucas. He must not have been able to prevent it. And he wouldn't have dumped Lucas' body like this, either.

At that moment, Caroline masked her fear with a show of bravado, and then turned to walk toward Mike's car—the one she had driven today because John's car had been low on gas.

She had no idea what was going on in the house, but instincts told her she wouldn't be able to do anything about it...at least, not alone. Dumb luck and distractions had gotten her out of the house before she found out what was happening. She feared her brother might be in trouble inside, or maybe worse. She refused to think those kinds of thoughts.

She tried to act normal and pace her steps. If someone was watching from inside, she didn't want them to think she was doing anything other than getting her purse or something from the car.

When she opened the driver's door, she reached in as if she was trying to find something, then sat behind the wheel and leaned over as if she was getting something from the glove compartment. After a moment, she sat straight up. Caroline quickly turned the key that had been left in the ignition, and hurriedly backed out of the driveway. She waited to close the driver's door when the car was in reverse motion. When she was safely on the road and pointed in a forward direction, she floored the gas pedal to make her fast getaway.

* * * * * *

The two men lurking silently in the Sanderson house finally spoke to each other.

"Wonder what tipped her off?" Carlo asked.

"For some reason I'm thinking it was a dead dog, you imbecile. She was looking at something in the car, too, and she was holding a baby blanket. I'm betting she had the baby in the car with her." Tony deduced.

"Go get our car from the next street over, and let's get out of here. NOW!" Tony barked.

"Right away, boss," Carlo responded without batting an eye. He quickly left through the kitchen door.

Tony reached in his pocket, pulling out J. Sanderson's BNL badge the Viper had given him a few short hours before. He glanced at the man's badge picture once more, concluding that the guy had looked much better in person.

Too bad nobody will ever get to see that charming face no more, eh? Tony thought as he carefully wiped away his fingerprints from the badge. He tossed it on the kitchen counter as he strolled one last time toward the master bath.

Peering into the tub to see the faceless corpse of his latest victim didn't affect Tony in the least. In fact, Tony smirked when he took the matchbook from his pocket and lit the first tiny stick.

After raking the single flame along the decorative nylon shower curtain, Tony carefully ignited the entire book of matches. As it instantly combusted, Tony dropped the flaming matchbook on the woven bath mat lying adjacent to the tub. He could smell the thick smoke billowing behind him as he left the bathroom to make his way back into the kitchen.

"Might as well bag up the pizza," Tony said aloud to himself as he realized he was getting hungry. "Shouldn't let it go to waste. That'd be a crime," Tony chuckled to himself as he grabbed the takeout box and exited the smoldering house.

CHAPTER 9

Monday, December 5, 1994

She was on the brink of hysteria, and her reckless driving confirmed it. Caroline had no idea where to go or what to do next. Moving toward the house she shared with her brother was the subconscious direction she took. However, she wondered if Mike's house would be a *safe* place to go.

No matter, she had to chance it. She had to grab as many of her clothes and personal belongings that she could. She knew in her heart that bad people would be coming for her next since they had found John's house so easily. Caroline was afraid to think about her brother; she feared something awful had happened to him inside John's house. If she thought about it too much, she would break down and be of no help to anyone. She had to stay focused for just a little bit longer.

What was going on? What prompted someone to kill a sweet little dog like Lucas? And where was Mike? Was he hiding somewhere?

The only thing different in all their otherwise boring lives had been John's rescue of the baby from the wreck. That child must have belonged to someone very important—or very powerful. Scary powerful.

Caroline circled the block around her brother's house several times. On the fourth trip around, she convinced herself that nothing looked out of the ordinary on his property. She pulled into the driveway, slowly got out of the car, and casually made her way to the door. She pushed the center of the door but it held steady. The key turned in the lock, indicating that Mike had locked up when he left. When she entered the house, she

peeked around the door jamb to scan the room for disruption. Everything looked as it had that morning.

Quietly stepping inside the room, she picked up an umbrella that had been leaning by the door. It wasn't much of a weapon, but it was better than nothing. She stealthily made her way through the living room. Caroline passed into the undisturbed kitchen, then walked slowly into Mike's bedroom to find everything in place. Her own room looked just as she had left it. There were no boogie men in the bathroom or behind the shower curtain.

Taking a deep but quivering breath, Caroline grabbed all the clothes that she could and stuffed them in her luggage. Her mind was functioning well enough to remember her check book and various banking papers. She also retrieved her passport and anything else she believed necessary for the long-term. Caroline had no idea when she'd be back—if ever.

She carried out her belongings and stowed them in the back of Mike's Jeep Cherokee. She almost left before remembering something important. Climbing back out of the car, she ran to the door, and entered the house in search of pen and paper. She found a notepad magnetically stuck on the refrigerator with a pen attached to it. She had to let John know how to find her. She wrote:

> *"Let's meet at the place where we had our first date. I think we still have things to talk about. See you at 8:30."*

She didn't sign or date the note, but left it in plain sight. Caroline thought the message was adequately encrypted. It could have been left at any time in the past; also, it could have been written by anyone for anybody. If John came there looking for her, he would recognize her handwriting and realize the note was for him. If she had to, she'd be at the designated

spot for several nights in a row to connect with John, since she had no idea when he planned to return.

She prayed John would stop by Mike's first before going home. Otherwise, she feared he would join her brother in whatever horrible nightmare Mike might be enduring.

* * * * * *

Caroline had only made it a couple of miles from Mike's house when concern for her brother's well-being overtook her. She pulled into a convenience store parking lot; she sat in her car trying to think of what she could do to track down Mike—or save Mike. Finally, she got out of her car, scanned the light traffic, and walked a few feet to a pay phone. She dialed 9-1-1.

"9-1-1, what's your emergency?" the dispatcher asked.

Caroline coughed, but then said, "There's a disturbance at my neighbor's house. It's bad. Could you check it out? It's at 189 Briarwood Street in Hicksville."

The dispatcher was quick to answer. "You mean the fire? That's already been reported, ma'am. Are you close to the residence now? Do you need assistance, ma'am?"

Caroline hung up without answering the dispatcher. *Oh my God! The house is on fire! Where's Mike? Oh God, please let Mike be safe!* Caroline thought as her heartbeat rapidly increased.

* * * * * *

John Sanderson was listening to radio music and singing along with popular songs as he drove the VW Beetle from Virginia back to New York. His spirits were high, and he was making great time. He expected to arrive in Hicksville by 7:00 p.m. He hoped Caroline would join him for

dinner so he could fill her in on the day's events. He was pleased that the baby's handoff had gone like clockwork.

He didn't expect to hear from Doug until the next day, but he found himself anxious to know how the baby was doing. He wondered if Stella had been alert enough to hold him yet. John smiled as he imagined all the lovely scenarios that could be happening at that very moment in the Brantley household—all because John had acted on his instincts when God revealed the baby to him at the accident scene. John couldn't help but smile. He felt a sense of joy and overwhelming peace that he hadn't experienced since before he and Caroline divorced.

* * * * * *

Even in her anxious state, Caroline was smart enough to know she shouldn't leave any financial paper trail behind until she was convinced no one was hunting her. She stopped at the local branch of her bank, catching the teller just as she was about to lock the door for the night. Caroline told the lady that there had been a family emergency prompting her to withdraw funds from her account. She had to have money for travel expenses, Caroline explained.

Taking pity on Caroline and her sob story, the teller opened the door to help Caroline with her transaction. Minutes later when Caroline left the bank, she had a little over $7,500 in cash in her purse.

* * * * * *

At 7:05 p.m., John Sanderson drove the teal blue VW Beetle into a Hicksville gas station to fill up the tank. He owed Caroline at least that, considering how he had taken her car without her explicit permission. John was confident he would be forgiven if he showed up with a full gas tank when he exchanged cars with his ex-wife. He got out of the car, stretching his aching body for a moment before reaching for the gas nozzle. A whiff of stale smoke drifted through his nostrils as he turned to

look for evidence of a nearby fire. He saw billows of smoke coming from the direction of his neighborhood, but he was too far away to be certain.

He finished fueling the car and walked briskly toward the windowed cashier station situated in the middle of the station's plaza. Without conversation, John slid a $20 bill through the tray. The cashier was preoccupied, listening attentively to a police scanner perched on a side table near his chair.

"Something going on around here? Where's that smoke coming from?" John asked casually.

As he reached for the money, the cashier never looked at John's face. He made the proper change, pushed it back through the sliding tray toward John, and unemotionally commented, "House fire on Briarwood Street. Total loss, I think."

At that point, the cashier lit a cigarette and turned back toward the scanner. John returned to his car, wondering if the neighborhood streets would be too congested with emergency vehicles for him to make it home. It didn't occur to John that his house might be the one on fire.

As he approached his neighborhood, John began to wonder just how close the fire might be to his own home. When John pulled up to the stop sign to make the right turn onto Briarwood Street, the roadway was blocked by sawhorses and policemen diverting traffic to a detour. John leaned as far as he could to the right, trying so see past the officers before he made forward progress.

Instantly, he knew the fire was either at his house or was engulfing one of his adjacent neighbors' houses. Beginning to feel panicky but still not believing what he was witnessing, he finally drove straight through the intersection. He followed the policeman's directions for the detour, but he had to find a way to check his house. He had to know exactly which house was ablaze. If it was his, where was Lucas?

John parked next to the curb on the detour street as he tried to form a quick plan of action. He didn't think he could drive through Briarwood Street from the other end because of more road blocks. His only solution was to walk. He turned off the motor and got out of the car.

A pedestrian came around the corner from Briarwood Street, walking slowly and shaking his head. As he approached John coming from the other direction, he nodded hello and kept walking. John nodded back, but quickly decided to ask about the status of the neighborhood fire.

"What's happening down there? Could you get close enough to see anything?" John asked the stranger.

"I couldn't get any farther down the street than the second house on the left because of all the fire trucks and equipment blocking the road. But the fourth house—you know, the small gray one with the white trim on the left side of the street? That house is nothing but ashes now. Apparently it's been burning for a while. I really hope no one was inside, because they couldn't have survived that. Looked pretty awful to me. What a shame, and right before Christmas, too." The pedestrian shook his head in pity.

John smiled weakly, thanking him for the information. As the pedestrian moved past John on the sidewalk, John slowly returned to the VW Beetle. He believed he would pass out if he didn't get off his feet quickly.

John sat down in the driver's seat attempting to catch his breath and to comprehend the bad news. His fears about Lucas now shifted to concern about Caroline. He had to find her. He had to find her fast.

* * * * * *

When John pulled into Mike's empty driveway, there were no lights on in the house. Wondering if Caroline's key ring held a house key, he made his way to the front door. He was surprised to find the door unlocked.

He stepped inside the house and called out. "Caroline? Mike? Anybody here?" No response. He switched on a table lamp as he passed by the couch. He quickly made his way through the small home, taking note that the room Caroline occupied had been emptied of clothing and personal effects.

He hurriedly entered and scanned the kitchen, spying a pad of paper lying in the center of the breakfast table. Realizing that there was something written on it, John picked up the pad and read Caroline's handwritten message. The hairs on the back of his neck prickled. He felt a sense of urgency to leave.

It was 7:45 p.m. by the time he backed out of the driveway. He headed toward the rendezvous point, fearful of what he was going to discover when he talked to his ex-wife. He prayed she was all right and that Lucas was with her. John had so many questions about what had happened in Hicksville during the past fourteen hours. Unfortunately for John, the inner peace he had felt on the drive from Virginia was now transformed into confusion and anguish.

* * * * * *

Caroline had parked the Jeep Cherokee in the parking space right in front of the entrance to the American Diner. Several years ago, she and John spent their first date at this establishment.

Even then, John knew Caroline wasn't one for fancy restaurants. After hours of torturous deliberation, he finally settled on taking her to the American Diner. Years later, they both laughed about his choice of restaurants, joking that John could have at least splurged on a "real" dinner instead of treating Caroline to a cheeseburger, fries, and a milkshake.

She took a seat in a rear booth, selecting the spot carefully. The location was perfect for a private conversation since most of the few customers

sat nearer to the front or at the counter. She ordered a large chocolate shake while she monitored the distant front door for traffic.

Within a half hour, she spotted John approaching the door. He looked worn out, and his face wore an apprehensive expression. She half-stood and waved in an attempt to get his attention. He hurried to the back of the restaurant to join her, leaning over to give her a quick embrace before he took his seat. When he was positioned across the table from her, he noticed her tears of relief. He reached across and took her hand.

"Talk to me, Caroline. What's happened? Where's Lucas?"

Instead of responding, Caroline buried her face in her hands and sobbed openly. John moved to her side of the table, wrapping his arms around her as best he could within the confines of the padded booth.

Finally, Caroline was able to give John a rundown of everything that had happened since he had left her asleep in his home. He listened solemnly, taking in every word. He cried when he heard about Lucas, and became outraged when he thought Caroline had been in danger. John was trying to make sense out of the house fire, realizing that Caroline's getaway had to have happened right before the fire started. He didn't understand any of this, and neither did Caroline. They both tried to figure out if Mike had managed to escape.

"I can't imagine why I am being targeted, Caroline," John thought aloud, "unless someone knows I took the baby from the wreck. I had on gloves, so there couldn't have been fingerprints. I would have sworn there were no other cars anywhere around when all that happened." John was stumped.

"Could you have lost your work badge somewhere around the accident scene? Wouldn't that have identified you? You already said you couldn't find it, and you retraced your steps at home several times," Caroline innocently asked.

John's eyes got wide when he realized Caroline was probably right. "If someone's looking for me, then they aren't doing it just to make a new friend. Oh shit, Caroline, what have I done?"

Caroline responded, "We have to *carefully* think through this, John. We need to get out of sight and go underground for a few days until something clicks or makes sense." Caroline made eye contact with John, both becoming more fearful and anxious as the minutes ticked by.

"How much did you pack when you left, John?" Caroline asked.

John closed his eyes as if he was taking a mental inventory. He sighed when he answered, "I didn't pack anything. It was just a day trip, Caroline. Everything I have is at home—was at home." John looked at his hands, feeling very defeated.

Caroline tried to form a cautious mental plan, but everything she thought of required one more visit to Mike's house. "Okay, John. I have some cash, so I want you to check into a nearby motel using a fake name. Pay cash and don't show your ID. Just get us a room, and then come back here. Sit in this same booth and wait for me," Caroline directed.

"I'm gonna go back to Mike's and pick up some of his things for you to use. I suspect the clothes will be a close fit; but if you can't fit into them, you can wear his sweats and tee shirts until we can get you something else. I'm going to try to grab some of his legal papers, too. It might help in the long run. Okay?" she asked.

Again, John realized Caroline always took control. This time, however, he was thankful. "Okay, Caroline. See you back here."

Caroline left a $10 bill on the table to cover the cost of the milkshake. They made their way to the front door where they hastily parted. Each of them was embarking on a dangerous mission that would forever change their lives.

Sacrificial Sins

CHAPTER 10

Monday, December 5, 1994

Cathy Giordano had been functioning robotically ever since her precious baby had been taken from his crib and spirited away by the unidentified intruders. During the past two days, she had paid little attention to her daughter or the newborn son the abductors had ignored. Cathy felt as though a part of her heart had been ripped from her chest; her soul had been savagely dissected, vulnerable to siege by despair. She tried to make herself believe that her baby boy would be recovered unharmed. She would be reunited with him once again, somehow.

The clock moved in slow motion for the anxious mother. Every minute that ticked by seemed more like an hour to Cathy. She refused to take any more sedatives, fearing she would not be alert enough to fully experience the baby's safe return. In desperation, she put her faith in the police department, believing that their investigation and quick response would surely lead them to the discovery of her missing baby. She was praying constantly; she had to have faith.

Lorenzo had been on edge and jumpy, and appeared to be easily agitated. To Cathy, abnormal behavior was to be expected under the circumstances; however, when she made optimistic remarks about getting their newborn back home, Lorenzo only frowned and exited the room. Cathy was left alone with her misery. Lorenzo planned to return to work on Tuesday after only one full day at home with Cathy, her mother, and the children. She would be glad when he left the house, even though she

couldn't understand how he could make himself do it so soon. How could he even *think* about anything but their loss?

Genevieve, Cathy's mother, had been no help to her daughter. Instead, she had continuously recounted the horrific incident to her multitude of friends in Nashville. As soon as she was clear-headed enough to carry on a conversation, she phoned her social circle members to inform them of the tragedy. It was apparent to Cathy that Genevieve was more concerned— maybe even excited—about her own dramatic experience than the safe recovery of her grandson.

Cathy allowed the nanny Lorenzo hired to care for her two children's immediate needs. She believed that it would take a little while for her to pay them the attention they deserved. Feeling alone and helpless, she settled in on a chaise lounge in the expansive windowed sunroom.

With the television news channel switched on for background noise, she surveyed her elegant surroundings. Cathy found herself loathing the house that had once been her dream home. She was beginning to detest her husband, her mother, and her own shallow life. All she could do effectively was drink wine and cry.

* * * * * *

Tony Caprio and his sidekick, Carlo, stood outside the mahogany front doors of the Viper's Southampton mansion. Tony cleared his throat, rang the doorbell, and wiped a stray hair off his coat sleeve. Carlo stood at attention directly behind Tony on the porch.

The butler opened the door, recognized the visitors, and promptly ushered them inside. They followed the butler to the den where the Viper sat waiting in his favorite leather chair.

"Sit down gentlemen. Tell me some good news," the Viper commanded.

"Well, we located J. Sanderson, but he acted like he didn't know nothing," Tony started. "We squeezed him some, but he still acted dumb. He tried to get away, so we had to take care of him. He had seen our faces, you know."

The Viper glared at Tony. "What exactly did you do?"

Tony nervously cleared his throat, pulling at his collar to give himself more breathing room. "Well, we had already cased the house, and there was nothin' there that made us think a baby had been there. We laid low inside until Sanderson drove up in his car. We surprised him when he came in, and knocked him around a little. He was so scared I thought he was gonna piss his pants." Tony chuckled, but the Viper saw no humor in the remark. Carlo's stoic expression didn't change.

"Uh, hum, anyway," Tony continued, "he tried to take off and we jumped him again. He fell down on the floor and hit his head, hard enough to cause brain damage even. He told us he was just doing what Caroline told him. That's his ex-wife. We're going to run a check on her now to find out where she lives and works. Should have the information by late tonight or first thing tomorrow."

The Viper continued staring at Tony. "You still haven't answered my question. What did you do with Sanderson?"

Tony hesitated, then said, "He got shot in the face. He's now been cremated because we set fire to the house before we left. No evidence left behind, and no witness either."

The Viper closed his eyes, wondering why he ever allowed a hot head like Tony to take charge of something this important. Calmly, he stated, "So now there will be an arson investigation, they'll discover the body with a bullet still in his head, and once again we have to pay off somebody to keep a lid on this shit. Am I saying all this right?"

Tony looked at the floor. "Well, when you say it like that, it don't sound so good, eh? But we can handle all that. Believe me, we'll get this ex-wife. She drove up while we were there, and we almost had her anyway. She took off before she came in the house the second time. And, she had a baby blanket in her hand. Carlo and I think maybe the baby was in the car with her when she brought in the pizza."

The Viper looked back and forth between Carlo and Tony. "She brought in pizza. So she came in the house while you were there and brought in pizza? Why did you let her leave?" The Viper was trying to maintain his cool, but it was getting harder by the minute.

"We were waiting in the living room, just like when we waited for Sanderson. We heard her come in the back door, we could smell pizza, and then she yelled for the dog. When he didn't come to her, she stepped back out the door to look for him, I guess. It all happened fast. She never came back in the house. But we watched through the window and saw her take a baby blanket out of Sanderson's car. She took it to her car, got in, and took off like a speed demon."

The Viper was fuming. *How could these supposedly "experienced" mob men act like such bumbling unprofessional idiots?* "What happened to the dog? You said there was a dog?"

"We cut his throat and took him in the back yard at the corner of the house. We covered him with a blanket," Carlo volunteered this information.

"**DAMMIT, YOU IDIOTS.** You killed a man before he could give you any real information, you killed an innocent dog for no good reason, and you let our last hope of getting any solid information about the baby **ESCAPE!** Then you draw attention from the **WHOLE FUCKING TOWN** to the little bonfire you set, which—by the way—happens to have mixed in with the ashes and debris a **HUMAN BODY WITH YOUR BULLET IN IT.** Your little

fire stunt invites the city government to take charge of this case and start an official investigation." The Viper was shouting so forcefully that spittle shot through the air when he emphasized his words.

Both Tony and Carlo were petrified. Neither had been on this end of the Viper's wrath, and it wasn't where they ever wanted to be again.

The Viper stopped shouting and rubbed his hand across his forehead. He sighed, taking several deep breaths to calm himself. He once again got his emotions back in check. Vincenzo looked at both men, then calmly said, "I expect you to find the ex-wife and the baby. I'm giving you 48 hours to find them both. Report back to me by Wednesday evening at eight o'clock— or before if you make progress. Otherwise, I'll be forced to deal with you two directly. Now get out of here. Your clock's ticking."

Both men looked as though they had been given two days to dig an escape tunnel to China without shovels. It might as well have been that assignment, because the one they were given was going to be hard to deliver. They hadn't started the inquiry into Caroline Sanderson's demographics; however, now that the clock was ticking, they knew better than to procrastinate. They had to get on top of it, NOW.

* * * * * *

Doug Brantley decided to take the whole week off from work, using the remaining available vacation days he had accumulated for use before the end of the calendar year. He had planned to use those vacation days during the Christmas holidays, but his plans had changed now that little Teddy needed his full-time attention.

When he mentally replayed his arrival with the new baby, he couldn't help but smile broadly. What a wonderful night! He walked in holding the baby in his arms, finding Stella in the bedroom groggily rousing from her nap. The substitute bear was lying on Doug's pillow on his side of the bed. Before Stella could focus well, Doug had laid the baby down in the

center of the bed next to his wife. He asked her, "Stella, don't you think it's time you took over full time care of our baby? I can't do it all the time. You know I have to work." His questions were posed as if Stella intentionally had been ignoring her baby in favor of a toy.

Stella looked at Doug questioningly, and said, "I thought I was doing pretty well. Is there something I need to do differently?" She was trying to remember the past weeks, but her drug-induced memories were not clear.

"Honey, we'll work together with Teddy this week, and then next week you can do it all by yourself. Maybe by the end of next week you'll feel up to coming by the plant so I can show off my son. How would you like that?" Doug beamed, hoping she was going to become as excited as he was.

"Do you think I'll be up to it, Doug?" Stella asked, still feeling woozy.

"Absolutely. Now why don't you feed our son. I'm pretty sure he's hungry." Doug handed Stella a fresh bottle of formula, leaving her alone in the bedroom to reacquaint herself with her baby boy.

* * * * * *

While John was busy getting the couple a motel room, Caroline swiftly pulled into her brother's empty driveway. Knowing that time was not on her side, she trotted to the unlocked front door.

As she entered the dark house, she felt her stomach begin to knot up. Tiny beads of sweat formed on her forehead. Caroline's heartbeat quickened as she raced with the clock.

Mike's room was always neat, so finding clothing and personal items for John to borrow was easy. She pulled her brother's old suitcase out from under the bed, stuffing it full of the items she had gathered. The harder

quest was locating Mike's important papers. He had a desk in the corner of the bedroom, but the drawers were locked.

No longer concerned about avoiding property damage, Caroline grabbed a hammer from the kitchen's tool drawer and pounded the lock area of the center desk drawer. After a few hard knocks, the desk drawer sprung open. To her surprise, the center drawer's release also unlocked the side file drawers.

Caroline raked the contents of the center drawer into a gym bag that had been stowed in the floor of her brother's closet. When she opened the desk's side drawers, she found them overflowing with files holding household bills, bank statements, and other miscellaneous papers. He had years' worth of medical files, including corresponding insurance policies. His tax returns for the past seven years were neatly lined up in hanging file folders with annual labels clearly marked. Caroline was amazed that Mike had been so diligent in recording and maintaining his personal documents.

Ignoring the household records, Caroline grabbed the medical files and tax returns. She then stuffed a few other personal files in the bag for good measure. Miscellaneous financial information and the bank statement file was loaded last before she zipped up the gym bag.

She had no time to take an inventory of the items she took. She knew her time was limited, and she had to swiftly get out of the house and out of the neighborhood. Grabbing the heavy suitcase and bulging gym bag, she left the house through the front door.

She circled the Jeep and loaded the baggage through the rear cargo door. She hurriedly got in the driver's seat and turned on the engine. She tried to calm herself. Praying there was nothing left inside that could tip off an intruder about her daily habits or routines, she made a split-second decision.

Forgive me, Mike. I hope you can understand someday how scared I am for us both. I'm so sorry. Caroline struggled with her thoughts for only a moment. She left the vehicle running in the driveway as she ran back inside the house.

Sacrificial Sins

CHAPTER 11

Monday, December 5, 1994

Diego Moretti had been patient with his wife ever since the accident. Each time she unexpectedly burst into tears at the slightest thing—even television commercials for baby shampoo set her off—he tried his best to comfort her. But enough was enough. She had been a mess far too long, in his opinion. She had to get herself together. Besides, he hadn't had a drink since Sunday afternoon, several hours before the now-missing baby was handed to them through the car window. He had to get out of the apartment and take a break from Juliana's hysterics for a while.

"Juliana, I think I'll run down to the corner bar and catch up with the guys. You want I should bring you a sandwich or something?" His superficial smile turned to an expression of trepidation as he approached the chaise lounge on which she reclined amid a massive group of silk and satin pillows. Her loathsome glare pierced his thin armor of courage. He knew that look.

"Get the hell out of my sight, you worthless piece of shit. If it hadn't been for you, we'd still have that baby. You disgust me. This is all *your* fault, you know. You did this." With that, she picked up a heavy ash tray from the side table and lobbed it toward his face. As Diego ducked, she started wailing again.

"Juliana, ...baby. Calm down. We'll get this fixed. Your father's on top of it," he said with a waning amount of patience that he didn't realize he could muster. His fear of Juliana's wrath was only surpassed by the fear he harbored toward her father.

"Just go, Diego. Just leave me alone." Her answer was muffled as she hid her face behind a plump pillow.

Taking no chances, Diego took the escape Juliana offered. He moved quickly toward the door and was gone in a flash. When Juliana looked up again, she realized she was thankful for her solitude. Diego had been smothering her with his constant questions about how she was feeling ever since they had left her father's house in Southampton.

Without her father to take care of her, she was certain she would have left Diego a long time ago. He gambled too much, and he drank far too much. There was no telling where they would be living if her father hadn't allowed them to move into his empty penthouse apartment overlooking Central Park. Their car had been his, too. Between the two of them, she and Diego really had nothing but an affinity to have a good time and party with rowdy friends. Now that she had a tiny taste of what a family could mean, she realized the two of them didn't have enough things in common anymore. It was time to grow up and assume some responsibility. The problem, it seemed, was that neither of them knew how to take the first step. The status quo was too easy, and the financial help from her father was more than convenient.

She slumped back into her pillows and thought about her future. For a second she thought the unthinkable: maybe Papa could get rid of Diego for her and she could start over. She gasped as she realized what that actually could mean. *No, No, No. Don't go there.*

She had to get up the nerve to ask Diego for a divorce. It had been a long time coming, anyway. He came home drunker and higher all the time. She had put up with his antics for longer than she thought she ever would. Why? It was probably because she didn't want to admit to her father that she had made a mistake. She didn't want to hear his "I warned you..." lecture. Her father disliked Diego from the time he first laid eyes on him.

It ought to be easy enough to start the divorce proceedings. If Diego protested, **then** she could go to her father for help. Whatever help he could provide would be fine with her as long as she didn't know all the details.

She smiled for the first time since the baby vanished from her arms. Maybe if she was free again she could find someone her father would welcome into the family—someone who wasn't sterile like Diego—someone with a fascinating future to offer her. And babies. Lots of babies.

* * * * *

Caroline had mixed feelings about what she was getting ready to do. She knew that Mike had recently been in trouble at work when he started a scuffle with one of his co-workers. One of the crew started teasing him about his dating history—or lack thereof—resulting in name calling and punch throwing.

All his life, Mike had been shy around women, especially good looking women. He took his sister, Caroline, to his senior prom because he was too afraid of rejection from any of his female classmates. Since then, he had notoriously been labeled as a "queer" or "fag," which Caroline believed was totally untrue.

Still, he had suffered most of his adult life because of his crippling shyness toward women, and eventually learned to ignore the rumors and slurs. Caroline was proud of Mike for standing his ground with the bullies at work. Unfortunately, now she was going to become an honorary member of the bully club, too.

As she looked in the pantry of the rental house she and her brother shared, Caroline found the can of black spray paint Mike had bought for touching up his rusted wrought iron patio chairs. He hadn't gotten around to it last fall when the idea was fresh on his mind. The unopened

can still stood in the same spot where it was initially placed when he brought it home from the store.

She opened the lid and hurried toward the living room, aiming the spray nozzle toward the blank wall above the couch. She purposely sprayed the words, "GET OUT FAG – WE WILL CUM FOR YOU" in huge letters on the beige wall. She turned and sprayed again, this time on the front of Mike's Sony television. She sprayed "QUEER" across the big screen.

She moved quickly through the house, pulling out drawers and dumping contents as if someone had purposely ransacked the place. She dropped dishes on the floor and smashed the oven's window door with the same hammer she had used earlier to open the desk. She emptied the refrigerator's contents onto the middle of the kitchen floor.

Knowing time was of the essence, she grabbed a box of matches from the kitchen junk drawer, then hurried outside the house. Looking cautiously around the quiet neighborhood, she took her next bold step. She painted the front siding of the house with the same cruel words she had written inside. It looked ominous and threatening. Surely, it would be perceived as a menacing threat to the house's occupants—perhaps enough to make them vacate the house in the middle of the night.

The final step in her plan was the most dangerous. She took the empty aerosol can and threw it on the fringe of the trash heap that Mike's neighbors had so conveniently built and then ignored. As she tossed a lit match toward the edge of the pile, she watched the flicker of the flame begin to grow. She ran to her car and backed out of the driveway as quietly and quickly as possible.

She was less than a mile away when the flickering flame went out. The trash pile smoldered slightly where the match had landed, but only a scant bit of smoke now swirled around the edge of the pile. The spray can

remained untouched by the flame, as did most of the trash Caroline had hoped to turn into a raging bonfire.

* * * * * *

John Sanderson nervously played with a plate of french fries in the back corner booth at the American Café. He had been there for over fifteen minutes expecting Caroline to appear at any second. He wondered why it was taking her so long to pick up a few things at Mike's. He was getting anxious.

When she rushed through the restaurant door, he sighed with relief. He suddenly felt hungry, and pushed two fat potato slivers into his mouth.

Caroline slid into the booth next to him, relieved to see John back from his errand of securing a motel room.

"Is that all you've eaten?" she asked John. He nodded as he chewed.

"Let's get an order to go and get out of here. I don't think we should discuss anything important in public. Want the usual?" she asked her ex-.

Again, John nodded as Caroline went to the counter to order their take-out dinner. She added two desserts to the order, plus an extra side of fries. They would get soft drinks from the vending machine at the motel. For now, this would have to get them through the long sleepless night ahead.

* * * * * *

"Holy shit, Carlo, would you look at that," Tony exclaimed as they slowly approached the house where Caroline Sanderson had been residing for the past two years.

"Looks like somebody has a grudge or something," Carlo stated the obvious.

113

Tony shook his head in disgust. "You know, I don't like fags. They give me the creeps. But vandalism like this is going too far. Probably the work of juvenile delinquents who need their asses kicked. What's the world coming to, eh?"

Carlo, nodded his head in agreement. Tony seemed to have no trouble rearranging a victim's face or tiptoeing around gore. But... graffiti? Neither of the thugs understood defacing property like that. It seemed disrespectful.

Carlo pulled the Cadillac over to the curb in front of the vandalized house. They scanned the surroundings before exiting the vehicle. Tony kept his hand on his holstered pistol, but Carlo walked up the driveway as if he owned the place. When he got to the front door, he turned to see if Tony had caught up to him.

"What? Go on, you goon. I'm right behind you. I got you covered if a boogie man jumps out of there," Tony chuckled. Carlo gave Tony a reprehensible look, then pushed open the unlocked door.

"Jeez, boss. Looks like somebody did a number on this place. Whoever this fag is, somebody's got it in for him. You sure this Caroline person lives here?" Carlo questioned.

"Yeah, I'm sure. She's used this address on everything from her telephone bill to her driver's license. This is the place." The two walked silently through the mess, each wondering if their informant really had been mistaken.

"Look here, boss." Carlo stopped to pick up a picture frame that had been broken during the fracas. "Here's a smashed picture of a woman with the guy we took care of today. Her ex-husband that we had to ..."

"Yeah, I know who he is. I remember, okay? That's the same woman we saw in the driveway there, too. So our info's good. This place is hers, and

she keeps pictures of her ex- around. Must have still had a little thing going on the side, eh?" Again, Tony sniggered.

Carlo threw the picture back down on the floor and moved toward the kitchen. Tony took a final walk down the hallway and peered inside the empty back rooms. "Looks like if she did live here, she's gone now. The closet doors are open in the bedrooms, and there's no clothes left in them. We might as well get outta here before somebody calls the cops and fingers us for this mess."

"Yeah, boss." Carlo turned to exit through the kitchen door for a final look at the back of the house. As he opened the door, he lit a cigarette. He filled his lungs with nicotine-laced smoke and inhaled deeply. Tony followed closely behind with his right hand still resting on his holstered gun.

Seeing nothing of interest in the back except rusted patio chairs and an old charcoal grill, the two men began their trek back to their car. As Carlo took a long drag from the cigarette, he flicked the hot butt toward a pile of garbage that occupied the strip of land adjacent to the Sanderson woman's driveway.

In a matter of seconds, both Tony and Carlo heard a loud "ka-boom" behind them as the aerosol paint can exploded. Along with the explosion came a tall flame in the middle of the trash heap. Lights began to come on in the neighboring houses, and heads were starting to peek out of windows.

Tony and Carlo sprinted toward the Cadillac. Carlo made it into the vehicle without trouble, but Tony's holster strap got hung on the side of the passenger seat. He spent valuable seconds trying to get his holster untangled so that he could sit down and close the door. The whole time he wrestled with the strap, the dome light of the car brightly illuminated his face. He cursed and spat while he tried to free himself.

When he was able to finally sit down and shut the car door, someone from close by was yelling at them to stop. Neither Carlo nor Tony turned to see who the person was, because neither man cared. At this point, they just wanted to be gone. They floored the Caddy and got the hell out of Dodge.

* * * * * *

Upon entering the room at the Sundown Terrace Motel, Caroline headed straight for the television and tuned it to the local news channel. While John set the table in the corner using the motel's hand towels for placemats, Caroline was busy trying to get the best reception she could from the NBC station affiliate. John unpacked their fast food dinner, and Caroline arranged the two straight back chairs so that they could both get a clear view of the TV while they ate.

Within ten minutes, the news anchor announced the afternoon's "tragedy in Hicksville, New York, that took the life of a local resident … ."

Caroline and John both stopped chewing and gave each other looks of incomprehension. John turned up the volume of the broadcast as they both stared at the screen in bewilderment.

The video that ran while the announcer spoke showed firefighters and paramedics on the scene as John's house was engulfed in flames in the background. It was evident that the house was a total loss, but what held their undivided attention was the interview with the Fire Chief. With a mournful expression on his ash-smeared face, the chief revealed the discovery of human remains—possibly the homeowner's—in the rubble. Positive identification would be forthcoming as soon as the victim's relatives could be contacted, he said. He described the victim as being burned beyond recognition; however, he indicated that from what they could hastily discern, the victim was a male in his thirties or forties. He also pointed out the homeowner's car was parked next to the house but

was untouched by the fire. The chief asked if anyone had information about the fire or homeowner, to please contact their local police department. As the chief closed his remarks, the video panned to the coroner's vehicle as it pulled into the driveway, parking directly behind John's car. The studio newscaster shook his head and mumbled, "*Such a tragedy*," as the station switched to the local weather report.

Sacrificial Sins

CHAPTER 12

Monday, December 5, 1994

The Viper sat alone in his den. He rose from his favorite chair and switched off the television news. The late broadcast had covered the Sanderson house fire in excruciating detail. His thoughts wandered to how Tony and Carlo had let the situation get to such an irreversible point. Professionals? Please. They were heavy-handed thugs who wanted to show off their muscle and their guns. They'd be a better fit in a street gang. He was going to have to get them in line or get rid of them.

As he ambled toward his wife's makeshift hospital room, he reflected on how his life had recently been in upheaval. Nothing seemed to be going right for him lately. The turning point was when Lucinda asked him for a divorce two years before. Thank God no one knew about that except her lover, who by now had quietly resumed his solitary life. He wondered if letting him go unharmed had been such a good idea after all. Maybe he talked? Probably not. To the public, Lucinda's fall had been accidental, and she was still alive—maybe not so much mentally, but physically she had recovered. No one ever suspected foul play, at least not by anyone stupid enough to publically voice the concern.

The nurse was reading a book as she sat close to his wife's bedside. Upon his entrance, she stood and passed by him, silently exiting the small room to give them privacy. The nightly ritual of a kiss on the forehead and a pat of Lucinda's hand took less than ten seconds, but it was an expected ritual. He never smiled while he performed this duty. But tonight, he felt the urge to try to communicate with his comatose spouse. As he leaned forward, he whispered the first words he had spoken to her in months.

"Lucinda, I'm gonna get our grandson back. If it's the last thing I ever do, I'll get him back. Our Juliana won't be childless for long. Mark my words."

* * * * * *

Tony Caprio glared at his partner as Carlo recklessly maneuvered the Cadillac through the Hicksville streets. He was on the way to Highway 495 where the two believed they would be more likely to blend in. Merging into the busy highway traffic would provide their best escape from the nosy neighbors and the vandalized house they left behind.

"Boss, you think we should be looking out for cops?" Carlo asked naively.

"Dummy, what do you think? We oughta lay low for a while, capisci? We don't know who saw what back there." Tony was agitated at his partner's lack of comprehension of the trouble they had created during the last several hours.

"Where you want me to go, boss? You wanna get in touch with the Viper?"

"What the hell? NO, I don't want to get in touch with the Viper! You crazy or something? He gave us 48 hours, and we've screwed up the first two. Jeez, Carlo. You surprise me how thick you are sometimes." Tony nervously tapped the side armrest of the Caddy.

"Just pull into the next all-night café you see. We'll get back in a corner somewhere and try to regroup. I don't exactly know what the hell we oughta do next."

Carlo nodded in agreement and complied with Tony's suggestion. He pulled into the first restaurant parking lot he saw with a flashing "Open" sign in the window. Carlo parked the Caddy near the rear side of the small diner situated next door to the Sundown Terrace Motel.

* * * * * *

John Sanderson knew from years of medical experience that his ex-wife was in shock. She lay on the motel bed, head buried in the pillow, emitting guttural sounds and gasps as she tried to control her breathing and sobbing. John lay behind her, spoon positioned, trying to help her calm down. He wished he could provide her with medicinal care, but he had nothing like that with him. Instead, he gently rocked her and laid his cheek on her spasming shoulder as she continued to mourn the apparent loss of her innocent brother.

After a while, Caroline's breathing returned to normal. John relaxed his hold around her slender frame, trying to give her some space. Caroline scooted her body back against her ex-husband as if physical closeness was what she needed most to maintain calmness. John pulled her closer, and they resumed their spooning. He tenderly kissed the back of her head, and she put her hand across his as he held her tighter. Neither of them spoke or moved, choosing to lie there, silently reflecting on the unbelievable happenings that had transpired in less than a day's time: the horrific chain of events that set their lives reeling off-course and ending the promising life of Mike Lewis.

* * * * * *

When he was certain Caroline had drifted off to sleep, John eased himself from the bed and grabbed his coat. He quietly approached the door and opened it slowly. Peering outside into the night, he cautiously walked to the vending machine. Having incorrect change, he mumbled, *"shit"* under his breath and looked around for a change machine. Instead, his eye caught sight of the open diner near the front of the motel's adjacent parking lot. *Maybe coffee would be better, anyway,* he decided.

He started walking against the cold wind, keeping his head down to brace himself as he trudged through the slush that had accumulated between

the tire tracks in the lot. He stepped over a few puddles here and there, but eventually made it to the diner's front door without issue.

He approached the counter which was attended by a bleached blond waitress who looked as though she had seen better days. Fatigue etched her face, but her smile seemed genuine.

"Coffee, mister?" she asked as she held up a freshly brewed pot in her right hand.

"Sure, and a cup to go please." John tried not to look directly into her face, but he also didn't want to appear suspicious. He glanced around the small dining room in an effort to avoid too much eye contact with the waitress. She pulled a cup and saucer from below the counter and filled the cup to the brim. She pushed a miniature aluminum pitcher of cream toward him and placed a spoon on a napkin next to the steaming cup. She then went to fetch the to-go order for John as he doctored his black coffee to minimize the bitterness of the brew.

Hunched forward on the counter stool, John sipped his coffee silently. He was deep in thought when two men emerged from a table in the back of the diner and appeared at the other end of the counter. The shorter of the two men dug in his coat pocket for cash, while the taller, more muscular man stood closely behind him. John overheard part of their verbal exchange while the weary waitress cashed out their ticket.

"Boss, we gotta find that woman tonight. She's gotta have that baby with her," the muscular man tried whispering, but his voice was still audible within a few feet.

"Shut up, you imbecile. You wanna broadcast everything to the world?" Tony's forehead wrinkled as if he had just taken a shot between the eyes with a water pistol. Not following his own advice, Tony answered, "That Sanderson broad's around here somewhere, and we'll find her. Just shut up. Jeez, Carlo." Tony took his change from the bleached blond waitress

and threw a dollar back down on the counter. She scooped it up and put it in her apron pocket as the two men exited the diner.

The waitress ambled back toward John just as he was preparing to stand up and follow the two strangers. He fished in his pocket for his wallet.

"Don't you want your takeout coffee order, mister?" the waitress asked as she put the brown bag on the counter in front of John.

"Yeah, I was just about to ask for it," John replied, trying to look as though lost seconds didn't matter.

He laid a five dollar bill on the counter in front of her as he grabbed the bag. "Will this cover it?" he asked impatiently.

"That and more, honey. Thanks." The waitress smiled at him again, then stuffed the fiver deep in her apron pocket. She returned to the coffee station and started brewing a fresh pot as John hastily headed for the front door.

* * * * *

John didn't make it to the parking lot in time to hear any more conversation between the two men, but he did see them drive away in a Cadillac. He caught the last few digits of the New York tag number, but nothing more. He watched them head east, and he could tell they seemed to be in a hurry.

John knew he had to get back to the motel and move the cars from highway view before these guys—or someone even more sinister—got another chance to spot them. Next he had to tell Caroline everything he had overheard and what he had surmised in the short time he'd had to process it. He hoped Caroline would be alert enough to be of help by the time he got back to the room. If not, he'd have to take control of the situation himself, and Caroline would just have to deal with it.

* * * * * *

Cathy Giordano couldn't sleep. She paced back and forth between her daughter's room and the open doorway of the nursery. It was as if she was keeping vigil—standing guard—in an attempt to ensure nothing would happen to her remaining two children. Lorenzo had tried to urge her to come to bed, but she knew that was impossible. Even if she *had* been sleepy, she was reluctant to share the bed with him. He seemed like a different man to her.

The last twenty-four hours had turned him into a man seemingly without compassion—a man who acted more like a ticking time bomb than a soothing refuge. Perhaps he was holding all his emotions inside. More likely, he was trying to heal himself at the expense of everyone who was hurting around him.

She needed the old Lorenzo—her husband—her love. She wanted the Lorenzo who shed a tear of happiness when they spoke of naming their babies. She desperately needed to see him break free from the hardened shell he had wrapped around himself and his feelings.

Tired and mentally drained, Cathy stopped mid-way down the hall between the children's rooms. She leaned her back against the wall and slid down until she sat spraddle-legged on the floor. She wondered how she could ever fill the void left in her heart now that her son had been taken from her. Was it even possible? Could the remaining son somehow make up for the one she lost, or would he be a constant reminder that her other son was still absent?

Struggling with unanswerable questions made her head pound. She couldn't think anymore, and she had given up on prayer. The first 48 hours after a kidnapping are usually the most critical, one policeman had told her. Half of that was already gone, and they knew nothing more than they had the first hour after it happened.

She had to assume the baby was dead. Otherwise, how would she ever go on living as a whole person again—wondering—hoping? How could she ever smile again?

She shook her head in surrender as she formed her contingency plan for tomorrow night. She would make herself wait until 49 hours after the baby was taken.

*I don't have to be whole or happy. I don't even have to **be** ...*

She laid down in the hallway between her children's rooms and went to sleep.

Sacrificial Sins

CHAPTER 13

Tuesday, December 6, 1994

When Caroline awoke, she glanced around the unfamiliar room in an attempt to get her bearings. Immediate thoughts of yesterday's tragedies flooded her mind as she blinked her eyes to focus in the dimly lit room. The bedside clock's bright red numbers indicated the time was 4:18 a.m., which meant she had been asleep for over four hours.

"John, where are you?" she mumbled as she patted the covers on the other side of the double bed.

"Here. Over here," he answered as he concentrated on the letter he was writing at the table where they sat only hours before watching the evening news.

"What are you doing?" she asked John as she struggled to rise and sit on the side of the bed.

John kept writing for a few more seconds before he looked up to answer her. "I'm setting up our plan. I'll explain everything to you after you shower and get yourself ready for what might be a very busy day for us. There's a cup of cold coffee on the chest in a bag, if you can manage to drink it at room temperature. If not, we'll get something later."

He started writing again—head down with lips tightened—as he carefully pondered his next written words. Still too groggy to protest, Caroline made her way to the bathroom to follow his orders.

* * * * *

Juliana had made herself so comfortable on the overstuffed chaise lounge that she hadn't moved from it since Diego left hours before to have a beer with "the boys." By the time sleep overtook her, she had lost interest in Diego's return, hoping that he would stay away for days instead of hours.

At about the same time Caroline Sanderson was rousing from her slumber, Diego was unsteadily opening the door to the penthouse apartment he shared with Juliana. He tried to creep inside without alerting his wife of his late return and avoid the corner of the massive room where she lay curled up on the big chair. There was too much alcohol in his system for him to be anything but clumsy. He noisily bumped into the couch's side table and shattered an expensive lamp as it tumbled with a crash on the hardwood floor. Juliana sat straight up with a gasp, spying a dark figure awkwardly moving on the other side of the room.

Diego stood up and laughed—an uncontrollable drunken laugh—that made Juliana even more irritated with her bumbling husband.

"What the hell? Diego, look what you've done! That was my mother's lamp that she loved so much! You stupid asshole! Papa's gonna be so pissed!" Juliana screamed at the top of her lungs. "Get out of here NOW. Go back to your "boys" and let them sober you up. You are so screwed!" she yelled.

Diego stood stiffly with a piece of broken lamp in his hand. "Juliana, I –," he started.

"NO. No more excuses. Just leave and don't come back. I'm over you and your little boy attitude. I need a man, not a *drunk*. You're no good, and you're no good for *me*. Just get out." Juliana jumped from the chaise lounge and raced toward the front door. "NOW, Diego," she ordered as she opened the door and held it for his exit.

Having no good retort, Diego lowered his head and slowly made his way to the door. As he crossed the threshold into the plushly decorated hallway, he turned back to face his seething wife. "Juliana, please ..."

Her response was to slam the door in his face, leaving him stunned and staring directly at the elaborate door knocker that prominently displayed the name "**Moretti**."

* * * * * *

Rising early for his 5:00 a.m. sauna, Vincenzo DeLuca made his way to the west wing of his palatial home where the indoor spa was located. He took a fresh towel from the linen area and removed his robe. As he wrapped the towel around his waist, his butler approached and cleared his throat.

"What is it?" Vincenzo asked without looking up.

"A call, sir, from your daughter. Shall I tell her you'll return the call shortly?" the servant asked in a matter-of-fact tone, holding his hand over the phone's mouthpiece.

"Give me the phone. I'll take it now," Vincenzo sighed.

Dutifully, the butler half-bowed his head as he extended the phone's receiver to his employer.

"Juliana, why are you up so early?" Vincenzo asked with concern.

"Papa, it's about Diego. I can't stand him anymore. He just keeps acting out and coming home drunk all the time. And ...you know he's not doing such a good job running the chop shop for you. He never goes in to work. If it wasn't for the crew, that business would go under if it was left up to Diego. He came home wasted tonight. Then he bumped into a table and **BROKE MAMA'S PRECIOUS LAMP**! I'm gonna divorce him, Papa. I can't take it anymore." Juliana started sobbing on the other end of the phone.

"Juliana, calm down. We can fix this." Vincenzo's thoughts were already forming a plan.

"How, Papa, how?" Juliana sobbed even harder.

"You can't divorce him, Juliana. Not now, anyway. You need to wait a little while. Besides, DeLucas don't get divorced. We take our vows seriously. We'll have to find another way. Let me figure something out." Vincenzo paused for a moment. "Where is Diego now?" he asked.

"I don't know, Papa. I threw him out. He knows he's not welcome here right now. I told him not to come back." Juliana was calmer now.

"I'll send one of the guys over to change the locks on the apartment. You stay put and don't answer the phone for a little while. Don't talk to Diego anymore until we get back in touch. Call me if you need to reach me."

Vincenzo smiled ever so slightly when he disconnected the call. He realized his family life was about to take an immediate turn for the better.

* * * * * *

Tony and his partner, Carlo, sat in a booth at Denny's off Highway 495 near the cut-off to Highway 27. They were slowly making their way back to the Viper's home in Southampton, but were not in a hurry. They dreaded having to report the details of the most recent debacle that had foiled their plans to locate Caroline Sanderson. They planned to make a call to Caroline's employer that morning when the law firm opened up, but that was still three or four hours hence. They concluded that if she reported to work, they could catch her when she exited the building. She had to eat sometime. Meanwhile, having breakfast would be the most comforting thing the men could do for the moment.

As Carlo scraped the last of the syrup onto a speck of uneaten pancake, Tony finished his coffee and chewed on a toothpick as he imagined how the day would end.

"Carlo, what did you say the name of that law office is where the Sanderson broad works?" Tony asked.

"I dunno exactly, but it has the name "Norton" in it. You know, like on the *Honeymooners*?" Carlo chucked as he did his best celebrity impression, "You know, like 'Hey, Norton!' What Jackie Gleason always said." Carlo laughed at himself.

"Yeah, yeah. We'll go look at the phone book before we leave here. After we tell the Viper what we plan to do, we'll get back over to the west side of the island, make the call, and then stake the place out. This broad may not have a clue what's going on. On the other hand, she might be running scared," Tony mused.

"Like us, boss?" Carlo innocently questioned.

"Yeah, kinda like us, Carlo. We gotta pull this off soon or we'll be running with her." Tony raised his cup toward an approaching waitress, hoping the extra helping of caffeine would make him more alert than he felt at the moment.

* * * * * *

The Viper postponed taking his sauna for later, deciding instead to handle the more immediate family issue that Julianna brought to his attention. Wrapped only in the towel, he sat on a teakwood bench outside the steam room, holding the phone receiver against his right ear.

"Westside Shop," the voice on the other end of the phone answered.

"It's me. Is Diego there yet?" he asked the mechanic.

"Yeah, boss. He must have really tied one on last night. He's sleeping it off on the office couch. You want me to go get him for you?" the nervous mechanic asked.

"No, just let him sleep. Time enough later to catch up with him." With that statement, the Viper disconnected the call without further comment.

Next the Viper dialed another crew member, giving discreet instructions to his employee. "Diego deserves a promotion. Get Tony to take care of it before he does anything else today."

The person on the other end of the phone responded, "Got it," as they simultaneously hung up.

Now, Vincenzo thought, *a nice steamy sauna and a glass of fresh kale juice will make me feel like a new man. It's already starting off to be a better day than I expected.*

The Viper dropped his cover towel and opened the door to the sauna. He already felt the cleansing power of the steam as he placed another fresh towel on the spot where he liked to relax and think.

As he sat down, he wondered who he should give the chop shop management to when Diego received his "promotion." He laughed out loud as the refreshing hot steam engulfed him.

Sacrificial Sins

CHAPTER 14

Tuesday, December 6, 1994

Doug Brantley awoke to the smell of brewing coffee and frying bacon. He propped himself up on his elbows, taking a quick look around the bedroom. The morning sun was peeking through the cracks around the shades that didn't quite cover the window. Listening closely, he could hear the faint sound of someone humming a familiar lullaby; he recognized Stella's out-of tune voice immediately.

The momentary smile that crossed his face was suddenly replaced with a look of concern. He quickly pulled back the covers and trotted toward the kitchen clad only in his boxers.

When he rounded the corner to the kitchen, he saw Stella standing in front of the stove flipping bacon in the cast iron skillet that had once been her mother's.

"Where's Teddy?" Doug asked shakily, trying to disguise his concern with a quick clearing of his throat.

"Good morning, Doug." Stella turned and smiled at her husband. "He's asleep. I fed and changed him a couple of hours ago. You were sawing logs and snoring so loud, I was afraid you'd wake him up when he drifted back off." She turned her attention back to the bacon.

"Hmm," was all Doug said. He moved slowly toward the coffee pot and poured himself a cup of morning caffeine.

"Uh...how are you feeling, Stella?" he asked while her head was still turned toward the stove.

"I'm sleepy and maybe a little less jittery than yesterday, but I'm good." She dished up the dripping bacon on a ripped open paper bag that she had set aside on the counter. "This will drain off the grease in just a minute so we can eat it when the eggs are ready."

She was already moving toward the refrigerator when Doug commented, "Why don't we skip the eggs and just have toast and bacon. I don't feel like eggs, and you look like you may still be a little sluggish. Why don't you save your strength for Teddy today. Whatta you say?" He smiled at his wife.

"Whatever you want. That works for me," Stella replied, suddenly feeling weak in her legs and clutching the back of a kitchen chair. "Maybe I oughta lie down for a little while. Will you watch Teddy?"

"Sure, hon. Get some rest while you can." Doug was wondering how she had the strength to get up with the baby and then start cooking breakfast. He had given her half the usual dosage of Valium the night before, expecting her to wean from the medication within a week or so. He didn't expect her to try to take complete charge of the baby and the household so soon. He knew she needed more time. If she pushed herself, that would be a big mistake. He knew she wouldn't be back to normal for a while.

He followed her as she walked to the bedroom. "Stella, you still need your medicine until your infection is knocked out."

She looked puzzled. "What infection?" she asked.

"You probably don't remember, but you had an infection in your uterus a few weeks after delivery. Your fever was so high you thought the teddy

bear was the baby. You've been on a constant dosage of antibiotics laced with sedatives to help curb the pain. Don't you remember?"

She looked confused.

"Remember now, you have to take *all* the medicine to make sure the infection is totally cleared up." Doug hated lying to Stella about her health, but he reasoned it was a better explanation than the truth.

"Oh. I don't know why I wouldn't remember something like that, Doug. But now that you mention it, I do remember thinking that the baby was sick... or I was sick ... or something bad had happened." Her brow was wrinkled as she tried to recall clouded details.

"Well, everything is fine now, but we have to keep up precautions. Take this pill now and get some rest. You don't want to overdo it, especially now that Teddy's getting accustomed to you again." Doug smiled as he handed her the next dose of Valium.

She took the pill as she sat on the bedside. She curled up under her blanket and fell asleep within minutes.

Doug dropped his head in shame as he exited their bedroom. As he entered the nursery where the baby peacefully slept, he recalled the day he secretly buried his firstborn. This child reminded him so much of his own dead son that by now, he couldn't remember their physical differences. The substituted child had morphed into the baby he had helped Stella deliver weeks before. To Doug Brantley, this child *was* Teddy Brantley—for now and for evermore.

* * * * * *

Within an hour of the Viper's call, his messenger tracked down Tony and Carlo. They were parked between fuel pumps at a Texaco station off Highway 495. Carlo was pumping gas into the Cadillac guzzler as Tony,

seated regally in the passenger seat, squinted at the tiny print of the Long Island phone book he had lifted from Denny's.

The messenger tapped on the passenger side window with the large gold ring on his left hand. Startled, Tony lowered the window and stared with impatience at the familiar bearded man.

"Yeah, Gino?" Tony asked, praying he wasn't being summoned by the Viper to make another personal appearance in Southampton.

"Boss said you should go give Diego a promotion. He's sleeping one off in the shop office, and we ain't supposed to let him leave 'til you get there." The message was delivered loud and clear.

"Wait, Gino. The boss already got us on assignment. When are we supposed to do this?" a puzzled Tony asked.

"Boss said to drop everything else and handle this. He wants it done first." Gino turned and walked away, leaving Tony staring at the man's back as he walked briskly away.

Carlo, who had overfilled the 15 gallon gas tank, stepped back a few feet and lit a cigarette. When a messenger tracked down another employee, privacy was expected. He knew not to intrude during the hushed but brief conversation at the car window. Besides, he also knew Tony would fill him in when he got back in the car, provided the information was meant to be shared with him.

When Gino departed, Carlo took his cue to return to the driver's seat. He flicked the lit cigarette butt toward a tall utility pole several feet from where the car had stopped parallel to the pumps.

Starting the car and, as always, stomping on the gas, Carlo took off and merged recklessly into traffic. A few seconds later, a loud explosion erupted from somewhere behind them. Carlo scanned the rearview

mirror and saw dark smoke forming a cloud in the distant sky. Tony turned around and peered through the back window of the sedan.

"Jeez, Carlo. Whatta you think that was? Looks like a bomb went off back there!"

"I dunno, but that was close. If we'd hung around a few seconds longer, we coulda been in the middle of that… boom. Looks like it might have gone off somewhere around the Texaco station!"

Tony contemplated what Carlo just said, immediately jumping to the conclusion that perhaps the Viper was sending them a threatening message. He hadn't seemed too happy with their performance lately.

Or maybe— just maybe—that Sanderson broad was a step ahead of them. But how could that be? She worked in a law firm—probably a secretary or something. How would she know how to plant a bomb? Maybe it was Gino's car that blew up? Oh Jesus, Mary, and Joseph. We gotta watch our backs!

The two bumbling hit men kept driving. Tony's thoughts were mixed with foreboding from the near-miss explosion and anxiety about the new assignment from the Viper. Carlo only thought about how fast he could put miles between them and the "bomb site."

When they were a safe distance away, Tony revealed the new priority mission to Carlo. Recklessly, the Caddy abruptly changed directions as the two assassins made their way to the Westside Shop.

Meanwhile at the Texaco station, customers scurried to avoid flying debris as employees tried to extinguish the flames around the gas pump nearest the highway. The explosion was caused when a hot cigarette ricocheted off a light pole, landing butt-down in a fresh gas puddle created when a careless customer in a Cadillac overfilled his tank.

* * * * * *

Caroline sat on the side of the unmade motel bed with her legs tucked under her and her wet hair wrapped in a dingy but clean towel. She stared at her ex-husband in disbelief as he repeated the conversation he overheard hours before at the diner.

"Are you sure they said 'Sanderson woman?' Are you sure you heard right?" Caroline wanted to know.

"I'm telling you, Caroline, that's exactly what I heard. They also mentioned a baby. It's not that hard to do the math," John replied.

As she drained the cup of cold coffee in her hand, Caroline whispered, "Good Lord, John. That means everything that's happened to us has been intentional. We were right to assume the worst. And poor Mike ... he didn't stand a chance," she whimpered as her eyes pooled with tears once again.

John left his chair and joined her on the bedside. He wrapped his arms around her and let her cry it out on his shoulder. Neither of them would be able to take appropriate time to mourn Mike's probable death, considering the predicament they found themselves in. Still, he thought she deserved this few minutes of unabated grief. He kissed the top of her head for the second time during the last few hours while gently rocking her in his arms. She collapsed against him and cried until there were no tears left within her.

* * * * * *

Once Caroline regained her composure, John moved from the bedside back to the table he had been using as a writing desk for the past few hours. He began to explain the preliminary plan he had been hatching all night.

"I've written letters that you'll need to deliver, Caroline. Do you think you're up to that?" John asked his ex-wife in the most unruffled voice he could muster.

Caroline nodded her head. "Okay. Explain the letters to me, please. Maybe it'll help."

"Okay," John began, "try to follow me and please don't interrupt. The most important letter is my suicide note. I ... ."

Caroline gasped. "What?" she barked from the side of the bed. She jumped up and was standing in front of his chair in a flash. She leaned down, grabbed him, and hugged him tightly.

"No you can't do something so stupid. Don't leave me in the middle of this alone. John, I don't know what to do if you're not with me!" He could feel her heart frantically beating as she hugged him to her chest so tightly his breathing was temporarily constricted.

"Caroline, back up. You're choking me, and I'm not going to kill myself." With that, she backed away a few inches and locked eyes with him. Posed nose to nose, John felt the sudden urge to kiss his ex-wife. It was apparent that his timing was off, so he pushed her further away. She returned to the bedside and caught her breath.

"Explain, you bastard. You scared me to death," she responded with panic still evident on her face.

"Like I said, don't interrupt. Please. This suicide note says I've been despondent lately, regretting our divorce and the lonely life I've let myself lead since then." He glanced at his silent ex-wife. She made no comment, nor did her facial expression change.

He cleared his throat and went on with the explanation. "It also says that I don't know how to carry on without you. My life's not worth living—I'll

never find another love like you—all that kinda stuff." As his explanation became more detailed, John became more and more uncomfortable. He stopped to clear his throat again, not chancing so much as a glance in Caroline's direction.

"So the note will explain the reason for the suicide and how it was done. Since we don't know the details except what we heard on the news, I've tried to keep the actual suicide sketchy but still believable. This note will substantiate that whoever they found dead in the house fire was actually me."

"So how did you say you did it?" Caroline inquired.

"I said I was a coward and didn't want to be in pain when the house fire spread, so I made sure I was dead first. I'm instructing you in the letter to tell the coroner that you should collect my body—the ashes, whatever—to have a private service. That I want to punish you by making you look at the urn for the rest of your life so you can remember the pain you've caused me by not taking me back." He stopped but kept his eyes on his hands instead of directing them toward Caroline.

"Is that true, John? What you said about your feelings in the letter?" Caroline softly asked him.

"Well, you know, Caroline. I wish things could've worked out differently. I do miss you sometimes." He grinned sheepishly as he got up the courage to make eye contact with her.

When the awkward moment subsided, Caroline asked John how he supposedly got the letter to her before he died.

"Just say I left it stuck in the door of your house sometime yesterday, and you found it yesterday afternoon. Tell them that you thought it was just theatrics on my part, and that I'd threatened to kill myself before when I wanted your attention."

Even to Caroline, John's explanation sounded convincing.

"Where am I supposed to say I was last night while your house was burning and my house was vandalized?" she asked, trying to cover all the possible bases.

"You were driving your brother to a motel where you dropped him off. He'd been getting death threats, and he wanted to get away from the house for a few days." John again dropped his eyes from her face, trying to conceal the pain he felt when he thought of Mike.

"Okay. I guess I better start by calling in at work and explaining why I didn't come back yesterday after I left for lunch. I'll let them know about your house and apparent suicide, too. That will be a good excuse to take a few days off to handle personal affairs."

"Yes, and you need to make another call, too. My boss needs to be notified that I won't be back at BNL after my untimely demise." He smiled ever so slightly.

Caroline nodded agreement, and picked up the phone book.

"Write down the numbers, but you should go up to the diner to make the calls from their pay phone. We don't want any records that put us in this motel. Remember, I checked in under an assumed name."

Caroline was amazed at how John had taken control of the plan and was being so thorough. She nodded again, but she still had one remaining question.

"What about the other letters you were writing?" she asked.

"Later, Caroline. Let's take care of this one first." Saying nothing else, he dismissed her by turning on the television. He wanted to know if the local news channels had reported anything more on the events of Monday evening.

* * * * *

Diego was still sprawled on the worn-out office couch of the Westside Shop when Tony and Carlo entered the concrete building. He had been trying to open his eyes for nearly half an hour, but he couldn't take the overhead glare from the flickering fluorescent lights. Besides, his head hurt like someone was taking a jack hammer to it, and he needed to puke.

Carlo came into the office first, seating himself at the desk. He swirled the chair around to face Diego some six feet away. Tony stood directly over Diego and peered down at his head from the side of the couch.

Diego peeped out from under his arm which he had slung across his face to shield his red eyes from the ceiling lights. "What's up, Tony? You need a car or something?" Diego squeaked as he tried to minimize his movements.

"No, the boss wants me to take you out for a little spin. We've got some important news to tell you. You know, the Viper has taken a special interest in you, being his son-in-law and all. He wants to show you his appreciation." Tony smirked as Carlo grunted from the desk chair.

"You're kidding, right? I don't even know if I can move for another couple of hours. Can't you just tell me whatever it is and leave? I ain't up to it right now." Diego wanted to be left alone to wallow in his misery.

"You can't disappoint the boss, Diego. Come on. Get up. Splash some water on that pretty face, and let's get going. Take an Alka-Seltzer or something." Tony reached down to grab Diego by the upper arm, but Diego lashed out with the back of his hand. Carlo stood at attention, ready to pounce at Tony's command. Tony stepped back, away from Diego's reach.

"Okay, okay. I'm getting up. Jeez. A man can't even be sick around here without somebody bothering him." Diego sat up painfully, running both

his hands through his greasy, unkempt hair. He gingerly got to his feet and stumbled toward the office's private half-bath. He shut the door behind him, the clicking of the lock making an echoing sound. Soon, both Tony and Carlo were serenaded by the sound of Diego vomiting in the toilet. He exited minutes later looking more alert and somewhat more presentable.

"Anything you need to do before we leave the office? We may be out a while," Tony asked considerately.

"Nah. It's all good. The boys can take care of it for the rest of the day. Let's go get some 'hair of the dog', guys."

Diego now lead them from the office, through the garage area, and toward the alley behind the building. He said nothing to the crew who was left to handle the shop.

Stepping into the sunlight, Diego immediately dug his sunglasses from his shirt pocket. Carlo opened the trunk and asked, "Diego, you know what this loose part is? Something's making a rattling noise back here, and it's driving us crazy."

Carlo stepped back as Diego came around to the rear of the Cadillac. When he bent forward to inspect the trunk, Carlo whacked him on the head with a tire iron. As he collapsed forward, both Carlo and Tony lifted Diego's legs and shoved him farther into the cavernous area of the big car. Slamming the trunk shut, Carlo and Tony chuckled at how easy that had been.

They both looked around for witnesses and, seeing none, made their way onto the main highway once again.

"Ain't it time for lunch yet, boss?" Carlo asked enthusiastically.

"Is that all you think about, you goon? You wanna eat all the time. Jeez, can't you wait a while?" Tony asked, exasperated with his partner.

"You know I got the sugar, boss. I gotta keep something in my stomach to keep from passing out. It ain't pretty when I fall on the ground." Carlo responded.

"You ain't pretty when you're upright either," Tony retorted, laughing at himself.

"C'mon boss. Let's go back to that diner we stopped at around midnight. It's close, and Diego's not gonna make any fuss. I knocked him out pretty good. Besides, he was already hung over. He'll be out for awhile," Carlo reasoned.

"Okay, but you better eat good while you're there. We won't stop again for a few hours 'cause we can't afford to waste any more time. We're still on the countdown, and the Viper won't give us any grace period." Tony took a deep breath and shook his head, while Carlo happily sped toward the diner where the bleach blond waitress worked. Carlo thought she might have smiled at him, and that didn't happen very often.

CHAPTER 15

Tuesday, December 6, 1994

In her opinion, Caroline had spent too many hours cooped up in the motel. She was relieved that John wanted her to go to the diner to make the calls. She could use some fresh air.

It had taken her longer than she expected to dry her hair because the motel's sorry excuse for a hair dryer had the wattage of a nightlight. She decided against make-up, even though she had remembered to throw her kit into her luggage when she first left Mike's house.

She selected a pair of sweatpants to wear outside, along with an oversized sweatshirt that had once been Mike's. Her tennis shoes would be fine for trudging across the parking lot in the slushy remains of the weekend's snow.

She tucked her shoulder-length hair behind her ears and donned a Yankees baseball cap that had also belonged to Mike.

Before leaving the room, she hoped to talk to John more about the contents of his suicide letter. She thought better of interrupting him, since he seemed to be engrossed in the television news broadcast. Stopping at John's chair, Caroline turned to watch the last few seconds of the updated Sanderson fire story.

The fire chief was wrapping up an interview that he had been obviously cornered into giving that morning. A brassy reporter had caught him as he was leaving his house for work, meeting him at his front door with

bright lights shining in his eyes and a microphone stuck toward the center of his face. The reporter asked the question everyone in town was wondering: "Sir, do you have any idea who the person was that was killed in the Hicksville fire?"

The fire chief frowned, but stumbled for an immediate answer. "We don't know for sure, but we hope someone from the victim's family will come forward to help with identification. We could use dental records or most any other viable identification sources; but, the police have the investigation now. They need some direction from the family." The fire chief tried to step forward but was blocked by the aggressive reporter.

"Sir, can you tell us how the victim died?"

The fire chief looked like a scared rabbit trapped in a snare. "They don't know if the gunshot was self-inflicted or if it was the result of a homicide. But, they are on top of the investigation."

At that moment, the fire chief knew he had given away more information than he was supposed to reveal. He pushed the microphone away from his face. With a grumpy response, he declared, "That's all. Let me get to work." The camera followed him to his car parked in his driveway. As he opened the door, he looked back at the reporter with a sneer. That was the last image caught on camera of the fire chief that day. He stayed in his office with his head down for the entirety of his long shift, afraid to open his mouth again for fear of yet another seething reprimand.

* * * * * *

When Lorenzo arrived at his Manhattan office on Tuesday morning, no one from his office wanted to be the first to approach him. Even though from outside appearances he was the same man, every member of his staff felt tongue-tied and unsure of how to start a conversation that wouldn't send him spiraling into an emotional crash.

He passed the reception desk, nodding a silent hello to the young lady who handled that position for the group of physicians. As he rounded the corner to the break room for his morning coffee, he heard chatter coming from the group already in the room.

When he appeared in the doorway, the chatter immediately stopped. All eyes were on him for a split second; then the eyes averted and found other objects on which to concentrate. The silence uncomfortably lingered.

Realizing that he was most likely the topic of their chatter, he cleared his throat. He poured his half-cup of coffee and turned to face the assembled staff.

"I know you are all sincerely sorry to hear about what happened with our family this past weekend. We—Cathy and I—appreciate your concern and your prayers. The police have assured us that they are doing everything they can. Meanwhile, all we can do is hope that our son will be returned to us unharmed and soon. We will ensure that you are among the first to know of any new developments; but for now, all we can do is carry on and hope for the best. I plan to try to stay busy, and Cathy will do the same with our other newborn and one-year old daughter. I know I speak for Cathy when I say we both need your continued support, but we beg for privacy as it relates to our personal lives. We won't speak of this again unless something changes with the investigation."

Again he cleared his throat and took a sip of coffee. Not knowing what else to say, he looked at the pitying faces of the office staff. He added, "So, let's get to work, shall we?" Lorenzo sadly smiled, and walked out of the silent break room. Behind him, he heard chairs scuffing on the tiled floor as the sorrowful staff began to disperse to their assigned work stations.

After he closed his mahogany office door, he leaned backwards against it, sighing with relief that the initial contact with the staff was over. He crossed the room to his executive chair, placing his coffee cup on a leather coaster in the center of his desk as he took his seat.

Once again he found Sunday's bottle of single malt scotch, generously splashed it in what was left of his coffee, and prepared himself for the day ahead .

* * * * * *

"Does this information change anything?" Caroline wanted to know.

"No," John answered, "but now we know Mike was shot. At least we can assume he didn't suffer through a fiery death." John suddenly got quiet. After a pause, he asked Caroline if Mike owned a gun.

"Yeah, he had a pistol of some kind. A Smith Western, I think." Caroline obviously didn't know much about firearms.

"You mean a Smith & Wesson." John laughed and then snorted. Caroline didn't see the humor in her remark.

"Whatever, John. Before I go over to the diner, maybe I should look through the stuff I brought from Mike's to see if there's a gun in it. I don't remember one, but I'm not exactly sure what I threw in the suitcase or the duffle bag. I was in too much of a hurry to take inventory," Caroline retorted.

Pouting, she turned toward the corner of the room where she had put Mike's suitcase. She had already opened it to get out the sweatshirt she was wearing. She was almost positive it held nothing but clothing and a few personal effects. The duffle bag, however, should have been full of odds and ends from the desk, along with Mike's select business papers

she had purged from the file drawer. She looked around, but the duffle bag was nowhere in sight.

"John, did you move the big duffle bag I brought from Mike's?" she asked as she scanned the other corners of the room.

"Nope," he answered. "Haven't seen a duffle bag. Did you leave it in Mike's Cherokee?"

"I must have. I'll go check." Caroline opened the motel door, but neither the Jeep Cherokee nor the VW Beetle was parked in front.

"Where are the cars? Have they been stolen?" Caroline turned to look again at John who was smiling broadly by now.

"Settle down, darlin'. I moved them last night. They were too obvious from the highway parked right in our front door. They're on the other side of the building. Just go through the open corridor where the ice machine is. It's open all the way through to the back side of the motel. The cars are right there." John pitched the Jeep's keys toward her. She caught them and gave him the bird, holding her middle finger stiff and straight.

"That's my girl," he said as he returned to the table to make a list of things for Caroline to pick up after she ran the day's necessary errands.

* * * * * *

Some 300 feet away from the Sundown Terrace Motel, the diner's parking lot was filling up as the late breakfast/early lunch crowd arrived. Someone had parked a big Cadillac across two spaces in front, oblivious to the lot's painted lines that were meant to corral parked vehicles in the most efficient and orderly fashion.

Carlo entered the diner first, scanning the serving staff for the good-looking blond he had seen several hours before. Tony, with a toothpick stuck in the corner of his mouth, lagged behind Carlo. He was in no hurry to eat again, although he wouldn't turn down a fresh cup of coffee and a piece of pie. Pecan, if they had it—apple, if they didn't.

They took an empty table in the back corner, just a few spots over from where they had recently sat. Carlo seemed disappointed when a young waiter asked them if they wanted coffee while looking over the menu.

"Where's that blond waitress that was here late last night?" Carlo asked as nonchalantly as he could.

"Oh, you mean Martha? Her shift ends at 2:00 a.m. She won't be back until around 6 o'clock tonight. I'll tell her you're looking for her, if you want. Or you can just come back when she's here." The waiter reached for the coffee cups that sat upside down on saucers in the middle of their table. He flipped them upright and filled them quickly. "I'll be back to take your order in a jiff," he said as he sailed toward another table to fill more empty cups.

Carlo tried to whisper, but he could never control his volume. "Tony, you think that guy's a little light in the loafers?" The occupants of the next table shot quick glances toward Carlo, then Tony.

"I don't know, and I don't care. Shut your trap, you imbecile. Jeez, I can't take you anywhere." Tony cleared his throat and tried to look interested in the laminated menu.

Carlo was already licking his lips imagining the feast he was about to order. His stomach growled just thinking about it.

In the trunk of the big Cadillac, Diego stirred enough to find a more comfortable position in which he could continue nursing his headache. He wasn't sure where he was, but he liked the darkness.

* * * * * *

"There's no gun in here," Caroline remarked as she dumped the duffle bag contents all over the bed. John stood next to her and surveyed the pile of papers and sundries that came out of Mike's desk drawers. He picked up a roll of tape and held it in Caroline's line of vision. "At least if I get tired of hearing you nag, I've got something here to close that mouth of yours," he laughed. She picked up a stapler and lunged toward John. "I've got my own weapon, mister," she teased. They laughed together for the first time that day.

"If he still owned the gun, I suppose I missed it when I tried to clear out the house. I couldn't look everywhere, so it must still be there. You know, it's possible he got rid of it." Caroline didn't think that had happened, but she didn't know for sure.

John picked up some scattered files and opened the one labeled "Credit Cards." Inside he saw a list of all the credit card accounts Mike held. The same information was listed for the three credit cards he carried: Card Company, Card Number, Expiration Date, numerical security code, and his full name as listed on the card. The phone numbers were neatly listed for each card company's customer service departments, as well as numbers for reporting lost or stolen cards. Recent statements for the three cards he carried were also in the file. Mike didn't owe much in the way of outstanding balances; but, among the three cards he was issued, he had available credit limits totaling almost $18,000.

"Looks like I have a call or two to make." John set the file aside. "I think I may be posing as Mike for a while."

"Let's see what all we have in here. Something else may pop up that we can use for a few days." Caroline started digging.

She plucked a file from the bed and held it in the air as if she was getting ready to yell **Bingo**. "His bank records—his latest statement—and he had

a little over $4,300 in there a week ago according to this. His November 30th statement shows him with $4,372.59 in his checking and savings accounts combined." Again, Caroline smiled.

John countered with a find of his own. "Here's his passport stuffed in a file with his birth certificate. We've struck the mother lode. Caroline, you were smart to think of all this stuff. I don't believe I would have been able to think that clearly if I had been in your shoes. You always were the smartest one of us all." He reached to give her a high-five. She responded in kind.

Caroline looked over the heap of papers and desk supplies. "Mike would have wanted us to do whatever we *have* to do—I *know* he would want us to use whatever he could provide to get us out of this mess and still make it out alive. Something he obviously couldn't do for himself." She was about to become emotional.

John took her by the shoulders and looked deeply in her eyes. "Caroline, get strong, honey. There will be time enough later to feel sorry about all this. But we don't have enough time right now to screw around with grief or pity. Get strong. Do it for Mike. Do it for me."

This time it was Caroline who felt the urge to kiss her ex-husband. She moved her head upward to catch his eye for a signal, but he had already half-closed his lids. Their lips gently touched; for a brief second, it felt like familiar love. When John reached around to pull Caroline tightly to him, he felt as though every loving emotion he had ever had—every feeling he wanted to express to Caroline—every bit of passion that was deep within him—was culminating in this one kiss. The kiss of love past, love lost, and love recovered—an all-encompassing joy with a depth of meaning that surpassed anything he ever felt before. Caroline responded as if her kiss would be the last she would ever give John. It was this kiss of the Sirens—the bonding of ethereal spirits—the melding of the souls—that overtook them both and plunged them back into the spirit of sacred love.

* * * * * *

Tony and Carlo eventually left the diner, but not until after Carlo finished every bite on his plate. Carlo made Tony wait an extra five minutes while he placed a take-out order to have with him as they completed the Viper's assignments during the rest of the afternoon. As Carlo again explained, he "had the sugar" and had to be prepared. Tony just thought he "loved the sugar" and couldn't be without. It didn't matter anyway, as long as Carlo did what he was told and kept the Viper off their backs.

When the front door of the diner opened and Tony stepped outside, he heard dull thumping sounds coming from near the road. Upon closer inspection, he realized the thumps were coming from the trunk of the Caddy.

"Carlo, get us outta here. Now." Tony hastily settled into the Cadillac's passenger seat while Carlo jumped in to drive.

"Where to, boss?" Carlo wasn't sure what was about to happen.

"Go to the back of that motel over there on the other side of the lot. Let's see how many people are around. If it's not too busy back there, maybe we can persuade Diego to shut up, eh?"

Carlo took off toward the Sundown Terrace Motel, bypassing the rooms facing the front, turning to go around the building. The extended parking area allowed them to park as far to the rear of the lot as possible. He backed the Caddy in a space that was bordered in the rear by a retaining wall. Carlo left just enough room between the bumper and the wall to walk behind the car and open the trunk.

The tire iron was behind the driver's seat where Carlo had thrown it after knocking out Diego in the shop's alley. He grabbed it, carrying it as extra protection if Diego pulled a fast one when the trunk was lifted.

The two of them approached the trunk slowly, as if they expected Diego to pop up like some sinister jack-in-the-box and attack them there on the spot. Once they made it between the wall and the car, Tony screwed the silencer on his gun just in case Diego was feisty. Tony told Carlo to go ahead and open the trunk as he took the safety off his gun and pointed it forward.

Carlo put the key in the trunk's lock and felt it turn. The trunk popped slightly upward, requiring some muscle to push it all the way open. Carlo did the honors, finding Diego once again sprawled out over the large rear area. His head had a chunk of raw, clotted flesh above his ear, but otherwise he was fine. He snored as if this was the best sleep he'd ever had.

The two men shook their heads and simultaneously closed the trunk together.

"Where was all that thumping noise coming from if he's asleep?" Tony asked his partner.

"Maybe he was bumping against the trunk lid when he tried to turn over and get comfortable? I dunno, boss. I never did really hear it."

"Well, we might as well finish him off in New Jersey at the drop-off site. Let's get rolling, Carlo."

Tony was making himself comfortable again in the passenger seat as Carlo pulled the big Caddy forward toward the motel building to find the exit. As the car passed the building, Tony looked down the row of parked cars and spotted a woman carrying an overstuffed duffle bag. She disappeared through the open corridor of the building before he could get a good look. She seemed vaguely familiar, but Tony couldn't place her.

"Carlo, swing around in front of this motel building, will ya? I want to look at something. Park a couple of rows out in the lot and face the building, eh?"

As Carlo pulled the car to a stop, the woman Tony saw was entering a room. She shut the door behind her so hastily, he still only got a glimpse.

"Hmmm. She looks like somebody I oughta know. Let's ride back around and see where she was coming from."

Staying silent, Carlo drove around to the back of the motel and parked a couple of rows away from the building. Tony scanned all the vehicles in the first two rows. Finally Carlo pointed out the Jeep Cherokee.

"Boss, don't you think that Sanderson broad was driving a car like that one? See that Jeep over there?" Carlo pointed toward the Cherokee.

"Yeah. YEAH! That's the Sanderson broad's car! That was her! Jesus, Mary, and Joseph, she's here. Right under our noses and she's HERE! Hey, let's go call the Viper and let him know what we found, eh?" Tony was elated.

Carlo said, "Sure boss. Let's go. Where you wanna go again?"

Tony was frustrated with Carlo, but he was so excited about locating Caroline that it didn't matter anymore. "Go up there to those phone booths outside the diner and let me out. I'll do the calling. You just sit here and listen for thumps and movement from back there." Tony nodded his head toward the trunk as he finished his instructions.

"Ok, boss." Carlo parked as close to the phone booths as he could. As soon as Tony got out, Carlo lit a cigarette for a quick smoke break. He rolled down the window and held the lit butt down near the side of the door, attempting to keep the smoke and smell from overtaking the car's interior.

153

Tony was back within a few minutes. He was frowning, shaking his head.

"The Viper said to take care of the promotion first, then come back and take care of the broad. I told him she could get away if we don't stay on her tail, but he don't care. He said **he'd** take that risk. I hope he remembers that when our 48 hours are up and we can't find the broad 'cause she took off."

Carlo nodded his agreement and flipped his cigarette out the window, watching it land on a dry piece of concrete. He pulled out of the parking lot, steering the big Caddy toward the out-of-state location where they dumped their special garbage.

They were travelling to a secluded area off the New Jersey Turnpike where "promoted" associates were relocated into what the Viper referred to as the "group home."

CHAPTER 16

Tuesday, December 6, 1994

By early afternoon Caroline was ready to make the necessary phone calls to John's boss and to her own employer. She believed those calls would be easy enough to handle. There would be no need to conjure up fake emotions. All she had to do was to think of her brother's tragic fate.

John's boss, the Medical Director of BNL, picked up the phone immediately after his administrative assistant informed him that a member of John Sanderson's family was calling. He said he was saddened to receive the call, but he had been expecting to hear from someone from the Sanderson family. He offered condolences and pledged to support the family in any way needed. He volunteered to handle all the required BNL paperwork and notifications to "terminate" John's employment. A grateful Caroline promised him she would be in touch with BNL's Human Resources Department as soon as she received John's official Death Certificate.

Next, she called her own boss, Perry Walker Norton, Esquire.

Perry was the 59-year old nephew of one of the original founding partners of Walker, Harrington, Norton and Stone, a prominent law firm with offices in both Manhattan and Syosset, New York. He was the attorney for whom Caroline performed clerical and paralegal duties in the firm's Syosset office.

She wasn't sure how her call would be received since she disappeared after lunch the day before, informing no one of her whereabouts or status since. Unless the office staff had connected her with the news about last

evening's fire, she knew she would have additional explaining to do. She called Perry's direct line, and to her surprise, he answered himself.

"Perry, this is Caroline Sanderson. I'm afraid there's been a terrible tragedy, and I wanted to tell you firsthand ...," she started.

"I know, Caroline. One of the legal secretaries told us about the fire and the ... uh, the loss of your ex-husband. I *assume* that was your ex-husband's home that was featured on the television news last night?" he asked kindly, listening to Caroline's sniffles as he spoke.

"Yes." She remained silent but sniffed again. She dug for a tissue from her jacket pocket.

"Well, take the rest of the week off to handle his affairs. If I'm not mistaken, he doesn't have any other family in New York, correct?"

"Right. His elderly parents live in Tennessee, and they haven't been notified as far as I know. I'm on my way to the Coroner's Office now to see what I can do to help." She again sniffed and moved the phone away from her face to blow her nose.

"Let us know if you need anything, and don't worry about your job. It'll be here when you get back." He tried to sound empathetic, but found himself mentally reviewing Caroline's recent history of tardiness. He realized he knew very little about Caroline's personal life and wondered what she must have been going through recently. He decided she deserved to come back to a clean slate at the office. He'd make sure the written warnings for tardiness were expunged from Caroline's official personnel file. He felt sorry for her, for some reason. She sounded so pitiful.

* * * * * *

Caroline drove the Jeep Cherokee to the Coroner's Office, praying that the appointment would be something she could do without breaking down into a sniveling lump of jelly. By far, this situation would require more concentration and self-control than anything she'd ever done before in her entire life. She would have to identify the charred remains of her precious brother as being that of her still very much alive ex-husband.

She parked at the side of the brick building and followed the signs to the public entrance. Once inside, she approached a middle-aged woman with half-glasses resting on the end of her nose. She peered over a file drawer, oblivious to anyone else in the room. When Caroline cleared her throat for attention, the woman jumped with a start. Her glasses fell from her nose and hung on the black beaded chain that secured them to her neck.

"Oh, I'm sorry," Caroline apologized sincerely. "I'm here to identify a body …, uh remains. I'm here to see the coroner, I guess."

The woman still held her right hand atop her sternum as if that would make her heart jump back into normal rhythm from the scare. "He's in his office. May I tell him which case you're here about?"

"The Hicksville fire. I believe the victim was my ex-husband. It was his house that burned." Caroline raised a tissue to her left eye and shakily wiped beneath it. Trying to hold back tears, she inhaled deeply.

The woman said nothing more, but turned briskly and took off down a back hallway. Caroline could hear the faint tap of knuckles rapping on a door, followed by screech of a rusty-hinged door as it was pushed open. Momentarily, the woman returned to the public area with a gray-haired gentleman trailing behind her. He stopped in front of Caroline and extended his hand. "I'm Ralph Carey, the County Coroner. And you are …?" he prodded.

"Caroline. Caroline Sanderson. I'm the ex-wife of John Sanderson, the owner of the house in Hicksville that burned last night. John hasn't ... I haven't heard... I don't know where John is. He hasn't checked in today, and I'm so afraid." Caroline burst into real tears, allowing her grief to reveal itself fully to the coroner and his file clerk.

"There, there, child. Please. Sit here. Take a few minutes to get yourself together," the kind man said as he steered Caroline toward a bench that appeared to be older than she was. Caroline allowed herself to be comforted by the gentle man as he sat beside her and patted her hand. "You probably have to do this a lot, don't you? I mean, in your job you must meet lots of grieving people, I guess," Caroline managed to say between sobs.

"Unfortunately, yes, and it never gets easier with practice," he said solemnly.

* * * * * *

The Cadillac made good time on the New Jersey Turnpike, traffic seemingly mild for a Tuesday afternoon. By the time Carlo reached the construction site that was owned by one of the Viper's off-shore shell companies, he was getting hungry again.

"Boss, you think when we get through here, maybe we can swing through the city for a pit stop at Patsy's? I'm thinking a big plate of spaghetti would hit the spot. That's the kinda meal that sticks to you, don't you think?" Carlo remarked as he pulled the car up behind some heavy equipment stored at the empty site.

"Do you EVER think about anything but food, Carlo? *Ever?*" Tony was exasperated.

"Yeah, boss. I like a good, cold beer, too," Carlo smiled.

"Just get the job done so we can get outta here. Jeez." Tony walked away, searching for a private spot to relieve his bladder.

With tire iron in hand, Carlo approached the Caddy's trunk. "Come out, come out, wherever you are," he playfully sang as he unlocked the trunk.

As the lock released, the trunk came flying up toward Carlo's face, catching him under the chin. As he sprawled backward on the graveled lot, Diego lunged up and out of the trunk that had held him captive for hours. Carlo had dropped the tire iron when he fell, and it lay nearby on the ground as an enticement for both men to grab. Scrambling toward the substitute weapon, Carlo and Diego tried crawling over each other to reach it first. Diego, being smaller and now filled with adrenalin, was able to reach it first, maneuvering the iron like a tennis racket, initiating a backhanded strike against Carlo's head. Stunned, Carlo laid his head back on the gravel, trying to reorient himself.

Diego took advantage of the momentary pause, and positioned himself over Carlo, readying himself to deal the final blow. Carlo looked up and saw two of Diego, his vision affected by the blow to the head. "Don't, Diego...no," he started to say.

Carlo shut his eyes tightly, afraid to watch the tire iron descending toward his face or the hatred in Diego's eyes as he swung it downward. Instead, a loud "pop" filled the air around him, and he suddenly felt the dead weight of Diego's body as it fell atop him.

"Son of a bitch, I can't trust you with anything, you moron. Get up and help me get rid of this body, Carlo. Jeez, a man can't even take a piss in peace with you around." Tony holstered his gun and zipped his pants. He shoved a fresh toothpick in the corner of his mouth as he waited for Carlo to squirm out from under Diego's dead body and get to his feet.

"Thanks, boss. I thought I was a goner, you know?" Carlo mumbled as he managed to get to his knees and eventually stand. He felt of his bleeding

ear where Diego had hit him, realizing he was beginning to get a massive headache.

"Yeah, yeah, yeah. Now let's drag this asshole to the group home over behind the building." Tony felt rejuvenated now that he had made another kill—another completed assignment that the Viper would more than appreciate. He was feeling more confident, with only one other loose end to tie up. If they timed it right, maybe they could still take care of the Sanderson woman before dark.

Each man grabbed a leg and dragged Diego's lifeless body away from the parking area to the rear of what used to be the main office of the now defunct construction company. They struggled with the weight, but finally managed to toss Diego's body into the abandoned well.

"Can we go to Patsy's now, Tony?" Carlo asked with begging eyes, still acting a little disoriented.

"You can't go anywhere looking like you just got mangled in a dog fight. We better let the Viper know what happened, and then we'll figure out dinner, capisci?" Tony explained.

"Yeah, catfish sounds good, too," Carlo said with the ringing in his ear getting louder with every second.

* * * * * *

Caroline was losing her nerve. The coroner had led her into a large room that reminded her of a hospital operating room. This definitely wasn't that kind of area. There were sheet-covered bodies on stainless steel tables and some still in body bags. She began to feel nauseous, unsure of where to go if she had to throw up. She kept the tissue over her nose to deflect the unpleasant odor of death that shrouded the room.

"Miss Sanderson, after reading your husband's ...uh, ex-husband's suicide note, I have no doubt the unidentified remains we collected belonged to him. However, I must do my due diligence in his positive identification through other means. You do understand, don't you?" the coroner looked at her with sympathy.

"Of course, but after I see him, I believe I can positively tell you if it is him or not." Caroline was firm.

"That's highly doubtful, Miss Sanderson, but you can try." He took a few more steps and stopped before a deflated body bag. At first Caroline wasn't entirely sure it contained anything at all. But, when the coroner unzipped the bag, she realized he was right. There wasn't much left to identify.

"Oh, God," Caroline moaned. The coroner once again led her to a seat and patted her hand while she wept

* * * * * *

When Tony hung up the payphone, he cursed under his breath as he approached the car.

"What now, boss?" Carlo asked.

"We gotta meet up with my cousin the doctor, that's what. The Viper wants you looked at before we finish with the Sanderson broad. I'm supposed to reach out to Lorenzo and ask him if he can look at your head. But remember, moron, 'Enzo can't know nothing about this baby chase we're on. He still thinks the baby was taken to some good home somewhere. He can't know anything about what we're doing. Got it?" Tony explained.

"Yeah, boss. I won't say nothin'." Carlo was sincere, but Tony was doubtful of Carlo's ability to keep his mouth shut.

******

"Our options are limited, I'm afraid," the coroner told Caroline. Without immediate access to dental records, we may be able to rely on DNA comparisons. No matter what we do, the police will have to be involved. I'm afraid Mr. Sanderson's suicide note will be important information in the official investigation," he explained.

"You mean I can't keep John's letter? He wrote it to me. How can they take it from me?" she cried.

"I'm sure they'll return it after the investigation is closed. I could probably help make a strong case for closure if only I had some comparative DNA samples. Do you have anything of his that I could use, Ms. Sanderson?" he asked with genuine hope.

"I still have his toothbrush at home. I let him stay over a couple of weeks ago when he was painting around his house. He couldn't stand the fumes, so I gave him my couch. He left it in the guest bathroom, and I just didn't get around to throwing it away." Caroline realized she was doing a good job of fabricating a backup story.

"Well, why don't you go grab that toothbrush and bring it back over here to me. Maybe with that, I can establish positive identity—or at least, positive enough to convince the police to close the homicidal aspects of the case." He patted her hand again.

"I'll go get it now. Thank you so much for your kindness. This has been one of the hardest things I've ever had to do. I don't think I can stand to have it drag out for much longer." For the last time, she sniffed and wiped her nose. She managed a smile as the coroner allowed her to exit the building from the employee's entrance. She was no more than ten feet from the Jeep Cherokee, and she was ready to sit down alone and cry.

162

CHAPTER 17

Tuesday, December 6, 1994

There was no use pacing; it only made her more fatigued. The sunroom that usually felt open and airy was now no more than another den of captivity. Cathy Giordano had awakened that morning and found herself on the hallway floor between her children's rooms. Apparently, Lorenzo had stepped over her as he left the master suite on his way to work that day. He had hardly spoken to her during the last 40 hours or more.

Her mother had kept busy explaining to the children's nanny all the horrible details of the kidnapping event. And, to top it off, Cathy had overheard Genevieve repeat the story over and over to all her friends who would still pick up the phone when she called. Now the poor nanny was cornered in the nursery, forced to listen while Genevieve embellished the details of a story that had changed a little more each time it was repeated.

Cathy couldn't talk about it; not yet, anyway. She only wanted to discuss it with Lorenzo, but he wasn't available. He avoided the subject. He avoided her. He wouldn't look at her, or hold her, or cry with her. He seemed to be in denial. If not denial, he had placed more confidence in the police's ability to find the baby than she now had.

The hours were slowly ticking by. She knew what it meant if the evening came without the baby's return. The critical 48 hours would have passed.

She was watching the clock and watching the door.

If she didn't talk to Lorenzo soon, she would die of despair and anxiety. Maybe she should give him one more chance to express his feelings. Perhaps if he understood how helpless she felt all alone like this, surely he would come to her rescue. If he had an ounce of feeling left for her well-being, he would realize how close she was to leaping over the edge of darkness and never coming back. He couldn't have shut down completely, could he?

She stared once more at the clock on the mantle. The hands hadn't moved, or so it seemed. Was the clock broken, or were the hands going around in slow motion? She felt like she was going crazy.

She had to make Lorenzo open up to her before time ran out altogether. Cathy fell to her knees and prayed for answers.

* * * * * *

Juliana Moretti had spent the morning in a manic state. One minute she was crying because she felt like her life was going to hell. The next minute, she was making manicure-pedicure and spa appointments because she wanted to feel pretty again.

The apartment locks had been changed before noon, but she hadn't heard from her father. It was close to 3:00 p.m. when she remembered what he'd told her. *I'm supposed to call **him**, I think. He told me not to answer the phone and call **him** if I needed him. I can't believe I've been waiting for his call all this time. I'm so clueless, sometimes.*

She reached for the phone and dialed her father's private number. He answered on the second ring.

"Papa, have you talked to Diego? I've been here all day and the phone hasn't rung. Apparently he was too busy to try to call. Anyway, I wouldn't have answered, because you told me not to." Juliana was chattering away.

"Juliana, I hate to be the one to give you bad news. You've had enough already, but there's something you must know about Diego." The Viper waited for her response, but she didn't utter a sound.

"Diego has been having a serious relationship with another woman for over a year. I didn't want to be the one to tell you, even though I knew months ago. I thought you two could work it out on your own. The baby was supposed to be the motivation to get you two back together. When that didn't work out—and when you revealed to me how Diego had been treating you—I had to take matters into my own hands." He paused.

"Did you hurt him, Papa?" Juliana silently hoped he did—just a little, anyway.

"Now, Juliana, why would I do that? I had a serious talk with him, and of course, I asked him to make his choice. He chose to accept a considerable sum of money to start a new life with the other woman. He was very gracious and very relieved, I believe," he lied.

"Papa, I ... I don't know what to say. Part of me is hurt, and the other part wants to cut the balls off that bastard." Juliana whimpered as she realized she would miss Diego's company and affection.

"That's a natural reaction. Of course you're hurt. Who wouldn't be? But I'll make it up to you, Juliana. Mark my words; you'll be happier than you've ever been now that you're free of that fuck-up." Again he paused, then added, "And I'm sending you over a new car tomorrow. A red Maserati. My little girl deserves the best." He smiled to himself.

"Oh, Papa, that's the sweetest thing. I'm sorry I sound so confused, but it's been really hard since Sunday night. So much has happened... and now, *this*. I love you, Papa. Thank you for letting Diego get off so easy. He may be a fuck-up, but I loved him." She made a kissing noise and hung up the phone.

The Viper returned to his paperwork, studying the new inventory at the chop shop. It was lucky for him that he looked over the new acquisition list before Juliana called. The boys had plenty of time to turn the black Maserati into a red one by the time Juliana would need it tomorrow.

* * * * * *

When the phone rang on Lorenzo's desk, he was hesitant to pick it up. His secretary was supposed to be screening calls that afternoon, only allowing the most important ones through. Hesitantly he put the receiver to his ear. "Yes," he said quietly.

"Enzo, it's Tony. I got an emergency and I need for you to meet me real quick like. Bring your doctor kit. I'm with Carlo in the parking lot next door to your building." Tony listened closely when he finished his spiel, but he didn't hear Lorenzo on the other end of the line.

"You there, Enzo?" he asked.

"Yes, I'm here. Are you hurt, Tony? What happened?" Lorenzo asked, as he stood up from his chair and scanned the room for his medical bag.

"Not me, Enzo, but my buddy Carlo took a tire iron up side the head. He's a little woozy and says he's seeing double. He said his head was killing him. He's got a gash that might need stitches, but he can stand it if you need to sew him up."

Lorenzo figured whatever Tony and his buddy had gotten involved with, it had something to do with the Viper. He had sworn he wouldn't do anything to help the Viper again; but, Tony was family—not family to be proud of, but family nonetheless.

"Tell me where you're parked, and I'll be there in a few minutes," Lorenzo responded.

Tony told him, hung up the payphone, and jogged back to the car where Carlo waited.

* * * * * *

John Sanderson had just stepped out of the shower when he heard the motel room door open and close. "Hello?" he asked as he stood defenseless in nothing but a towel.

"Hello, back," Caroline shouted.

"I'll be out in a minute. Just drying off," he shouted. He was relieved that it was Caroline and not a housekeeper or intruder. He was beginning to feel anxious about occupying the room for too long. He thought perhaps it was time to relocate to another motel or a different city. He had a gut feeling about changing locations that he couldn't quite shake.

When he came out of the bathroom, he saw Caroline busily looking through the suitcase that held Mike's belongings.

"What are you looking for now?" John wanted to know.

"Mike's toothbrush, or his razor, or something with his DNA. The coroner says he can speed up the identity process, maybe even get the police to close the homicide part of the investigation, if I can provide Mike's –I mean, supposedly *your* DNA. I told him I had a toothbrush you had left at my house, and he seemed to believe it. If I can produce it, we might overcome a big hurdle." Caroline kept digging.

John went to the bed where all the duffle bag contents were still strewn. He moved around some papers, spying a comb that had been scraped out of the desk drawer with all its other random contents. He picked up a set of nail clippers, as well. "Do you think these are good enough to sway the coroner?" he asked Caroline.

She looked up and smiled. "Maybe, but I really wanted his toothbrush." She was about to give up when she noticed a white piece of hard plastic under the edge of the suitcase. She lifted up the suitcase corner to find the toothbrush she had been searching for. "Eureka! It's here! It must have fallen out when I pulled out this sweatshirt," she exclaimed. "And I'll take the comb, too. The nail clippers won't help." She smiled as she snatched the comb from John's hands.

"You're welcome, your majesty" John bowed and almost lost the towel that hung loosely around his waist.

"I see you've cleaned the family jewels," she said as she jerked the towel from around him. John stood there, naked and speechless.

"Keep up the good work. I'll be back shortly," Caroline teased as she kissed him quickly on the cheek. She moved toward the door, but abruptly retraced her steps. She kissed him hard on the mouth, then whispered, "We'll continue this later." She swiftly left the room, leaving John standing fully exposed with the towel at his feet.

* * * * * *

When Lorenzo found the Cadillac, Tony was pacing back and forth in front of it. Clearly, he was distressed.

"Where's your buddy," Lorenzo asked as he made his way closer to his cousin.

"Too late, Enzo. I think he's gone." Tony put the base of his palm against his brow and sighed deeply.

"Where did he go, Tony? I thought he was going to wait here for medical attention. Why didn't you make him stay?" Lorenzo questioned, irritated at his cousin for making him leave the sanctity of his office.

"No, Enzo. I think he's *dead*. Like permanent dirt nap *dead*. See for yourself, he's slumped in the front seat of the Caddy." Tony looked as if he was about to start crying.

Lorenzo opened the passenger door of the Cadillac. There he found Carlo slumped sideways, leaning with his head propped against the rolled-up window. Under other circumstances, he would have looked as if he was peacefully napping. The clotted gash on the right side of his head signaled otherwise.

Lorenzo couldn't find Carlo's pulse. Not a drop of fresh blood could be seen upon quick inspection of Carlo's violent head wound. It was obvious to Lorenzo that Carlo was no longer alive.

Tony came around to the passenger side of the car as Lorenzo got out of the Caddy and shut the door behind him.

"Well?" Tony asked.

"He's gone. His head injury would be more appropriately classified as a TBI—Traumatic Brain Injury—if my guess is right. Based on what you said about his vision and dizziness, that would be my initial assumption. And the headache symptom you mentioned, of course, make it a rather obvious TBI. Considering the hit he took with the..."

"Tire iron," Tony supplied Lorenzo's missing words.

"Yes, tire iron. Considering the force of the blow from such a heavy object, I'm surprised he didn't die on the spot." Lorenzo observed. "Keep in mind, I'm speculating. An autopsy would have to be performed to accurately determine the cause of death," the doctor clinically stated.

"No. No autopsy." Tony looked as though he had just taken a blow to the stomach. "Thanks, Enzo. I'll be in touch. But right now, I gotta go make some arrangements. I owe you one, Enzo."

Lorenzo turned away from Tony and the Cadillac, making his way back toward his high rise office building. As he got closer, he thought about bypassing the front door altogether and forgetting work for the rest of the day. He could use another drink, and his private office stash of single malt scotch had been depleted hours ago. Perhaps a brisk walk down the block to the liquor store would do him good. He could be back behind his impressive office doors before anyone missed him. He was already past his office doors and committed to a liquor store visit before he had time to change his mind.

* * * * * *

Cathy Giordano had talked with Lorenzo's secretary twice within the last half hour. He wasn't in the office, and hadn't told anyone where he was going. His calendar had been blocked out for the rest of the afternoon. The other office physicians had taken over Lorenzo's daily patients' appointments to give him some time to get back into the groove. Cathy left word for Lorenzo to return her call when he made it back to the office.

It was close to 4:30 p.m., and Cathy was becoming increasingly irrational. Her anxiety level had hit a new high, causing her to believe that she was capable of doing anything if it would reduce her pain and imagined guilt. *I should have been home Sunday night. Screw Lorenzo and his night on the town.*

Silently replaying the past Sunday evening's events over and over prompted her to doubt Lorenzo's innocence. **He** was the one who insisted she needed a night out when she was still recuperating from the delivery. **He** was the one who wanted to go out on the town the night before he was scheduled for surgery the next day. **He** was the one who tried to keep her from calling home to check on the children when her gut said she should never have left them to begin with. **He** was the one who

insisted everything would be fine when it clearly was not. **He** should be the one she hated right now, instead of hating herself.

If Lorenzo didn't call her within the hour, she would take matters into her own hands and do what she had to do.

CHAPTER 18

Tuesday, December 6, 1994

Tony drove the Cadillac to the rear of the Sundown Terrace Motel with his lifeless partner still slumped sideways in the front seat. It had taken all the strength Tony could muster to push the heavy man from behind the steering wheel and far enough into the passenger side for Tony to drive the big car.

This time when he parked the Caddy in the motel's back parking area, he chose a spot in the opposite left corner where a large green dumpster loomed. He backed in next to the trash receptacle, but at the last moment turned the wheel enough to stop the car at a 45 degree angle next to the towering steel box. He backed up slowly so that the passenger side of the Caddy formed a triangle of private space between the car and the bin.

As if carrying on his usual banter with Carlo, Tony said, "No, Carlo. I ain't dumping you here. But I have to get you in the trunk, somehow. Jeez, I wish you had been a skinnier guy." He chuckled to his lifeless friend. "Me and you had some real thrills the last couple o' days, didn't we, Carlo? You fucked up some, like always, but you came through. I'm gonna miss you, you big goon," he admitted to Carlo whose blank staring eyes were still wide open.

Tony got out of the car and immediately headed for the trunk. He opened it, leaving the trunk lid gaping as he moved to the passenger door of the Caddy.

As the wide Caddy door swung open, it created a temporary privacy shield between the front edge of the dumpster and the rear corner of the car. Tony looked up at the dumpster's small opening for a brief moment, toying with the enticing option of disposing of the body in with the motel's garbage. However, he'd promised Carlo he wouldn't do that just a few seconds earlier. Plus, as small as Tony was, he knew he'd never be able to lift Carlo high enough to get him shoved through that small opening.

Instead, he relied on his adrenalin and limited muscle power to pull Carlo from the seat and out onto the asphalt pavement. He caught his breath before he tried to pull the heavy body by an arm and a leg toward the rear of the car. Tony managed to move Carlo a few inches, but not quite far enough to make headway. The rough asphalt was snagging Carlo's clothing and hampering ease of movement.

"Jeez, Carlo. You should'a laid off the pancakes. You're a heavy son of a bitch." Tony breathed with effort, placing both his hands on his hips. The small man gazed up at the cloudy sky as if praying for more strength. He glanced around the parking lot once more before he looked down at Carlo again. "Sorry, big guy. I gotta move fast before somebody wants to empty the trash out here."

Tony went back to the trunk and pulled out a folded plastic tarpaulin stored there in case 'assignments' got messy. He spread it on the asphalt next to Carlo, hoping that he could manage to roll the body onto it. A big shove proved successful, and Tony grabbed the free end of the tarp and pulled with all his might. Carlo's lifeless form slid easily now.

With the body between him and the trunk, Tony now faced another monumental issue: lifting the dead weight up over the edge of the big car's bumper. He scratched his head and looked upward again. A thought crossed his mind.

Digging underneath the trunk pad, he exposed the spare tire and the jack positioned next to it. He grabbed the jack and attempted to position it under Carlo's buttocks. There was no way to get it wedged under the body considering Carlo was now sprawled flat on his back. Tony looked around, feeling hopeless and exposed in the private but public area. Thinking quickly, he sprinted toward the dumpster. Peering through the opening on tiptoes, he caught a glimpse of scrapped wood. Apparently there had been some recent remodeling done at the motel.

Tony hoisted himself up, precariously bending forward from the waist into the dumpster. His petite-sized feet dangled off the ground in his pristine Italian leather shoes. He managed to snare two short pieces of scrap 2" x 4", haphazardly dropping them on the ground from his side as he continued to hang from the dumpster's opening. He stretched for another one that was slightly out of reach, causing him to lose his balance and topple forward. He landed face first on a greasy piece of discarded pizza, which sadly reminded him that Carlo had asked to go to Patsy's for spaghetti. Tony burst into mournful tears as he climbed out of the dumpster, face smeared with tomato sauce, and his shiny Italian shoes now scuffed and soiled.

* * * * * *

When Caroline reached the Coroner's Office, she parked in the same spot she had occupied that afternoon. It was approaching 5:00 p.m. when she arrived, bringing the vehicle to a halt in the parking lot within minutes of the office's official closing time.

To save a few moments, she went directly to the employee entrance she had used when she left earlier. To her surprise the door was unlocked.

She stuck her head around the door and called, "Dr. Carey?"

Hearing no response from inside the building, she took a few steps forward into the hallway. The door shut behind her with a thud.

Dr. Carey appeared at the end of the corridor with clipboard in hand and a smile on his face. "Ah. Ms. Sanderson. Back so soon?"

"I brought you his toothbrush and his spare comb. I hope they can be of help to you," Caroline said as she carefully avoided using names. "Oh, and this..." she said as she took the Yankees cap off her head and extended it toward the coroner. "This was his, too."

Dr. Carey took the items from her. "These should do nicely. Perhaps within a few days and some urging, I can convince the police to close this part of the investigation," he said as he held the comb up in front of his face and inspected it. Then he added, "... pending matching DNA identification from these items, that is."

"Thank you, Dr. Carey. I'll leave you to it," she mumbled as she glanced once more at Mike's cap that the coroner was now holding. She turned to leave through the employees' door for the second time that day.

* * * * * *

Tony had managed to get the scrap lumber under Carlo's waist, but that only made matters worse. He had retrieved the tire iron from the car with which he planned to raise the jack (and Carlo). He twirled it around like a bloody baton while deep in thought.

Tony still struggled with how to get Carlo on top of the jack and moved into the trunk. Finally, he abandoned the idea of using the jack and threw the tire iron to the side. Tony sat defeated on the edge of the clear tarp next to his friend's body.

"Looks like we're stuck, Carlo," Tony said as he chewed on a fresh toothpick. "I thought the jack idea would work, but I guess I'm an imbecile, too. No wonder we worked so good together." Tony chuckled, but not from amusement.

Reaching over to pull the lumber out from under the corpse, another idea crossed his mind. He gathered the wood pieces in front of him and gazed at them as if they were his personal crystal ball. He was going to build an improvised ramp. *That could work!*

He laid the ends of the lumber pieces on the edge of the trunk opening, with the opposite ends wedged downward into the asphalt. Fearing the lumber would scoot forward with the moving weight of the body, he scouted for anything that could be used as a scotch to keep the ramp in place. He noticed loose pieces of concrete that had fallen from the retaining wall a few feet away, and Tony seized them. Now all he had to do was maneuver Carlo up the ramp and into the security of the big trunk.

* * * * * *

Satisfied with herself, Caroline carefully merged the Jeep Cherokee into traffic and halted at the stop light a hundred yards or so from Dr. Carey's office. She wondered if she should pick up some food to take back to the motel room. John had given her a list of items to pick up at the grocery store, but she didn't feel like shopping.

Contemplating her food options as she waited for the light to turn green, she glanced at the fuel gauge for the first time in hours. She still had a half tank of gas, but she also had a red "check engine" warning light that she hadn't noticed before. *Crap!* she thought as she wondered if she should try to get it checked or head back to the motel.

Rather than press her luck, Caroline pulled over into a convenience store parking lot. She parked on the side of the building feeling less conspicuous there. *I should check the owner's manual before I panic. It might be something as simple as a loose fuel cap.*

Caroline pushed the button to release the glove compartment panel. She reached for the owner's manual that she was certain Mike would have kept there. Her fingers brushed up against something cold and hard. She

leaned across the seat to get a better look. *Mike, you've surprised me again! That's your Smith and Western!*

She quickly closed the glove compartment, focused only on getting back to John with the pistol she had found. The "check engine" light didn't matter anymore, and neither did food or groceries. Now they were armed and ready to defend themselves, or so she innocently thought.

* * * * * *

To make the ramp idea work, Carlo's body had to be positioned dead center on the plastic. His head and feet had to be hanging over the short edges of the tarp so his body could be rolled up like a fancy appetizer. *What are they called? Oh yeah, pigs in a blanket.* Tony grinned as he thought about how Carlo now reminded *him* of food.

Pulling the tarp's edge as close to the end of the ramp as possible, Tony began his magic trick. Getting Carlo to the base of the ramp wasn't as hard as he thought; however, when he tried to push Carlo upward, Tony's back sent a shock of electricity through his small body. Carlo rolled back down to the pavement in his plastic wrap, and Tony bent forward in pain.

"Jesus, Mary, and Joseph, that hurt," was all Tony could say. More determined than ever and ignoring the searing lumbar pain, Tony climbed in the trunk to survey the problem from an alternate view.

"Okay, Carlo. We're gonna make this happen any minute now." Tony climbed back down, gathered the opposite ends of the tarp and held them together as if he were folding a sheet. With Carlo's body in the middle fold, Tony worked himself backwards into the trunk once more. He sat down, pushing his feet against the open trunk's inside edge, getting leverage as he pulled with all the strength he could gather with his arms.

He felt Carlo's body moving forward while he grabbed more of the tarp and gathered the excess plastic in his hands. Again he pulled with all his

might, trying to maneuver himself more upright so he could gauge the progress. The massive body was now safely over and above the scotches.

Holding on with a Herculean strength he didn't know he had, Tony managed to get to his knees without losing an inch of forward progress. He straightened himself as well as he could. His short stature came in handy as he tried to half-stand in the back of the Caddy's gaping trunk. He rose slowly, still maintaining his grip. With a final heave backwards, Tony lost control of the plastic, losing his left hand's grasp; but, he still managed to get Carlo turned head upwards on the rickety ramp.

Tony climbed out of the trunk and jumped down on the asphalt. Amazingly, the thrown-together ramp was still holding the heavy weight of the dead man. Also to his surprise, there had been no activity in the parking area while he had been parked there.

Turning back to his challenge, Tony pushed Carlo's deadweight an inch at a time up the remaining distance. Eventually, he was able to pull the wood out from under Carlo's lower half and work the big man's legs into the trunk. It had been a massive undertaking for such a small man, but he had done it. He threw the wood in the trunk with Carlo, kicked the concrete pieces back toward the wall, and at the last second, remembered the useless jack and tire iron. He threw it in the trunk as well, and climbed in the driver's seat. He had to clean himself up a little and report to the Viper before he checked up on the Sanderson broad.

He started the engine and sat silently for a moment, making the sacred sign of the Holy Cross on his chest. *"Rest in Peace, you heavy bastard. My back will never be the same."*

* * * * * *

When her stomach growled loudly, Caroline admitted to herself that food was, indeed, her real priority instead of rushing back to the motel. She didn't fancy anything from the diner next door to the motel, but she could

be tempted with fried chicken. Looking up and down the highway for a suitable restaurant, she slowly traveled in the highway's right-hand lane causing impatient drivers to pass her by. Finally, Caroline spotted a familiar red sign with a southern gentleman smiling toward the roadway. Her mouth began to water as she pulled in to the parking area.

Meanwhile, John had repacked all Mike's papers in the duffle bag and closed the suitcase full of Mike's clothes and other personal items. With that taken care of, he started packing Caroline's personal items so that the two could quickly relocate to another motel that evening.

Caroline's toothbrush, hair brush, and makeup kit were on top of the bathroom vanity. As he reached to collect them, John suddenly thought of the other letters he had written that morning before Caroline awoke.

He approached the bedside table where he had hidden the folded papers. He opened the drawer and found them where he had left them: safely stuck inside the Bible that had been placed there years before by the Gideons. He took the letters back into the bathroom, sliding them deep inside Caroline's zippered makeup pouch.

* * * * * *

Ever since Lorenzo had gotten back to the office, he had postponed talking to his persistent wife. Cathy had called repeatedly, and he had instructed his secretary to tell her he was in a meeting. It was 5:30 p.m. now, past office hours, as he sat with his scotch in hand. The phone on his desk rang again. He ignored it.

Cathy Giordano was obsessed with contacting her husband. She hung up the phone and waited a few minutes before dialing his number again. Still no answer.

She wandered to the kitchen to pour herself another glass of wine, resigning herself to wait for Lorenzo to come home instead of trying to

get him to answer the phone. The kind of conversation they needed to have should be done face-to-face, anyway.

When Cathy reentered the sunroom, she found Genevieve Parker, with bandaged nose and raccoon eyes, sitting in a plush side chair a few feet from the chaise to which Cathy was returning.

"Cathy, darling, I've been thinking," her mother began. "I don't seem to be of any help here with the nanny taking care of the children. You apparently don't want or need my emotional support through this nightmare." Genevieve looked accusingly at her daughter whose facial expression remained stoic.

"Perhaps you can be better served with some psychiatric counseling. Heaven knows you must need it after losing your baby to those monsters ..."

"SHUT UP, MOTHER!" Cathy finally broke her silence.

"I beg your ..." Genevieve started to respond, but her daughter cut her off.

"JUST FUCKING LEAVE!" Cathy commanded as she watched her mother shrink back in surprise.

"Cathy, please calm down. I'm not suggesting I abandon you altogether. I just think ..."

"I don't CARE what you think, Mother. I just want you out of here. I'm sick of hearing you tell everyone how you cheated death when those hoodlums took your precious grandchild! This is not about YOU! Please, just go back to Nashville. We'll manage without you. I'll call you when I'm ready to talk to you again, but for now—GO!" Cathy turned her head away from her mother as Genevieve slowly rose from her chair.

Genevieve dabbed at her eyes with a lace handkerchief. "I'll make arrangements to leave tonight," she said with a hint of hurt in her voice. She left the room and closed the door behind her.

Cathy arose, threw her wine glass at the clock on the mantle, and went back in the kitchen to get a fresh glass.

CHAPTER 19

Tuesday, December 6, 1994

Vincenzo DeLuca wasn't surprised to hear from Tony. It was dinner time when the call came through, causing the Viper to push aside his fresh cob salad when the butler handed him the telephone.

He wiped his mouth with the tail end of the linen napkin tucked in his collar before he answered, "Yeah."

"Boss, Diego's at the group home all tucked in, but we have another problem. You know Diego whacked Carlo with a tire iron before I could put him down completely. It took a few hours, but now Carlo's dead. I tried to get Lorenzo to him in time for some help, but he died anyway. Lorenzo said it was from B-I-T or something. Carlo got some kind of brain injury trauma. Not to worry, I'll take care of Carlo, too; but, I gotta say I'm sorta shaken up." Tony stopped abruptly.

The Viper chewed what was left in his mouth, swallowed the food, and took a gulp of wine before responding.

"So the good doctor helped you out?" the Viper asked as he leaned back in the captain's chair of the heavy dining room suite.

"Yeah, he's family, you know. Came right away when I called him," Tony responded.

"That's good. That's very good," the Viper said as he swirled the dark wine in the crystal glass. "So, are you back on the trail of the Sanderson woman?"

"Yeah, Boss. I gotta clean up a little, but I'm jumping right back on it. I'm across the street from the motel where she was this afternoon. If she hasn't skipped by now, she should be easy enough to corner."

The Viper smiled. "Good. I'm sorry about Carlo, but our business is risky. He knew that. Keep me informed, as usual," the Viper commanded as he hung up the phone.

Tony left the payphone and headed toward the diner's front door. He had wiped the pizza sauce from his face already, but he knew he looked as though he'd been in a street fight. He slithered through the entrance and headed straight for the men's room in the rear of the restaurant. He caught a glimpse of the bleached blond waitress—was her name Martha?—as he weaved through the rear tables. It must be after 6:00 p.m., he thought as he remembered what the waiter told Carlo about her shift schedule.

* * * * * *

The two Sandersons feasted on a meal of fried chicken, potato chips, and biscuits, saving the two fried cherry pies for later.

After their meal, John had been taken aback when Caroline pulled the Smith & Wesson from her purse and pointed it toward him. "Surprise! Look what I found in Mike's glove compartment," she beamed.

"Whoa, Caroline. Don't point a gun at any target unless you intend to shoot it!" John barked.

"Sorry, John. I'm not used to handguns. I think maybe you better give me a little instruction before I have to really use it." She laid the gun on the bed next to her ex-husband. He agreed and started his instruction.

"Caroline, this is a magazine and it holds the bullets. See?" He released the magazine to reveal a row of copper-colored bullet tips poking from

behind their brass casings in the slender cylinder. "Let me show you how to load the magazine. Watch."

John emptied the bullets on the bed and reloaded the magazine half full. "Now you try." He handed the magazine to Caroline. She fumbled with the bullets, trying to put the first one in backwards. When she realized her mistake, she turned the bullet around and wedged it on top of those already secured in the magazine.

"That's hard to do," she remarked.

John nodded and said, "Yes, but you have to be able to do it. Speed is important if you're in a tight spot. Either that, or you better have extra loaded magazines to use just in case." He took the gun from her and emptied the chamber. A lone bullet fell on the bed beside him.

"I'm glad you didn't pull the trigger when you pointed this thing at me. It had a bullet in the chamber. I should have checked that first. First rule—always assume *any* gun is loaded and empty the chamber first thing unless you're trying to kill someone." John picked up the bullet and rolled it around in his hand.

"We've got a completely empty gun here now, so let's get you familiar with how to hold it and work on your imaginary aim."

He pointed the pistol toward the rear of the room. He held the gun almost level to his shoulders with both arms extended rigidly. His grip on the gun was firm; the handle was cupped between his palms, with his right pointer finger extended straight down the side of the barrel but away from the trigger. He showed her how he overlapped his thumbs to perfect the hold. He pointed out how the gun rested on his slightly cupped left hand and how much steadiness that simple adjustment provided for straight sighting. Finally, he showed her how to work the thumb safety.

Next, he let her try, handing over the unloaded pistol to Caroline who had never fired a gun before. She soon got the hang of how to hold the weapon and was ready to proceed to the next lesson.

They sat down on the bed again, and he explained how to release the magazine and insert it again. She found the magazine release button easily and soon was repeating the process with ease.

He knew she would have trouble getting a bullet in the chamber; cocking a gun was simple enough if one went about it the right way. With the magazine out of the gun, he told Caroline to pretend she was going to empty the chamber. Immediately she tried to grasp the top of the semi-automatic weapon and pull backwards with her left hand. It didn't work. She didn't have the strength.

"Ok, Caroline. Try this. Put your hand across the top of the gun and hold tightly around the slide. Now your job is to keep that slide from moving." She followed his directions and stood waiting for the next step. "Now, with your right hand, PUSH the gun through the slide—don't let your left hand move forward—only your right hand should move when you push."

Caroline looked at him tentatively, and shoved her right hand forward, holding the slide as steady as she could. To her amazement, it worked!

"That wasn't hard at all!" she exclaimed. She hugged John tightly in celebration of her new gun knowledge.

They worked a while longer loading bullets and extracting the magazine until Caroline felt much more comfortable with the gun in her hand.

"Now, let's get the bullet out of the chamber and reload the full magazine. I'm not sure I want you loose around a cocked gun just yet. You'll get there soon enough, though. You've caught on quickly." John let Caroline handle the final gun processes. She seemed excited, but he was

still planning on being on the back side of the gun while she finished the task.

* * * * *

Lorenzo opened his front door a few minutes before 7:00 p.m., surprised that no one seemed to be stirring in the house. He removed his suit jacket and laid it on a brocade chair of French design that Cathy had picked up at an antique store. She brought it home a few years ago announcing how the chair would "look marvelous" in the square foyer. It was rarely used except to hold jackets or purses.

Considering the hour, he expected the baby to be asleep in the nursery. Usually, Sophia would have already eaten dinner and be in the throws of preparing for her bath and subsequent bedtime stories with the nanny. Lorenzo was glad he had hired the woman to help. He never expected his mother-in-law to be anything except a hindrance. Genevieve had insisted that her presence was required, even though Cathy never invited her to visit. He hoped she planned to leave soon. She was irritating.

He bypassed the children's rooms and proceeded straight to the master suite. He thought about tossing a few pillows and a blanket into the hallway for Cathy to use during the course of the night. She preferred sleeping on the floor near the kids, apparently. He didn't want to talk to her until he had to because all she did was wring her hands and cry. It made him feel guilty to look at her. He didn't have any extra sympathy to give her. He was using all of his pity supply on himself. He loathed himself for his betrayal to his son and to his wife. Cathy didn't deserve to pay like this for his stupid mistakes.

He poured himself a stiff drink from the portable tray bar in the sitting area of the large suite. He half-reclined in an overstuffed chair and propped his feet on the edge of the antique coffee table to his left. He

swirled the brown liquid, swallowing hard as it rolled down the back of his throat. It burned just enough to feel good.

A soft knock on the closed double doors delayed his second gulp.

"Yes," he answered.

The door cracked open and the nanny, Miss Elmore, stepped in.

"Mrs. Giordano wants to know if you would join her in the sunroom?" she asked as if she needed to wait for a reply.

"Of course I will. And the children... are they ... "

"They're fine, Doctor. The baby is no trouble and Sophia is a delight. I have a cot set up in the baby's room and plan to stay here 24/7...at least for the rest of this week. I hope that's still the arrangement?"

"Yes, of course." He smiled and started to rise from the chair, but the nanny made no move to leave.

"Sir, may I ask a question?"

"Yes, what is it?" Lorenzo looked quizzically at the uniformed woman.

"Is there some reason Mrs. Giordano slept on the hallway floor last night? I would think she'd have been more comfortable sleeping in one of the guest rooms." The nanny was afraid she had overstepped her boundaries, but she was concerned for the mentally frail Cathy.

"Don't worry about Cathy. She's dealing with this tragedy in her own way. By tonight, I'm sure she'll rest comfortably in a bed instead of the floor. Last night was hard for her. She must think she needs to protect what's left of the family. Quite honestly, I don't know what she was thinking or trying to do. This whole fiasco has left a mental scar on her that I can only hope will someday heal." Lorenzo didn't know what else to say.

Miss Elmore looked at him and shook her head in reluctant agreement. "Well, if I can do anything for her, I'm available." She exited the room quietly, leaving Lorenzo staring at the closed door.

* * * * * *

It had been more than thirty minutes since Lorenzo had come home. She knew because she heard him open and close the front door. She had been waiting hours to talk to him, but apparently he wanted to continue avoiding her.

Earlier when the nanny came through the hallway passage to warm the baby's bottle, Cathy stopped her as she exited the kitchen. Asking her to summon Lorenzo was hard to do, but Cathy didn't want to confront him in the wing where the bedrooms were located. She thought the nanny might be the nosy kind who liked to spread gossip or insinuations about other people. It was bad enough that Genevieve had filled the nanny's ears with all that nonsense and the theatrical reenactments. Cathy was thankful that Genevieve had left for the Waldorf or Ritz or wherever she had decided to stay for the night. *Good riddance*, she thought as she drained another glass of wine.

* * * * * *

Tony nursed a cup of the diner's take-out coffee from the driver's seat of the Cadillac. He had moved the car to the center of the motel's parking lot for a closer view of the rooms. He pushed the seat far enough back to give his aching spine more comfort. The way he was positioned, he still had a direct view of the motel room that the Sanderson woman had entered earlier.

She had pulled into the parking lot about the same time Tony hung up with the Viper from the payphone outside the diner. She parked the Jeep behind the motel again, taking bags of take-out food inside with her when she entered the room. The drapes had been closed all day, but Tony

could tell she had left the lights on when she went to get food. *Typical broad. Afraid of the dark.*

He sat patiently, eventually emptying the cup and feeling like he needed to take a good piss. He squirmed in his seat and tried to control his bladder. *Think about something else. Jeez. Always with the bad timing.*

The more he tried not to think about it, the more he had to take a leak. He looked at his empty coffee cup, wondering if it would serve as a temporary toilet. *What are you thinking? That little cup will overflow in your lap, you moron.* Tony laughed at himself for a moment. *Now you're talking to yourself like you used to talk to Carlo.*

Five seconds later, Tony started the Caddy. He drove back up to the diner, believing he probably wouldn't miss anything happening at the motel if he hurried.

* * * * * *

"I think moving is smart, John. We shouldn't stay anywhere too long. Our chances of being discovered are bad enough as it is," Caroline agreed. Do you have a suggestion on where to go next?" she asked.

"No, but maybe another motel on the other side of town would be a thought. If we jump around and don't stick in the same area too long, we'll probably be okay for a while longer."

John pointed to the bags he had already packed in the corner of the room. "Well, we're ready to go whenever we decide. All that's left is to load the cars." John picked the gun up off the bed where Caroline had laid it.

"And you should keep this in your purse at all times. Just remember, there is no bullet in the chamber right now. You should cock it if you think you're in danger, and hopefully before you need the fire power." He smiled as he handed the pistol to her.

She took it without making any comment, realizing how serious their situation had become. She never thought she would need to be armed to feel safe.

"How about I take my suitcase to the Beetle and load it up. I'll scout around for another motel and be back as soon as I can. I'll bring us some ice cream to top off those fried cherry pies," she grinned as she pecked him on the cheek. "Maybe after we get settled somewhere else we can take up where we left off ... family jewel inspection, remember?" She giggled and left the motel room. She smiled broadly as she turned the corner into the open corridor heading for her car.

At that exact moment, Tony was staring at graffiti scrawled in ink on a paper sign above the urinal in the diner's bathroom:

Carlo loves Martha

Ah, Jeez, you big goon. I thought you hated graffiti. Tony shook his head as he zipped up his pants.

* * * * * *

Lorenzo left the bedroom wing of the house dreading the moment he had to look his wife in the eyes. He took his time as he walked through the huge house, trying to delay his entrance into the sunroom. Cocktail glass in hand, he turned the corner at the end of the corridor that led toward the kitchen. He wasn't the slightest bit hungry; but, once there, he picked up an apple from the island's fruit bowl, then dropped it back in, before he entered the adjoining room where Cathy waited.

"So you decided to join me after all?" Cathy sneered. She downed the last of her wine and threw the glass at the mantle—the fifth one within the last hour.

"Do you recall where we were exactly 48 hours ago, Lorenzo? We were walking into a fucking Broadway show, about to take our seats. Do you remember what I told you, dear husband? I said, 'something feels wrong,' I think. Yes, those were my exact words. And how did you react? You **didn't listen** to me. Oh, no. You dragged me back in that theater and made me sit there while you tried to act like you enjoyed that miserable play." She tried to get up to get another glass of wine, but her legs were too wobbly. She eased herself back down in her seat and continued her rant.

Lorenzo stood uneasily near the door adjacent to the mantle, staring blankly across the room. He hadn't had the chance to seat himself before Cathy started in on him.

"And get *this*, Doctor. You'll find this amusing. The *great* neurosurgeon who was interrupted last Thursday because his wife had twins, you know the guy I mean? Well, he had to prepare Sunday afternoon for an early operation scheduled for the next morning. So he spent the afternoon at his office. What a dedicated doctor, wouldn't you agree? Well, I, *for one*, think it's strange that suddenly—instead of needing his rest after all that preparation—the good doctor decides his wife needs a night out on the town! Imagine that! How considerate of him! *Especially* after she had just gotten out of the hospital the day before. She didn't need recovery time from delivering *TWO* babies. Oh, no. She just wanted to make her doctor husband happy; so, she went along for the ride. Now, how sweet was that? Sound like a marriage made in heaven? The joining of one stupid, submissive woman with a selfish bastard of a man? Hardly."

"Cathy, you're drunk. Please stop before you say something you can't take back," Lorenzo pleaded without looking in her direction.

"And just why would I want to take anything back that I say, Lorenzo? It's all true. You know it is." Cathy lowered her head and her tears flowed

freely. Lorenzo stood as stiff as a guard at Buckingham Palace, never moving and looking straight ahead.

"Lorenzo, I need to hear the truth from you. Do you know anything about why our baby was taken? Did you play some part in it? Is that why you won't talk about it?"

Cathy tried to stand again, and this time she was successful. Gripping the back of the chaise with one hand, she unsteadily approached Lorenzo. She leaned against the mantle, stepping barefoot on a piece of broken glass, but it didn't seem to faze her. She continued to stand there, rocking back and forth, as she held on to the mantle's edge. The glass was embedding itself in the ball of her foot, but it didn't matter to her. That pain was nothing compared to the heartache she was harboring.

"Lorenzo, please answer me. I need to hear the truth. Please help me understand," she sobbed.

He turned to face her, but he didn't expect to feel the overwhelming sense of pity he felt for the broken woman standing before him. "Cathy, I don't know where our baby is. If I could get him back, I would. I hate to see you suffer this way. I can't stand to look at you this way. Please believe me." He reached for her, but she jerked away.

"NO! NO! You didn't answer the questions. I asked you if you knew *why* he was taken! I asked you if you had *anything* to do with it! ANSWER ME!" she screamed, then bent over and sobbed from deep within her soul. She was consumed with a toxic mixture of rage and grief.

"Please, Cathy! I'm *trying* to answer you. I would never do anything to put our children in harm's way, you know that."

She looked up at him with fiery eyes and growled, "I know nothing of the kind. I don't even know you anymore." She turned and moved quickly

toward the kitchen, leaving bloody footprints behind on the hardwood floor.

Lorenzo followed her, but she hadn't gotten very far. She had stopped at the kitchen's center island. She leaned unsteadily against the granite top while she tried to get her emotions in check. She wanted to finish the conversation before Lorenzo tried to calm her with medication. For the first time in her marriage, she was afraid of him.

"Cathy, don't be like this. Please listen to me." Lorenzo stood behind her, feeling helpless.

"*Now* you want to talk, Lorenzo? Really? I've been trying to talk to you ever since this happened, and you just ignored me. If you want to talk, tell me the fucking TRUTH!"

Lorenzo took a deep breath and a gulp of his liquor. "All right, Cathy. I'll tell you the truth. I got in gambling trouble with a crime family and owed more money than I could get my hands on. They took the baby to settle the debt. I was told the baby would be placed with a loving family, and we should never worry about him. He's alive and well somewhere, Cathy." Lorenzo emptied his glass and turned his back to Cathy. He couldn't look her in the face now that he had admitted his guilt.

He leaned forward, facing the counter that lined the kitchen wall as he waited for her reaction behind him. He expected her to come at him with her fists or kick and scream, but he heard nothing. Wondering if she had fainted or done something even worse to herself, Lorenzo slowly turned around to face her. He was met with a chef's knife pointed directly under his chin. Cathy had taken it from the knife block on the island while his back was turned.

He raised both his hands in surrender as he tried to talk her down, "Cathy, put the knife down, baby. Don't do this. Not here. Not with the children in the house ...and the nanny. Don't go to jail over my stupidity. We can

work this out somehow. I'll go to the crime family and explain. I'll find a way to get our baby back. Please, Cathy. Be reasonable, honey," he begged.

Her facial expression changed from rage to something different. He couldn't quite read her, but he thought her hardness had relaxed. It seemed as though she was thinking about what he said, rolling the options over in her mind. *Could he get the baby back*? Then she changed again. Her eyes became fiery once more and the sneer returned. She pushed the knife tip up under his chin causing a drop of blood to ooze out onto the shiny blade.

In the only defensive move he could think of, Lorenzo moved his foot slowly and then stepped hard on Cathy's glass-embedded foot. It stunned her enough that she tried to shift backwards, allowing enough time for Lorenzo to grab the edge of the chef's knife and extract it from her hand. He cut his hand, but not deeply, as he grabbed for the blade.

 Cathy ran toward him as soon as she was back on her feet. She wanted to punish him for his idiocy and for making her suffer.   Both of them were inebriated to the point that wrestling for the knife was more like performing a wild dance. But Cathy was determined, and the strength she displayed was remarkable.

For a moment she had the blade pointed in the direction of Lorenzo's stomach. But, at the last second, Lorenzo managed to push Cathy's wrist backward. The knife was now pointed at her chest.

They stopped struggling for a moment and looked into each others' eyes. She smiled slightly. He looked at her questioningly. She closed her eyes and lunged forward against the sharp blade. Before she took her last breath, she mumbled, "You killed me, Lorenzo. Now you can live with that, too."

Sacrificial Sins

CHAPTER 20

Tuesday, December 6, 1994

Sitting in silence behind the steering wheel of the Cadillac made Tony realize how alone he was. He missed his big thug of a friend, even though he hated to admit it. It was unpleasant running a stake-out without Carlo to talk to or to joke with. Carlo was *there*, of course, but he was in the trunk and very dead.

Tony would need some help from the Viper's crew in disposing of Carlo's body after the Sanderson woman was handled. Until then, the two would be together a little longer, even if it was in opposite ends of the Caddy.

Tony just hoped that Carlo wouldn't start to stink up the car or leak anything out while he was in cold storage back there. *Thank God it's freezing outside* was the only positive thing Tony could think of about the entire situation.

Maybe circling around the motel parking lot would help pass some time. He felt certain the broad hadn't left the room since she went in with the fast food bags. *Yep, driving around back would be a good idea. Maybe it's time to get things rolling.*

He might as well try to meet the Viper's 48-hour deadline early. That was a much better alternative than being late or missing it altogether.

He tried not to look conspicuous as he drove the big Caddy slowly around to the back of the building. He proceeded to the far corner of the lot where not long before he had wrestled with Carlo's body near the dumpster. He didn't stop the car there, however. He kept moving;

and, as he circled the lot and drove closer to the building, he spotted the Jeep. It was still parked where the broad had left it. That meant she was still in the room. She hadn't skipped. *Good girl.*

Tony drove slowly back to the front of the motel. He parked near the walk-through corridor, a few doors down from the woman's room. He lingered in the car for an extra few minutes while he scoped the area and made a quick plan to get inside the room without alerting her. Surprise attacks always worked best for Tony. Soon, he was screwing the silencer on the barrel of his handgun, holstering the weapon, and digging in his wallet for a credit card. At the last minute before he exited the car, he reached into the glove compartment and grabbed a roll of duct tape and put it in his jacket pocket.

He walked swiftly to the door of the motel room, smiling when he surveyed the doorknob and lock more closely. *This is gonna be easy. Someone with the right skill can get through h one of these doors with a quick flick of the wrist.* His Diner's Club card was good for more than dining.

Trying to peer through the peephole from the outside didn't provide him with the good view he'd hoped. He listened closely, hearing only the sound of the television in the background. Tony tried to peep through a small open sliver between the pulled drapes, but he couldn't see anything. Taking a deep breath, he slid the credit card between the door frame and the door, maneuvering it just right to disengage the lock. He stood still, expecting some acknowledgement from inside the room. Nothing happened.

Drawing his pistol, he held it in front of him with his right hand while he slowly turned the door knob with his left. He pushed gently against the door, trying to peer inside as it moved inward. No one was in the room.

When the toilet flushed behind the closed bathroom door, Tony smiled. As quietly as possible, he eased into the room and closed the door behind him. He moved to the table in the corner, took a seat facing the bathroom, and waited.

John opened the bathroom door as he wiped his hands dry with a small dingy towel. He threw the towel backwards toward the sink and took a step forward.

"Hello, handsome," Tony said with the gun pointed squarely toward John's chest. John stopped in his tracks, mentally calculating whether he should recoil into the bathroom or try to run past the guy without getting shot. Both ideas would only get him shot, he reasoned. He didn't make a move as he stared at the intruder.

"Somebody in the bathroom with you? A pretty broad, maybe?" Tony quizzed his prey. John shook his head, afraid to open his mouth.

"I'm Tony. And you are ... ?"

"J- - Mike." John replied nervously.

"J'mike, like Jerome?" Tony chuckled.

"I was gonna say 'Just Mike' but my tongue got tied. Guns make me real nervous," John moved his eyes toward Tony's gun barrel and then back up to Tony's face.

"I guess if I was on the other end of this baby, I'd be a little nervous, too," Tony smirked. "Well, 'Just Mike,' why don't you raise both yours hands in the air and come on over here. Sit down in that empty chair and keep your hands high. I think there's some things you need to tell me about your Sanderson girlfriend." He paused. "By the way, where'd she go?"

John moved slowly in the direction of the table's remaining vacant chair, trying to think of how to escape or, at the very least, prolong what he feared was eventually coming. If he could stall long enough, maybe he could overtake the little guy before Caroline came back. He didn't want her to have to deal with this dangerous-looking hoodlum.

"My girlfriend? I don't have a girlfriend." John moved to the chair and sat down, hands still held high.

"Don't fuck with me, 'Just Mike.' I'm a little tired from chasing that bitch around town. I don't have time for twenty questions. If you don't want to play nice, I'll be forced to return the 'favor.' You don't want to see my bad side, pal."

John could tell that the man named Tony was irritated. John didn't know how long he could steer the conversation away from Caroline, but he was going to try. He started to lower his arms, but Tony stopped him.

"Ah, ah, ah. Arms stay up, Mikey." The barrel of the gun remained pointed menacingly at John. Tony reached in his pocket for the gray duct tape and placed it on the table close to John's chair. "Now with one arm still up, take the other hand and pick up the tape," Tony instructed.

John reached for the tape and held it in his left hand.

"Now I want you to do exactly as I say, 'cause I don't want to have to end our conversation just yet. Hold the roll of tape over your head and pull off about two feet," Tony commanded.

John did as he was told. When the tape was extended the appropriate length, Tony told him to rip it off and drop the roll on the floor behind his chair.

John struggled to rip the tape while holding it above his head. When the tape fell loose from the roll, John gripped the heavy roll and threw it hard toward Tony. John tried to stand and lunge at the intruder, but Tony managed to evade him. Instead, Tony came down hard with the gun and hit John on the side of the head. John fell with a thud at Tony's feet.

"Jeez, Mikey. I told you we needed to talk. Now look what you made me do." Tony shook his head, disappointed that he would have to put even more stress on his aching back to get this bastard in the right position.

* * * * * *

He could tell she was dead. It was obvious. Lorenzo stood over his wife's body staring at the big knife that she had forced into her own chest seconds before while looking into her husband's eyes.

Blood was pooling around the blade, and it would only be a matter of seconds before it started running down her side onto the tile in a crimson puddle. He knew better than to pull the knife out until he could find something to help contain the flow.

How could she do this to herself? Why didn't she listen to me? Now what am I going to do?

He looked around the kitchen quickly, spotting decorative kitchen towels folded neatly on the end of the island. There were plastic garbage bags under the sink, he remembered. That would have to do.

He held the towels close to the knife's blade as he extracted it from Cathy's lifeless body. As the knife ejected, he pushed as much of a towel's edge into the open wound as possible. He pressed the other towels on top, trying to provide additional layers of fabric as a buffer to

the flow. He grabbed a tall kitchen garbage bag and slit both sides with the bloody weapon.

When extended, the single ply garbage bag was a narrow but long plastic sheet. He did the best he could, trying to slide it under Cathy's dead weight and around her body to create a big plastic bandage. He did the same thing with another garbage bag—and another—until he thought he had contained the flow.

Lorenzo stood up and quickly surveyed the kitchen area. The bloody knife was in the stainless steel sink where he'd dropped it after he'd sliced open the garbage bags. He quickly rinsed the knife and stuck it in the top rack of the dishwasher. There were a few spots of blood on the floor, but thank goodness he had attended to the blood flow quickly. There wasn't much to clean up there.

The next important thing he needed to do was change out of his blood-smeared shirt. That had to be done before he checked on the nanny and the children. Removing and wadding the Brooks Brothers shirt in his hand, he walked bare-chested to the laundry room located adjacent to the kitchen. Occasionally, the maid would hand wash and hang up some of his pricey cotton sweater shirts on the folding drying rack. He was relieved to find a dry shirt waiting for him there. He quickly washed his hands in the big laundry sink, ran cold water over the stains on the front of his Brooks Brothers shirt, and dropped the shirt in the empty washing machine. He slid a clean light blue sweater over his head and arranged his clothing to look as presentable as possible.

Before he left the kitchen, he looked again at his wife's lifeless body. From the kitchen's entrance, she wasn't visible. She lay on the floor between the island and the back counter wall. He could leave her there for a few more minutes while he made sure the nanny had not heard their ruckus.

When he got to the bedroom wing, he peeked around the corner of the nursery to find the nanny gently rocking Ricky to sleep. Sophia was playing with her blocks on the round plush rug in the center of the room. In the background, toddler music was playing while Sophia tried to follow along in her own style of singing. The nanny, though not asleep, had her eyes closed and a smile was on her face.

Lorenzo did not interrupt or call attention to himself. Instead, he made his way down the hall to the master suite to gather Cathy's purse and coat. He found a large overnight bag, and he stuffed it with essentials (or what he thought were necessities) for a few days' stay away from the house. He took a few of Cathy's hanging clothes, intentionally creating a wide gap in the middle of her closet area between her favorite dresses. Shoes were next, and then underwear. He had already gathered a hair brush, toothbrush and some makeup from the top of her vanity.

He worked hastily, even though he was in the suite with the door closed. He didn't want to take a chance that the nanny might decide to get something from the kitchen before he could move Cathy's body.

He picked up the packed bag along with his wife's coat and purse. He moved quietly back down the hallway, glancing one last time toward the nursery. Nothing had changed. Miss Elmore still had her eyes closed peacefully rocking the baby, and Sophia was arranging her blocks in a big pile.

He made it to the kitchen without discovery, but was faced with the problem of moving Cathy's body. He set her purse on the kitchen counter, opened it, and retrieved her keys. Once he had them, he picked up the bag, coat and purse and went outside to her car.

The big Lexus SUV was parked close by on the brick driveway that branched off from the front circle drive to the side of the house. He

opened the SUV's rear door and placed Cathy's things on the back seat. Then he started the car and backed it as close to the mudroom's entrance as he could. He lifted the SUV's cargo door and hurried back inside the house.

His plan was to drag Cathy's body as fast and far as he could through the mudroom, through the side door, and out to the car. He knew he could do it. His daily workouts had certainly paid off. Lorenzo's upper body strength was phenomenal.

All it would take to get this problem behind him was a few more uninterrupted minutes and a lot more luck.

* * * * * *

Caroline had chosen a motel about fifteen miles away from the Sundown Terrace Motel. She and John had agreed that jumping around Long Island might be smarter than staying in the same vicinity. This time she headed northwest to Commack before starting to scout for new accommodations.

When she spotted the small motel situated next door to a doughnut shop, she couldn't resist. The location was off the main drag, but still easily accessible. The room set-up was similar to the room they occupied at Sundown Terrace, but it was a newer building. There was also an available room in the back that faced the rear parking lot and not the highway. She took the room, paid in cash, and used a fake name. There were no questions asked as she paid for two nights in advance.

After she unloaded her suitcase, she went into the bathroom to make a much needed pit stop. She looked at her reflection in the vanity mirror. Surprised, she thought she saw her mother's face staring back. Caroline thought she had aged twenty years during the last day and a half.

Finishing her bathroom duties, she locked the room and headed back to the VW. She noticed that John had filled the tank when he'd brought her car back from his trip on Monday. Sometimes he could be so damned thoughtful. She realized she had fallen back in love with her ex-husband in the short time they had been on the lam together.

Deep in her heart, she believed that they could still have a future together. They had learned to like each other again, perhaps. She knew the love between them had never really gone away.

Smiling at that prospect, Caroline started the car and exited the parking lot. On her way back to the Sundown Terrace, she would make one more stop for ice cream. She envisioned the two of them making passionate love in the new motel room, topping off the glorious evening devouring a sinful dessert of cherry pie a la mode. What a perfect way to celebrate their holy reunion.

* * * * * *

Lorenzo had been driving for such a long time, he kept wondering *how much further could the place be?* He didn't travel to Southampton often, and he had forgotten how far across Long Island really was. *It sure has the right name,* he thought.

Lorenzo was driving carefully and going the speed limit and no more. He couldn't afford to be stopped by a policeman for speeding or running a stop sign. With the cargo area of the Lexus holding a dead body, he had to be careful on all counts.

Eventually, he arrived at the large mansion where he parked Cathy's Lexus in the private driveway. Lorenzo headed up the steps and across the porch to face the heavy mahogany door. When he rang the bell, it was answered almost immediately by a butler in formal attire.

"I need to see Mr. DeLuca. I'm Lorenzo Giordano. It's urgent."

The butler showed Lorenzo into a large foyer and asked him to be seated while he checked on Mr. DeLuca's availability. Lorenzo was too anxious to sit and chose to stand, shifting back and forth on his feet.

When Vincenzo DeLuca entered the foyer, Lorenzo started moving quickly toward him. The Viper cautiously reached for his concealed pistol before he realized Lorenzo was not there to harm him.

"I desperately need your help, Mr. DeLuca. My cousin Tony speaks highly of you, and he's said many times you're the kind of man who can get things done. I need the kind of help I've never had to ask for before. I don't know what to do. Maybe you could give me some assistance or advice. I'm so desperate right now, sir."

Surprised, the Viper asked Lorenzo to join him in his private den so Lorenzo could explain his predicament. The Viper was already thinking of ways Lorenzo could repay whatever debt he was about to incur.

* * * * * *

John had trouble opening his eyes. He had been knocked out, but he had no sense of how long he'd been out. It must have been several minutes, though. He was now lying atop the double bed, wrists bound with duct tape around the headboard posts. His ankles were taped together, as were his knees, since there were no foot posts on the bed to accommodate a spread-eagle position.

His mouth was not taped, and he was surprised. He looked at his captor, wondering what was about to happen.

Tony said, "So 'Just Mike' has snapped out of it. Good for you, Mikey. Now we're gonna play a little game. It's called 'tell me what I want to know or start losing parts of your body.' It's fun if you're the one *asking* the questions." Tony's smile was pure evil.

"So, Mikey, where's your girlfriend?" Tony asked.

John said nothing.

"I want to show you something, Mikey." Tony reached inside his jacket and withdrew a knife. He popped it open to reveal a switchblade that looked as if it could slice a single hair into two.

"Don't you think this is the most evil looking blade you've ever seen, eh? Well, it is. I'd say it's been introduced intimately to maybe ten or twelve other people who used other words to describe it besides 'evil,' and I think you know what I mean."

John's eyes got wide with terror, wondering what torture he'd have to endure if he kept his mouth shut.

"Yeah, I think you get the picture, don't you, pal?" Tony smiled his friendliest smile. "So, Mikey, let's start over. Where's the Sanderson woman?"

John responded in a shaky voice, "She left already. She took her bags, and she's going to visit her family somewhere in the Midwest."

"Okay, but I see bags over there in the corner, Mikey. Maybe you ain't telling the truth. And if you lie to me, you'll have to suffer for it." Tony walked to the suitcase and duffle bag that Mike had planned to take to the new motel in the Jeep Cherokee.

When he unzipped the suitcase, all he saw was men's clothing and some toiletries. However, when he opened the duffle bag, he saw piles of paperwork atop a mound of sundries that looked as if they had come from an office.

He picked up a piece of paper on top, reading the bank statement for Michael Aaron Lewis.

"Okay, so you got a little cash, Mike Lewis. So, tell me, who is this Sanderson broad to you anyway?" Tony started again.

"A friend. She asked me to get her a room so she could rest for one night before she left town. Her house was vandalized, and she couldn't stay there." John said earnestly.

Tony nodded. He knew about the house being vandalized. He'd seen it himself.

"So, Mikey, what's this?" he asked as he picked up a folder of life insurance records. He thumbed through the pages but stopped when he saw a copy of Mike Lewis' beneficiary designation. "Says here you'll leave 100% of your insurance benefit to your sister, Caroline Lewis Sanderson." Tony glared at John. "So she's a friend, eh? Remember what I said about lying? I'm sorry, pal, but you lied and now you pay."

Tony moved slowly toward the bed where John lay helpless. The switchblade glinted under the overhead light as he walked with it pointed forward. When Tony got to the side of the bed, he nudged the blade's point at John's wrist. "Would you like to donate some blood to a good cause, Mikey?" Tony's eyes looked mean and hateful.

John's eyes were wide and frightened. He held Tony's gaze as long as he could, then squeezed his eyes shut and held his breath. Tony took the knife tip and sliced into John's arm, beginning at his wrist and moving another four inches up his inner forearm. Blood immediately began dripping at a steady pace from John's arm as he struggled to pull himself free from the bindings.

"Now, the other arm still looks good for the time being, but maybe you need a matched set, eh?" John shook his head and struggled.

Tony continued taunting his victim, "Of course, I can stop the bleeding and get you fixed up any time I think you're cooperating. But, truth is,

you don't seem the type. So, let's try it once more. This broad's your sister, so you know where she is or where she's going. So let's hear the story, eh?"

John was in emotional and physical pain, but he tried to hold on to his mental clarity as long as he could. He knew soon he would become lightheaded. If he was unable to talk from loss of blood, he would be left to die anyway.

"Bandage me and I'll talk to you," John said. "Stop the blood."

Tony got up to get something that he could wrap around John's arm to form a temporary tourniquet. He dug in the suitcase looking for a belt. Not finding one, he grabbed a tee shirt and ripped it, forming a long cotton strip.

John watched Tony walk to the bedside and reach up to loosely tie the cloth strip above the deep cut. He didn't tighten it immediately.

"You were saying, Mikey?" Tony stood there ready to cinch the band around John's arm.

"She's my sister. It was my house that got vandalized because some people think I'm queer. I'm not a fag. I was tired of all the bullying, and Caroline wanted to help me. She put me in this room and gave me the car to get the hell out. She didn't tell me where she was going, but I think she might be going out of state for a while. She thinks I'm going to stay with some college buddies in upstate New York, but that's not true. I can't go back there."

Tony tightened the strip on John's bleeding arm just a little, but not enough to be effective. "Okay, but I don't give a shit about any of that. Where is the fucking baby? We already took care of her husband, so she has to have the baby. Where. Is. IT?" Tony raised his voice as his rage was getting harder to control.

"Caroline never had a baby. She didn't want to have babies when she was married." John mumbled, beginning to feel faint.

"Well, her motherfucking husband stole ours. I mean the one we took... Never mind! I just have to find that baby. Now tell me where the fuck that baby is. Tell me NOW!" Tony pulled the fabric strip off John's arm to emphasize he meant business. Tony would never save him if he didn't provide the information he wanted to hear.

"Sh..she never had a baby. I don't know what you want me to say ..." John was fading fast.

"You son of a bitch, you know something but you're not telling me. Let's see if we can give you a little more encouragement, eh?" Tony sprinted around the bed to John's other wrist and made the same upward slice on it.

"I'm gonna sit right here and watch you bleed out, you motherfucker. And when you're dead, I'm gonna cut out your tongue—since you don't want to use it while you still can—and stick it as far up your ass as I can shove it. We'll let the police try to figure out what that means, right? Now TALK!" Tony shouted.

John was beginning to feel queasy and light headed. He had lost a lot of blood during the course of Tony's interrogation. Within minutes he passed out, never uttering another word to Tony.

CHAPTER 21

Tuesday, December 6, 1994

Vincenzo "the Viper" DeLuca was a very gracious host. After offering Lorenzo a stiff drink to calm his nerves, he sat back in his chair and listened intently as the good doctor made his confession from the couch.

As his guest explained the events of the evening, Vincenzo studied Lorenzo's face thoroughly. The sorrow in his eyes and the panic on his face made Lorenzo easy prey. Vincenzo almost felt sorry for him.

"Where is your wife's body now, Lorenzo?" Vincenzo asked calmly.

"The Lexus is in your driveway. I drove straight here. I didn't know where else to go or how to … ."

"I understand," the Viper said as he silently wished the body had already been dumped. But, how could he expect that kind of action from someone so clearly inexperienced in the disposal business?

"I'll take care of it. Don't worry. So explain to me how you've covered your bloody tracks, pun intended, of course." Neither Vincenzo nor Lorenzo smiled at the remark.

Lorenzo tried to remember every detail as he verbally checked off his cover-up actions. "I put the knife in the dishwasher after I washed it off. I took dish towels off the island counter, but they were red Christmas towels, and we have more like them. I can put more out before anyone

notices they're missing, I think." Lorenzo closed his eyes as he recounted his steps.

"Good. What else?" Vincenzo inquired.

Lorenzo studied hard. "I cleaned up the bloody spots on the floor, but there weren't many."

"What did you clean with?" Vincenzo asked.

"I used wet paper towels. I didn't have time to do anything else," Lorenzo looked worried.

"All right, keep going," the Viper instructed.

"I put the towels deep in the kitchen garbage can under other trash. I can take care of that when I get back home. I washed my hands in the laundry room sink, and rinsed out the shirt I was wearing that had a blood smear on the front from when Cathy slid down. It's in the washer right now. But, you can't see where the blood was," Lorenzo added.

The Viper was taking mental notes. When Lorenzo stopped talking, Vincenzo took over.

"Lorenzo, considering you had to react with split second impulses, you did well. To make sure you thoroughly complete the job, there are a few loose ends to tie up." Vincenzo squinted his eyes as he leaned his head forward and peered at his guest.

"First, take care of the obvious. Take the shirt out of the washer and bag it up. Empty your garbage where the wet paper towels were disposed. Put both bags in another trash bag and tie it up. Put it in the back of your car for tonight, and I'll send someone for it tomorrow.

"Next, look at every inch of your kitchen floor and cabinet area to scan for blood spatter. Use a flashlight and magnifying glass if you need to; but, if

any trace of blood is still there, you must find it. Make sure you use a disposable cloth that you can dab bleach on for the small spots. Just find them." As an afterthought, he remarked, "You can add the bleach rags to your trash bag."

The Viper continued. "The knife needs to be wiped with bleach, too. Scrub it with dishwashing soap afterwards, but put it back in its proper place after you finish. Nothing in the kitchen should look as if it was disturbed. It can't look like a sloppy crime scene or a tidied up one, either.

"And as you suggested, replace the towels. Can you remember all of this, Lorenzo?" Vincenzo asked.

"Yes, I think so," Lorenzo nodded.

"Good. The car and the body are matters that I can handle from here. If anyone asks, Cathy was in a drunken, grief-stricken state. She was angry at you after your quarrel about her drinking too much, and she left. You had both been drinking, so you weren't in any condition to chase after her. You don't know where she went, but you suspect she went to join her mother. She packed some things, saying nothing to you as she left the house."

"What if the nanny realizes I've been gone for a while? My car is still in the driveway at the house?" Lorenzo worried.

"If that's so, just tell her you've been jogging around outside trying to clear your head. Make up any excuse that will keep her happy. If she doubts you, say what you have to until we can convince her she was mistaken." The Viper's grin looked more evil than comforting.

"Right," Lorenzo commented, then looked helplessly at Vincenzo, "but I hope it won't come to that."

"So do I. Now, I'll have my driver take you home. Remember your instructions. Cover every detail." As a last thought, he added, "Oh, and leave the keys to your wife's car with my butler." The two men stood and made their way back into the impressive entry foyer.

As they shook hands, Lorenzo suddenly looked puzzled. "Mr. DeLuca, I know you don't work *pro bono*. What will I have to do in return for your help?" Lorenzo questioned.

"Absolutely nothing that you can't easily handle, Lorenzo. I'd like you to continue as our family's on-call emergency surgeon. You've done an excellent job with that. And my comatose wife needs a new physician. I think you may have a better bedside manner than the doctor who has been ineffectively treating her for so long."

Lorenzo considered Vincenzo's requests. "I can agree to those terms, certainly."

The Viper smiled again and added, "One other small thing, Lorenzo. I believe you and my daughter would make a beautiful couple. After a reasonable time of mourning for you both, I'll arrange a social gathering where I'm confident you two will experience love at first sight."

The Viper turned, re-entered the den, and closed the French doors behind him.

* * * * * *

While the DeLuca's driver delivered Lorenzo to his home in the Town of Oyster Bay, the Viper was on the phone arranging for the new manager of the Westside Chop Shop to make a pickup in Southampton. There would be a new Lexus SUV on the vehicle acquisition list tomorrow. By that time, Cathy Giordano would have already settled in with Diego Moretti at the group home.

* * * * * *

Caroline hummed to herself as she pulled into the Sundown Terrace motel parking lot. Her favorite singer, Elton John, was performing, "Can You Feel The Love Tonight," on the VW's radio. She thought about what those words meant. She hoped John would understand the lyrics' special meaning before the night was over.

Parking next to the Jeep Cherokee, she grabbed her purse and the brown paper bag that contained a pint of French vanilla ice cream. They still had plastic eating utensils left over from their fried chicken feast. She hoped John hadn't gotten the munchies while he waited for her to return. If he had, the ice cream would still be a good late night treat even without the pies.

She entered the motel's open external corridor and made the left turn toward their highway-facing room. For a second, Caroline felt something similar to what she experienced when she stood in the driveway at John's house—an indescribable internal danger alert. She stopped in her tracks before she got to the door of the room. Setting the bag of ice cream on the sidewalk, she opened her shoulder bag purse and touched the gun. *Am I being paranoid?*

She looked around the parking lot, seeing nothing unusual. There was a huge gas guzzler Cadillac parked nearby that she hadn't noticed before, but nothing else seemed different. She removed the handgun from her purse and moved forward with caution.

When she got to the door, she stood silently without moving again. She had the room key in her left hand, and tried to insert it as quietly as possible. She wanted the gun in her right hand in case she had to fire it. *You're being silly, Caroline. All this talk about needing a gun for protection is getting to you.*

Hearing the sound of the television from inside, she clicked the lock open and gently pushed the door forward a few inches. She caught a glimpse of John sitting up against the headboard of the bed, arms outstretched, with both hands bound to the headboard posts. She tried not to gasp out loud.

There was so much blood! He couldn't be alive with all that blood loss! His head was slumped to the side, and he appeared either deeply unconscious or dead.

She stepped in quickly, holding the gun in front of her at shoulder level just like John had instructed. A strange man was across the room, back turned to the door with his head down. He was digging through papers in Mike's duffle bag. With the television going, he hadn't heard Caroline enter.

"Hands up, you bastard!" Caroline yelled.

Taking Tony by surprise, Caroline moved to the side of the table where Tony had recklessly laid his gun with the silencer. She picked it up, shifting Mike's Smith & Wesson to her left hand. She aimed the loaded pistol with the silencer toward Tony.

Still in a crouched position, Tony turned and slowly started to stand.

"Hands in the air. Clasp them on top of your head NOW!" Caroline demanded.

"We finally meet, eh? Caroline, this could have all been avoided if you'd just given back the baby. Just tell me where you've stashed him and this can all go away. You can still get help for your brother. Mike said you … ."

Caroline interrupted. "Don't say another word until I say you can. Now clasp your hands on top of your head or I'll shoot you dead. NOW!" Caroline yelled. Tony followed her instructions.

"I need to call an ambulance, so don't you move, motherfucker!" she screamed.

"Don't do that just yet, lady. Please. Let's just talk for a minute. We can figure this out," Tony pleaded and started to take a step forward.

"I said stop right there," Caroline exclaimed as she aimed the gun. He stopped.

Caroline went to John's side, laying Mike's gun on the empty chair next to the bed. Feeling for a pulse on his neck, she found a weak one. She turned to Tony.

"Get your ass in that other chair. Slowly." Caroline was more calm than she thought she would be in such an encounter.

Tony took small steps and found the chair. He sat, leaving his hands clasped on his head as Caroline had told him.

"Now what, lady? You can't tie me up unless you use both hands. You know I'll get the best of you when you don't have that gun to hide behind." Tony chuckled as if he was making fun of her inexperience. That pissed her off.

"You know, you're right. I'll just have to use the gun first, I guess. Thank you for pointing out the obvious," she smirked as she aimed the gun toward Tony's genitals.

"No, lady, please. Please don't do that," the scared man pleaded. "I'll tie myself up or something. I won't move. Don't point that thing at me. It's dangerous!" Tony realized he should never have opened his mouth to chide her.

"No, you were right the first time," Caroline answered. She suddenly shot Tony in the upper thigh, dangerously close to his crotch.

217

Tony screamed in pain as he felt the burn. He looked at her with both fear and anger in his eyes, determined to think of a way to stop her from completing her mission of revenge.

"Lady, please. I beg you. I'm only the messenger for another guy. I have to get that baby back or I'm a dead man," he begged.

"Why don't you fill me in on what this chase has been about. Maybe I'll show you some mercy if I understand more. But you better talk fast, because now you have lots of blood flowing, too." Caroline sat down in the other chair and stared at her captive. "Let's hear it before I get trigger-happy again. I kind of like the way this gun feels in my hand."

"Okay. Okay. The Viper told me to kidnap one of the twins and take it to his daughter ..."

"Hold on. Pretend I don't know these people. Give me names. Hurry up." Caroline glanced at John, hoping that there'd be time to save him. She was racing against the clock now.

"Okay. The Viper is Vincenzo DeLuca. The twins belong to Lorenzo Giordano...he's my cousin, so I knew they were expecting twins. Lorenzo's a doctor. He owed the Viper a big gambling debt but didn't have enough money to cover it. Lorenzo agreed to give him one of the babies to clear his debt because the Viper wasn't ever going to have grandchildren. DeLuca's son-in-law is—was— sterile. The stolen baby was taken to his daughter, but they had a wreck." Tony was talking so fast he thought he was going to pass out. He paused to catch his breath and tighten the grip on his bleeding leg.

"Finish! Hurry up!" Caroline demanded, losing her patience and fearing she was also losing John.

"Your husband took the baby from the wrecked car, but he lost his work badge on the seat. That's how we fingered him. The Viper is trying to get

the baby back. That's it. End of story. Please get me some help." Tony pleaded, almost to the point of tears.

"Thank you for explaining everything." Caroline smiled sweetly as she lifted Tony's pistol and pointed it straight at his face. She stood up and approached him as he sat there helpless. He had pressed both his hands over the bullet wound in his thigh, unsuccessfully trying to slow the rapid blood loss. She kept her eyes locked on his, then abruptly dropped her aim. "Why don't you use that tape over there to bind your ankles together, asshole," she suggested with authority. Tony nodded.

Having no idea how crazy the woman could be, Tony's eyes located the duct tape on the floor near his chair where he'd tossed it after binding John to the bedposts. "Slowly, asshole. No sudden moves," Caroline warned.

Tony painfully leaned to reach for the tape, and Caroline watched his every movement. He managed to snare the roll with the tips of his fingers without raising his wounded leg from the chair. With bloody hands, he ripped off a long section of tape and looked at Caroline for approval.

"Now toss the tape roll on the bed... slowly," Caroline directed. Again, a scared Tony did as he was told. Caroline stepped to Tony's right side, indicating with a wave of the gun for Tony to proceed with binding his feet. As Tony leaned forward, she mercilessly shot him in the right temple. His dead eyes were still open when she turned quickly toward John.

She tried to rouse John, but by then he was gone. He had lost too much blood, and there was no pulse. She sat back down in the empty chair and sobbed for love found and love lost.

CHAPTER 22

Tuesday, December 6, 1994

Through the dark tinted glass of the limousine, Lorenzo wondered if the man in the moon was sneering at him. Was that a look of disappointment or disgust he imagined in the moon man's face?

Are you staring at me, old man? Are you trying to read my mind? Well, good luck because there's nothing left to read. Pretty sure I've lost it.

Lorenzo closed his eyes and listened to the winter sound of traffic on the salted highway pavement. Even at the late hour, vehicles were being reckless on the icy pavement; drivers obviously still in a hurry to get somewhere—anywhere—besides out in the weather on the lonely highways. Horns blasted, brakes squealed, and slush splashed on windows creating a harsh background symphony that Lorenzo tried hard to tune out.

Feeling remorse, shame, and various degrees of angst, Lorenzo tried to imagine what the scene would be inside his home when he arrived after his lengthy evening absence. Would Miss Elmore be waiting at the door? Not likely. Would she question him when he finally ran into her—either in the kitchen (*oh, please, not while I'm removing the evidence*), or would she meet him at the door when he entered the house? Lorenzo tried to imagine how to respond to each hypothetical scenario, but his mind was too active and the "what if's" were too varied. He was making himself more frustrated by the second. He tried to turn off his thoughts, but then he would hear Cathy's last words haunting him.

Finally, the limo stopped fifty feet from the gated entrance to Lorenzo's circular driveway. The driver said nothing as the engine idled quietly. Taking his cue, Lorenzo got out of the car and watched the limo make a U-turn so as not to pass by the front of the Giordano house. Cautiously, Lorenzo waited five minutes before using his private entry code to enter through the driveway's tall wrought iron gate.

The lights in the house were on brightly in the kitchen/sunroom wing of the house. The other wing—the bedroom chambers— was dark with only faint light showing through the nursery's plantation blinds. If he was quiet, he could get his clean-up tasks handled before Miss Elmore would suspect he had re-entered the house.

* * * * *

Caroline stared at the gun in her hand. A day ago she would have been afraid to get near a pistol, much less fire one. Now she felt as though the pistol was suddenly her trusted friend. It came through for her when she needed it, and John had taught her how to defend herself... sort of.

John. Poor John. Sweet John.

Everything happens for a reason, Caroline.

"Oh does it, now? I suppose there was a reason that I am involuntarily involved in this **MESS**, right? I was doing everything I could to stay away from John. I wasn't involved with him at all, except for Lucas's custody. Then **HE** calls **ME** and pulls me into something that causes me to lose my brother, my dog, and **HIM**. On top of that, I've got blood on my hands, too. I've killed a man," Caroline whimpered to herself in between sobbing outbursts. "I'm going to Hell." She abruptly stood up and paced the area between the foot of the bed and the television set.

Caroline sat down again on the end of the bed with her back to John's lifeless body. To her left, Tony sat slumped over in his chair next to the

round table where she shared her last meal with John. Tony's body looked as though it would topple over onto the floor with no more than a hint of a breeze.

What now, Caroline? What are you going to do now?

 "I'm going to do what I always do. I'm going to weigh all my options and make my best judgment call. I have to push my emotions aside and try to be smart." Again she struggled to organize her thoughts into viable options. Finally, it came to her.

 She looked at John's body. As if she could convince him to respond to her, she audibly addressed her ex-husband's corpse.

"Mike's already been identified with your DNA, so that means *John Sanderson* is officially dead in the morgue. That also means the real John Sanderson will now have to become the dead Mike Lewis. You'll eventually wind up in the same morgue, I suppose. The duffle bag has all your important files and paperwork, your passport, your medical records, and other stuff in there that will identify you as Mike. Mike's car is parked out back. Those are Mike's clothes in the suitcase. All I have to do is take your identification—*John Sanderson's* identification and wallet—so there's no initial confusion about who you are supposed to be."

Getting no response from John, she turned back around and stared at the television screen.

Something was missing. Trying to find the loophole in her state of mind would have been as easy as spotting a white pearl in a pile of marbles. But try, she must. When it occurred to her what she must do, she sat on the floor and cried. *I can't do that. I just can't.*

* * * * *

Lorenzo was in luck. He entered the mudroom side entrance, hearing no stirrings in the house. Apparently, everyone was sound asleep, and he would have free reign of the house until he had tackled every item on the Viper's cleanup list.

Walking slowly and peeping around doorways to check for room occupants, he made it undetected to the kitchen, proceeding straight to the garbage bag supply under the sink. He pulled out two bags and went to work.

He took the blood-smeared shirt from the washer, wrapped it in a bag and then stuffed it in the other empty bag. He was "double-bagging" it, just like the Viper instructed.

Next he took the almost full bag from the kitchen trash can and replaced it with a clean one. He cinched up the full bag filled with the kitchen garbage and bloody paper towels, then poked it in the big bag with the shirt.

He brought two fresh red Christmas hand towels from the laundry room, folded and ready to be put away. Except Lorenzo didn't put them away; he put them on the top of the kitchen island where the others had been before he ruined them with Cathy's blood.

The kitchen knife was still in the top rack of the dishwasher where he had left it. He found some bleach under the sink and thoroughly doused it. He then hand washed it, dried it, and positioned it back to its place in the knife block.

All that was left was the blood spatter inspection. He was so exhausted he considered waiting until the morning to look for it. He knew better than to delay; but, he was more than ready to go to bed to sleep off the nightmare evening.

Avoiding the last task, Lorenzo took the garbage bag of evidence to his car and stowed it in the rear cargo area. He wasn't sure when the Viper's guys would get it, but he was positive the bag would not be in his car by the time he left his office the following afternoon.

Glancing at the floor and cabinets, Lorenzo saw nothing that looked like blood spatter. The cleaning exercise was easy to procrastinate. He was mentally drained, and it was past time for another drink before bed.

He turned off the light in the kitchen and followed the long hallway toward the bedroom wing. As he tiptoed past the nursery door, he spotted Miss Elmore asleep on the cot. If she had ventured into the kitchen during his absence, she would probably have stayed up to ask him about anything strange she might have noticed. Either that, or the police would have been waiting for him when he came in the house. Since neither had happened, Lorenzo sighed with relief.

Sophia was sound asleep, as well. A fairy princess nightlight stood guard from the far corner of the toddler's pink room. No harm would come to Sophia as long as the princess's magic wand glowed faintly but fiercely over the child's presence.

From the looks of things, Lorenzo could go to bed without a confrontation or explanation of his whereabouts tonight. That pleased him greatly.

He closed the door to the master suite, turned around, and leaned against it for a moment. Closing his eyes, he could still hear Cathy say, "You killed me, Lorenzo. Now you can live with that, too." He quickly moved to the portable bar, poured a stiff drink, and gulped down his generous nightcap of strong scotch.

Before he allowed himself to rest, he made himself walk into the master bathroom. There, he looked through pill bottles previously stored in Cathy's medicine cabinet for the family's potential needs. He found a xanax bottle, shook out a single pill, and swallowed it dry.

Praying for a dreamless and restful sleep, Lorenzo laid across the king-sized bed in his clothes, arms crossed over his eyes, and felt his anguish escape through his tearful eyes. Eventually he drifted off to sleep, dreaming of ghosts, gore, and the horrors of prison.

* * *   * * *

Caroline carefully pointed Tony's "silenced" gun toward the body. She knew her aim wouldn't miss her target because she was standing so close to the victim.

Struggling to make herself go through with her plan, she tried to remember the reasons it had to be done. First, there can be no question as to identity. Second, with the passport in the duffle bag, the face can't be identifiable. Lastly, since there is already DNA matching John Sanderson at the morgue which was taken there to identify Mike Lewis's body (what a mess), there must be no way anyone would ever suspect this body belonged to the real John Sanderson. No third-party DNA profiling.

Caroline peeked out the draperies and looked around outside as best as she could. Seeing no movement, she approached the television and turned it up louder. She tried to find a western with some gun fighting action to drown out the noise.

Satisfied with the program she chose, she turned back to John. She tried to hide her body behind a towel and part of the sheet, fearing more blood would splatter back toward her. She had never done anything like this before, and had no idea what would happen when she pulled the trigger.

Her goal was to blow his face off. She didn't know how far back from his nose she should be to accomplish that, but she had to try—even if it took multiple attempts. At least John and Mike had similar physical features ... brown hair, brown eyes, same complexion, almost the same height,

similar build, and they were born the same year. In this case, the coincidence was working in her favor.

After two shots – timing them carefully with the television's gun slingers' battles—she managed to obliterate John's face to the point that facial recognition would be impossible. She cried, and talked to John as if he was there in the room and heard everything she was saying.

"Forgive me, baby. I didn't want to do this to you, but I think it's the only way right now. I know you tried to save me. I wish I had saved you. Forgive me."

Caroline took a washcloth from the bathroom and dipped it in the pool of blood clotting on the bed under John's wrists. Even though the sticky blood was hard to work with, she was still able to write "FAG" on the wall above John's sagging, mutilated head.

Next she went to Tony's slumped body. She put his gun in his right hand. With a single bullet still in the chamber, she held his arm up and helped the dead man fire a bullet straight at John's body. Gunshot residue was now on Tony's hand. The knife he had sliced John's arms with was lying on the floor with Tony's fingerprints on it.

After she wiped down the room of her own fingerprints, she took John's wallet out of his back pocket. Now the only evidence of his identity would be that of Mike Lewis, stowed so conveniently in the duffle bag in the corner.

She looked out the draperies once more and then opened the door. She didn't look back. She couldn't. That faceless corpse wasn't John anymore.

Face forward and chin held high, she would leave the premises in the VW Beetle and head to the new motel room across town.

The duo was now a solo act.

CHAPTER 23

Wednesday, December 7, 1994

That loud-ass mockingbird—chirping his head off outside the window—is making me want to kill something.

Vincenzo DeLuca opened his eyes and stared at the intricate Italian ceiling medallion from which the bedroom's overhead chandelier hung. The craftsmanship and detail were extraordinary; even in the shadowy light of early morning, its artistic beauty was breathtaking.

Lucinda had chosen it while visiting Milan, most likely asking her lover's opinion before making her final selection and shipping it home. That had been four, possibly five years before. So much had changed in such a short span of time.

He smiled to himself before pushing back the heavy brocade comforter and sitting straight up in bed. When the mockingbird started chirping again, Lorenzo cupped his hands over his ears and yelled, "Shut up" toward the window.

Hearing his employer's outburst, the butler gently rapped on the bedroom door. He entered, balancing a silver tray that held the morning newspaper and a glass of freshly blended kale juice. Wordlessly, the butler set the tray in its usual bedside spot, slightly bowed his head to excuse himself, and was gone before Vincenzo had time to glance at the morning headlines.

* * * * * *

"Is Mrs. Giordano here, sir?" Miss Elmore asked as she entered the kitchen to prepare a freshly made bottle of formula for Ricky.

Perched on a bar stool at the kitchen island, Lorenzo looked up sheepishly as she approached.

Don't volunteer too much information. It can be used against you.

"No, she and her car are both gone. There are things missing from her closet, so I assume she left on a mental R&R." Lorenzo sipped his coffee and munched on a toasted bagel, avoiding eye contact.

Miss Elmore looked puzzled, but continued her quest to find a sterile baby bottle for Ricky's breakfast formula. She opened the dishwasher door to see if any clean bottles were there.

Lorenzo peripherally watched her movements, knowing that the dishwasher hadn't been run since the prior morning. Paranoia was difficult to fend off now.

Simply saying "hmm" to herself, she closed the dishwasher door and turned to search the wall cabinet across from it. "Here we go," she mumbled as she found a row of cleaned, sterile bottles.

Lorenzo continued to eat his bagel, although by now he had lost his appetite. He wished he had cleaned the kitchen more thoroughly the night before. In broad daylight, every speck of dust showed on the cabinet tops. The floor was just as bad. He made no comments to her as she continued with her task.

She warmed the bottle in an electric appliance made specifically for that purpose. As she tested the formula's temperature on her wrist, she looked again at Lorenzo.

"I wish your wife could conquer her drinking before it becomes a problem for the family. Uh, I hope I'm not speaking out of turn, doctor." She lowered her eyes and started to leave the room, but Lorenzo unexpectedly responded.

"We had a little tiff about that subject last night. I hope we didn't disturb you." His facial expression was meant to look like embarrassment. "I asked her to stop trying to drown her sorrows in alcohol. She's not made for drinking, you know. It affects her badly. She was very angry with me. She threw a wine glass—several, in fact—so there may be some shards of glass still around. Be careful. I tried to clean some of it up, but when she stepped on a piece and cut her foot, she got even angrier." He paused, his face a forlorn mask. After a deep breath, he added, "I suspect she'll be back by the end of the day when she realizes how she's acted." He gave Miss Elmore his most pathetic smile.

Her sympathetic look made Lorenzo believe his brief summary had covered any loose ends that might have been left hanging in her curious mind.

She tried to comfort him saying, "I know she's having a hard time. Any mother would that has suffered what she has. But don't you worry, doctor. She'll come to her senses and get her strength back. Your family will be back together soon, I just know it." She gave him another encouraging look, took the warm bottle of formula, and headed to the nursery to the low cries of the hungry baby.

As soon as Miss Elmore was out of sight, Lorenzo got off the bar stool and dumped his half-eaten bagel in the empty garbage can. He rinsed his plate under the faucet, and carefully loaded the dish into the dishwasher. He couldn't help but notice a faded red dot in the bottom of the dishwasher. It could have been a diluted drop from a rinsed glass that had once been filled with tomato juice or wine. More likely, it was a drop

of water that drained from a rinsed knife that had previously been covered in blood.

His heartbeat quickened as he filled the dishwasher's dispenser with soap. He started the machine and leaned against it until he felt the gushing of water saturating the dirty dishes inside. Only then did he move.

His next quest was to check every single inch of the kitchen's surface and floor. If the nanny came back in, he'd just tell her he was looking for stray pieces of Cathy's smashed wine glasses. He realized how stupid he had been to circumvent the Viper's expert advice.

It's the little things that trip you up.

* * * * *

After the commode flushed, she refused to move. She sat there on the porcelain throne for several minutes trying to wake up before she finally mustered the effort to stand.

The mirror was not her friend. She tried not to look at it while she washed her hands. Concentrating on the sink's water temperature was better than following the path of etched lines and dark blotches on her face.

What the hell is that? She peered closely at her fingernails on her left hand—then her right. *Rust? How ..?"*

For a second she had forgotten. For a brief second her world was automatically functioning like an engine with pistons pumping, oil flowing, and gasoline running. *Not oil flowing, though...**blood** flowing?*

The room was painted red now. Red everywhere. Even the whites of her eyes were red.

Her mind replayed the events of the prior evening in fast forward mode. She saw it all as if she were a bystander watching through the window. She saw herself raise the pistol and fire point blank at John's face. John's beautiful face. She saw herself walk out the door as if she had just left a successful business meeting. She saw everything.

Her eyes were now clenched shut. Caroline reached above her ears and grabbed her hair with both fists. She suddenly thought she was going to be sick.

She slowly slumped down to the floor and felt the coolness of the linoleum align with her cheek. Holding back the animalistic, guttural scream she wanted to emit, she cried and cried until she could cry no more.

* * * * * *

"Papa, why don't you come into the city and treat me to a spree at Tiffany's?" Juliana cooed into the telephone. Despite the early hour, she sounded fresh and alert. She knew the best time to catch her father in a good mood was after he had his morning kale cocktail and was reading the paper.

"I have business today, Juliana. Why don't you drop by the house this evening for dinner? I'm sure your Mother would like for you to visit." Vincenzo said absently, picking up the newspaper from the silver tray. Realizing what he said, he waved the newspaper in front of his face as he gestured. "But make sure it's after 6 o'clock." Instead of opening the paper, he laid it down again next to the tray.

"Papa, she doesn't know if I'm there or not." She paused for a moment to let the guilt sink into her father before she added, "I miss her, don't you?" Juliana was using her best little girl voice. She knew that always got her father's attention.

Vincenzo pinched the bridge of his nose. "Of course I miss her, Juliana. Your Mother was ... is a wonderful woman. Now go treat yourself to a spa day or hairdressing appointment or whatever it is that makes you feel good. I'll see you tonight at 6 o'clock." He hung up the phone without saying goodbye.

Realizing that his morning bodily functions were more urgent than reading the news from the comfort of his bed, Vincenzo swiveled to drop his bare feet to the floor. Still clutching the newspaper, he padded across the room to the bathroom. He entered the huge master bath suite and closed the door behind him. As he sat on the toilet, he unfolded the local Long Island newspaper. When he read the front page, his eyes widened unnaturally and the vein on his temple began to pulsate to a quickened heartbeat.

"**Damn imbeciles**!" he screamed as he wadded up the paper and threw it across the room at an imaginary target.

The butler stood outside the bathroom door waiting for his inevitable summon.

* * * * *

She had nothing to eat for breakfast. It didn't matter about that because she didn't think she could eat anything, anyway. But coffee. That was different. She remembered a small coffee maker taking up too much room on the small vanity. She didn't remember, however, if there was any coffee to go with it.

Searching around the small brown cafeteria-like tray that held the machine and its accoutrements, she found one green plastic bag of decaffeinated coffee grounds. The red caffeinated bag was conspicuously missing. Damn housekeeping! And the serving size was a small four-cup pot. Roughly translated, that was about one and a half cups of liquid.

234

She started the brew and once again found herself perched on the end of a motel room bed staring at a television set. She saw her reflection, pitiful as it was, through the blank screen. To rid herself of the image, she switched on the set.

It seemed all she did lately was cry and watch the news. She had hardly ever watched television before the past weekend. Mike always liked TV, and his favorite shows were *ER* and *Chicago Hope.* She didn't have any favorites, but occasionally she would watch *Murphy Brown* because she likes the painter guy. He was funny. She smiled remembering better times.

When the screen came to life, the volume was muted. As soon as she realized what was being reported, she quickly turned on the sound.

"... happened sometime last evening here at the Sundown Terrace Motel. The crime scene was discovered shortly after 9:30 p.m. when another motel guest reported a television playing too loudly from a nearby room. The motel manager told us that he tried several times to get a response from the motel guest before he entered the room with his pass key. Once the manager entered, he found the grisly crime scene and immediately called the police.

"We know very little about what went down here, with the exception of information provided to us by the motel's manager. What we know, but has not yet been officially confirmed, is that two male bodies were found inside, victims of an apparent murder/suicide. Another body has been found in the trunk of this Cadillac which you can see behind me here in the parking lot. Police have that immediate area and the vehicle cordoned off with crime scene tape, awaiting arrival of a special crime scene unit to tow the car to a location for further analysis.

"Police believe they know the identities of two of the victims, but that information will not be officially released until notification of next of kin.

The third victim remains unidentified as the investigation now intensifies. Police have assured us that there will be an official statement released within the next few hours. We will keep you updated as the news comes in. For now, back to you at the station, Ed."

Caroline sat stunned as she realized how close she had come to discovery. Perhaps if she'd turned down the volume of the television, the bodies would still be undisturbed. She wondered if a few hours lead time would matter in the long run. It was just a matter of time before she was called in for questioning; after all, she was the "sister" of the victim they would soon identify. She prayed that she left behind nothing that would indicate she had ever been in that room.

Maybe it was time to consult with a lawyer.

CHAPTER 24

Wednesday, December 7, 1994

The pin-striped suit was still a classic. Besides, it was Armani. Armani never goes out of style.

A dashing figure at age 50, Perry Walker Norton stood in front of his full-length tri-fold mirror in his closet's dressing area and critiqued his image. Approving of what he saw, he returned to his dresser and splashed on a hint of cologne—not too much, of course—just enough to carry an expensive but musky scent in his wake.

His attaché case was on his desk downstairs. Since his wife left him several years before, he had converted her reading room to his personal office sanctuary. He called it his "study" but it looked more like an expansive library now, filled with leather-bound first editions showcased in the hand-crafted bookcases that lined the room's walls. He had purchased a desk once owned by Dwight Eisenhower (or so he was told), that fit perfectly in the center of the magnificent room. The solid cherry plant column standing next to the French doors was originally a part of the Kennedy White House décor, chosen by Mrs. Kennedy for use in one of the public hallways. Surrounded by walls of knowledge and the furniture of the nation's past aristocracy, Perry Norton often found himself imagining he was in the center of the intellectual universe when he entered this room.

Today's office agenda was light, his calendar filled with a few afternoon appointments; but the morning was reserved for the Syosset office's

weekly staff meeting and routine conference calls with the Manhattan office executives. Being the nephew of a founding partner (Wallace Edward Walker, his mother's brother and Perry's middle name-sake) had its perks, however. If he felt like handing off his morning's responsibilities to a junior partner, his dearly departed uncle Wally wouldn't mind. In fact, allowing others to handle such menial tasks had become the recent habit of Perry Norton as he gained seniority among the partners and staff.

Perry had meandered downstairs and was reaching for his attaché case when the doorbell unexpectedly rang. Glancing at his Rolex, he wondered who the surprise visitor could be so early in the morning. Cautiously, he stepped to the front window of his study, peeked through the curtains, and attempted to get a look at his early visitor. When he realized who was on his doorstep, he hurried to the door.

"Caroline! What on earth?" her boss asked her with astonishment.

At that moment, Caroline burst into tears and meekly said, "I think I may need a lawyer."

Perry reached for her arm and pulled her inside the house. The young woman looked as if she'd been run through a wringer. She seemed to have aged since he'd seen her last, and his heart went out to her.

He motioned her into his study and urged her to sit in one of the broad-backed leather chairs that faced his desk. While she sat stiffly trying to control her emotions, he called his Syosset law office. "I may not be in today. Cancel my appointments," he barked into the telephone.

Perry Walker Norton never wasted his perks at Walker, Harrington, Norton and Stone, Attorneys at Law. Plus, he could never ignore a damsel in distress.

For once, Caroline was thankful that this handsome but arrogant man was giving her his full attention. She secretly hoped she could afford his services.

* * * * * *

Once the Viper had calmed down and finished his toilet duties, he exited the bathroom to find the butler standing at attention nearby.

"Prepare the sauna. Then set up a meeting with Dr. Lorenzo Giordano for 11 o'clock this morning. Tell the good doctor that he's to make a house call to check out his new patient, my wife. Also, inform the kitchen staff to prepare dinner for two this evening. Juliana will be dining with me at 6:00 p.m. sharp."

"Very good, sir." The butler again excused himself with a bow of the head.

When the butler was out of earshot, Vincenzo picked up the bedroom telephone and dialed the Westside Chop Shop. When Gino answered, the Viper was clearly pleased that the new manager had reported to the shop early.

"I see you are taking your new responsibilities seriously, Gino. That's good. That's very good. Now, I need to check on your progress with the Lexus. Will it be ready to ship out by late afternoon?" the Viper asked.

"Yes, boss. After the other delivery was made, the boys brought the car in, and it's almost ready now. The boys worked on it all night. You want me to handle the transport personally?" Gino inquired.

"No, you got enough on your plate. I'll get someone else to handle that one. But I do need you to reach out to your contact at the police department and see what's happening with Tony's Cadillac. We need some intel on the bodies they found—Tony and Carlo. We've got to be

sure the cops don't link this fiasco to the shop or to me personally. Think you can handle that, Gino?" the Viper asked even though it wasn't really a question.

"I'll handle it, boss. I'll get the latest and make sure everything is nice and clean. No ties to the shop or the family. I got a couple of solid police contacts on our payroll that can give us inside information with no questions asked."

Vincenzo smiled. "Good, Gino. Call me with any news. And try to keep all this low-key today. If the other boys haven't heard about Tony and Carlo, they can stay in the dark a little longer. I don't want anybody getting antsy." He put the phone in its cradle giving his orders to Gino no further thought.

With the critical business behind him now, Vincenzo could look forward to his favorite activity of the day: his steam bath in the scorching sauna.

* * * * *

The coffee cup was real china. The ornate pattern of the 24K gold rimmed cup was mesmerizing to her. *This cup is much too perfect to hold regular coffee,* Caroline thought as she puckered her lips and gingerly sipped the steaming dark roast brew. She was nervous, and when she set the cup in its companion saucer, it rattled.

"I'm sorry, Perry. I don't even know where to start. So much has happened. There's so much to tell you. My brother and my ex-husband are dead now, and I may be next." Caroline started to visibly shake, her nerves getting the best of her as she dropped her guard.

"Why don't you just start at the beginning, Caroline. But first, there's a dollar there on the side of the desk. Why don't you hand it to me," he urged.

She picked up the dollar bill and immediately handed it to Perry.

"Great. Now, I am not only your employer, but I am also your attorney. What we discuss will be subject to attorney-client privilege. You understand how that works, I'm sure."

Caroline nodded, and shakily lifted her cup to take another soothing sip of her caffeinated coffee.

"So, now. Tell me everything that's happened since you were last at work. Don't leave out anything, and provide as much detail as you can. I am not going to record our conversation, but I will take notes if that is agreeable to you?"

Again, Caroline nodded her consent.

"Fine. So go back to the beginning and bring me up to speed." Perry Norton smiled at her as if he was taking on the most important client in the world. Perhaps he was.

* * * * * *

The medical staff at Lorenzo's office still walked on eggshells around him even on his second full day back at work. There was no denying that Lorenzo's mind wasn't focused entirely on medicine. Most of the staff wondered why he was at work at all. When tragedy strikes a family, isn't it normal to drop daily routines and band together in a familial network for strength and mental stability? Apparently, that particular idea never crossed Lorenzo Giordano's mind.

Lorenzo was relieved when he received the summons to the DeLuca home for an 11:00 a.m. appointment with his new patient, Lucinda DeLuca. He could use the time away from the office staff's whispers. As much as he didn't want to be at home, the office was even more uncomfortable for him. He found that paranoia grew in the most unexpected places, and the

office was providing a robust harvest of the stuff. He was grateful for a legitimate reason to escape Manhattan.

* * * * * *

At precisely 11:00 a.m., Dr. Lorenzo Giordano rang the doorbell at Vincenzo DeLuca's palatial estate in Southampton. Within seconds, the same stoic man who ushered him in the night before answered the door. A few feet behind the butler, Vincenzo DeLuca was approaching the front door to personally greet his guest.

"Doctor, how good of you to come on such short notice. I realize you're a very busy man, but I believe it is important to establish our routines, don't you? Wednesday mornings are usually quiet here in the household, and I am delighted that your schedule will allow you to be here each week at the same time for Lucinda's examinations. I'm sure you will be able to set this time aside on your schedule for our weekly visits." The Viper never gave Lorenzo an opportunity to protest or negotiate the arrangement.

"Now, let's introduce you to your new patient." The Viper turned toward his right and began to walk in the direction of Lucinda's medical room, formerly the one guest bedroom that was smaller than the others.

As the two men entered the room, the duty nurse rose from her chair and disappeared out the door. Vincenzo closed the door behind her for privacy.

"Lorenzo, my wife has lingered too long. We see no signs of improvement, only comatose stability without progress. I know my wife wouldn't want to live this way. We need to talk about alternatives... alternatives of mercy." The Viper touched his wife's hand with no response from her.

Lorenzo hadn't been in the Viper's house more than ten minutes, and he was already being coerced into a mercy killing.

"Mr. DeLuca, before we can jump to such a conclusion on what is best for your wife, perhaps we should run some tests to find out if there is any brain activity, whether or not she has been on the correct medication regime, and several other things we need to know for certain before making such an irreversible decision. That particular action can never be overturned. Once done, it's done. I know you understand this." Lorenzo had to do his due diligence before agreeing to something so radical for a patient he hardly knew.

"Lorenzo, she has been this way for years now. She doesn't get better. She doesn't improve. I want her to suffer no more, if you understand what I mean." Vincenzo was beginning to look irritated.

Lorenzo came up with an idea. "Why don't we do this: I can arrange to have medical equipment delivered next Monday, and we'll run the tests we're capable of from right here. After that, if we decide additional tests at the hospital are required for a final diagnosis, we'll figure out how to make that happen. But we'll expedite the process and have it all completed by next Thursday—just seven more days . By then, we should know if there is any reason we shouldn't pull the plug, and we can make a final determination then. You've waited this long. One more week won't make much difference, I wouldn't think." Lorenzo stared the Viper straight in the eyes.

"All right. You've got your week. No delays." Vincenzo looked first at his wife and then back at Lorenzo. "Go ahead and do her routine exam today, and have the butler find me when you're finished." Vincenzo left the room, closing the door behind him once again.

Lorenzo was now alone with Lucinda DeLuca. He began his examination by lifting her eyelids and looking at her eyes. He listened to her heart and chest with his stethoscope. He examined her ears, and checked her chart to determine her regime of medications. He sat on the side of the bed and held her right hand, attempting to feel her pulse. As he started to

pull back his hand, he thought for a moment she had tried to touch his little finger. He looked at her expressionless face and allowed her fingers to brush his for a moment. He watched her eyes move under the lids. He gently laid her hand on the bed and disengaged his hand from hers. He moved to her other arm and did the same thing. She again tried to brush his hand, but she never opened her eyes. He tried applying limited resistance to her hand, but she met the resistance with a faint pressure in her fingers. Lorenzo smiled. These were good signs.

He spoke to her as if he knew she could hear him. "Mrs. DeLuca, I am Dr. Lorenzo Giordano. I am here to help you, not to kill you." He paused before saying anything more just in case he could get a deliberate response from her. She did nothing. "Mrs. DeLuca, if you can hear me, please try to open your eyes. Your husband has left the room. Only you and I are involved in this examination." He waited for a few moments and finally saw a slight flutter on her right eyelid. She was trying.

"Please try again to open your eyes. Give it all you've got so I can see your lovely eyes! Come on!" She tried again, this time resulting in a slight fluttering of both eyes, but she wasn't able to open her lids.

"This is remarkable, Mrs. DeLuca. You're doing great. I don't want you to tire yourself out, but I want you to keep trying to open your eyes as often as you can. You may be able to do it easily by the time I check on you again. That would be wonderful. Now, let's try one more thing. Can you lift any one finger on your right hand for me?" He stopped and stared at her right hand lying at her side on top of the plush blanket. He kept staring until he thought he imagined a movement. He leaned in closer and saw it! Her pointer finger did move!

"Mrs. DeLuca, you have just begun the first day of your new life. I will be ordering physical therapy, several new tests, and whatever we can think of to get you back to a functioning woman. I think your husband will be amazed at the progress we can make." It was then that Lorenzo saw the

solitary tear roll down the side of Lucinda DeLuca's face. He wondered if the tear was from fear or joy.

* * * * * *

Five long hours after Caroline rang Perry Norton's doorbell, she sat back in her chair and declared, "And then I came here." She glanced around the unfamiliar home, noticing how empty and hollow it seemed. She had imagined it to be more lively, somehow. Having only been there to deliver work papers to her boss, she had never once stepped inside the threshold before that morning. She let her mind come back into focus as she studied Perry's somber demeanor.

Perry had gone through four full yellow legal pads taking notes on everything Caroline had told him. He seemed particularly interested in the original kidnapping of the Giordano baby. He asked questions about the DeLuca family and their businesses that she might know about. Caroline explained that she had never heard of them until their thug spilled the information at the first threat of being killed.

"Have you ever dealt with the DeLucas, Perry? Are they tough clients to take on?" Caroline innocently asked.

Perry's face remained stern. "The DeLucas are a crime family. They are in all sorts of illegal activities including sex trafficking, gambling, drugs, chop shops, murder for hire, you name it. They have been around a long time, and it doesn't look like they're losing any of their strong holds. They have enough money to tie people up in court for years. They have enough power to sway judges and jurors or witnesses, if the truth be told. They have policemen in their pockets and politicians who ask the Viper for instructions on how to run the government. The DeLuca empire is built to last. If seriously challenged, that family would go down fighting; but, I don't think we'll ever see them going down at all. They're too well-connected. And, if they ever find your weakness, they use it ruthlessly against you. Eventually you'll fall to your knees and beg them to do things their way because it would be less painful."

"Sounds a lot like you've been there, done that." Caroline observed.

Perry sighed, withholding his answer. "What do you say we go in the kitchen and rustle up some lunch, okay? After that, let's talk strategy about what should happen next. I think I have an idea that might keep you out of trouble with the cops if you go along with it. Sound like a plan?"

Caroline nodded. She had not had breakfast and her stomach was growling loudly, which was probably why Perry suggested they stop to eat. She was seeing him through different eyes today. He was a man who cared about people. She would have never believed that before this morning.

CHAPTER 25

Wednesday, December 7, 1994

It was time to make a decision. If she went back to Nashville without so much as a word to her daughter, Genevieve Parker would never forgive herself. On the other hand, it was Cathy who demanded she get out of her house. Genevieve had only been trying to help, in her own way.

*And look how much **I've** suffered in just the short time I was there. A broken nose! My dignity ripped from me while I sat mortified in that chair—on the precipice of death—losing bladder control and fearing for my very life! And then to lose my grandson to some indignant kidnapper who couldn't have cared less for the sanctity of family! The nerve! My daughter is the one who owes **me** an apology for my pain and suffering!*

Looking around the plush Waldorf suite, Genevieve felt like an outcast. Of course, Lorenzo had never liked her. She never liked him, either. He was too handsome. Even though Cathy was beautiful in her own way, Lorenzo was the eye candy of the marriage. Her daughter should never have to take a back seat to any man, or so Genevieve thought. "Humpf," she said to no one.

Still, she had to make plans soon. She didn't want to spend extravagant dollars on the posh hotel any longer than she had to. Truthfully, she only checked in to the Waldorf to give Cathy time to settle down and subsequently beg her mother's forgiveness for her outrageous, drunken behavior.

I suppose I would go back to Cathy's if she asked me politely. My Nashville friends have cut our phone conversations short recently, and I haven't felt their support nearly so much as right after the tragedy happened.

She stared across the room at the fresh floral arrangement sitting atop an entrance table topped with marble. Wrestling with solitude was not Genevieve's strong suit.

When the idea struck her, she smiled broadly. Picking up the phone, she hastily dialed the Giordano house.

"Giordano residence," the pleasant voice answered after the second ring.

"Hello, this is Mrs. Giordano's mother, Mrs. Parker. I left the house rather unexpectedly and must have left some diamond earrings behind somewhere. Would you please ask Mrs. Giordano if she has seen them?" Genevieve asked in her most pleasant social voice.

"Mrs. Giordano is not here, ma'am. But I'd be happy to leave a note for her or Mr. Giordano to return your call," the pleasant voice responded.

"Do you know where I might contact her? I'm trying to make plans to leave the city and would rather not do that until I'm certain the earrings are located. They're very valuable—and sentimental to me," Genevieve prodded.

"No ma'am. Mrs. Giordano hasn't been here since last evening. I'm not sure where she went or when she will return. I'd be happy to leave a mess..."

"Never mind. I'll talk with Lorenzo later," Genevieve said, impatiently hanging up without waiting for a response from the other end of the phone.

Unless Cathy would have tried to come to me, I can't imagine where she might have gone. She didn't call me, though.

Puzzled, Genevieve placed a call to The Plaza Hotel, but discovered that Cathy had not checked in overnight. Next she tried the Ritz-Carlton, but her daughter wasn't there either.

She called the Waldorf's front desk to see if she had missed a message, but the desk manager assured Genevieve that no one had called for her, either in person or via telephone. As an afterthought, she inquired if perhaps Cathy had checked in the Waldorf overnight securing her own room. No luck.

Clearly confused, Genevieve made her "last resort" phone call. The receptionist at Lorenzo's medical practice was kind but generally evasive when Genevieve questioned her as to Lorenzo's whereabouts. "He had an appointment out of the office this morning, and I am not certain about his afternoon schedule. May I take a message?" the lady asked pleasantly.

"Yes, tell him to call Genevieve immediately at the Waldorf. If he doesn't call me as soon as he gets this message, let him know I will be standing in his office later this afternoon for a face-to-face ***discussion*** about my daughter. And if he tries to evade or avoid me, I'll call the police." Genevieve angrily slammed down the phone.

She reached for a piece of fruit from the nearby freshly-filled bowl. The orange she held was soon lobbing toward the fresh flowers in the crystal vase across the room. As the vase shattered into hundreds of pieces, Genevieve realized her life was about to succumb to a similar fate.

* * * * * *

The attractive brunette was typing frantically on a keyboard, watching her keystrokes turn into little gray word ghosts on the green computer screen. When she looked up from the screen, the massive alien-looking computer blocked her full view of the police officers who just entered the front door

of the office. She had to lean toward her right to make full eye contact with the policemen as they approached her desk.

"Good afternoon. Welcome to Walker, Harrington, Norton and Stone. How may I help you gentlemen?" she asked through a fake smile. She always felt nervous about interruptions when she worked on the new computer. Giving visitors her immediate attention usually meant she couldn't graciously take the few extra seconds to save a copy of her documents.

"We're here to speak to Caroline Sanderson. I believe she works here?" the older of the two officers responded after a brief introduction and show of badges.

"I'm afraid she's not here today. Could someone else help you?" she asked, still smiling but growing impatient to get back to her computer keyboard.

"I don't know. Is her boss or supervisor available? Perhaps he can help us?" the officer wondered.

"That would be Perry Norton, one of our partners. I'm afraid he is out of the office today. May I ask what this is concerning, officers?" The receptionist was more curious than nervous.

"Unless you can give us phone numbers for Miss Sanderson or Mr. Norton, we'll just come back later," the younger policeman said sternly without breaking eye contact with the brunette.

"If you'll wait over there, I'll try to reach Mr. Norton," she quickly offered.

"Thank you, ma'am," the older officer said and smiled easily.

When the receptionist swiveled around in her chair to pick up the phone, she inadvertently kicked the under-desk extension cord causing her green computer screen with gray letters to turn dark and blank. Sighing with

frustration, the brunette receptionist dialed Perry Norton's home phone number.

* * * * * *

"What if no one believes it? There's over twenty years of age difference between us. I'm not sure even *I* believe it. You could be my father." Caroline reached for her glass of iced tea.

It was past noon. The morning's unabridged dialogue—confessions, analyses, ideas, and hypotheticals—was swirling around in her head much like a swarm of pesky hornets. Swat one down, here comes another...the last more dangerous than the first.

By now they had gotten comfortable in each other's presence. Caroline was sitting curled up in an overstuffed side chair while her boss watched her from his seat on the large leather sofa. Before they settled into the den adjacent to the kitchen, Perry had changed into a cobalt-colored running suit (designer, of course). Caroline had kicked off her shoes, but still wore the sweatshirt and sweatpants she had been wearing the day before.

"It's not rocket science, Caroline. You have no idea how many men my age date women your age, and even younger. It's an unspoken sign of virility for the men, and often a step up the social ladder for the younger women. It's done all the time. Granted, it's not often that an eventual marriage comes into those pictures; but, it's a common practice. Believe me." Perry was giving his best closing argument.

"I don't know. The people in the office won't believe it, for sure. Most of them know you don't like me." Caroline quickly looked at Perry with an embarrassed smile. "Well, I mean, you were quick to point out my *occasional* tardiness and ..."

"Precisely, Caroline." He smiled. "That makes it even more convincing. We will let everyone think they've stumbled on to the big secret that we've tried so diligently to hide. They will all assume our mutual dislike was really our way of covering up our secret love life." Perry chuckled. "Actually, I think this could be amusing as well as beneficial for us both."

"How can it be beneficial to you, Perry? I'm the one in trouble. I'd say you're putting yourself at great risk. Are you willing to assume that risk just to help me out? Your lowly employee?"

Perry smiled again, this time more broadly. "Caroline, my life has been so boring for so long, I welcome the chance to help out an innocent person. Besides, I despise what has happened to so many innocent people in this situation. It's a matter of justice in this case. The most egregious crime I could ever imagine is if *you* were punished for your part in this whole scheme. You are not a hardened criminal, Caroline. You've lost two very precious people in a matter of days, and you have had to defend your own life. Someone has to step up and set things right before more innocent people are lost." His closing argument was now concluded. He crossed his arms across his chest and locked eyes with her.

"Well...okay, I guess. But what do I do now? Go get another motel room? John's house was destroyed and Mike's house is a vandalized mess. What do you advise, now that you're my attorney?" Caroline was clueless about what came next.

"Are your bags in your car outside?" Perry asked.

"Yeah, I felt very uncomfortable alone in the second motel, so I brought my things with me just in case my plans changed."

Perry grinned. "All right, pull your car up around back, then bring your bags inside. There are several guest rooms here from which you can choose. Pick any one you like. I suppose now is as good a time as any to get this fabricated love life started." Perry stood and held out his hand to

help Caroline from the chair. When she stood, she awkwardly embraced him quickly before going to retrieve her car. Before she had a chance to release him, Perry's house phone rang.

* * * * * *

"She said **what**?" Lorenzo was fuming. When the office receptionist handed him the pink message slip, he glanced at it assuming it was just another pharmaceutical sales rep trying to set up a sales pitch. When he realized it was Genevieve who had called, he was livid. The receptionist didn't help when she audibly quoted verbatim everything that his mother-in-law had said during the short conversation.

Lorenzo crumpled up the pink message slip and threw it at the receptionist. "Hold all my calls for the afternoon. And no interruptions until I say so!" he yelled as he rushed through the private doors of the "Employees Only" entrance.

When he reached the sanctuary that was now his office, he followed his standard procedure to reduce anxiety. He poured himself two fingers of scotch and swirled it around his glass. He wasn't sure who to call first: the Viper or Genevieve. He chose to call the greater of the two evils. He called his mother-in-law.

CHAPTER 26

Wednesday, December 7, 1994

The VW Beetle motor revved as she put it in first gear. Gently releasing the clutch, she eased forward carefully to miss the concrete curb as she pulled from the street into Perry Norton's bricked driveway. *The VW will look out of place back here among Perry's super cars*, she thought as she rounded the back of the house. She parked next to a pristine Bentley that looked as though it had just rolled off the showroom floor. *Hope you don't get piston envy sitting next to this heavyweight, little Beetle.*

Caroline chuckled to herself about the mental joke she had made and wondered if she would ever be close enough to Perry to repeat it. Probably not any time soon.

When the phone rang a few minutes before, Perry scurried off to answer it in his study. Caroline left the house to move her car to give him some privacy. However, when she returned to the den, Perry was pacing in the kitchen.

"Everything okay, Perry?" she asked casually.

"Probably. That was the office. There are two policemen waiting there who had initially asked to see you. Since you were out of the office, they asked to speak to me. I told the receptionist to let them know they can stop by here and talk to both of us at 4 o'clock." He paused, expecting an outburst of anger or surprise from Caroline.

She wore her most serious face, then grinned and winked. "Well, then *darling,* we'd better throw some of my stuff around the house to make it

255

Sacrificial Sins

look like a love nest should, don't you think?" she sniggered, trying to make light of the serious situation.

"Yes, *dear,* we should snap to it." Perry's eyes twinkled like a young boy about to get into some seriously punishable mischief.

* * * * * *

"Genevieve, our marriage is not your business. What Cathy and I argue about is no concern of yours," Lorenzo all but screamed into the phone.

"When it affects my daughter and her mental stability, it most certainly is my business! Now, tell me where I can find her!" Genevieve raised her voice to make the point.

"If I knew that, I'd go get her myself. I told you. I will tell you once *again*. Listen to me, Genevieve. She was drinking so much she was slurring her words. She was angry because the police haven't found the baby and haven't shared any leads... if there are any to share."

Genevieve thought about her own heated conversation with Cathy. She had seen the anger in her face and heard it in her daughter's voice. "Well, of course she was angry!" Genevieve could vouch for that, having been told to leave her daughter's home.

Trying to remain calm, Lorenzo lowered his voice another notch and continued. "Cathy would drink a glass of wine, then throw the empty glass at the fireplace and smash it. She did that four or five times. Cathy tried standing and couldn't, she was so drunk. She told me I didn't care about her or anyone. She said nobody cared about her..."

"That's not true!" Genevieve interrupted forcefully.

Lorenzo responded, "Genevieve, she was taking her anger out on me, but I was—am suffering, too. I didn't know how to calm her down in her drunken state. I just knew I had to get out of the room and away from the

argument and her craziness. I told her we'd talk when she sobered up and could control herself. I jogged and walked around outside the house and up and down the street for a while. When I got back, she was gone. No note, no goodbye, nothing. That's all I know." Lorenzo pinched the bridge of his nose as if to ward off a threatening headache.

Genevieve mumbled something unintelligible to herself. Finally, she spoke up and said, "Why didn't you go after her, Lorenzo? She was in no condition to drive if what you say is true."

"Neither was I, Genevieve. I believe Cathy and I both have relied on the bottle a little too heavily while trying to cope with this nightmare. Besides, I had no reason to think she would try to leave. By the time I got back to the house, I had no way to tell which direction she went or how long ago she had left. I assumed she'd ride around the block or go look at the ocean and meditate. I never dreamed she would stay away so long. I'm just as surprised as you are." Lorenzo was trying to mentally keep track of each detail he was providing. He expected he would have to repeat the whole story at least once more.

Genevieve stayed quiet on the other end of the line. Dead silence lingered until finally the frightened mother spoke again. "I am going to call our family friend from the FBI and ask him what we should do. You know as children, he and Cathy's father spent summer camps together and were college roommates at Columbia. We attended his wife's funeral several years ago when she died in an awful car crash. He and I still exchange Christmas cards, so he will certainly be responsive to my needs."

"Genevieve, why don't you wait a little while longer, and let's see if Cathy returns on her own volition. She may be sleeping it off at the Ritz for all we know."

"We **do** know that she **isn't**. I've personally contacted every 5-star hotel in the area, and she isn't checked-in at any of them. I even contacted the hospitals. Now you can either join me like a concerned husband, or ignore what might be your wife's last plea for help. But I intend to take action and get her home. Can I count on you, Lorenzo?" she demanded through gritted teeth.

"Genevieve…please listen. We've been fortunate to keep a lot of what's happened off the front pages of the newspapers. The law enforcement agencies have helped make that happen. They convinced the newspapers that too much coverage could incite the kidnappers to do something dreadful to the baby—maybe even come after Ricky, too. Not only that, sometimes sensitive investigative info is inadvertently printed, revealing too much detail and causing false leads. This situation is so delicate. Please give Cathy a chance to come back on her own before you make it public knowledge by involving the FBI or the police."

Genevieve was silent only for a second. "I'll consider it. But if she's not home by 8:00 a.m. tomorrow morning, I'm calling our FBI friend. If you want to be a part of that call, I expect to hear from you by then."

Lorenzo heard the line go dead. He poured more scotch and scribbled on a notepad, trying to relieve some of his incensed tension. His pen scratched repeatedly on the pad: "BITCH BITCH BITCH BITCH BITCH."

* * * * * *

The grandfather clock in the downstairs hallway chimed three loud times. Caroline was in the master bathroom stowing various feminine supplies in the medicine cabinet, makeup brushes and her toothbrush on top of the sink, and body splash, shampoo and conditioners around the tub. She laid a pink razor on the soap dish just for a speck of feminine color.

She had taken her suitcase to a guest room down the hall, but Perry had convinced her that it would be more appropriate to empty her belongings

in the master bedroom, at least for the time being. They were hastily staging the house for the policemen's visit. They weren't going to be arguing over splitting closet space anytime soon.

"We've got to make it look natural. Where would you put your things if you lived here with me? You'd be trying to overtake my side of the sink, I would suppose. That's what my wife used to do; so, make yourself at home," he laughed.

When Caroline opened the massive walk in closet, she was surprised to see several rows of women's clothing still hanging there. She turned to look at Perry questioningly.

"Those were my wife's things. Believe me, she's not going around naked. This was the stuff she wanted to take to the Salvation Army, but she didn't want to deal with it herself. I just haven't gotten around to handling it. Please...consider it yours. If you can wear any of it, be my guest. Otherwise, it will make the policeman believe you have a full wardrobe here. Consider it a stage prop, if you will."

Caroline smiled again, thinking that once the house was staged (and it was very close), they needed to work on their collaborating story. Appearance wasn't as much of a priority as having a cohesive account of the past events.

Perry had already told her to follow his lead. He believed he knew enough detail from the last few days' events that he could handle any question thrown at him. He wasn't sure Caroline had the grit to follow through if her emotions were on edge. But, as a new team, they both had the belief and the confidence to meet the police interviewers head-on. How much worse could things get, anyway? Things could only get better—she hoped.

* * *   * * *

Lorenzo made the next phone call, more as a courtesy than as a call for help. The Viper was brought to the phone by the dutiful butler and pleasantly greeted his caller.

"Dr. Giordano, to what do I owe the pleasure of a second chat in one day?" Vincenzo teased.

"I just wanted to update you on another family matter that may have some impact on my schedule over the next few weeks. I know how important family is to you, sir." Lorenzo paused.

"Yes, I understand. How can I help you, doctor?" The Viper understood that Lorenzo was attempting to provide serious information to him through an encrypted conversation.

"Well, last evening my wife left unexpectedly after we had an argument. You know how things like that can happen. But this time, she didn't come back. My wife's mother is very worried, especially after the kidnapping just a few days ago. Mrs. Parker thinks Cathy is in a precarious state of mind, all things considered. She believes that she should call her FBI friend for advice and assistance if Cathy isn't home by 8 o'clock tomorrow morning. If all this happens, especially after the loss we had over the weekend, I'm afraid I might be tied up in police stations giving interviews, or perhaps the newspapers will be brought in. I'm sure you know better than I that this could be negatively impactful to my schedule." Lorenzo waited for the Viper's comment.

"Of course, doctor. Your family comes first. We can always reschedule our appointments to work around your busy schedule. Don't worry about a thing. We can handle things from our side. Now, you make sure your mother-in-law gets a good night's rest at … where? Your house?" the Viper asked.

"No, she's at the Waldorf," Lorenzo volunteered.

"A fine establishment. I know several members of the staff there, and they are all well trained to take care of the customer. She couldn't have chosen a better hotel in the city. As I was saying, please make sure your mother-in-law rests well tonight, and remind her that her son-in-law knows how to get things done. She'll be reunited with her daughter in no time, I'm sure."

"Thank you for understanding, Mr. DeLuca. I certainly do appreciate your patience."

When Vincenzo hung up the phone, he smiled evilly.

Another opportunity to grab Lorenzo Giordano by the balls and move him right where I want him. He's making this much too easy.

CHAPTER 27

Wednesday, December 7, 1994

The grandfather clock's four loud chimes coincided with the first buzz of the doorbell. Perry Norton was ready, still clad in his designer running suit that so clearly matched his deep-set blue eyes. He took a deep breath, smiled broadly, and opened the door.

Two uniformed police patrolmen stood before him. With badges raised, the officers introduced themselves and waited for an invitation to enter the home.

"I am Officer Hopkins," the older man said, "and this is Officer Davis." The second policeman nodded his head in recognition of the introduction.

"Gentlemen, please come in. We'll be in the den this afternoon. It's more comfortable there. Please... follow me." Perry didn't hesitate to get the men inside the house and seated. "May I offer you something to drink? We have Perrier or something more substantial, if you prefer?"

"No thank you, sir. I understand Miss Sanderson is to meet us here?" Officer Hopkins was getting right to business.

"Oh, she's just finishing up her shower upstairs. You know how women are...always running behind when it comes to primping," Perry chuckled.

The two officers glanced at each other as if they had just found a hair in their casserole. Neither officer made a comment as Perry interjected,

"Let me see how much longer she will be. Please excuse me for a moment."

He left the room and entered the foyer. With a devious smirk on his face he shouted to Caroline from the bottom of the stairs. "Caroline, darling. Our guests are here."

"Be right there, Perry," she answered as if she had been putting on the last touches of her make-up. She sounded thoroughly relaxed in Perry's home.

Perry waited at the foot of the stairs for Caroline's entrance. As she slowly proceeded down the steps, he couldn't help but notice how different she looked. She was wearing one of his ex-wife's "discarded" lounging pajama outfits, complete with silk pants and flowing robe. It was sheer elegance. Wearing it, Caroline gave the impression she was the mistress of the house. Perry's eyes danced with excitement.

"Darling, you look fabulous! But then, you always do! Come, let me introduce you to the policemen. Perhaps they have some information to share about the dreadful fire at your ex-husband's home." That was Caroline's cue to resume her somber state of mind. *Let Perry handle the exuberance of new love. I still need to be the sad ex-wife. I don't know anything else ... remember your role.*

"Thank you, Perry. I hope you're right," she said as she took his arm. He escorted her to the entrance to the den where both officers turned and stood.

"Officer Hopkins, Officer Davis. Let me introduce you to Miss Caroline Sanderson." Both officers said, "Ma'am" simultaneously, and watched her closely as she put on her bravest smile. Caroline merely nodded politely in their direction.

Perry ushered Caroline to the same chair she had been occupying all morning. She gracefully sat, crossing her ankles, awaiting Perry to sit on the ottoman. He took her hand, and she held onto it firmly.

Officer Hopkins coughed, took out a notepad, and began. "Ma'am, I'm here to inform you of some very bad news."

Caroline squeezed Perry's hand, and the two made eye contact with each other. Both showed a sense of fear and anticipation of Officer Hopkins's next words.

"We believe your brother, Mike Lewis, was one of the victims of a murder/suicide last evening. We aren't sure of his identity; however, various documents and clothing found at the scene point directly to the victim being your brother. We would like for you to identify the body at the morgue, if you would, please." Both policemen stared expectantly at Caroline.

"I...I... I thought you might know something about my ex-husband...what do you mean... Mike?" she stammered. Tears were pooling in her wide eyes. Perry gently pulled her as close to him as he could from his position on the ottoman. She collapsed toward him, taking deep breaths, allowing him to drape his arm around her shaking shoulders.

"Ma'am, that case is still open, I believe. After your visit to the coroner's office yesterday, the police chief accepted the recommendation from Dr. Carey on positive identification. As far as we know, your ex-husband's suicide note is being reviewed and considered as a material part of the investigation. I don't know if the case is considered closed yet, but I'm sure the Chief will be in touch on that."

Bingo! Perry's mind was mentally updating his checklist of hurdles to overcome.

"But, Mike? That's impossible! Mike would never hurt anyone!" Caroline wept genuine tears of grief.

"Ma'am, I know this is a lot to take in, especially after what happened to your ex-husband. But we need to talk about your brother...his friends... the last time you spoke to him. We need to find out whatever we can leading up to his death." Officer Hopkins was all business.

"No. You said yourself I needed to identify him. Until I see for myself, I refuse to believe my brother is dead. He was too gentle to be part of a murder or suicide. That is not the Mike I know. He absolutely is NOT dead." Caroline began to sob hysterically, and Perry kissed her on the forehead in an obvious show of affection.

"It's all right, dear. You're right. You don't have to believe it for now. Go back upstairs and rest. I'll work with these gentlemen until you feel better. Go now," Perry cooed, and released the broken Caroline from his embrace. He handed her a tissue from the side table, which she accepted to wipe the tears streaking down her face.

She stood shakily, and Perry asked in an endearing voice, "Can you make it up the stairs, darling? Here, let me help you." He started to rise from the ottoman, but Caroline stopped him.

"No, I'll be fine. You help these officers. Make them understand that Mike is not dead." Caroline's grim expression was noted by the officers who tried not to make eye contact with the pitiful woman.

Caroline made her way out of the room without theatrics. Every horrid detail of the past few days was rushing through her mental theater and projecting in bloody color before her mind's eye. She gasped as she realized how much raw emotion she had pushed into the depths of her mind's darkness in order to get through the recent hours. She truly believed she was on the cusp of a nervous breakdown. Sobbing loudly by

now, Caroline made her way slowly up the steps and into the master suite. The door closed loudly behind her as she screamed in anguish.

Taking matters into his own hands, Perry shook his head somberly and addressed the officers. "As you can see, Miss Sanderson wasn't expecting this news. It saddens me, of course, because I know how close the two were. Such a tragedy." Perry looked questioningly at Officer Hopkins. "Are you absolutely certain the victim you are trying to identify is Caroline's brother? Couldn't you identify him yourself? After all, I would expect there must have been some kind of picture identification somewhere at the scene? If it's avoidable, it would be best if Miss Sanderson could avoid another upsetting encounter like that at the morgue."

Officer Hopkins looked helplessly at his partner before answering Perry's question. "I'm afraid the body couldn't be identified by facial recognition. Mike Lewis' passport was among the personal documents we found at the scene. However, …"

"Are you saying his body was also burned beyond recognition? What kinds of monsters are loose in this town? What Caroline went through yesterday was a futile attempt to identify nothing but burned flesh and ash…a horrid experience no one should have to endure needlessly. I must insist that she forego this identification farce if it's the same situation." Perry sat down on the ottoman and sternly stared at the officers.

"Sir, the situation is nothing like that. I assure you, it's different." Officer Hopkins was attempting to explain without providing investigative details.

"So how is it different if a legal document's photograph is not useful? I don't understand." Perry crossed his legs and leaned back against the arm of the chair. "Please, explain."

Officer Davis reluctantly responded to Perry. "Mr. Norton, the victim suffered close-range gunshot wounds to the face. His other physical

characteristics...hair color and facial shape, for example... bear a strong resemblance to the photograph; but without facial detail, DNA, comparative fingerprints, or positive identification by next of kin, we're just making an assumption. We believe Miss Sanderson would be able to tell us what we need before extensive testing is done during the autopsy process. We're trying to get a jump on the case, as I'm sure you can understand."

Perry's mind was working fast. There was a glitch on the horizon that neither he nor Caroline had anticipated. He sat silently for a few seconds, then nodded his head.

"Yes, gentlemen, I do understand. I will see what I can do to get Miss Sanderson to the morgue as soon as she's mentally stable enough to look at another dead body. It's possible I may coerce her into getting this ghastly task over with first thing in the morning."

Perry looked concerned and then asked another leading question. "When is the autopsy scheduled for the victim? I would prefer Caroline view the least amount of disfigurement possible. It will be bad enough to have to look into the decimated face of her brother. I don't want to add additional trauma to her fragile state by having her view more mutilation than what she must." Perry's worried expression showed his concern for Caroline's welfare.

"Sometime tomorrow, I believe. If I were you, I'd get to the morgue when the doors open if you want to get this done before the coroner starts the exam procedure. I can't blame you for wanting to get it over with. If I were Miss Sanderson—considering what the last couple of days have been like for her—it would be hard to get me off the couch to face this kind of reality. I'm really sorry about all this," Officer Hopkins offered sympathetically as he stood and held out his hand to Perry.

"Thank you, Officer Hopkins. And, thank you, too, Officer Davis." Perry stood up and shook hands with both the men.

"We'll be in touch, sir," Officer Davis responded.

Perry smiled and ushered them hastily to the front door. As soon as the policemen were out of his yard and approaching their vehicle, Perry ran up the stairs.

"Caroline! Caroline! We've got a big problem!"

* * * * * *

Housekeeping had already cleaned up the shattered vase and removed the scattered cut flowers. Already in its place sat another fresh arrangement, this time in what appeared to be a much less expensive vase of cut glass.

It had been hours ago that she spoke with her shifty son-in-law. He had asked for a little time to locate Cathy, which was probably reasonable. Still, she had been pacing the Waldorf suite like a cat in heat that couldn't get through a glass door. She was restless and nervous, and more than a little paranoid. She had no one to discuss her feelings with, and that was important to her.

I want to see my grandchildren. Maybe that would take the edge off. Besides, I can talk to that nice lady that's taking care of the children. She's a good listener and a pleasant enough person. And if Cathy comes home while I'm there, I'll know it without having to wait for a call.

Genevieve picked up the phone and ordered a limousine. If she left within half an hour, she could get there before Lorenzo came home.

She decided against checking out of the hotel just in case Cathy might try to get in touch with her there.

Lorenzo probably wouldn't want me staying at the house after the conversation we had today, anyway.

She grabbed her Chanel purse, threw on her sable wrap, and left the room to meet the limousine waiting downstairs.

* * * * *

The butler brought the telephone to the Viper and announced a waiting call. "Sir, it's Mr. Gino from the Westside office."

Vincenzo took the phone without comment and held it to his ear. He remained silent until the butler closed the door behind him.

"Boss, you there?" he could hear Gino asking from the other end of the line.

"You have information for me, Gino?" Vincenzo asked impatiently.

"The car you were asking about has been towed to a secure lot close by. So far, nobody's touched it. I've been told it will still be there a few days before they can get around to it. As for the people you were asking about, they're already ID'd." Gino waited for the Viper's reaction.

"Have they tracked down their families?" the boss wanted to know.

"No, those tracks are covered." Gino proudly reported.

"Fine work. There's one more thing that will require some coordination on your part. Reach out to your friend at the Waldorf and ask him to be on alert for a job tonight. Details will be passed to him some time later in the evening. Would you do that, Gino?" the Viper asked.

"Sure, boss. Consider it done. And, by the way...we have that Lexus SUV all finished. It's a real beauty. The boys did a great job on it. It looks just

like it came from the factory, but now it's solid black. I'd like to have a car like that myself, someday," Gino hinted.

"In time, Gino, in time. This car can't stay too close to home. But, there'll be others. You've earned a bonus for taking over so efficiently in the middle of our crunch time. We'll find you something special."

The Viper disconnected the call, leaving Gino on the other end of the line holding the receiver to his ear with a wide grin on his face. "Hot Damn," he said to himself.

CHAPTER 28

Wednesday, December 7, 1994

Juliana DeLuca Moretti pulled the red Maserati into the driveway of the Southampton mansion and parked it near her father's garage. Since she was expected for dinner, she entered the home through the veranda entrance, just as she did when she was a teenager residing there.

The butler met her as she crossed the jungle-like sunroom that provided a panoramic view of the Olympic-sized swimming pool.

"Mrs. Moretti, would you like a cocktail before dinner?" he asked politely.

"No, thank you. I'm going to peek in on my mother for a minute, and later I'll have something with Papa in the den," she replied as she headed for the guest room-medical suite. She left the butler behind her as she rounded the corner to the hallway toward the room of her unconscious mother.

Opening the door cautiously so as not to alarm the nurse, Juliana tiptoed to her mother's bedside. On cue, the nurse picked up the book she had been reading to take a quick break to allow the mother and daughter a private moment.

The room was sparse with only medical equipment surrounding her mother's bed. All of the beautiful furniture and paintings that the room once held were now somewhere catching dust in the attic storage area.

A plain bedside table—not unlike the kind used in public hospital rooms—was positioned next to her mother's bed. On top of the cheap veneer surface was a plastic water pitcher, plastic cups, and a box of tissue. It broke her heart to see her mother lying in such a cold, sterile room when Lucinda DeLuca had once been a successful interior designer. Her mother had lavishly furnished the entire Southampton mansion before her accident. Now she lay in a room stripped of all its former beauty and vitality, much like Lucinda herself.

"Mama, I wish you could hear me. I would love to tell you about my life." She patted her mother's still hand and held it gently.

"Diego left me for another woman, Mama. My guess is she's a tramp. I never thought he would desert me, Mama. I really thought we could be happy together, but I guess it wasn't meant to be. Now I'm all alone, and I have to start my life over. I wish you were here to advise me. I miss you so much." Juliana smiled weakly at her unmoving mother. For a moment, she thought she saw a tear forming in the corner of her mother's eye, but she dismissed the idea. If it was moisture, it was probably from her dry eyes. She patted her mother's hand again and released it. It was time to go get Papa for dinner.

* * * * * *

"Such beautiful children," Genevieve said under her breath.

"Ma'am?" Miss Elmore asked while she folded the children's clean laundry at the changing table.

"I was just saying the children are beautiful. Sophia has the most gorgeous dimples, doesn't she? She reminds me so much of Cathy when she was that age. And of course, Ricky is as handsome as they come." Genevieve was in the rocking chair usually occupied by the nanny. The tiny baby Ricky was sound asleep in her arms. Sophia was planted on the rug in the center of the room occupying herself with a train set.

"Yes, ma'am, they are beautiful children. They come from beautiful parents, so I guess it was inevitable." Miss Elmore turned to smile at Genevieve.

"It's too bad their father is such a bastard," Genevieve declared without looking away from Ricky's face.

"Ma'am?" the nanny asked and stopped folding clothes. She turned to face the grandmother.

Genevieve sighed before she started her story. "Well, you know he's driven my daughter to drink. He mistreats her, you know…leaves her here all alone without anyone to talk to. No wonder she's depressed! I tell you, she hasn't been herself in a *long* time. I think he completely ignored her while she was pregnant, and now he's deserted her in the face of heartbreak and tragedy. No, he's not a kind person. There's not a kind bone in his selfish body. I wouldn't doubt if he hasn't been seeing another woman the way he leaves Cathy all alone to handle everything here," she declared.

"I thought it was the Missus who left the doctor?" Miss Elmore curiously inquired.

"I deeply doubt that. Why would my daughter leave the security of her own home to run off to some place unknown? Why would she abandon her two remaining children? I don't think that sounds like my daughter at all. I suspect there's foul play somewhere. I just don't know how to find out what's really happening. Granted, Cathy has been irritable and easily provoked lately, but who wouldn't be in her situation? I think Lorenzo knows a lot more than he's telling. The police should be talking to *him*…about *several* things, if you want my opinion."

The sound of Lorenzo's car pulling in the driveway caused Genevieve to hush and halt the rocking chair in mid-rock. The nanny turned back to the clean laundry and resumed folding a baby blanket.

Genevieve rose from her chair, laid the sleeping baby in his crib, and declared, "I'm off to spar with the devil himself."

* * * * *

The twilight sky had a hint of rose coloring streaked across the graying blue background. The sun had almost set completely, but it was still light enough outside to see the early evening joggers trotting through the upscale neighborhood.

Caroline left the window and returned to the leather chair in Perry's study. She sat across from him as he leaned back in his executive chair behind his Eisenhower desk. With his hands clasped behind his head, he gazed upward as if the solutions he sought were written above him on the ten-foot ceiling.

"How do we get out of this one, Perry?" Caroline picked at her fingernails, still not over the emotional roller coaster ride from which she had just been ejected.

"I don't know, Caroline. This is all so complicated." He studied the ceiling some more before he sat straight up in the oversized chair and turned his head to face her. "There are two bodies at the morgue: John and Mike. Except Mike is John and John is Mike, as far as anyone else knows. I don't believe I've ever had to work through an issue so royally fucked-up."

Caroline looked up quickly, taken by surprise by Perry's outburst of profanity. She'd never heard him utter anything of the kind.

"Sorry," he muttered as he realized what he'd said. "But Caroline, how can they identify John as Mike if they do the autopsy and try to match fingerprints or DNA? We're screwed. We're royally screwed." Perry was deflated. "John's fingerprints will be on file with the Department of Energy. If his prints are run through their federal database, John will be identified for the second time by the same coroner."

"Well, maybe the coroner would take my word for it again and won't go to that trouble," Caroline thought aloud. "What if they can match the prints right there in the morgue? Wouldn't that keep them from tapping into another source to verify his identity through fingerprints?" she mused.

"Maybe, but it's not guaranteed. But what about his DNA? The coroner will still do blood tests, won't he? I don't know what kind of tests they could run from blood samples, but I'm guessing DNA might be one of their routine panels," he remarked.

"What if I demand that the coroner release both bodies as soon as possible for a joint memorial? I'm the grieving sister *and* ex-wife. I know the coroner already feels a lot of sympathy for me, and Mike's death will conjure up more, I'd bet. If he will buy off on my evidence, could we have them both cremated immediately to stop any other potential exams… legally, I mean?" she asked.

"That is something only you can find out when you make your request, or better yet, demand. I can go with you to identify Mike's body, but you'll probably have to do most of the talking. So, I guess the answer to your question really depends on how persuasive you can be with the nice Dr. Carey." Perry looked at his Rolex.

"Caroline, it's almost 6:30 p.m. Where can you get John's fingerprints or DNA to pass off to Dr. Carey tomorrow morning. Do you have anything here with you?"

"Only John's billfold. I don't think that will be useful. Let me think about it for a little while," she said as she rose from the chair.

Perry stood up as well. "Why don't I order-in something for us to eat while you're looking through your things?"

"That'd be nice, Perry. But don't order much for me. I don't have much of an appetite these days."

Caroline left Perry standing in his study trying to figure out what to feed Caroline for dinner. He had no idea what kind of food she liked. He had no idea about *anything* Caroline liked. His lack of knowledge about Caroline wasn't restricted to food.

* * * * * *

"Tell me again why you're in my house, Genevieve," Lorenzo demanded as he threw his jacket on top of Genevieve's purse and sable jacket. The French chair in the foyer was finally getting some use.

"I came in case Cathy came back. I wanted to be here for her, since you never seem to be," she screeched at her son-in-law.

"Leave. Now! I told you I'd let you know when she came home. She didn't want you here, and I don't want you here. Leave before I call the police," Lorenzo warned.

"Why don't you do that, Lorenzo? Call the police? That's what I've been trying to get you to do all day!" Genevieve sneered at her son-in-law.

Trying to remain calm, Lorenzo spoke more softly. "Look, Genevieve, we've all suffered lately and we're all under a lot of strain. You included. But please back off. You and I already agreed to wait until morning to give Cathy time to come to her senses and come home. I promise to call you the minute she comes through that door, or if she doesn't, I'll talk to you at eight o'clock in the morning. We'll do the right thing. Please, just honor our agreement for tonight." Lorenzo's face was a blank as his eyes pleaded with his mother-in-law.

"Then perhaps I'll just spend the night with the grandchildren, and we'll face the morning together." Genevieve was testing Lorenzo's patience once again.

"Genevieve, after tonight you can stay here all you want. I need an evening alone to absorb everything that's happened...maybe even figure out where Cathy's run off to by herself. I'll try calling some of her friends. But please, I don't want to discuss this all night with you. We've talked about it enough for today. I'm begging you, Genevieve. Go back to the hotel and wait to hear from me. If Cathy's not home by morning, you can move in here for all I care. Just give me one night of peace before our lives are thrown into the second ring of this circus." Finally, Lorenzo's eyes were filling with tears.

Embarrassed by Lorenzo's unexpected show of emotion, Genevieve jerked her wrap and purse out from under Lorenzo's jacket in the chair. Her eyes were clouded over with mist as she took her things into the sunroom.

Lorenzo could hear her calling for a limousine to take her back to the Waldorf. "Thank God," he murmured under his breath.

* * * * * *

"I was expecting something a little more healthy considering the kinds of food you usually prefer, Papa." Juliana took another big mouthful of the homemade lasagna that was the specialty of the DeLuca's chef. "This is so good. I've missed good Italian cooking, Papa," she remarked as she took another long gulp of her wine. She speared more Caesar salad with her fork and shoved it in her mouth. She rolled her eyes with delight as her father watched her eat.

"You'll be on the market for a new husband before long, Juliana. Don't start over-indulging on good food. I know it's tempting, but there's plenty of time for that after you catch your next victim," Vincenzo laughed.

"Stop it, Papa. I look pretty good now, don't I?" she countered.

"You're beautiful, my darling. I am a very proud father, and you are a wonderful daughter. You make me a very happy man just being here with you like this," he said sincerely.

"Aww, Papa. Thank you! And thank you for the car! I love it!" She left her seat and went to her father's side. She leaned down and kissed him on the cheek, smearing meat sauce on the side of his face. Giggling, she playfully took his napkin from his lap to wipe off the sauce before returning to her seat.

"Juliana, I think we need to talk about your mother," Vincenzo said, breaking the jovial mood.

"What about her, Papa? Is she getting worse? She looks the same to me," his daughter asked with apprehension.

"That's just it, Juliana. She's no better at all. She's been the same for years now, and perhaps it's time to consider alternatives." He couldn't make himself look at his daughter's pained eyes.

"Oh, Papa. Isn't there anything we can do? Anything?" she asked as tears welled in her eyes.

"We have a new doctor who will be running some tests. I believe the doctor she's seen for so long is not trying hard enough to help her. If the new doctor thinks there's hope...well, that's one thing. But if, after all the tests he plans to run, there appears to be nothing more to do, then we'll have no choice but to discuss other alternatives." Vincenzo looked at his hands in his lap. He didn't want to lie to Juliana, but he had to lay the appropriate ground work for when Lucinda drew her last breath. Lucinda's death would have to appear as though there was no other alternative except pulling the plug.

CHAPTER 29

Wednesday, December 7, 1994

The VW Beetle looked like a tin wind-up toy parked next to the bulky silver Bentley in Perry's back driveway. Perry had offered to let her use the luxury car, but Caroline thought it best to keep a low profile considering what she was about to do. She didn't need to draw any extra attention to herself.

Her stomach felt nervous as she got into the Beetle. Two spring rolls and a hearty bowl of egg drop soup were still sloshing around uncomfortably in her stomach. Thankfully, Perry had listened and hadn't ordered much food for her. She mechanically ate what was in front of her, stopping when the food was gone. Her mind was not on the food she tasted, but on the impromptu scavenger hunt that was ahead of her that evening.

She drove carefully in an attempt to look like any other driver who blended in with the evening's light traffic flow. As anxious as she was about her mission, it was difficult not to speed through the streets of the calm neighborhood.

Her thoughts kept her occupied as she drove on auto-pilot toward Hicksville. Before she knew it, she had arrived.

There had to be something in John's soot covered car that would provide a good DNA or fingerprint sample for the coroner. If it was there, she was going to find it. It was her only hope.

* * * * *

Before leaving for the Manhattan penthouse apartment, Juliana wanted to peek in on her mother one last time. Vincenzo accompanied his daughter to her mother's bedside, expecting a brief interlude of goodnight kisses before he walked his daughter outside to her car. He was looking forward to the pleasure of his evening pipe and the comfort of his favorite chair. He had a lot of thinking to do.

Again, the attending nurse removed herself from the room, providing the expected privacy between the family members and the patient. Juliana stepped to the bedside the nurse had just left and sat in the vacated chair. She leaned forward with her crossed arms over the side rail of the bed and stared at her mother's face. "Papa, she is still beautiful, isn't she?"

Vincenzo said nothing.

"I miss her, Papa. I would give anything to have her back in our lives. A daughter needs her mother. They have a special bond that no one else can ever understand. I've needed her so many times. Times like this, when I've been deserted and left to start over." Juliana reached for her mother's hand through the bed's side railing and held it gently. She lowered her chin and wept silently.

Vincenzo moved next to his daughter and put his hand on her shoulder. "Juliana, your mother is feeling no pain. She is comfortable. If she could be here for you, she would. You mustn't grieve what is not yet lost. The new doctor may be able to work a miracle for us... maybe not...but at least he will try. Now why don't you kiss your mother goodnight and make your way back home. You have a long drive ahead of you." Lorenzo tenderly smiled at Juliana.

Without warning, Lucinda slowly lifted her pointer finger a half inch from the mattress. Juliana felt the movement just as she started to release her mother's hand. The stunned daughter jerked her head up to look at her

mother's frail hand. The finger slowly lowered to a flat position on the sheet.

Juliana shot quickly to the head of the bed so she could gaze intently into her mother's face. She could see her mother's eyes moving under her closed lids, something similar to REM sleep movements.

"Mama, if you can hear me, try to raise your finger again. Please, Mama" Juliana pleaded. There were no hand or finger movements. "Mama, please try!" Still no movement from Lucinda. Juliana's tears fell from her face onto her mother's cheek. "Oh, Mama, please come back to me!" she sobbed. Vincenzo watched helplessly as his daughter embraced Lucinda's rigid body—a healthy woman who had once been the epitome of strength and energy. "Mama, PLEASE!" Juliana screamed through her tears.

"Juliana, come here, darling. You're making yourself too upset," her father begged.

As she started to turn away, Juliana peripherally glimpsed a slight movement around her mother's eye. She immediately faced her mother and clearly saw another twitch—Lucinda was struggling to open her eyes! She couldn't get them open, but she was trying! This was miraculous!

"PAPA! LOOK! MAMA IS TRYING TO WAKE UP!!" Juliana started laughing and crying simultaneously. Vincenzo was dumbstruck. *If Lorenzo noticed this earlier, he hadn't spoken of it. This is terrible timing.*

"Papa, I'm staying here with Mama tonight in case she tries to get her eyes open… or if she starts talking… or if she needs anything," Juliana proclaimed. She announced her new evening plans without pausing to take a breath. "If she needs me, I can stay here all the time. I can move in to help care for Mama. Papa, this is the answer to my prayers!"

Vincenzo smiled pitifully at his daughter. He tried to mask his concern about his wife's sudden change in condition. "Juliana, please don't get

your hopes up. I've been warned before about reading too much into involuntary muscle spasms of comatose patients. They do that occasionally, but it's not always a clear signal that the patient is about to wake up." He smiled a weak smile.

"But, Papa..." she began, but her father interjected his command.

"Go up to your old room and get settled in for the night. We'll call the nurse back in and let her go through her nightly routine with your mother. She will alert us if your mother shows any more positive signs or movements." He paused as he barely smiled at his daughter.

"For now, go get your room ready, and let's don't wear your mother out. If this is an actual improvement, we'll have her new doctor examine her tomorrow and verify it for us. We can have him come out here first thing in the morning, I'm sure." Vincenzo was trying to hide his alarm. If Lucinda awoke, he knew things could get exponentially uglier in the DeLuca household.

"Papa, who is Mama's new doctor? Do I know him?" Juliana asked.

"His name is Lorenzo Giordano. He's a neurosurgeon from Manhattan. Have you ever heard of him?" he cautiously inquired.

"No, doesn't sound familiar. But, I'll be here to meet him tomorrow. I want to know everything that's happening with Mama. We'll be doing exactly as the doctor tells us, no exceptions. Right, Papa?" She looked at her father with little girl eyes.

"Of course, Juliana. And I *want* you to spend time with the doctor. You need to be around more professional people instead of people like Diego and his low-life friends. You never know how quickly your life can change given the right circumstances."

Juliana happily shook her head, kissed her father's cheek, and hurried upstairs to her old room. She was feeling like she belonged somewhere once more. She adored feeling like a part of a strong family again. It was a pleasant change from her recent lifestyle. She could get used to around-the-clock servants and gourmet food pretty darn quickly.

Suddenly, she felt as giddy as she once did as a privileged teenager. She felt like the DeLuca princess she once was. For the first time in a long while, she felt alive and vibrant. She had new hope on so many levels.

* * * * * *

John's car was unlocked, thank goodness. She wasn't sure if she had his car key in her purse mixed up with all the others she had collected during the past few days.

She briefly pointed the lit flashlight through the driver's side window, but the ash dust was too thick to see through. With a quick look around the area, she extinguished the light and reached for the door handle.

She sat in the driver's seat to scope out the interior of the vehicle, feeling in between the front seats and the console searching for anything that might have John's fingerprints on it. Nothing.

Caroline leaned as far over the passenger seat as she could reach. She felt around in the floorboard area, trying to keep the flashlight off until she really needed it again.

There her fingers brushed the edge of the portfolio that John sometimes brought home from work. It had his handwriting all through it—the same handwriting in the fake "suicide" note from John (aka Mike from the fire) that the coroner and police had seen. Anything with John's real handwriting on it had to be automatically eliminated. She couldn't risk the coroner concluding that the identity of his two new corpses had been

switched. She would have to take John's portfolio back to Perry's house and get rid of it along with John's wallet.

The whole fiasco was getting even more complicated. Even Caroline was having trouble keeping the story straight. She silently hoped Perry had taken good notes. Knowing him, he probably flowcharted the whole process.

She turned on the flashlight briefly for a final quick splash of light in both front floorboards. She didn't want to overlook any object that might help. There was nothing of use there.

Caroline got out of the front seat and opened the rear door to the backseat area. She leaned in, looking for anything she could give the coroner if he insisted on performing a DNA panel.

John, you were as messy with your car as you were in the house. What a load of trash back here!

Then she spied the hard plastic coffee cup that John used to drink from on his way to work every morning. She remembered his routine: he filled the ugly brown cup at home, sipped from it on his drive to work, left the empty cup in the parked car, brought it back home every night, and rinsed it out. Then the next morning he would refill it with fresh brew and drive back to work. Same process every day, like clockwork.

However, the cup had been carelessly left in the car, apparently missing its last nightly rinse. Rings of dried coffee circled the bottom of the sturdy plastic and greasy smudges adorned the outside of the vessel.

I'd bet this little item will work for both fingerprints and DNA, if the coroner wants to go that far.

She exited John's car carrying the prized cup and the notebook. Caroline trotted back to her VW.

No neighbors bothered or interrupted her while she was on John's property...probably because they had seen her car often enough over the years to know she once belonged there. *Belonged there with John... I wish I could turn back time.*

Rather than getting sentimental, she attempted to focus on the next twelve hours which would be crucial in determining whether or not she remained a free citizen, an incarcerated citizen, or a potentially dead citizen. She backed the car out of the driveway and drove cautiously toward the Norton home.

* * * * * *

"Would someone please come up to my suite and take this huge room service table out of my way? My dinner has been over for at least an hour, and this enormous cart is blocking off the entrance to my bedroom. Please have someone get up here immediately to take care of this."

Genevieve wondered why the Waldorf would put up with such lazy employees. *This is supposed to be a 5-star hotel, but now I wonder.*

Within minutes, she heard a light tapping on her door and a low masculine voice announcing "Room Service."

"*Finally,*" she said aloud, not caring if the employee heard her remark or not.

As she opened the door, an unfamiliar dark complexioned man stood at attention. "You want the room service cart removed, right ma'am?" he asked with a clearly superficial smile plastered on his face.

"I most certainly do, young man." She ushered him into the room. Genevieve turned away when she saw him preparing the cart for removal.

Reaching for her nearby Chanel purse, she struggled with her conscience. It was customary to give a generous tip for the excellent service of the

hotel staff; but tonight's service had not been up to par, in her opinion. As she contemplated the minimum acceptable tip amount, she kept her back to the housekeeping employee. She opened her designer purse and withdrew a $5 bill.

When she turned back around, the young man was standing within inches of her. His hand was rising quickly, aiming toward the middle of her face. Before she realized what had happened, a foul smelling cloth had been clamped painfully across her broken nose, making it difficult for Genevieve to breathe. Within seconds, she was knocked out cold.

The assailant reacted efficiently, catching her slumping body before it hit the floor. He dragged her limp body to the large dining cart and stuffed Genevieve Parker underneath its white cotton side skirts. She was perfectly concealed from public view; he was thankful she was petite— easy prey.

Thinking fast on his feet, he grabbed her small purse and shoved it under a dish cover, concealing it effectively. He threw the chloroform rag under the table on top of Genevieve's face... just in case she got a big enough whiff of fresh air to rouse before he made it to the basement and safely to the black Suburban.

Moments later when he pushed the heavy cart into the empty service elevator, he knew he was home free. From there, everything about the trip to New Jersey was planned out in detail.

He had been told that this lady was "dying" to meet up with her daughter who had recently become a permanent resident of the infamous group home. It was his job to reunite them. A smile crossed his face as he rode the elevator down to the garage level. He was really good at following orders.

Maybe the boss will give me a bonus if I do real good on this job, he thought as he whistled a happy tune.

CHAPTER 30

Thursday, December 8, 1994

"I'm sorry, sir. The room does not answer. Would you like to leave a message for our guest?" the hotel desk clerk offered.

"Yes. This is my third call within the last half hour. She's expecting to hear from me. Would you please have someone take a message to Mrs. Parker's room?" Lorenzo requested.

The desk clerk chose the nearest pen sporting the *Waldorf-Astoria* label on its black barrel, then scribbled the message on the cream-colored notepad displaying the same prestigious name. "Yes, sir. I've got it. I'll have it delivered *post haste*." He stuffed the note in a coordinating hotel envelope and quickly wrote Genevieve Parker's name and room number on the front.

The desk clerk snapped his fingers to summon the closest bell boy. The uniformed young man took the envelope without hesitation, glanced at the handwriting on its front, and trotted swiftly toward the elevator.

* * * * * *

"Are you certain they open at 9 o'clock, Caroline?" Perry wondered as they pulled in the coroner's crowded parking lot at 8:45 a.m. "It appears there's quite a gathering here this morning. Do you suppose they open earlier... say 8 o'clock?" he quizzed.

"It's on the door there... see? We're early," she responded, pointing to the black lettering on the entry door that displayed the office hours. She was tightly gripping the paper bag containing John's coffee cup close to her body. "Maybe they're having a staff meeting or something. Let's see if the public door is unlocked." Caroline started to exit the Bentley when Perry grabbed her left forearm.

"Remember, let me do most of the talking until you have to identify the body. Okay, Caroline?" he asked. "Say as little as possible until then."

"Okay, Perry. I'll try not to mess anything up," she responded, grateful that she had someone with her to visit the coroner this time around.

The front door was indeed locked, but Perry rapped on the clear glass to get the attention of the employee in the lobby. Caroline recognized the same lady from yesterday behind the front counter, half-glasses still perched on the end of her nose. Today she was punching holes in paperwork, then carefully sliding the pierced contents onto two silver prongs that impaled the back of a stiff manila folder. It appeared she was busy creating a stack of new "patient" files.

Unlike the day before, the middle-aged woman wasn't startled when Perry and Caroline appeared unexpectedly at the front door. Since before 7:30 a.m., she had been constantly interrupted by persons trying to gain entrance into the building. The coroner had scheduled a 'before hours' instructive autopsy on a victim of the recent motel shooting. The event was an open forum for medical students and investigative policemen, alike. At that very moment, a dozen or more people were crowded around the autopsy room to observe the famous Dr. Ralph Carey at work.

* * * * * *

A low murmur filled the room as Dr. Carey removed his blood stained gloves and apron, signaling the end of the autopsy. Some of the room's occupants remained to speak with the coroner, visibly impressed with his

expertise when he sliced and diced the body that had once been a living man. Others were making a quick escape to the fresh air of the corridor, wiping the Vick's VapoRub from below their noses as they choked back the urge to revisit their breakfasts.

Caroline and Perry sat huddled in the corner of the frigid lobby, watching the procession from the interior door as the autopsy's audience members took their leave.

"That was one of the victims from the motel killing," one young student remarked to another as they passed through the small lobby. "I'd hate to have suffered like that," he continued as he pushed open the front door to exit the building.

Suddenly alarmed, Caroline grabbed Perry's arm and squeezed tightly. "You don't think they were talking about our...Mike, do you?"

Perry took her gloved hand in his. "If they were, we'll still offer Dr. Carey the cup. Maybe he won't run the samples through the federal databases. Just stay calm, dear." He smiled, trying to convince himself to stay positive for her sake.

Fifteen minutes later, a refreshed Dr. Carey made his way to the lobby and approached the waiting Caroline and Perry.

"Miss Sanderson. I was told to expect you today," the kind doctor remarked as he extended his hand to her. She stood and grasped his welcoming hand, now scrubbed clean of any trace of his earlier activities.

"Dr. Carey, may I present my dear friend, Perry Norton?" she said as she turned her head to meet Perry's eyes. "He's here for support," she uttered in a low voice as the coroner looked at Caroline's guest.

"A pleasure, doctor," Perry said as he shook the coroner's hand.

Dr. Carey gazed at Perry's face for an extra moment before releasing his hand. "You look very familiar, Mr. Norton. Have we met before?" he inquired.

"I don't think so, doctor. But you may have seen my picture in the newspapers from time to time. I'm an attorney with Walker, Harrington, Norton and Stone. I've handled a few high-profile cases in my time," Perry replied, still smiling.

The coroner looked at Caroline quizzically. "Is Mr. Norton your attorney, Miss Sanderson?"

Before Caroline could answer, Perry volunteered the response. "Miss Sanderson and I...how can I put this delicately...have a more personal relationship." Perry paused for effect. "Don't we, darling?" Perry smiled as he draped his arm around Caroline's shoulders.

Caroline looked into Perry's eyes and smiled weakly.

"Well, let's proceed to the business at hand, shall we? I hope you don't mind that two police officers have asked to join you during the identification process. If you prefer privacy that is your decision to make, of course."

"Police officers, doctor? Why are police officers here?" a stunned Perry wanted to know.

"Oh, they were here earlier while a group of medical students observed a routine autopsy. The policemen had an interest, since the victim was found at the same crime scene as your brother. Assuming he is, in fact, your brother, Miss Sanderson. I don't believe the officers routinely view these types of examinations, though. Neither looked very comfortable during the procedure." The coroner chuckled.

"Caroline, I'm sure it will be fine for the policemen to be in the room when you make the identification, don't you? I'll be there for you to lean on, darling," Perry sympathetically offered.

"Of course, as long as you are there with me, Perry." Caroline raised her chin high. Grasping the paper bag firmly, she took Perry's arm as they followed the coroner down the hall to the familiar room of death.

* * * * * *

"She isn't answering the phone. I've tried several times and finally left a message for her to call me back. Do you know anything about this?"

The Viper could hear Lorenzo's rapid breathing through the telephone.

"Don't worry about that for now. I can assure you everything there is fine." Vincenzo paused briefly. "I called you about Lucinda. While Juliana and I were in her room last night, my wife's finger slightly moved. Juliana is excited and anxious for you to examine her mother."

"That sounds very positive," Lorenzo remarked without enthusiasm.

With irritation in his voice, the Viper continued. "I've told her that involuntary spasms don't always mean a medical breakthrough. I expect you to tell Juliana the same thing. She can't be expecting something positive to happen when you and I both know how this story ends. Be here in an hour, and plan to stay for a while. You and Juliana need to get to know each other. She needs to learn to trust you—the sooner, the better." Vincenzo slammed down the phone.

Lorenzo stared at the dead phone in his hand as he let his mind wander. *That evil man is Satan's spawn, no doubt about it. He won't allow me to mourn my wife or worry about my missing son. I can only imagine what's happened to Genevieve by now. He's ripped my family apart, shred by bloody shred. And **now** he wants me to downplay his comatose wife's*

potential medical progress! He must have **put** her in that bed—he must have orchestrated her accident. Why else would he want to plan her death when she may be coming out of the coma? Unless... is there someone else he wants to be with?

Putting that thought aside, he assumed it was more likely Lucinda was being punished for something. It didn't matter what caused her to be in that bed; helping her was the important thing in Lorenzo's mind. Medical expertise was the only revenge skill he readily possessed, and he intended to use it with a vengeance.

* * * * * *

Officers Hopkins and Davis stood solemnly across the gurney from Caroline and Perry. As they waited for the coroner to unzip the body bag, Officer Davis held a protective tissue across his mouth.

"Are you ready, Miss Sanderson?" the coroner asked as he grasped the zipper pull.

Perry once again wrapped his arm around Caroline's shoulders as she nodded. Dr. Carey pulled the zipper down quickly, exposing a faceless corpse.

Caroline gasped and turned her head into Perry's shoulder. She moaned the guttural sound of a tortured animal.

"Miss Sanderson, I realize this is difficult. Lord knows you're being challenged far too much this week. But if you can manage it, please look again. Do you know of any identifying physical characteristics that your brother may have that could positively identify him?" the coroner softly asked the shaken woman.

She slowly turned, breathed heavily and made herself look into the mangled face of her ex-husband—the handsome face that she had disfigured. As her tears flowed, she openly sobbed.

"That's him. That's ... Mike, my brother. Oh, God! Look at him!" she moaned as she turned back to the comfort of Perry's shoulder.

"Could you think back, Miss Sanderson? Does your brother have any scars or tattoos? Anything you can think of?" the coroner wanted to know.

"Darling, be strong. Think," Perry cooed.

"Mike ... he had an emergency operation as a teenager. He had to have his appendix out. I remember that," Caroline meekly answered while her head was still turned.

The coroner unzipped the body bag and made a quick inspection of the victim's abdomen. He found the scar and swiftly zipped the bag closed.

"He has the appendectomy scar. That is very helpful. We'll schedule the official autopsy for tomorrow, if that's all right with you."

Caroline audibly gasped. She looked up at Perry with a terrified look on her face.

"Doctor Carey, Miss Sanderson brought you a coffee cup that her brother left in her car." He took the paper bag from Caroline and held it toward the coroner. "We thought perhaps you could retrieve his fingerprints or DNA samples from it to hurry this matter along. As you can see, Caroline remains very upset and traumatized over these recent events. She would like nothing more than to have the bodies of both her brother and her ex-husband released for an expedient joint memorial service. To use her words, she doesn't want her brother autopsied or mutilated any more than he already is." Perry patted Caroline on the back as he held her close to his body. She kept her face buried.

"That would be a matter for the police to decide. I will release the bodies to the family as soon as they give the approval." The doctor looked beseechingly at the police officers. "Gentlemen, pending Mr. Lewis's identification from the evidence submitted by Miss Sanderson, how soon can we expect the bodies to be released?"

Officer Davis suddenly volunteered an answer. "I'll go check in with the Chief," he blurted as he hastily departed the room.

The second the door closed, the sound of vomit splattering on linoleum echoed through the spotless corridor as Officer Davis found a moment of physical and mental relief.

CHAPTER 31

Thursday, December 8, 1994

Gino Pucci was helping the crew wipe down a Porsche that had come in the afternoon before, readying the sports car for a brand new paint job and owner. Gino envisioned himself behind the wheel of the glamorous machine. *Maybe this will be the car the boss will hand over to me. He told me I deserved a bonus 'cause I've been doing so good.* He smiled and worked harder.

He kept wiping even as the office phone started to ring. By the third ring Gino managed to pick it up.

On the other end of the line, his boss was clearly agitated. "I just got a tip about a fire at the New Jersey construction site. The place is swarming with cops right now, and I need to know everything on our end is under control. Get somebody on it. And Gino...watch yourself. We could have a mole."

The Viper disconnected, leaving Gino standing with mouth agape and thoughts running rampant. "Oh, fuck!" Gino said, as the crew members stopped their work and stared blankly at their new manager.

* * * * * *

"Mrs. Moretti, your father is right. The slight movements your mother may involuntarily make don't necessarily mean she is mentally responsive. Your mother has been comatose for quite a while. I've recommended some extensive testing that your father has agreed to begin immediately. Once we get the results, we'll have a better idea of your mother's prognosis. I'm sorry if you got your hopes up, but we'll know more soon."

Lorenzo was following the Viper's orders, giving Juliana no real basis to expect a positive change in her mother's condition. He wished he could tell her what he really thought, but he knew now was not the time.

Juliana looked disappointed. "Thank you for your honesty, Dr. Giordano. And please call me Juliana. I don't like to be reminded of my soon-to-be ex-husband. I plan to take my maiden name back after the divorce is final. I'm sure my father told you all about that, too."

Skirting her remarks, he simply said, "And you should call me Lorenzo. I'm sure we'll be seeing a lot of each other during the course of your mother's medical care. I intend to do everything I can—regardless of how long it takes—to bring your mother back to you." He gave her his most reassuring smile.

* * * * * *

Officers Hopkins and Davis waited patiently in the parking lot outside the coroner's building, leaning against the side of the police cruiser as they watched the building's front door. Breathing deeply, Officer Davis welcomed the cold December air on his clammy face and wished he could have made it outside before he got embarrassingly sick.

When Perry and Caroline came out, both officers snapped to attention. They watched as Perry took Caroline's arm and gingerly guided her along the sidewalk. The young woman looked fragile and pale; her older "friend" seemed genuinely concerned for her.

Officer Hopkins approached the two as they neared the end of the walkway.

"Miss Sanderson, Mr. Norton. Officer Davis and I would like to speak with you about your brother. Now that you've identified him, we'd like to get some information from you that might help with our investigation. The

sooner we get some answers, the sooner we can wrap up this case. I'm sure that's what you both want, too. Closure," the senior officer said.

Once again, Caroline tried to bury the side of her face in Perry's shoulder. He answered on her behalf.

"Why don't you gentlemen come by the house again today around one o'clock? For now, Miss Sanderson needs some time to process this morning's activities and to come to terms with the sudden loss of her brother. I'm sure you understand. We'll expect you then."

Perry led Caroline past the policemen in an effort to get her swiftly inside the Bentley and away from the officers. Within moments, he drove out of the parking lot, leaving the two policemen behind.

"Wanna go grab a doughnut and coffee?" Officer Hopkins teased his younger partner.

"Shut the fuck up, old man," Officer Davis replied , half-joking, half-serious.

"You pansy," Officer Hopkins teased again, this time punching the younger officer playfully on the arm. "Come on, tiger. We'll get you some milk to help settle your tummy," Hopkins laughed.

"You're an asshole, Hopkins." They both chuckled as they left the parking lot in search of a doughnut shop. "I'll eat a plain doughnut, okay? Will that make you happy, old man?" Officer Davis conceded as they pulled onto the main highway.

"I'll be even happier if you can keep it down, buddy," Hopkins laughed. "Don't upchuck in my car, man."

******

Gino slipped into the private office and shut the door. What he had to do didn't concern the chop shop crew. He had to reach his contact in the police department and find out what was going on at the construction site. He had no idea what was currently happening there.

When the call was answered, Gino simply said, "What's going on in New Jersey, buddy? I hear there are some flames and lots of company hanging around one of our favorite areas. What do you know?"

Gino listened carefully as the person on the other end of the line gave him details. His face remained somber as he listened carefully, learning more about the police involvement. When he'd heard the entire summary, Gino simply said, "thanks," and hung up. He shook his head as he imagined what was coming.

This is gonna piss off the Boss real bad. Guess I can kiss that sweet Porsche goodbye.

******

The place was crawling with policemen. Representatives of the local city and county law enforcement departments wandered around the scene trying not to get in the way of the multiple fire trucks that had been dispatched to douse the early morning flames at the abandoned construction site.

Had it not been for one hose-wielding fireman who tripped over a woman's expensive purse near the front of the building, the police probably would never have been summoned. The fire would have most likely been chalked up to malicious mischief by some prankster or teenage troublemaker.

* * * * * *

"Boss, it's bad," Gino began. "Looks like somebody was sloppy."

Vincenzo could feel his blood pressure rising. Through gritted teeth, he murmured, "go on," prompting Gino to provide details.

"Well, boss, my source says someone called in a fire in the area. When the firemen got there, the old office building was in flames. They almost had it out when one of the fire fighters tripped over somebody's pocketbook. I think it must have been a real expensive one or something. Next thing you know, all the local cops are there searching around everywhere. I think they brought in some dogs, too. They're still there, but my source doesn't know any more than that." Gino paused. "But, if this gets any bigger, they'll be calling in the Feds, too. I'll get an update as soon as anything else happens, and I'll let you know when I hear." There was nothing left for Gino to say. He fell silent waiting for his Boss to respond.

The Viper sat stiffly, pondering his next words. He tried to control his anger and carefully stated his response.

"Thanks, Gino. Don't discuss this with any of the boys in the shop. Just stick close to the phone," he ordered as he lowered the phone to its cradle.

* * * * * *

Promptly at 1:00 p.m., the doorbell rang at Perry Norton's front door. Caroline answered the door alone, leaving Perry waiting in the den for the officers' arrival. As if she were the lady of the house, Caroline ushered the two policemen to the same leather couch on which they sat the day before. Perry was once again sitting on the ottoman, reserving the matching chair behind him for Caroline to occupy. It was a déjà vu moment for them all.

Officer Hopkins started first. "Miss Sanderson, first let us say we're deeply sorry for the loss of your brother." A slight nod was Caroline's acknowledgement to the policemen's condolences as Perry took her hand.

"Can you tell us why your brother was at the Sundown Terrace Motel on Tuesday, December 6th?" the policeman asked. He already had his notepad ready to record Caroline's answer.

"Well, his house had been vandalized, and it was in no condition for anyone to stay there. Someone had written some offensive words all around, and broken up everything. It was a mess... heartbreaking, really. Mike told me he had been getting some death threats. So I took the vandalism seriously, and we got him checked into a motel. He was going to stay there until he could get the house back into shape," she volunteered.

"Yes, ma'am, we're aware of the vandalism. A neighbor called the police department that night and reported a fire in the yard. The witness also described a Cadillac and two men who were seen leaving the premises. We believe those two men were the other victims at the motel, based on the witness's description of the car and the individuals seen leaving the premises."

"Thank goodness for that. I suppose this information ties everything up, then," Perry declared.

"Not quite, Mr. Norton. Miss Sanderson, do you have any idea why these two men would vandalize your brother's house...or target him for murder?" Officer Davis asked.

"No, of course not. Mike was a sweet person. Most people didn't understand him, and he was often mistaken for a homosexual; but he wasn't gay. He was shy around women. He had been recently reprimanded at work for punching a bully who kept harassing him and

calling him names. Mike finally had enough and struck the man. And, I don't blame him for that at all. It was time he stood up to those jerks." Caroline looked away and dabbed a tissue under her eye.

Perry interjected, "Gentlemen, why don't you tell us everything you can and perhaps it would be easier for Miss Sanderson to fill in the blanks. It may be faster if you get to the point. I can't imagine what she can add to what you already seem to know."

Both officers glanced at each other briefly as if trying to silently agree with the proposal. "Well," Officer Hopkins began, "you already know what's been in the newspapers and broadcast on the television news stations. It appeared to be a murder/suicide. We believe your brother was murdered. If he was getting death threats, that adds up. And there was another graffiti word smeared on the wall in blood. The handwriting seemed to match that of the graffiti written on the inside and outside of your brother's residence."

Officer Hopkins waited for a reaction from Caroline, but she said nothing. He continued, "The suicide victim was well known in the area as being an enforcer."

"What's an enforcer," Caroline asked innocently.

The officer looked at Perry and then at Caroline. "The victim had been known around town as the right hand man of a local crime boss. He was the guy who would enforce the crime family's rules. He would collect their debts, so to speak. Do you understand now?" Officer Hopkins asked.

"I guess I do, but what does that have to do with my brother?" Caroline looked puzzled.

"Ma'am, that's what we're trying to find out. Unless this was just a pure hate crime, we don't understand the murder/suicide. What we're mainly

struggling with is the suicide. A 'connected' man like this wouldn't be the kind of man who would kill himself," the policeman declared.

Perry cleared his throat. "He might if he was ashamed of something. Caroline, don't take offense at this, please." Perry knew he was about to tread on thin ice when he offered his hypothetical theory to the policemen. "What if this man arranged...shall we say, a tryst with your brother?" Perry asked, looking directly at Caroline.

Caroline gasped. She covered her mouth with her hand as tears filled her eyes.

Perry continued, "What if the man was a closet homosexual himself, or maybe he wanted to test the waters? What if he met with your brother and then became disgusted with himself? His anger overtook him and he killed Mike, then killed himself," Perry then gazed at the officers hoping they might give his theory some credence.

"What about the other victim. How did he fit into this puzzle?" Officer Davis asked.

"You mean the man in the trunk? The newspapers never said much about that. Frankly, I don't know how he fits into this. Apparently he was dead long before Mike and the suicide victim, right?" Perry was once again fishing for information.

"Yes, apparently. So you think that death had nothing to do with the motel room activities, then?" Officer Hopkins asked Perry.

Perry smiled and shook his head. "Honestly, gentlemen, I have no idea what happened there. But it seems logical to me that if the body was in the trunk when the car was initially parked there, his death had to have occurred before the murder/suicide. How else could it have happened?" Perry surmised.

"True. That's a good point, Mr. Norton. We'll see what the chief thinks of your theory when we get back to the station." Officer Hopkins was writing as fast as he could so he didn't leave out a single word.

"What else can you tell us about the crime scene, officers? I haven't been allowed to go there so I don't know much about my brother's death. Would one of you please tell me what really happened?" Caroline begged. "Was my brother tortured? Please tell me he wasn't." Caroline started to get visibly upset again.

"Your brother was strapped by his wrists to the headboard of the bed. His feet were bound at the ankles with duct tape, as were his knees. Your brother's wrists were slit and then sliced further up the inner arms to create a stream of heavy blood flow. It probably didn't take long for your bother to lose consciousness, considering the amount of blood at the scene." Officer Hopkins recited these facts from an open page of his notepad. He looked up at Caroline and Perry, who both appeared shaken and horrified. "And as you know, your brother was shot in the face. The whole murder seemed very 'personal.'"

Officer Davis picked up the conversation. "Sometimes, these kinds of torture methods are used when the victim won't readily disclose some information the perp is trying to get from the victim. Other times, it's just for the pure pleasure of watching another person's life leak out of him. Who knows what thoughts go through the minds of criminals?"

Caroline put both hands across her mouth, and inhaled deeply. "Please tell me you don't think Mike could have known something this brute would have killed him over...Mike never did anything bad. He was an EMT, for goodness sake. He *cared* about people. He would *never* get mixed up with criminals." Caroline could hardly contain her emotions. She closed her eyes as tears rolled in steady streams down her face.

Perry jumped to her rescue. "I quite agree, gentlemen. Miss Sanderson's brother was a model citizen and neighbor. Despite the slight altercation he had at work when he finally... and bravely... confronted his tormentor, he'd never had any issues with anyone, to my knowledge." Perry pitifully looked at Caroline.

When his eyes met Officer Hopkins' eyes again, Perry continued his case. "I believe Miss Sanderson has provided you with everything you need, right gentlemen?"

Officer Hopkins closed his notepad, but Officer Davis clearly wasn't finished. "There is still the matter of the ice cream," he added.

The sobbing Caroline tilted her head back, keeping her eyes closed. She sniffed slightly before asking, "What are you talking about?"

"There was a brown bag containing a half-frozen carton of ice cream left a few feet from the motel room door. We wondered if you knew anything about it?" Officer David inquired, locking eyes with Caroline.

Perry could tell that Caroline had been taken off-guard, so Perry chose to respond for her. "The ice cream was intended for Mike, of course. Caroline and I planned to leave it with him after dinner that evening. When Mike didn't answer the door, Caroline just set it down outside his room. He must not have had a chance to retrieve it before ... "

Officer Davis looked questioningly at Perry and then Caroline. "You put it right outside the door, Miss Sanderson?"

Caroline nodded her response.

"And about what time was this, would you say?" Officer Davis inquired.

Caroline looked at Perry, and he smiled. "Tell them when and where we got the ice cream, darling. It's all right," Perry insisted. Officer Davis

looked impatiently at Perry, wishing he would be quiet and let the lady speak without coaxing.

"It was vanilla—a pint of French vanilla—that I bought for him at a convenience store a few blocks away. It was sometime around 7:30 p.m. or 8:30 p.m., I can't remember," Caroline offered.

"There was a receipt left in the bag from Korner Mart that showed the time of purchase as 8:18 p.m. on December 6th. We talked to the cashier who gave us a description of the customer. She described you perfectly." Officers Hopkins and Davis stared silently at Caroline while she sat unmoving in the big chair.

"And your point is?" Perry asked.

"You were most likely there either shortly before or during your brother's encounter with his assailant. Did you hear anything at all coming from the room? Did you see anything suspicious?" Officer Hopkins inquired.

"Oh, God. You mean that horrible man may have had my brother captive when I knocked on his door? Oh, no! Perry!" she screamed as she leaned forward to clutch Perry closely to her.

"Gentlemen, please!" Perry exclaimed, as he tried to comfort Caroline. "Please, I think she's had enough for today. If you have additional questions, please contact me tomorrow. For now, Miss Sanderson needs to recoup. You know your way out. Please."

Perry turned back toward Caroline and muttered, "There, there, dear. Sssshh." He looked up to see the two policemen now standing, but not moving from the front of the couch.

"Please, gentlemen. We will discuss this further tomorrow. Look what you've done to my sweet Caroline," he said as he turned back to her,

cupping the back of her head with his hand. She sobbed more quietly now. Perry closed his eyes as he held her tightly.

The policemen slowly found their way to the front door. Glancing around the luxurious home of Perry Norton, they opened the heavy door. As they walked slowly to their squad car, both men had a cloud of suspicion trailing behind them. The Sanderson/Norton romance didn't seem genuine to either of them.

CHAPTER 32

Thursday, December 8, 1994

While Officers Hopkins and Davis were being ushered into the Norton home, Vincenzo DeLuca was pacing back and forth in his den. The massive television in the corner was tuned to the local news, and the Viper was monitoring events taking place at an abandoned construction site in New Jersey.

Stupid imbeciles! If you want something done right, you've got to do it yourself!

Nothing was going as planned in the Viper's life. He had been cocky about having leverage over Lorenzo. However, the good doctor surprised him when he met privately with Vincenzo after that morning's visit with his wife and daughter. The bastard Lorenzo as much as told him he was going to do everything he could to keep Lucinda alive, at least for the time being. The doctor said the only way to quickly gain Juliana's trust and respect was for him to help her mother, not kill her.

*The bastard is trying to tell **me** how the future will turn out for the DeLuca family! Well, the doctor has balls—I'll give him that!*

Lorenzo's message didn't come without concessions, however. The good doctor did agree to eventually marry Juliana and allow her to be a substitute mother to his two children. He bowed to the Viper's wishes on that score.

The handsome doctor was definitely a charmer, but Juliana still had to fall for him. That would take time, and Lorenzo and the Viper both knew it.

Part of Lorenzo's proposed plan was to immediately take an extended leave of absence from his practice to be Lucinda's full-time, on-site, well-paid medical professional. He would temporarily move himself, his children, and Miss Elmore into the DeLuca mansion to "kill two birds with one stone." Juliana would become attached to the Giordano children over time, and perhaps even fall in love with Lorenzo—her mother's savior.

Meanwhile, Lorenzo would keep Lucinda in an induced coma while encouraging Juliana to remain hopeful for her mother's full recovery. Lorenzo even remarked that another few months to a year of Lucinda's extended comatose life shouldn't matter—unless the Viper had someone on the side he wanted to marry? That remark had infuriated the Viper, but he later conceded the point. Time didn't matter to Vincenzo, only Juliana and her happiness. The only 'other woman' in the Viper's life was his daughter.

In this instance, the doctor was right. Time would be needed for all things to fall neatly into place. Besides, if solitude was what the Viper eventually found he needed, he could find that at his Central Park penthouse apartment. It wasn't as though he was doomed to become a prisoner in his own Southampton mansion.

If Lorenzo was smart enough to pull off this proposal, perhaps the Viper could find him an executive position within the DeLuca family—a permanent position, provided he and Juliana tied the knot, and the doctor was found to be trustworthy. *Another plan, another time.*

For now, the Viper's primary concern was what the police were looking for at the construction site. Gino still hadn't called him back, so he assumed the search efforts had yielded nothing of serious consequence.

* * * * * *

"I don't like it. I didn't get a good feeling about that interview," a worried Perry commented to his new "romantic interest."

"Neither did I. They came out of nowhere asking about the ice cream," Caroline said.

"You didn't mention that to me, Caroline. I thought you told me every move you made that evening. I hope I didn't say something wrong," he wondered.

Caroline tried to think back to the previous Tuesday evening. It seemed like years before instead of two days. "I forgot. It didn't seem important, I suppose, considering every other detail I was confessing." She stared across the room at nothing in particular.

"Tell me about the purchase. Where did you park? How long were you in the store? Did you chat with the cashier?" Perry asked impatiently.

"I parked the Beetle near the front door. Not right at the door, but a couple of spaces away. The cashier's area was to the right of the entrance. She had her back to me when I walked in, and I think she was putting cigarettes in a display above her head, but behind her. I went straight to the freezer and chose the ice cream I wanted. Then I walked up to the counter and paid. I handed her a $5 bill. She said something like, 'cold outside,' and I said, 'yeah.' She gave me my change and that was it. No chitchat. In and out in less than five minutes." Caroline recounted the event with as much detail as she could.

"Do you think she watched you go to your car, or watched you leave the parking lot?" Perry inquired.

"I don't know. She turned back around to her cigarette display, I believe. I doubt she saw anything outside."

Perry studied for a moment before he said, "Okay. Let's straddle the truth. It's easiest. Tomorrow you explain to the policemen that they upset you when you realized you may have been able to prevent your brother's fate if only you had waited at his door. Tell them that they upset you so much, you couldn't concentrate on anything else they said. Are you following me, Caroline?"

Caroline nodded.

Once again trying to develop a cohesive timeline, Perry started thinking out loud. "I've already said we left after dinner to buy ice cream. So, if you left the Coroner's Office—the second time, that is— as they were closing, you had to go somewhere else in between buying ice cream and delivering it to the motel."

Caroline looked at Perry closely. "Of course I did. I bought fried chicken and I went back to the room where John gave me a gun lesson. Remember? Afterwards, I took my stuff from the room and put it in the Beetle because the check engine light was on in the Cherokee—which I left parked behind the Sundown Terrace. I took the Beetle and left in search of another motel. After I did all that, I bought the ice cream and went back to let John know where we were going to relocate. That's when I came in and found … "

Perry calmly smiled. "Clearly, your memory is unclouded. So, let's reconstruct, shall we? So, you could have arrived at my house by 6 o'clock by my calculations, don't you think?"

Caroline mumbled, "Yes, that would give me plenty of time to get here, but I had to change cars first. If the coroner or anyone saw me in the Cherokee, they'd wonder about the Beetle."

Perry continued, "All right. You went back to the motel to switch cars. Would you have checked in with your 'brother' to exchange car keys?"

"Oh, God. Yes, I would have done that. I never said anything to the policemen about my own timeline. We need to work that out!" Caroline excitedly proclaimed.

"I know, Caroline. We are. Right now, that's what we're doing. Don't get overly anxious. " Perry tried to comfort her. "So, you briefly saw your brother right after the coroner visit. You exchanged keys and you were on your way to meet me for dinner. If we'd eaten at a nearby restaurant, there would have been witnesses. Forget that. Instead, you and I ate here at my house. I made something simple—tomato soup and ham sandwiches—because you didn't feel like eating heavily after your ordeal." Perry smiled. "Can you remember that?"

"Of course, Perry. But why did we go back out in my car—not your Bentley—to take ice cream to Mike?" she asked innocently.

"Let me think," he paused, then smiled widely. "You thought you heard some rattling in the car and wanted me to hear it, too. You thought it might be time to trade, even though the car has sentimental value to you. You wanted to prolong trading it in as long as possible. How about that?" Perry looked pleased with himself.

"I suppose that could work. It is an older model, and it does need some work. And you're right about the sentimental part. John gave me that car when we got married." Caroline stared across the room again, thinking how in the course of a few days John had been permanently erased from her future.

Satisfied that they could stick to the story that was loosely based on truth, the two had tomato soup and ham sandwiches for dinner that night. Perry believed that experiencing (not just fabricating) an event would go a long way to reinforce the details of the recalled "memory" should the questions about dinner arise.

* * * * *

Dr. Ralph Carey had just finished writing his official report from the preliminary examination of the corpse of Mike Lewis. He sat back in his chair and rubbed his weary eyes.

Miss Sanderson has certainly been put under a lot of stress this week with the alleged suicide of her ex-husband and then the murder of her brother the next day. The timing seems so suspicious, but yet the circumstances seem mutually exclusive. There doesn't appear to be any tie to the two events, except the deceaseds' relationships to Miss Sanderson.

He scratched his head and pulled out a copy of the suicide note Miss Sanderson had provided that had been written by her ex-husband. He read it again. These were surely the words of a despondent man. He loved his ex-wife dearly and wanted to reconnect. But then he wanted to punish her and make her look at his urn for the rest of her life! He must have been mentally unbalanced! Regardless, there wasn't enough left of him to autopsy. As far as he was concerned, the remains of John Sanderson could be released to his ex-wife. The police didn't appear to be interested in that particular investigation since the note thoroughly explained the motive. Besides the victim's DNA matched that on the toothbrush brought in by Miss Sanderson.

But that left Mike Lewis, Miss Sanderson's brother. The victim of a horrible attack, just one day after his ex-brother-in-law dies. He's accused of being homosexual, his home is vandalized with graffiti declaring him a "fag," and similar markings are found at the murder scene. The man bled to death from his wrists and forearms, plus he was shot in the face—post mortem. His sister wants him to remain "unmutilated" as much as possible, but the poor man is already sliced and mangled.

I could still do a full autopsy on the body, but it is so evident what happened to him, it's a waste of taxpayer money. I've easily matched the

fingerprints from the coffee mug to get a quick identification. With all the new cases in the last few days, this office is swamped. I could cut a few corners here if the police chief agrees. Besides, that poor woman is trying to plan a joint memorial. She needs to get all this behind her, I'd suspect. She looks like a prime candidate for a nervous breakdown.

Dr. Ralph Carey, usually so precise and a strict follower of policies and procedures, was fed up with government red tape. He was also getting tired of his job, and was looking forward to retiring in one more year. Thinking of all the additional work ahead of him on the new cases, he found it easy to sign off on the reports for both Mike Lewis and John Sanderson. He identified them both through DNA and/or fingerprints provided by materials brought to him by next of kin, specified both the cause and manner of death of the two victims, as well as the location and time of each death. He wrote out the basic elements of their demise in a neat little package. He recommended that the bodies of the deceased be released immediately to Miss Sanderson. Besides, he needed the room in the morgue.

* * * * * *

By 5:00 p.m., Lorenzo couldn't wait any longer. He called the Waldorf-Astoria and asked to be connected to his mother-in-law's room. Instead of ringing the room, the desk clerk informed Lorenzo that Mrs. Parker was no longer a guest at the hotel. She hadn't bothered to officially check out through the front desk. He wondered if the credit card he had on file for her would be suitable to use to apply to the remaining costs on her bill.

Lorenzo didn't answer him, but instead asked questions, "Do you know where she went? Did she leave any messages for me? What time did she depart the hotel?" he inquired.

"Sir, she did not speak with the desk or staff that I am aware of, and did not disclose her plans to leave. None of her clothing or personal items

remain in the room. Generally, this indicates a person has intentionally left our establishment and moved on to other accommodations. As I said, there is an outstanding balance; and we will be charging her credit card on file—unless you would like to clear the bill on her behalf?"

Lorenzo answered immediately. "No, go ahead and charge her credit card. It was her decision to stay there, so she can handle the financial ramifications of that decision." He added, "If you hear from her for any reason, would you please have her call me? Dr. Lorenzo Giordano. She has the number."

"Of course, sir. Have a good evening," the clerk said before hastily hanging up. Lorenzo doubted if the haughty desk clerk even wrote down the message.

* * * * * *

The big yellow letters "F B I" were prominently displayed on the back of the jackets of the men walking the grids around the construction site. Dogs had picked up the scent of blood in the middle of the gravel parking lot and kept circling back to the same spot.

Law enforcement officers were rummaging through the remains of the now collapsed and burned abandoned office building. Scorched bags of leaking lime and other unidentified chemicals were found in the rear corner of the destroyed building. Some 100 feet farther back from the edge of the burned building, FBI and local officers were teaming up to walk the grid in an acre field area. In the center of the grid they planned to search was an abandoned well that looked as though it had not been used for at least half a century.

Expecting an update at any moment from Gino, the Viper sat stiffly in his den chair, favorite pipe next to him on the table, and his hands formed like a steeple around his nose. His chest was tight, and his breaths were becoming more shallow. He was beginning to feel slightly dizzy. He was

sweating profusely and his arm hurt. He tried to relax, but no position was comfortable. He rang the bell for the butler.

Within a moment, the butler was at his side. Within two moments, the butler had summoned an ambulance.

Juliana accompanied her father to NYU Mineola where emergency room staff diagnosed her father as having suffered a mild heart attack. The doctors insisted on keeping him overnight for further observation and suggested that Vincenzo's family contact his primary physician immediately.

Juliana agreed to take care of all the necessary calls and notifications and stayed with her father at the hospital throughout the night. By the next morning, Lorenzo was waiting in the Viper's hospital room, planning to consult with the physician on call about Vincenzo's episode. He needed to learn every little detail about Vincenzo DeLuca's current medical condition that he could.

CHAPTER 33

Friday, December 9, 1994

The polished conference room table was large enough to accommodate twelve people comfortably, but today there were only four men huddled at one end. Papers were scattered before them—the contents of two separate files—which were the subject of the morning's discussion.

Dr. Ralph Carey had finished presenting his preliminary findings to the police chief while two interested policemen listened intently to the coroner's words.

"Unless you have objections, I see no reason why we shouldn't release the remains to the victims' next of kin, Caroline Sanderson," Dr. Carey concluded.

The police chief studied the document he held in his hand. "But *is* Miss Sanderson the next of kin to Mr. Sanderson? They are divorced, aren't they?" he asked as he slid the single document toward the coroner.

"Mr. Sanderson's parents live in Tennessee, and they're both elderly, according to Miss Sanderson. They asked her to handle the process here on their behalf. They are in ill-health and in no condition to travel," the coroner stated.

"Is that so?" the chief responded. "And have you spoken with them yourself?" he asked.

"No, I haven't. But the letter that the deceased wrote to his ex-wife clearly stated that she should collect the remains for cremation. He

wanted her to have his urn. He was doling out punishment, as I understood his express intent." The coroner looked uncomfortable. "Some legal authorities might consider his note as a valid last will and testament, considering he provided a directive of how to dispose of his remains."

The police chief surveyed the faces of the gentlemen around the table. His gaze stopped on the face of Officer Hopkins.

"What do you say, Hopkins? You okay with letting the bodies go?" the chief inquired.

"Sir, as long as we don't automatically close the Lewis case, I don't think we need the bodies for anything else we're investigating. I think there's still some things to be uncovered in that case. Some of the information we're looking at just doesn't add up." Officer Hopkins stated as Officer Davis nodded his agreement.

"Fine. Release the bodies, Dr. Carey. Contact Miss Sanderson and let her know. As far as I'm concerned, the John Sanderson suicide case is closed. The Lewis case will remain open until further notice."

The police chief stood and Officers Hopkins and Davis followed suit. As the three lawmen exited the room, the coroner hastily collected his documents. Dr. Carey smiled as he realized he could officially close two more files and clear two more spots in the death room. In addition, Miss Sanderson could start planning the joint memorial. *Poor lady,* the sympathetic coroner thought.

* * * * * *

Perry left his downstairs study and made his way up the stairs toward the guest room Caroline occupied. He knocked gently on the door, hoping she was already awake.

"Come in," she said from the comfort of the large bed. She was snuggled under a fluffy white down comforter, and only her face showed as Perry entered the room. He stopped at the foot of the bed, not expecting Caroline to move from her comfortable position.

"Sorry to wake you, Caroline, but the coroner just called. Both bodies have been approved for release to next of kin—you. Would you like me to call a mortician and arrange for their immediate cremation?" Perry kindly offered.

"Uh…yes. But Perry….don't let them get the bodies mixed up. Please." Caroline didn't make any moves to leave the bed.

"I'll handle it, Caroline. Try to go back to sleep." Perry eased out of the room and slowly closed the door. He could hear Caroline begin to whimper even before the door completely latched behind him.

* * * * * *

The ambulance cautiously pulled into the driveway of the largest mansion in Southampton. Following closely behind was a red Maserati and a white Jaguar, the personal vehicles of Juliana Moretti and Dr. Lorenzo Giordano, respectively.

The butler opened the veranda's garden doors to allow for entry of the gurney into the first floor of the DeLuca home. Vincenzo, slightly sedated and still attached to an oxygen mask plus several intravenous [IV] solution bags, lay calmly as he was gingerly rolled through the house to his new temporary bedroom.

The den had been selected by Juliana as the appropriate place for her father to recover. It was near her mother's room, which would make it much easier for the doctor and nurse to monitor them both. Besides, it was where her father liked to relax and meditate. The den was his comfort zone.

A hospital bed had already been set up where the loveseat was once positioned. Next to his hospital bed, the Viper's favorite leather chair remained as a constant reminder that he too was vulnerable to life's little surprises. Out of his reach but also in his view was his favorite pipe, propped in its stand next to an ornately decorated, empty tobacco tin. All of the comforts of his den so close—but yet, so far and out of reach of the recovering man. Vincenzo grimaced as he tried to grasp the severity of the situation.

Once he was transferred from the gurney and lay safely in his new bed, Juliana sat down in the leather chair next to her father. "Papa, you do everything Lorenzo tells you. He had to pull some strings to get you home so quickly. You don't want to do anything that could set you back. You pay attention to him, okay Papa?" she said as she kissed his forehead. He groggily nodded.

As she rose, she locked eyes with Lorenzo who was standing near the door watching Juliana interact with her father. They smiled at each other, and Juliana took her leave. "He's in your hands, Lorenzo. I'll go check on Mama." Lorenzo gently patted her shoulder as she passed by. She glanced at him flirtatiously as she left the room.

As he strolled across the room to the Viper's bedside, Lorenzo stopped briefly to turn on the television set. From his position, the Viper had a direct view of the screen. Lorenzo adjusted the volume to the mute setting before he seated himself in the leather chair.

Lorenzo followed the Viper's eyes toward the television news broadcast silently playing on the large screen across the room. He could see the Viper's brow furrow as the news banner scrolled across the broadcast screen proclaiming, "**BODIES FOUND AT NJ CONSTRUCTION SITE.**"

"Terrible. Just terrible," Lorenzo commented. "So many bad people out there."

322

The Viper clumsily reached for his face, attempting to pull down his oxygen mask; but, Lorenzo stopped him. As he deflected the Viper's hand away, Lorenzo smiled slightly. "Don't do that, Vincenzo. Leave your oxygen mask where it is. I don't want to have to completely sedate you, but I will if you don't cooperate. Your only job right now is to get better."

Vincenzo's face looked stunned, as if he suddenly realized he was totally at the mercy of the man whose son he had abducted—whose family he had destroyed in less than a week. Lorenzo merely continued to smile menacingly at his confused captive.

"I think we need to get some things straight, Vincenzo. Just as you expect me to regulate the consciousness of your lovely wife, I find myself in the unique position to also regulate yours. If we're on the same page...and I believe we are...I expect some answers from you. Do you agree? Just nod your head," Lorenzo instructed. The Viper weakly nodded.

"Good. Right now, I believe what you need most is rest. Lie quietly, Vincenzo. I'll get you something to keep you calm for a few hours, and then I'll come back to check on you. Tonight after Juliana goes to bed, you and I will have a little talk. You can expect the sedation to fully wear off by then." Lorenzo patted Vincenzo's arm as he rose to adjust the intravenous medication. "Sleep well, Viper."

* * * * * *

The war room was filled with busy men and women, all sporting the same blue jackets with "FBI" written across the back. They were busy in segregated groups: some peering over printed maps, others on telephones excitedly speaking with other agents or law enforcement contacts, and many holding stirring discussions about the day's shocking discoveries. None had ever seen anything quite as appalling as the mass grave they had uncovered that morning after the construction site fire

had been extinguished. The room was abuzz with questions and theories about the dumping site that had apparently been used for many years.

In the rear of the room stood Alexander McNeal, the FBI's Unit Section Chief who was assigned out of the New York field office to lead the federal investigative unit. Throughout his long career with the Bureau, he had always been intent on pursuing and dismantling crime family enterprises.

He had a special interest in this case, however. The Chanel purse of a longtime friend's widow had been inadvertently uncovered at the site soon after the fire broke out. Alexander McNeal wouldn't rest until his unit resolved every unanswered question about the discovered bodies and the person ultimately responsible for such atrocious crimes.

* * * * * *

Caroline took her time getting out of bed. Not only had she become physically exhausted, her mind had become numb, as well. She had forced herself to play so many different roles during the past few days. At any given time, it was difficult to keep up with the persona she was supposed to represent.

She had not been allowed to grieve properly for her losses—her precious brother, Mike, who had never had a chance to be happy—and John, her ex-husband, lover and friend. When the full effect of her losses finally hit her, she suspected she would hide away somewhere to experience her grief to the fullest. She owed them that; they were the only two men she ever truly loved in her life. She owed it to herself, too.

Stumbling toward the bathroom, she planned to bask in the luxury of a long shower. As she turned on the water, she looked around the bathroom and noticed her personal items scattered across the vanity top.

I need to straighten up my things. I haven't taken time to do anything normal. The least I can do is try not to be a slob in someone else's house.

She turned her attention to the shower, tested the water, then stepped around the sliding glass door to feel the warm stream raining against her skin.

I've got to get myself together. It wouldn't hurt me to pitch in more if I'm going to stay here for any length of time. I'll organize my things, and then I'll offer to make breakfast.

* * * * * *

Perry had already settled in with a cup of strong coffee and the newspaper when Caroline joined him in the kitchen. She was clutching two pieces of paper to her chest, obviously upset.

Her host looked up from his newspaper, peering over the top of his reading glasses at the distraught woman standing on the other side of the table from him. Noting Caroline's demeanor, he asked, "Can I get you some coffee? You look like you could use it."

Instead of answering, Caroline extended the papers toward him. Perry took them and skimmed them both quickly. He didn't take the time to read every word.

"Oh, goodness. Where did you find these?" Perry quizzed.

Caroline poured a cup of coffee, then sat down across the table from Perry. "They were in my makeup bag, stuffed down inside. I don't know how I missed them. They were flat against the side of the bag, so I suppose I've just been sliding my hand past them as I took out my cosmetics. It's probably best I haven't seen them before now." She slurped the hot brew as Perry glanced over the pages.

325

"Did you know John had written these?" Perry wanted to know.

"I knew he'd written the fake suicide letter, and I remember now that he told me there were more letters. He never showed them to me, though. Honestly, I had forgotten." She lowered her head as she recalled the morning after the house fire when she woke up to see John writing at the motel room table.

Perry didn't continue reading. "This first letter to you seems to be of a very personal nature. Are you sure you want me to read it?" he considerately asked her.

"It doesn't matter anymore. You can read it. It says he never regretted our time together. He said if I'd thought he'd made a stupid mistake picking up that baby, nothing compared to the insane mistake he made when he let me go." Tears started to leak from her red eyes again.

"He was wise in his own way. I'm so sorry, Caroline." Perry returned to the page in front of him and read intently. "He says you'll be taken care of through all his work insurance benefits and savings program...and he asks you to *share* the benefits?" a surprised Perry inquired.

Caroline wiped her dripping nose with a tissue she had brought with her from upstairs. "Yes, the second letter to Doug Brantley explains all that. Looks like I'm going on a road trip as soon as I can pick up the guys' ashes."

Perry reached across the table to pat her hand. "If you don't mind the company, I'd like to join you," he said. "I've never been to Tennessee."

CHAPTER 34

Friday, December 9, 1994

The evening sun was setting, painting gorgeous pastel streaks throughout the darkening Southampton sky. Juliana and Lorenzo stood in the formal living room of the luxurious mansion that Lucinda DeLuca has so painstakingly decorated. They both gazed at the sky as they finished their after-dinner drink.

Juliana turned to Lorenzo and asked the question that she had had on her mind ever since she'd met him. "I thought you were married, Lorenzo. But Papa said you will be moving into the house with your children and their caregiver. Where is your wife?" she asked curiously.

Lorenzo finished his nightcap, set down the glass on a nearby table, and turned to face Juliana. "I don't know where she is. She left me recently," he told her with a pained look in his eyes. "She had just delivered twins—a week ago, actually. One was kidnapped the second night he was home with us." Lorenzo paused as if to get up enough courage to carry on. "The investigation hasn't provided any leads about the abduction, and my wife couldn't mentally handle it. She's mad at the world, especially me, for some reason. She left our house in a drunken rage, and I haven't heard anything from her since. This was right after she threw her own mother out of our house," Lorenzo explained with remorse.

"NO! That's horrible!" Juliana exclaimed, realizing that the story sounded too coincidental and much too familiar. "A little boy?" she gulped.

"Yes, only a few days old." Lorenzo began to choke up, having a hard time keeping his emotions in check.

"Oh, no." Juliana was breathing hard and rapidly. "Lorenzo...I...," she started, wondering if she should voice her concerns about what was going through her head.

"It's all right, Juliana." Lorenzo tried to smile bravely. "I have to believe everything is going to be all right. It's only been a few days, and I have confidence in the police...and Cathy, too. She'll show up again in a day or two. She's had a lot to adjust to, but underneath it all she's a strong woman. She's a good mother, and she won't abandon the children for long. She just needs to sober up and think things through." Lorenzo tried to project confidence in the words he spoke.

Juliana turned to face the sunset again, having a hard time looking at Lorenzo's sad face. He looked broken and discouraged despite his declaration of optimism. "I hope you're right, Lorenzo, for the sake of the children." Juliana downed the last of her nightcap. She turned abruptly, smiled faintly, and left the room.

* * * * * *

"Do we have preliminary identifications yet?" Alexander McNeal asked his unit members as they stood in a huddle in the war room.

The Special Agent in Charge (SAC) answered for the group. "Several bodies have been recovered, but there are more down there. So far, only two bodies have been tentatively identified: a man and a woman. The male is Diego Moretti, a man we've been tracking who has ties to the DeLuca crime family. His father-in-law, Vincenzo DeLuca, is also known as the Viper."

Alexander impatiently waited for the identity of the second body. "And who is the woman?" he asked the SAC.

"Catherine Parker Giordano, wife of Dr. Lorenzo Giordano and mother of the baby abducted from their Long Island home Sunday night." The SAC closed his notepad and looked at McNeal before continuing. "We were planning on notifying next of kin immediately after we talked with you."

McNeal pondered a moment before responding. "Hold off on that. I need to inform Washington about these developments. This is bigger than local kidnappings and homicides." McNeal turned away from the SAC and hastily made his way to the closest telephone.

* * * * * *

A clearly upset Juliana sat in the chair next to her father's hospital bed. She had been staring at him while he slept the peaceful sleep of sedation. He hadn't stirred since she had entered the room—only minutes after she had left Lorenzo standing alone at the living room window. She had waited almost half an hour for him to stir; but her father had not made a single move.

Is this where the baby came from, Papa? How could you do that to this innocent man and his wife? I guess I'm guilty, too—accepting the baby as a gift without questioning you. I was too excited and overjoyed to think about what his parents must have been feeling—I only thought of myself. I'm selfish, I know; but you taught me to be that way. Before tonight, I've never questioned anything you've ever done. There are so many things I need to know, Papa. I really wish I could talk to you! I need to understand! I want to help set things right!

Juliana stood to depart her father's bedside as she heard the door open. The butler stood stiffly at the threshold. "Ma'am, the doctor is preparing to check in on your father before retiring. I can tidy up the area around Mr. DeLuca's bed later, if you like. In any case, it should be done before Dr. Giordano comes in."

"I was just about to leave. Go ahead. I think I'll go to bed, too, after I say goodnight to Mama," she responded as she moved away from her father's bedside.

"Could I get you anything first, ma'am? A glass of warm milk or something else, perhaps?" the butler asked in his monotone.

"No, thank you. I'm fine. I'll check in on Papa first thing in the morning," she replied as she left the butler standing at attention.

* * * * * *

Lorenzo cut off the flow of the IV drip so that his patient would begin to slowly wake up from his restful sleep. It would take a little while for Vincenzo to come around, but that was all right with Lorenzo—he had plenty of time.

The television across the room was still muted and playing silently. The news station was recapping the day's noteworthy events, including reruns of updated segments recorded live from the active crime scene in New Jersey. Lorenzo settled himself in the Viper's cozy chair and glanced back and forth from his patient to the television.

The television reporter talked directly into the camera with a solemn expression, turning to look behind him, sweeping his free arm around to indicate the area behind him. As he continued to report, the banner across the bottom of the screen announced, "Bodies Found in Abandoned Well."

Still concerned about the Viper, the doctor checked the IV to ensure the liquid sedative flow had completely ceased. When he turned back toward the television, his eye caught something familiar in the background of the crime scene.

The reporter was still talking away in the forefront of the screen; however, immediately behind him, two black body bags could be seen positioned atop gurneys that were now being slowly pushed toward the waiting coroner vehicles. On top of one gurney lay a black crocodile purse, complete with monogram on the front closure flap. Even though the monogram couldn't be read by the television audience, the purse looked like the one Lorenzo had custom ordered for Cathy's Christmas present a year ago. It closely resembled the one he had thrown so carelessly in the back seat of her Lexus—along with her coat and bag—when he drove Cathy's car to the DeLuca estate. Before the gurney was lifted to roll into the ambulance-like vehicle, someone removed the purse and stuffed it into an evidence bag. The person to whom it was handed was off-screen, but the visible sleeve was covered in blue. FBI.

Now on his feet, Lorenzo sprang toward the television to turn up the sound. The reporter was signing off and tossing the report back to the station. The news desk anchor responded with, "Shocking news out of New Jersey today. In other news ..."

Lorenzo turned the volume down again, and paced back and forth in the room. He ran his fingers through his hair and then sighed heavily as his heart began to pound in his temples.

Moving swiftly toward the small bar, Lorenzo poured a stiff scotch and returned to his seat next to the Viper's bedside. It was then that he heard the Viper's low chuckle, followed by a weak cough.

Infuriated, Lorenzo turned toward the patient with hatred-filled eyes. "I ought to ..." Lorenzo started to say.

The Viper smiled weakly and coughed again. "You're screwed, Doc," he whispered, then tried unsuccessfully to laugh aloud.

Lorenzo violently pulled the IV needle out of Vincenzo's arm and scoffed as the Viper's face contorted with pain.

"Oops, let me fix that," Lorenzo said as he mercilessly jabbed the large needle back into the vein on the Viper's hand. Before he left he checked the IV drip, adjusting it to a heavier dosage of sedation than before.

He leaned over Vincenzo's face and smiled evilly. "I'm going to go wake up your wife." Lorenzo grinned broadly as the Viper's eyes fluttered closed.

* * * * * *

Every defensive thought Lorenzo had turned out to be a bad idea. He knew he had to get ahead of the police about Cathy's 'disappearance,' but he was already in deep trouble. The only thing he had going for him right now was the relationship he was building with Juliana. Perhaps she could become an unwitting assistant in solving his dilemma.

As he opened the door to Lucinda's room, he peeked around the door. There was Juliana, just as he suspected. She was staring at her mother intently, appearing worried as well as hopeful. Lorenzo tapped on the partly opened door to alert her to his entry.

"Come in, Lorenzo. I was just about to say goodnight to Mama." Juliana turned back to face her mother.

"Juliana, would you mind giving me some advice...about something personal? I know we hardly know each other, but in this case that's probably best. You won't be biased and you'll speak from the heart." Lorenzo gave her his most pitiful expression.

Juliana looked at her mother, leaned over, and tenderly kissed Lucinda's forehead. She touched her mother's still hand once more—lingering in case of a repeat performance of last night's moment of hope—then she withdrew from the bedside. "Let me get the nurse, and I'll meet you in the sunroom."

* * * * * *

A few minutes later, Lorenzo was inspecting the large plants that lined the massive sunroom. He touched the healthy leaves of the tall plants and bent over to inhale the fragrance of several potted flowers that adorned the room. He ambled to the wall of glass, standing within inches of his own reflection.

His eyes took in the outdoor swimming pool that was rarely used. He shifted his gaze to the ominous moon, just as he had on his ride home from the DeLuca house three short nights before. He opened his mouth to say something aloud to the damning man-like face of the moon that stared back at him, but he thought better of it. Instead, he stayed quiet and averted his eyes to his reflection in the glass. Moments later, he caught the reflective sight of Juliana approaching him and he turned to face her.

"How can I help you, Lorenzo?" she asked, concerned that he was going to confess something terrible to her about her father.

"My wife. I want to talk about my wife," he said, watching Juliana seem to relax when his words sunk in.

"Okay," she smiled. They sat down on a divan that was positioned to provide the best view of the well lit backyard landscape.

Lorenzo looked uncomfortable, but managed to speak as he clasped his hands in his lap. Avoiding eye contact, Lorenzo started talking.

"My wife left our house late Tuesday night. I haven't seen or heard from her since. Her car is gone, and so are some of her things from her closet and bathroom. I believed she would come back, and I still believe that. But do you think I should contact the authorities and report her as missing? Or do you think I should just wait her out? I'm really torn."

Juliana thought carefully before speaking. "Do you have any idea where she would have gone," she asked.

"I figured she'd run to her mother, but apparently she didn't. Her mother, Genevieve, came by the house the next afternoon looking for Cathy. She thought I should get the police involved since Cathy hadn't tried to contact her. I told her we'd call the police Thursday morning if Cathy hadn't come back home by then. Then Thursday when I tried to call the hotel to reach Genevieve, she had already left. I thought maybe she and Cathy had gotten together and left town, but I think Cathy would have let me know that by now. I'm confused. I'm worried." Lorenzo started to weep silently.

Moving closer to him, Juliana took his hand in hers. "If your heart tells you to be concerned, you should pay attention to your instincts. You've given in to logic and faith for over two days. Now it's time to contact the authorities and get some assistance. You can't shoulder everything alone, Lorenzo. Sometimes you have to get help. The police can start looking for your wife right away. If she's with her mother, they'll find out." She squeezed his hand. "Share your burden, Lorenzo. Why don't you call the police now?"

"Do you really think I should? If she drove home to Tennessee with her mother, it's possible they're just now getting there. Maybe she hasn't had time to call yet." Lorenzo wiped his eyes.

"That's possible, but what if she's not with her mother? What if she ran her car off the road or had an accident? She may be all alone out there waiting for someone to rescue her. It's time to involve the police, Lorenzo. You've given her more than enough time to come home." Juliana stood and pulled Lorenzo to his feet. "Go. Now. Either call the police or go visit them. Either way, you need to contact them," she urged.

* * * * * *

"Chief, a call just came in to the Nassau County police station from a Lorenzo Giordano. He told them his wife's been missing since late Tuesday night," the FBI dispatcher informed Alexander McNeal.

"What did they tell him to do?" the FBI Unit Section Chief asked.

"They took down the basic information and asked him to come in to file a missing person's report. He'll be there early tomorrow morning," the dispatcher replied.

"So will I. Thanks for the heads up," McNeal said as he hung up the phone.

* * * * * *

She lay in her bed, watching the shadows from the moonlight dance on the walls. She had left the heavy drapes open, exposing only the sheer curtain panels that covered the large windows. Tonight she didn't want to be draped in total darkness as she drifted off to sleep. She wanted the comfort of soft light.

Unable to sleep, she tossed and turned in the king sized bed. Juliana mentally replayed the two conversations she'd had with Lorenzo that evening.

During the first, he looked truly broken and sad, but he put on a show of bravado. The second? Well...that one was odd. She thought surely he was going to tell her that her father had stolen his baby. But then again, if he knew that, why was he helping her father? And mother? *Why would he willingly do that if he knew what Papa had done? How would Lorenzo feel about me if he knew I was excited about being the new mother of his baby? Then I literally lost the baby during the accident? He would hate me.*

335

It did no good to cry. Not for Lorenzo, and not for the baby. But now she was worried about his wife's well-being. As sinister as the baby's kidnapping was, she wondered if her father—or Lorenzo—could have engineered Cathy's disappearance. She knew her father had done some shady things in his life, but how far would he go to get what he wanted? She realized she had no idea.

She turned her face into the plump pillow. She would will herself to sleep. She had to stop thinking such unspeakable thoughts.

CHAPTER 35

Saturday, December 10, 1994

The winter sky was gray, filled with what he called "snow clouds" as a young boy. The landscape was already covered in a soft layer of fluffy snow, but the roads were not yet iced over. The wet, slick streets would succumb to the low temperatures soon enough, creating an ice rink surface for those drivers reckless enough to travel.

He had already kissed the children goodbye and left them in the care of Miss Elmore once again. When he told her about his plans to temporarily move the family to the DeLuca estate in Southampton, she seemed elated. She was busy making a relocation list of the children's necessities when he left the house.

Lorenzo was on his way to the Nassau County police station to officially file a missing person's report for Cathy. Throughout the night, he had rehearsed his story, praying that he wouldn't slip and say something that piqued any suspicion by the police. He was nervous, but thought he might be able to use that to his advantage.

When he arrived outside the station at 8:30 a.m., he took a deep breath, closed his eyes, and silently prayed for the first time in months. He needed strength and wisdom to get through the next few hours. He hoped that God would hear him and help him, but he wasn't sure God would be listening to his prayers today.

* * * * * *

Since 7:30 a.m., FBI Unit Section Chief Alexander McNeal had been briefing Sheriff Jack Harvey in an interview room at the Nassau County Police Department. As they sipped from the paper cups of strong black coffee, the sheriff became more and more intrigued with the gruesome story being told by McNeal. The sheriff knew about the abducted Giordano baby, but was flabbergasted when McNeal revealed that one of the bodies recovered at the construction site was apparently that of Mrs. Giordano. They compared case notes and waited anxiously for the arrival of Lorenzo Giordano.

When the door to the room opened, a deputy escorted a solemn-looking man inside as both the sheriff and McNeal stood. Lorenzo was introduced to both men and asked to take a seat across the wide table from the two gentlemen. He tried to smile, but found that particular expression uncomfortable. He nodded to the officers, foregoing the usual handshakes of introduction.

"Dr. Giordano, I understand you want to file a missing persons report on behalf of your wife?" the sheriff asked routinely.

Nervously, Lorenzo meekly answered, "Yes."

"Why don't you tell us why you believe she's missing. Start at the beginning, if you will," the sheriff directed.

"Actually, I'm not sure she *is* missing. But she's been gone long enough to make me wonder why she hasn't checked in with me," Lorenzo explained. "It's been over three days since I've heard from her, and this isn't like Cathy." Lorenzo reached for the cup of coffee that had been poured for him when he sat down a few moments before.

"Then let's start at the beginning. Recap for us what happened before she left. You don't mind if we take notes, do you Doctor?" the sheriff inquired.

Lorenzo felt nervous, but nodded his agreement for the note taking. Then he began his story, starting with the night of the baby's abduction through the evening he came home to find Cathy drunk and agitated. He was careful to detail her unstable state of mind—how she ejected her own mother from their home, flung wine glasses at the fireplace, and her unnatural erratic behavior. He cried real tears as he explained how his beautiful family disintegrated right before his eyes in just a matter of days. He ended his story by recounting his conversation with the nanny the morning after Cathy apparently left. He hung his head and closed his eyes, as if wishing he had the chance to go back in time to do things differently. Lorenzo was a very convincing interviewee.

The sheriff dropped his pen and leaned back in his chair. "Do you think your wife would have tried to find her mother?"

Lorenzo wiped his face with a handkerchief from his coat pocket. "I thought she might, but her mother contacted me at my office the next day looking for Cathy. She later came to our house to visit the children, and Genevieve was still there when I got home from work. She left our house to go back to the Waldorf after we both agreed to give Cathy another night to come back home. When I tried to call her at the hotel the next morning, Genevieve had already left. I assumed she and Cathy had gotten together and were going to Genevieve's home in Tennessee," Lorenzo explained.

"Why would you think that," the sheriff asked.

"Well, Cathy was in an erratic state of mind, and Genevieve never liked me. My mother-in-law and I are both stubborn, and we clashed often. And she still wanted to control Cathy, her only child. To say Genevieve

was an interfering person would be an understatement," Lorenzo explained.

"I see. Have you tried to contact your mother-in-law at her Tennessee residence?" the sheriff inquired.

"No, I thought Cathy would call me. Since Cathy had her car, I thought maybe they were driving there. It would take a while to make a trip that long. I wasn't sure when they left, so I haven't tried to call yet."

The sheriff nodded as he picked up his pen to scribble more notes. "So, if I understand you correctly, you and your wife had an altercation on Tuesday evening," he started.

"A verbal altercation, sheriff," Lorenzo corrected.

"All right. You two argued on Tuesday evening. Based on what you just told us, you had both been drinking heavily. Sometime after you left the house to clear your head, your wife left with some of her personal items in her vehicle, a new Lexus SUV. When you came back to the house, you realized she was gone. You cleaned up glass from the wine glasses she shattered, and then you went to bed to sleep it off. She wasn't back the next morning, so you went to work. You expected to hear from her, but she never called. Does that sum it up correctly?" the sheriff asked.

Lorenzo nodded.

"And since that time you have left the children in the sole care of a hired nanny, also correct?" the sheriff asked.

"Yes," Lorenzo meekly responded.

"And your mother-in-law, also concerned about Mrs. Giordano's whereabouts, had called your office and also visited your home the day after Mrs. Giordano left, also correct?"

"Yes," Lorenzo said.

"And now Mrs. Giordano's mother—Genevieve Parker—has also vanished?" the sheriff wanted to know.

Lorenzo cleared his throat. "I don't know if she's *vanished*, but she's no longer a guest at the Waldorf. I asked the desk clerk to have her call me if she returned, but I've heard nothing."

The sheriff stared at Lorenzo as if he didn't know what else to say.

At that moment, the FBI Unit Section Chief cleared his throat. "Perhaps I can take it from here, sheriff." McNeal took a sip of his lukewarm coffee before he began.

"Dr. Giordano, I'm very sorry your family has suffered so much recently. I know everything about your life must seem like a bad dream, but I'd like to help you. I'm interested in solving this case—the entire case as it applies to your family—with the full backing of the FBI and its resources. However, there are a few issues we need to clarify, and I think you can help us do that."

Lorenzo responded, "Anything."

"Fine," Unit Chief McNeal said, "let's start with Vincenzo DeLuca. How do you know him?"

Lorenzo's eyes widened and his worried facial expression changed to one of shock. "Wh..Why? What does he have to do with this?"

"That's what we're trying to find out," McNeal answered, watching Lorenzo's nervous reactions carefully.

* * * * *

Caroline hung up the phone with the mortician and turned toward Perry who was across the room reading the morning newspaper.

"The ashes will be ready first thing Monday morning. We're all set to pick up the urns after 9 o'clock." She made her way to the couch and picked up a magazine. She flipped a few pages, but couldn't make herself get interested in the superficial contents.

"You know, Perry. I should order name plates to put on the sides of the urns. That way there will never be any question about which urn belongs to whom."

Perry didn't respond, but Caroline went back to the phone again. She called the mortician, ordering the adhesive-backed name plates that would be mounted on the base of each urn. She instructed him not to adhere the name plates on the ash-filled urns before she picked them up—she wanted to do that herself. Satisfied with his response, she hung up again.

"Now, that's handled," she said.

Perry grunted from the chair, trying to acknowledge Caroline's comment without losing his place in the tiny print of the Stock Market column.

Suddenly, Caroline spoke. "Let's leave Monday after we pick up the ashes. It would be nice to take this trip in the Bentley, wouldn't it? We could take our time and see some of the sights along the way. What do you say, Perry?"

"If that's what you want to do, that's fine with me. But you'll have to help drive, Caroline. I'm more of an airplane man, myself." Perry grinned widely, happy to see Caroline showing some interest in something besides bereavement.

* * * * * *

"I'm not sure how much I can tell you without disclosing doctor-patient confidentiality," Lorenzo responded to McNeal.

"Dr. Giordano, we understand the need for confidentiality concerning medical conditions and so forth, but this is very important. It would be in your best interest to tell us what you know about Mr. DeLuca—on a personal level. That wouldn't violate any confidentialities, would it, doctor?" McNeal kept staring Lorenzo down.

"I don't suppose, but what can I tell you?" Lorenzo looked panicked. "My cousin, Tony Caprio, works for Mr. DeLuca. Mrs. DeLuca has been under a doctor's care since she fell down the stairs and hit her head. She has been comatose with no promise of progress by her previous doctor. My cousin told Mr. DeLuca about my neurological practice, and he asked me if I could help his wife improve. I've taken her case."

Maintaining steady eye contact with Lorenzo, McNeal said, "And that's all?"

Without hesitation, Lorenzo volunteered more information. "A couple of nights ago, Mr. DeLuca suffered a mild heart attack, and I met with his daughter at the hospital the next morning. I suppose you could say that he is under my care now, too. Although, unless something changes for the worse in the next day or two, I expect Mr. DeLuca will not need me any longer. He should recover, all things remaining equal in his progress."

"I see. And Tony Caprio is your relative, you say?" McNeal commented as he took more notes.

"Yes. On my mother's side." Lorenzo didn't add any further explanation.

"Do you know where to find your cousin, Mr. Caprio?"

343

"Not really. He usually gets in touch with me, but I haven't talked to him in a few days. We don't generally hear from each other very often." Lorenzo's mind was working fast. The FBI Unit Section Chief was going down a path Lorenzo hadn't anticipated. *Don't volunteer too much information!*

"Would you consider your cousin 'missing' too?" McNeal teased Lorenzo.

"I...I...What? I don't understand," Lorenzo stammered. "Why would I think Tony is missing?"

McNeal and the sheriff stared silently at Lorenzo. Finally McNeal responded, "Perhaps we need to visit some morgues, just in case one of your relatives happens to be there." He stood abruptly, causing the sheriff to do the same. Lorenzo kept his seat, wide-eyed and stunned.

"Wh...what are you saying? Are you going to look for my wife at the morgue? Oh Jesus, no! She can't be at the morgue. You haven't even started looking for her yet!" Lorenzo started to loudly sob.

The sheriff and McNeal looked unsympathetically toward the doctor. They waited until he had his emotions under control, then led him outside to the sheriff's squad car.

Even though he wasn't under arrest, Lorenzo felt shaken and paranoid as he sat in the rear passenger seat behind McNeal. The sheriff drove the familiar highways toward the Nassau County morgue where Tony Caprio's body waited.

The next drive would be to a morgue in New Jersey, where they would eagerly observe Lorenzo Giordano's reaction when the body bag was opened that held his wife.

CHAPTER 36

Saturday, December 10, 1994

Lucinda DeLuca opened her eyes briefly. The indirect lighting was harsh to her sensitive eyes, even though the lights were on their dimmest setting. She had not experienced the light of day for years, but she had no awareness of time. Her thoughts weren't making sense, and her head was throbbing. She didn't know where she was.

Deeply enthralled in her book, the nurse who sat nearby didn't observe her patient's sudden activity. It wasn't until she glanced at the silenced monitor above the bed that the nurse realized Lucinda's blood pressure and pulse rate had risen. The nurse watched her patient's face carefully, noticing the slight fluttering of Lucinda's eyelids.

Running from the room, the nurse found the butler arranging flowers in the foyer. Out of breath from the quick sprint, she approached him with the news. "Mrs. DeLuca seems to be stirring! Where's the doctor? Where's Mrs. Moretti?" she asked excitedly.

"I'll summon Mrs. Moretti, and I will try to reach the doctor," he said calmly as the nurse trotted back to Lucinda's room.

Meanwhile in the den, the Viper slept the peaceful sleep of sedation in his new hospital bed, unaware that his wife had any cognitive life left in her.

* * * * * *

"Why are we here? Do you have a Jane Doe here that might be Cathy?" Lorenzo excitedly asked McNeal as the men pulled into the parking lot of the Nassau County Coroner's Office.

No one answered the doctor. Instead the two men exited the parked vehicle, with McNeal opening the rear door of the squad car to allow Lorenzo to get out. Lorenzo followed the silent men to the front door of the building.

An older gentleman was waiting inside, expecting the visitors. He had opened the office at the request of McNeal and as a favor to the sheriff. Dr. Carey unlocked the door and ushered the three men inside the lobby.

"Right this way, gentlemen," Dr. Carey said without an introduction to the third man of the group.

The four men walked down a spotless corridor, proceeding to the room that held the bodies of the recently deceased. Dr. Carey led them to a gurney that held a sheet-covered corpse, recently autopsied, and ready for release to the victim's family. He reached for the top edge of the sheet and looked up at McNeal for permission to proceed.

McNeal nodded, and the coroner pulled the sheet down to mid-chest of the corpse. Both the sheriff and McNeal watched Lorenzo carefully as the body was unveiled.

"Oh, God! That's Tony! What happened? *When* did this happen?" Lorenzo was clearly surprised.

"That's part of what we're trying to find out, Doctor Giordano. He worked for DeLuca. Now you work for DeLuca. And now, your baby and your wife are both missing." McNeal stopped for emphasis. "You seem to be embroiled in a crime spree, whether you are a willing participant or

not." McNeal motioned for the coroner to cover the body again with the sheet.

"*Willing participant*? Are you *crazy*? I hardly know DeLuca!" Lorenzo yelled, trying to control his fear.

Awkward silence followed. Lorenzo got his wits about him and stood straight. "Am I under arrest for something? Do I need to contact my attorney?" Lorenzo stiffly asked.

"Relax. We aren't charging you with anything, Dr. Giordano. We just want your assistance. We have one more stop to make, if you're up to it," McNeal stated. "After that, you're free to go."

At that precise moment, the pager that Lorenzo always carried started to buzz. Taking it from his coat pocket, he viewed the message. His answering service wanted him to call in immediately.

* * * * * *

"Were you able to reach Lorenzo?" an eager Juliana asked the butler.

"His service assured me he would get the message immediately, ma'am," the butler answered in his monotone voice.

"Let me know the minute he calls or gets here—whichever," Juliana ordered.

Returning to her mother's bedside, she reached between the rails to hold Lucinda's hand. She squeezed firmly. To her surprise, Lucinda lightly squeezed back.

"Oh, Mama! Can you open your eyes? It's me, Juliana. Oh, Mama!" she exclaimed through tears of joy.

Lucinda tried to look, but her lids were so heavy. The faint light in the room was so bright to her eyes that had experienced nothing but

darkness for so long. She fluttered her lids, then clenched them tightly as her eyes watered. She wasn't crying, but her eyes were full of moisture from the brief second she held them open when the nurse was reading. She still didn't understand where she was, but she recognized Juliana's voice. She tried to squeeze Juliana's hand in recognition.

Juliana smiled broadly, and firmly held onto her mother's hand. "Mama, this is so wonderful! Lorenzo is a miracle worker! You're awake after all this time! I love you, Mama! I've missed you so much!"

A faint smile seemed to be forming on Lucinda's face, although her strained eyes remained closed.

Juliana bowed her head and thanked God for the miracle of her mother's response and for the man who prompted it, Dr. Lorenzo Giordano.

* * * * * *

"Emergency, doctor?" the sheriff asked Lorenzo.

Lorenzo had used the telephone at the coroner's reception desk, learning from his answering service that Lucinda DeLuca had stirred slightly. He advised the service to call the DeLuca residence and relay his instructions to the attending nurse as to what she should do until he could return. He didn't provide his expected arrival time. He didn't know what else the FBI Unit Section Chief had in store for him. As long as the nurse was there and followed his instructions, everything would be fine.

"More of an update than an emergency," Lorenzo responded casually. *My patients are none of their business. Especially the DeLucas.*

Within minutes, they were in the squad car moving south toward New Jersey. The sheriff and McNeal were discussing various sports, none of which interested Lorenzo. He sat quietly from his back seat position, silently reviewing everything he had told the two men when they

questioned him at the station. He believed he had said nothing suspicious that would cause them to suspect his involvement in the disappearances of the baby or Cathy. He prayed he could keep his stories straight for the rest of the day. He promised God he would become a better man if the next dead face he looked into was anybody's but Cathy's. He couldn't guarantee a surprised reaction if he looked into her dead face once more.

* * * * * *

This time the body was in a black, zippered body bag. Lorenzo held his breath, fearing the worst. McNeal gave the same approval nod to the New Jersey Coroner who carefully started the process of unzipping the bag.

Lorenzo held his right hand at his chin, fingers spread loosely over closed lips. With the same anticipation of watching a car wreck in slow motion, Lorenzo breathed deeply as the tight zipper carefully made its way open.

When Cathy's gray face appeared between the edges of the gaping zipper, Lorenzo gasped audibly, immediately turning his back to the corpse. He fell to his knees, both hands now covering his face, as he wailed with grief. The three men who watched him appeared to sympathize with the sorrow-filled man; however, FBI Unit Section Chief McNeal never took his eyes off Lorenzo. His body language would tell a story, too.

McNeal was surprised at his interpretation of Lorenzo's stunned reaction: The doctor was either a genuinely distraught, grief-stricken man, or he was an excellent actor whose performance was worthy of an Academy Award.

* * * * * *

Finally calm enough to maintain his composure, Lorenzo sat in the New Jersey Coroner's private office, joined by the sheriff and the FBI Chief. He

had stopped weeping, but still intermittently sniffed to control the dripping flow of his runny nose. Finally, he reached into his pocket and retrieved the same handkerchief he had used that morning in the sheriff's office.

"Dr. Giordano, I'm sorry for your loss. I truly am. But considering where your wife's body was discovered, we believe her apparent murder was a part of something much bigger. It's possible the abduction of your son may have also been a part of the same crime spree—we just don't know yet. We're still searching for any information or leads that will clarify the mysteries. Until then, we'll need your cooperation and your silence," McNeal stated.

Lorenzo looked blankly at McNeal, wondering what was about to happen.

McNeal continued, "We request that you don't disclose anything that you've learned today, not even to your family members or close friends. I realize that's a difficult request, considering your wife is supposedly missing. But now you know the truth. You cannot reveal that truth to anyone yet. We need some time, here."

Not quite understanding, Lorenzo looked at McNeal quizzically. "I can't take Cathy? I can't send her to a mortician? She has to stay in that God-awful body bag?" he asked as tears streamed down his face again.

"I'm sorry. This investigation is active and crucial to another parallel investigation we have going right now. We will stay in constant touch with you, Dr. Giordano. I promise you that. Meanwhile, we'd like your assurance that if you learn anything about either your wife's or child's situation, you'll contact us right away."

"Wh..what about my mother-in-law? What am I supposed to tell her if she calls?" Lorenzo asked as innocently as he could.

McNeal answered, "I'm sure your mother-in-law will reach out to you, if and when she can."

Lorenzo nodded with the blank stare of a dazed man. Finally he said, "Would you take me back now? I still have a patient to look in on."

The Chief nodded his agreement. As the three stood, Lorenzo commented, "What I'd really like to do is just go home and drown myself in a bottle of scotch. But, I guess that will have to wait."

The sheriff lightly patted Lorenzo on the back as he allowed the doctor to go first through the office doorway.

As Lorenzo approached the back door of the squad car to enter, he quickly turned and unexpectantly vomited on the pavement in the parking lot. Both the sheriff and FBI Unit Section Chief watched the new widower forcefully empty his stomach's contents until Lorenzo began to dry heave.

"You sure you're up to a patient call, Doctor?" the sheriff asked with concern.

Lorenzo used his handkerchief to wipe his mouth. "I'll be fine. I don't usually have a weak stomach, but today has been challenging." He took a deep breath and murmured, "Let's go, please. The sooner, the better."

* * * * * *

Pulling the Jaguar into his driveway, Lorenzo made his way through the side door of his house to find the children's nanny in the kitchen. She was preparing a bottle of formula for the sleeping Ricky, due to wake up at any moment ready for a diaper change and feeding. Sophia was sitting beside the breakfast table, strapped in her high chair and cramming Cheerios into her toddler mouth. She beamed with happiness when she saw her father enter the room.

"Daddee," she squealed with excitement. Lorenzo walked to her immediately and kissed her forehead. She tried to feed him a Cheerio as he lingered in his bent position to gaze at her cherubic face.

"Daddy's not hungry for Cheerios, baby girl," he said as he smiled broadly at his first born. "You eat them, Sophia." He rubbed the thin hair on the child's head, as he stood straight again. He looked at Miss Elmore, still smiling.

"She's precious, Dr. Giordano. I'm already attached, I'm afraid," she commented.

"It's hard not to get attached, isn't it? I just wish her mother..." he stopped mid-sentence.

Miss Elmore smiled again, this time with sadness in her eyes. "I know. But she'll come around, just wait. I can't imagine how she could bear to be away from these babies much longer."

Lorenzo nodded. He moved toward the refrigerator in hopes of finding something there that would fill the void but not upset his stomach further. He chose a carton of yogurt. Settling in at the island where the busy nanny was mixing formula, he faced her but did not look into her face. He sat blankly on the barstool before he realized he hadn't fetched a spoon.

Miss Elmore reached into the cabinet drawer nearby, grabbed a spoon, and slid it across the countertop to her employer. She continued with her task.

"When do you think we'll be going to stay in Southampton?" she asked as she placed the filled bottle into the bottle warmer and switched it on.

Lorenzo thought for a minute, then responded, "Can you get everything together by Monday?"

"That depends on what we need to bring from the house. Will there already be baby furniture there? You know, the baby will need a crib, and he loves being rocked to sleep. The rocking chair will have to go with us if there isn't one there already," she explained. "I've made a list of clothing, toys, bottles, nursery supplies, and other things. I've accumulated most of it in the empty crib." She put her hand over her mouth as if she had said something wrong. "I'm sorry, Doctor."

"That's all right. I'm glad you've taken initiative. If you'll just get all the children's personal things together, I'll have some rented furniture sent over to the other house. Be ready to leave by early afternoon on Monday. Be sure to pack what you'll need for a few weeks, too. I expect we will be back here before you know it." Lorenzo announced.

The nanny seemed happy about the change in routine. She had spent many lonely hours in the Giordano home without the company of an interesting adult. She hoped the Southampton residence would at least provide that.

Lorenzo finished his yogurt, scraping the small cup to capture the last bite of creamy vanilla. "I'm going to freshen up and get some things from my office. I probably won't be back home tonight, if you're all right with that. My Southampton patient seems to be making some progress, and I need to be there in case anything significant occurs. It's rather miraculous, really," he declared.

Miss Elmore merely nodded agreement as the doctor left the room.

* * * * * *

Juliana had been anxiously awaiting Lorenzo's return, making trips between her mother's and father's bedsides, monitoring the status of each as best she knew how. Nothing had changed with her father—he still slept soundly. But her mother's status was another story altogether. Lucinda had been squeezing Juliana's hand every time her daughter took

her hand in hers. Lucinda occasionally tried to open her eyes, but she was weak and her head still pounded.

Her daughter had been talking non-stop. Juliana had recapped the events that had occurred before and on the day of Lucinda's horrible accident on the stairs. Grasping some of what Juliana said, Lucinda's memory could only recall minor things. She remembered buying a Faberge egg with someone—a man, perhaps—but she remembered so little detail. She was aware that the egg was on a table in Vincenzo's den. Nothing more. Her head throbbed too hard for her scattered thoughts to gel into memories. Lucinda just wanted the pain to subside and Juliana's voice to halt. She needed quiet for a while longer.

* * * * * *

The butler watched the Jaguar make the turn around the corner of the driveway to its designated parking spot at the rear of the house. Anticipating Lorenzo's entry, the butler met him at the veranda door. As the door appeared to magically open for Lorenzo, the butler stalled the doctor a few steps inside the room to give him an update of the morning's events.

"Mr. DeLuca appears to be stable with no change. He sleeps soundly. Mrs. Moretti has been by her mother's bedside, reporting that Mrs. DeLuca has repeatedly responded to touch. However, she has not yet opened her eyes for any period, nor has she tried to speak, to my knowledge. The attending nurse will be at your disposal for a more professional update, sir. If you'd like me to summon her, I shall have her join you privately in the living room." The butler stood stoically, awaiting Lorenzo's response.

"Thank you, but I will speak with the nurse later. I'd like to briefly check on both my patients first." Lorenzo answered as he briskly walked through the sunroom.

* * * * * *

The Viper lay motionless as Lorenzo entered the room, oblivious to the muted television still playing in the corner. The local news channel was reporting an accident that had just occurred on Highway 495, warning travelers to expect delays if they were traveling Eastbound. There was no banner announcing breaking news headlines. The traffic story was fading into a commercial that told shoppers about the best Christmas deals ANYWHERE on just-reduced 1994 automobiles! The audience was warned that 'these deals won't last long.'

Scanning the monitor for Vincenzo's vitals, the doctor seemed pleased with his patient's status. He once again lowered the sedative flow of the IV drip so that Vincenzo's alertness would return within a short period. They still had things to discuss.

Moving now to Lucinda's room, he was met at her door by Juliana. She threw her arms around Lorenzo, as she excitedly thanked him for her mother's progress.

"Juliana, this was just coincidental. I did nothing to prompt your mother's recovery," he said as he allowed her to cling to him.

"Oh, Lorenzo, that's not true. She seemed better shortly after you saw her for the first time. I know it was you. You don't have to be modest!" she explained. "Thank you from the bottom of my heart," she said as she squeezed him to her once more.

Lorenzo gently pushed her to his arm's length. Grinning, he merely nodded. "Well, let's try to keep that positive momentum going. How's our patient now? I understand she's been responsive?" he asked as he reached to take Lucinda's hand. He gently squeezed, and she weakly squeezed back.

"Mrs. DeLuca, you'll be as good as new before you know it! You're getting quite a grip. Can you try to open your eyes for me?" he asked softly.

For a second, Lucinda's eyes fluttered. "Juliana, turn off the lights, please," Lorenzo directed as he took a small flashlight from his pocket.

"Can you try again for me, please?" he asked in total darkness. He counted to three, then flashed the pin light quickly across her face. Her open eyes blinked and closed again when the light moved across her face.

"Great, Mrs. DeLuca. Your eyes are understandably sensitive to light now, and I'd bet your sensitive to noise as well. We'll keep the lights lowered in here until you can get used to it, and we'll keep your visitors silent, as well." He turned to Juliana. "No long conversations with your mother for a few days, all right?"

Juliana nodded, disappointed that it would still take time for her mother to get back to normal.

"Mrs. DeLuca, instead of trying to open your eyes, can you open your mouth for me?" the doctor asked persuasively.

Her lips were stuck together. She tried to pull them apart, but they were too dry. "Juliana, would you ask the nurse to bring in some petroleum jelly?"

Juliana did as she was told. In a few seconds, Lucinda's cracked lips were greased lightly and her mouth opened just a little.

"Look at that!" Lorenzo said a little too loudly. "Your mother just moved her lips!" He stared excitedly at his recovering patient.

"Mrs. Deluca, would you like an ice chip in your mouth? I'm guessing your mouth is very dry," he asked her softly.

Lucinda raised her pointer finger.

356

"Does that mean 'yes?'" he asked. "Raise your finger once for 'yes,' or twice for 'no,'" Lorenzo instructed.

Her pointer finger raised again, only once. "We'll get you some ice chips. Good. But let's be certain you understand. Show me that you can respond 'no.' Raise your finger twice in a row, please." Lorenzo and Juliana watched her hand intently.

Slowly her pointer finger raised, lowered, then slowly raised again.

"Excellent, Mrs. DeLuca! Now we can communicate. But we aren't going to tire you. We'll have plenty of time for conversation later."

Juliana slipped an ice chip between her mother's lips, watching her mother's mouth closely. "Want another ice chip, Mama?" she asked.

Lucinda raised her finger once again. Thrilled, Juliana fed her another small piece of ice.

"Juliana, that's enough for now. I'm going to give your mother a light dose of pain medication to help her rest. She most likely has a massive headache, so let's make her comfortable. Let's leave her in dim light for now. And, if you have some extra sunglasses around, you might want to let your mother use them," he said happily.

Juliana embraced him again. "I'm so grateful to you! I've never been happier!" she said as she released him so she could go in search of sunglasses.

* * * * * *

The butler answered the door to find two gentlemen that weren't expected.

"I'm FBI Section Chief Alexander McNeal. This is the Nassau County Sheriff, Jack Harvey. We're here to speak with Vincenzo DeLuca," McNeal said.

"I'm sorry, but Mr. DeLuca is unavailable. You will have to return another time," the butler said as he closed the door.

McNeal rang the doorbell again. The butler opened the door and started to repeat the message when McNeal interrupted him.

"We are trying to track down Mr. DeLuca's daughter, Juliana Moretti. Is there anyone here who might know how we can reach her?"

The butler hesitated, then ushered the men into the foyer. "If you will wait in here, please," he said as he pointed to a formal living room to the right of the entrance hall. The two men made themselves comfortable as they scanned the luxurious room. "I'll bet that painting over there cost more than I could make in ten years," the sheriff commented. McNeal agreed.

A casually dressed Juliana came swiftly into the living room, startling both men. They had expected the butler to return with an address—they didn't expect Juliana to be there.

"I'm Juliana. You wanted to see me?" she asked curiously. She remained standing in the doorway.

"Yes, ma'am. The body of a deceased male was recently recovered during an investigation the FBI is conducting. We wondered if you might be able to identify the deceased from a picture, rather than escorting you to the coroner's office," McNeal stated bluntly. Both he and the sheriff got up from the couch and walked toward her.

"Me? I'm not aware of...why me?" she inquired.

"If you'll just look at this head shot, ma'am, perhaps you will be able to help us," McNeal said as he reached in his coat pocket and extracted the picture taken from the coroner's table in New Jersey. Except for what appeared to be a head injury above his face, the victim appeared to be asleep.

Juliana looked puzzled, but took the picture from McNeal's hand. Her facial expression changed from one of irritation to one of alarm. She looked into McNeal's face, searching for answers to questions she hadn't yet formed. McNeal took her arm and led her to the couch.

"Do you know this man, Mrs. Moretti?" McNeal asked calmly.

"That's Diego, my husband," she answered, still stunned. "What happened to him?" she asked pitifully.

"That's what we're trying to piece together, ma'am," McNeal said. "We believe your husband's death may be linked to another investigation we're working. Now that his identity has been confirmed, we ask that you keep this information confidential. Discuss this event with no one, not even your family members, until we contact you again. We'll let you know as soon as your husband's body can be released, but that won't happen for several days. Do you understand, Mrs. Moretti?" McNeal asked.

The good news about her mother was now shadowed by the notification of Diego's death. She suddenly felt numb.

"I suppose so, but I still don't understand any of this. Diego left me for another woman! How could he be dead?" she said through tears.

"Ma'am, we'll find out. Who was this other woman? We'll need to talk to her," McNeal stated matter-of-factly.

"I..I.. don't know. Papa didn't tell me her name," she stuttered.

"Papa? Is that your father?" the sheriff inquired.

"Yes, my father. He told me that Diego left me for another woman. Papa even gave him some money to keep him from bothering me again." Suddenly, Juliana looked frightened.

"Is your father available, Mrs. Moretti? We'd like to ask him a few questions about this other woman," McNeal eagerly asked.

She shook her head. "Papa had a heart attack yesterday, and he's being treated here at home by a private doctor. He's unconscious right now. Should I get Dr. Giordano? He's in the room with Papa now."

The two men looked at each other uneasily. McNeal responded for them both. "No, ma'am, we'll come back when your father is able to talk to us. Thank you, Mrs. Moretti, for your help. I'm sorry for your loss," McNeal said as he moved toward the front door. The sheriff meekly said, "I'm sorry, too," as he followed McNeal out.

Juliana remained on the couch. *How can I keep this from Lorenzo? I was so excited and happy about Mama's progress, he'll be sure to notice my mood change. I'll just have to tell him and make him promise not to say anything.*

She sat there for a while longer, letting her sorrow for Diego overtake her. Only the butler interrupted her, bringing her a cocktail to help calm her nerves. He had heard everything from his post outside in the foyer.

CHAPTER 37

Saturday, December 10, 1994

The DeLuca residence was finally quiet. Everyone had retired for the night except Lorenzo, who graciously volunteered to monitor both of his patients to give the attending nurse and family a reprieve.

He hadn't spoken with Juliana since early afternoon. Lorenzo had assumed she would be constantly trekking in and out of her mother's room, checking every little while for new signs of Lucinda's impending awakening. However, that had not been the case, and he wondered why. Considering the excitement Juliana had shown when her mother raised her finger in response to his 'yes' and 'no' questions, the doctor assumed Juliana would have to be barred from the room to allow her mother an appropriate amount of uninterrupted rest.

During his recent patient round at 10:30 p.m., he noted that Lucinda continued resting comfortably. Her sensitive, closed eyes were now masked by large sunglasses, reminiscent of Jackie O's popular style. Lorenzo left the door to Lucinda's room cracked as he quietly made his way to the den for Vincenzo's next status check.

The Viper was clearly agitated, trying to escape from the bedside restraints Lorenzo had so cautiously applied. Vincenzo was still groggy, not yet able to comprehend everything that Lorenzo was putting him through. When Lorenzo entered the den, Vincenzo grunted.

"Get these damn straps off me! NOW!" he demanded with a voice that sounded rough and gravelly.

"They're for your own good, Vincenzo. You'd be better served to relax and let your body heal," the good doctor said with a grin. "A heart attack is a serious matter. You don't want to have another one, now do you?"

"I want to see Juliana! I demand to see my daughter!" Vincenzo snapped.

"She's already in bed, and so is everyone else in the house. It's just you and me, Vincenzo," Lorenzo replied as he poured himself a drink from the crystal decanter on the small sidebar. He walked back to his patient and sat in the oxblood leather chair.

"Would you like to watch some television, Vincenzo? A lot has happened—especially in New Jersey—while you've been resting. Several bodies have been recovered from an old well on the property of an abandoned construction site. Some of those bodies have been identified. I would think you'd find that interesting. I know I did." Lorenzo took a drink of his scotch, and swirled the remaining liquid around in the Waterford glass. His eyes were filled with anger.

"Damn it, let me out of this bed. I've got to make some phone calls!" the Viper demanded.

"Not yet, Vincenzo. First, you need to help me understand a few things. There are some questions you're going to answer or I'll be forced to sedate you again—this time I'll induce the same coma you and your previous doctor crony forced on your wife. And, by the way, your wife is trying to wake up." Lorenzo smirked, "You're welcome."

"You're just as stupid as everybody else. You're better off staying ignorant, if you know what's best for you," Vincenzo snapped again.

"That may be true, Vincenzo, but I want to know what happened to my baby. I have no idea where you stashed my son. I want to know what happened, and you're going to start at the beginning. Start talking, or I'll

adjust your medication so that you'll never talk again," Lorenzo threatened.

He reached for the IV, posing his fingers around the drip control. He glared at Vincenzo, "Are you going to talk?" he asked one last time.

"All right, but you really don't want to hear this," Vincenzo warned.

Lorenzo released the IV and sat in the leather chair facing his patient. "I'll be the judge of that," Lorenzo answered as he discreetly reached in his pocket and removed a small handheld dictation recorder. He transferred it to his hand that was closest to the Viper, careful to keep the device out of his patient's line of vision. He flipped it on "record," keeping his finger posed over the "pause" button in case he had to quickly censor comments concerning his complicity in the confessed crimes.

*** * ***

In his weak voice, the Viper began to recount the criminal events of the past week.

"Your gambling debt was a sham. Tony told me your wife was having twins, so I figured one of your babies would help cancel that debt." The Viper stopped to catch his breath, and Lorenzo paused the recorder.

Lorenzo commented, "That part I know. What did you do with the baby? Did you sell him?" Lorenzo asked as he discreetly turned the device back on "record."

The Viper coughed, then started again, "I had my men break in while you and your wife were out and take one of the babies. Your mother-in-law was there, but they didn't seriously hurt her. All they wanted was the baby," he stopped again, prompting Lorenzo to pause the recording once more.

363

Lorenzo gave the Viper a sip of water, then asked the next question. "What did you do with my son?" he asked right before he switched the recorder back on.

"My men took the baby and delivered him to my daughter, Juliana. I had called her earlier and told her I was going to have a surprise delivered to her. She didn't know anything about it beforehand. When the baby was dropped off, Diego had a wreck in the snow. The crash knocked Juliana and Diego out. An ambulance took them to the hospital, but the baby wasn't in the car," the Viper said. Lorenzo stopped the recorder again.

"What happened to my son?" Lorenzo said loudly, then hit 'record' once more.

"Somebody took him out of the car—some guy who dropped his work badge at the site when he took the baby. His name was John Sanderson, but Tony and Carlo killed him before he had a chance to tell us what happened. Then, they started tracking Sanderson's ex-wife for more leads, but she must have skipped town. She disappeared, too. I know that somehow Carlo wound up dead, but I haven't heard anything else from Tony," he concluded as Lorenzo shut off the recorder.

"Tony's dead. I identified his body this morning. I was also escorted to New Jersey by the sheriff and an FBI agent to view my wife's body. Your little plan to have an instant grandbaby has turned into a major federal investigation," the doctor explained to an astounded Viper.

"Let me up. I can fix this if you'll just let me have the phone," the Viper pleaded.

"You're not done yet. Tell me what happened to your wife. I'm curious why she's been fed a constant drip of heavy benzodiazepines. You and her previous doctor colluded to keep her in an induced coma, and I want to know why." Lorenzo switched on the recorder.

"Lucinda was leaving me for another man. She packed her bags and was heading downstairs when I pushed her. She fell down the staircase and hit her head. There was a lot of blood, and I expected her to be dead. But, when I got to her, she was unconscious but still breathing.

"The butler heard the commotion and came in the room, so I couldn't finish her off right then. He called the doctor, and after a while, I paid him a lot of money off the books to keep her comatose. After two years, I threatened to cut off his payments if he didn't go ahead and let her slip away. He said he would never do that, but he agreed to keep her sedated for a while longer. When I hired you to be Lucinda's doctor, I hoped you would be swayed to do what the first doctor wouldn't." Vincenzo showed no remorse as he looked at Lorenzo. The recorder was paused again.

"What about your son-in-law? I hear he's dead, too," the doctor asked, then switched on the recorder for the last time.

"My daughter is better off without her deadbeat husband. She was going to divorce him, anyway, so I just speeded up the process. I had Tony and Carlo take care of him. Juliana thinks he's run off with some woman," he snickered.

Shutting off the recorder and slipping it back in his pocket, Lorenzo left his seat to pour another drink. As he approached the Viper's bedside, he kept his eyes locked with the helpless man strapped in the bulky hospital bed.

"Now are you going to get me out of these straps and get me to a telephone?" the Viper pleaded.

Lorenzo dropped his head and sighed. "I wish I could, Vincenzo, but you need more rest before you get upset about things that are no longer in your control." The Viper's eyes had turned into angry beams focused on the doctor.

 Before Vincenzo could voice his protests, Lorenzo adjusted the sedative IV to a steady drip.

"Good night, Vincenzo. Sleep long and well," Lorenzo chuckled as he watched the Viper's eyes flutter closed.

CHAPTER 38

Sunday, December 11, 1994

Juliana sat in the dining room in the chair her father usually occupied at the head of the table. The chef had prepared a breakfast buffet on the sideboard, and Juliana had served herself an English muffin and fruit. Except for her strong coffee, she had scarcely touched anything.

Lorenzo entered the dining room and nodded his greeting to Juliana. After he served himself a cup of coffee, he sat down in the seat next to hers along the side of the long table.

"I didn't see you yesterday afternoon or evening. I was surprised you weren't checking in occasionally on your mother," Lorenzo commented as he added cream to his black coffee.

"I had some family business," Juliana said, trying to avoid further questions.

"Oh," Lorenzo muttered. Without thinking, he reached for the morning newspaper that had been placed in the center of the table. Juliana watched him, thinking Lorenzo looked pensive.

They sat silently for several awkward minutes before Juliana spoke again. "After you talked with me about your missing wife, I started feeling like we were becoming close friends," she said as she stared blankly at her plate.

"Of course we're friends. Juliana, have I done something to upset you?" Lorenzo wanted to know.

"No, no. Nothing like that. I just believe that if we're good friends, we should be able to talk to each other without worrying that the other one will repeat the details of those conversations. Don't you agree?" She looked at Lorenzo with expectant eyes.

"Yes. I agree. That's what friends do for each other...true friends, anyway. Juliana, what's happened?" he asked sincerely, as he put down the unread paper and turned toward her from his chair. He gave her his full attention.

"Yesterday afternoon I had visitors. I thought maybe you were aware of that, since the butler showed them in." She looked at Lorenzo for confirmation of her suspicions.

"No, he never said anything to me about it. Who were they?"

Juliana sighed deeply, and answered, "The Nassau County Sheriff and an FBI Chief. They came to show me a picture of Diego. He's dead." As soon as the words left her mouth, the new widow began to weep.

Averting his gaze from her, Lorenzo stared across the room in an attempt to conceal his true emotions. Instead of feeling sorry for Juliana, he was angrier than ever at her father. Lorenzo could envision the Viper's vicious plan unfurling: steal the baby and force Cathy to go crazy... get rid of Diego ... clear the path for his daughter's solid marriage to a widower... instant grandchildren... get a new family doctor thrown in the deal for good measure! If that *wasn't* the original plan, it had certainly shifted in that direction through lots of bad luck!

Lorenzo stood and threw his napkin on the table, clearly upset. "Juliana, I'm sorry about Diego. I, too, had a similar meeting with the sheriff and FBI Chief yesterday. My wife's body was found, and I identified her in the morgue. Seems we've both had our share of bad news lately," he said as he abruptly left the room.

* * * * *

Juliana found Lorenzo in the sunroom, standing at the tall glass window and gazing outside at the pool. He was standing exactly where he had been when she joined him two nights before—when he asked her advice about reporting his missing wife. The difference now was acute—Cathy Giordano was not his missing wife…she was his *dead* wife. He no longer needed her advice.

"Lorenzo?" she said as she quietly approached him. He continued to stare out of the window as if he hadn't heard her. She walked to the divan and sat down, hoping he would turn and join her.

Instead, Lorenzo remained in front of the glass, eventually talking as if speaking to himself. "I was told not to talk about this to anyone because there's an ongoing investigation. I can't even tell the family about this yet. They plan to keep her body for God knows how long. It's disgraceful," he said as he began to weep. When he turned toward Juliana, he saw that she was also crying softly. He moved to the divan and sat beside her.

"That's what they told me, too. I've been dying inside wishing I had someone to talk to about this. I'm sorry it had to be you, Lorenzo," she admitted.

"I guess we both needed somebody to share our grief with today. It's been a hard night for me, too," he said as he took her hand in his. "We're both strong people. Together, we can brave this storm. Right?" he asked.

"Right," she responded, trying her best to smile.

He gave her a look of encouragement as he said, "Come on. Let's go check in on your mother."

* * * * * *

The nurse sat quietly in the darkened room reading with a small book light that clipped on the pages of a romance novel. Keeping the lights dim in Lucinda's room had hampered the nurse's ability to read while her patient slept, but it was worth it to see the patient improving.

Lucinda had slept soundly through the night, according to Dr. Giordano. The nurse was happy that she hadn't been required to check the patient periodically during the night. It felt good to sleep eight full hours straight without the alarm waking her every three hours to take vital readings.

She realized that she liked Dr. Giordano more and more every day. He really cared for his patients, their families, and even the hired hands. He made everyone feel important. It didn't hurt that he was so handsome, either. He would have been a perfect model for the cover of the book she was holding—she could picture him as the hero of the story.

Juliana peeked through the door and motioned for the nurse to join her in the hallway. Once the nurse arrived, her face turned bright crimson when she realized Dr. Giordano was waiting there, as well.

"Are you all right? You look overheated. Is the room too warm?" Juliana asked.

"No, I just need a little air, I think," the timid nurse responded. "This is a good time for a quick break. I'll go splash some cold water on my face," she said as she swiftly moved past the doctor with her head down.

* * * * * *

After Lorenzo adjusted Lucinda's IV medication, he left Juliana sitting with the nurse in Lucinda's room. He instructed them to let him know when Lucinda began to stir. He expected more progress today, he explained, as he made his way to the den to check on Vincenzo.

Nothing had changed in the Viper's condition. His vitals were still good, and his pulse rate was slow, but still in normal range. He watched the monitor that showed his heartbeat at a steady rhythm.

Turning up the television volume, Lorenzo settled in the chair beside the sleeping man. He made himself comfortable as he prepared to watch the news. Today's broadcast was focused again on the New Jersey crime scene, where two more bodies had been recovered from the well. Identifications were pending notification of next of kin. Lorenzo expected someone to be calling about Genevieve soon. He started thinking about what he would have to say to the FBI Unit Section Chief if he received the call. The man looked pretty sharp, and he certainly had an intimidating way about him.

Lorenzo leaned back and rested his head against the padded chair. His mind wandered. It wasn't long before he realized his exhaustion and fatigue were stronger than his will to think. Soon he was lightly snoring, dreaming about his lost son.

* * * * * *

"Lorenzo! She's awake!" he heard someone say in his dream. Rousing from his sleep, he found Juliana standing next to him, shaking his shoulder.

"Mama's awake. She said my name!" Juliana said as she rushed out of the den to join her mother down the hall, leaving Lorenzo behind to catch up.

When he entered Lucinda's room, he found her propped on a pillow, sunglasses still on, and faintly smiling. She clasped Juliana's hand in hers, as she tried to squint through the sunglasses to focus on the handsome doctor.

"Mama, this is Dr. Lorenzo Giordano. He brought you out of your coma!" Juliana excitedly said.

Lorenzo approached her bedside, and Juliana let go of her mother's hand to step aside. "I'm thrilled to finally meet you, Mrs. DeLuca," Lorenzo said as he genuinely smiled at her.

"Thank you," she said in a low, weak voice. "Where's my husband?" she squeaked.

"Mama, here. Take a sip of water," her daughter urged.

After Lucinda sipped a small amount of iced water through a straw, she asked again, "Where's Vincenzo?"

"He's recovering in another room. He had a mild heart attack a few days ago. He's sedated and resting," Lorenzo explained.

Fearing her mother would be upset at the news, Juliana moved past Lorenzo to take her mother's hand again. Lucinda squeezed her daughter's hand as tightly as she could.

"It's all right, Mama. He should be fine," Juliana offered encouragingly.

"No, don't let him recover. He'll try to kill me again," Lucinda said shakily, as her blood pressure and pulse rate escalated.

Stunned, Juliana said, "What? Did Papa cause your accident?" Juliana looked panicked.

"I was leaving him. He pushed me. That's all I remember," Lucinda cried.

Lorenzo looked sternly at Juliana. "I'll give your mother something to help calm her down."

Then Lorenzo bent down over Lucinda's bedside and gently touched his patient's cheek. "You don't have to worry about anything anymore, Mrs. DeLuca. Your husband will stay sedated as long as I think it's medically necessary. Get some rest, now," he whispered.

He watched her fall asleep as her daughter stood nearby, filled with amazement, anger, and grief. Too many emotional jolts had hit her in too short of a period. She sat down in the nurse's chair, looking limp and defeated.

"Juliana, come with me. We have some things to discuss, and some of them won't be pleasant," Lorenzo commanded. She followed robotically, wondering what could be worse than her father attempting to kill her mother.

* * * * * *

Lorenzo explained that her father had told him what he thought to be his "death bed" confession. Complicating matters was the fact that Lorenzo recorded it unbeknownst to Vincenzo. Lorenzo clarified that he thought Vincenzo was going to talk about distribution of assets or something that would benefit the family. He told Juliana that he never dreamed Vincenzo wanted to confess his crimes.

When Juliana asked Lorenzo to play the tape, he cautioned her that she might not want to hear the atrocities outlined in her father's confession. When she disagreed and demanded to hear her father's words, he rewound the tape still in the miniature recorder and played it for her. She listened intently.

> *"Your gambling debt was a sham. Tony told me your wife was having twins, so I figured one of your babies would help cancel that debt.*
>
> *"I had my men break in while you and your wife were out and take one of the babies. Your mother-in-law was there, but they didn't seriously hurt her. All they wanted was the baby.*
>
> *"My men took the baby and delivered him to my daughter, Juliana. I had called her earlier and told her I was going to have*

a surprise delivered to her. She didn't know anything about it beforehand. When the baby was dropped off, Diego had a wreck in the snow. The crash knocked Juliana and Diego out. An ambulance took them to the hospital, but the baby wasn't in the car.

"Somebody took him out of the car—some guy who dropped his work badge at the site when he took the baby. His name was John Sanderson, but Tony and Carlo killed him before he had a chance to tell us what happened. Then, they started tracking Sanderson's ex-wife for more leads, but she must have skipped town. She disappeared, too. I know that somehow Carlo wound up dead, but I haven't heard anything else from Tony.

"Lucinda was leaving me for another man. She packed her bags and was heading downstairs when I pushed her. She fell down the staircase and hit her head. There was a lot of blood, and I expected her to be dead. But, when I got to her, she was unconscious and still breathing.

"The butler heard the commotion and came in the room, so I couldn't finish her off right then. He called the doctor, and after a while, I paid him a lot of money off the books to keep her comatose. After two years, I threatened to cut off his payments if he didn't go ahead and let her slip away. He said he would never do that, but he agreed to keep her sedated for a while longer. When I hired you to be Lucinda's doctor, I hoped you would be swayed to do what the first doctor wouldn't.

"My daughter is better off without her deadbeat husband. She was going to divorce him, anyway, so I just speeded up the process. I had Tony and Carlo take care of him. Juliana thinks he's run off with some woman."

Juliana sobbed hysterically. It was hard for her to grasp what her father had done to his own family, as well as Lorenzo's.

"I'm so ashamed, I can't believe Papa could look me in the face and act like he was some kind of great benefactor. For all I knew, he bought the baby from an orphanage for me. He never tried to explain, especially after the baby disappeared from the car. He just told me everything would be all right," she blubbered and continued.

"I swear, Lorenzo, I had no idea the baby he sent us was taken from you and your wife. I had no idea! When you told me the other evening that your son had been kidnapped, I was afraid it might have been the one Papa got us, but I didn't want to believe it. I wanted to talk to Papa and be sure before I said anything to you. Can you ever forgive us, Lorenzo? Please forgive us!" she wailed.

The expression on Lorenzo's face was solemn, but he understood how the Viper's "princess" daughter had always come to expect miracles from her father. He had given her everything she'd ever hoped for all her life. She never questioned his actions, always assuming the best and trusting in her father to do the right thing. He felt sorry for Juliana.

"I don't blame you, Juliana. You've lost quite a bit yourself: years without your mother, your husband, and God knows what else."

She studied the wadded tissue in her hands for what seemed like forever. When she finally looked Lorenzo in the face, she meekly asked, "What do we do now?"

"I think we keep your father asleep for a little longer until we can figure that out. Maybe we should get an attorney's counsel before we go any further," Lorenzo offered.

"Maybe you're right. If we can get some good legal advice, the attorney will tell us what's best to do." Juliana continued to weep silently.

Cathy and I use an attorney in Syosset. He prepared our wills for us, and he's set up an educational trust fund for Sophia. We hadn't had time to set anything up for the twins before …"

"I'm sure he's a good attorney. What's his name, Lorenzo?" Juliana asked as she dried her eyes.

"His name is Perry Norton. He and his firm are well-known and have a good reputation," Lorenzo replied.

"Okay, let's call Perry Norton. Maybe we can reach him at home, if we can find the number," Juliana said.

* * * * * *

"Caroline, what's a seven letter word for 'pavement?'" Perry asked as he laboriously worked the crossword in the *New York Times*.

Lounging on the leather couch reading *To Kill A Mockingbird* for the fifth time, she promptly answered, "Asphalt," without looking up from her book.

"I knew that," Perry said to himself, proud that he had almost finished the puzzle.

Caroline laid the book on the couch and moved upward into a sitting position. She was becoming stir-crazy, or so she had recently told Perry. They had not been out of the house except to identify dead bodies or secure evidence for the coroner. She was beginning to attach morbidity to Perry and his home. The overcast sky and snowy weather wasn't helping her mood.

"I'm anxious to go on our trip. I think we both need to get out of here for a while," she said blandly.

"What have you decided about the ashes? Are we taking them on the trip, or should we bring the urns back here first?" Perry asked. He wasn't sure of Caroline's total plan.

"I thought maybe John's mother might like to at least see his urn. But, I don't want to leave his ashes in Tennessee with her. If she got the wrong idea, it would be awkward to take them away from her," voicing her thoughts aloud.

"Then leave the urns here and just visit. Tell his parents stories about him, make them smile as much as you can. Let them remember the good things, but don't tell them exactly how he died," Perry advised. "They don't need to know those details."

"Hmmm," Caroline agreed. "So I guess I'll pick up the urns while you pack the car. We can leave after I get back."

"Perfect," Perry responded.

Perry finished the crossword, forcing a word or two until he had all the spaces filled. Caroline resumed her position on the couch and started to nod off when the phone loudly rang. Startling both of them, Perry jumped to answer it, trying not to rouse Caroline. She rolled over and resumed her nap while Perry talked quietly.

He listened carefully to the caller, responded appropriately, and hung up after a few minutes had passed. He ambled to the couch and stood at the end, wondering if he should wake Caroline. She stirred, and he cleared his throat. She jerked her head up and saw Perry standing at the end of the couch. "What?" she said, sleepily.

"I'm afraid we may need to postpone our little trip to Tennessee," he said.

"Why?" Caroline said, as she tried to clear her head from sleep-fog.

"I have an appointment with a current client—and a new one—set for tomorrow morning at nine o'clock in my office," he responded.

"Can't somebody else take the meeting?" Caroline asked.

"Not this one. The client is Lorenzo Giordano. He's bringing Juliana DeLuca Moretti with him. I think I need to handle this myself," he smiled.

CHAPTER 39

Monday, December 12, 1994

An inch of snow was nothing to New Yorkers. Most residents drove in snow routinely every winter, hardly taking note of a little white stuff scattered around or ice patches on the highways. Caroline was no different and didn't hesitate to scrape the powder from her windshield and rev up the Beetle. She wanted to get her day's errand behind her, looking forward to having her loved ones' urns in her possession. She planned to mourn them privately while Perry was meeting with his clients. While she had precious time to herself, Caroline would give her undivided attention to the special memories she harbored of her brother and her ex-husband.

She pulled the Beetle onto the slushy roadway and babied the car as it sputtered in the cold. "Come on, girl," she urged the VW as the engine finally warmed up enough to run more smoothly. "Let's go get the boys," she said as she shifted the Beetle into fourth gear.

* * * * * *

Inside the lavishly decorated reception area of Walker, Harrington, Norton & Stone, two well-dressed clients waited nervously to be ushered into a private office setting with their legal counsel. To an unknown person, the two could have been mistaken for brother and sister, considering they both had dark hair, similar complexions, and their mouths turned downward wearing grim expressions. Both were apprehensive, silently staring at the expensive paintings that covered the opposite wall from their seats.

Promptly at 9 o'clock, an administrative assistant entered the lobby from a side door. She perkily announced, "Doctor?" as she looked in Lorenzo's direction. He and Juliana rose from their chairs, acknowledging that they were the party being summoned.

They followed the assistant through the private door and down a long hallway before they were ushered into a small conference room. Within seconds, Perry Norton entered the room and shook Lorenzo's hand and introduced himself to Juliana.

As they seated themselves, Perry picked up the phone sitting mid-table. Without asking his clients of their preferences, he requested a pot of freshly brewed coffee and a pitcher of iced water for the three of them. Juliana thought how much this man reminded her of her father, in some ways. He was decisive and sure of himself. He was in control.

"Now, let's get started, shall we?" Perry remarked as he officially began their meeting. He had a yellow legal pad in front of him, and his pen was positioned in his right hand.

 "Thank you for seeing us on such short notice, Mr. Norton," Lorenzo began. "Mrs. Moretti and I have recently suffered tragic losses in our respective families. We're here together because we believe that those losses may somehow be connected. We're here for legal advice."

Looking up from his legal pad where he had written the clients' names and the date, he put down his pen.

"Let's suspend the formalities, if that's agreeable to you. Please call me 'Perry,' and I'd like to refer to you both by your first names... if you have no objections," Perry said as he tried to make the anxious clients feel more at ease. Both nodded agreement to Perry's request.

As if on cue, a clerk rolled in a serving cart loaded with the coffee, water, and breakfast rolls. Perry poured three cups of coffee, serving them to his

clients and placing his own cup next to his legal pad. Everyone passed on the breakfast rolls but gladly accepted the coffee.

When they were settled once more, Perry said, "So, tell me what's brought you here today."

Juliana's eyes locked with Lorenzo's, as if mentally deciding who should start the conversation. Lorenzo took the lead.

"Well, it's a long story," Lorenzo started.

* * * * * *

Three hours and two pots of coffee later, both Lorenzo and Juliana had finished their recitations. Lorenzo was careful not to incriminate himself in the kidnapping of his son or his wife's death. Juliana kept insisting that she had no prior knowledge of her father's kidnapping scheme or his criminal affiliations.

Somewhere near the mid-point of the meeting, Lorenzo had played the "deathbed confession" tape of Vincenzo DeLuca. As Perry heard the revelations, he became more and more agitated as he listened to the Viper's unemotional voice. Throughout the entire recording, Vincenzo DeLuca's voice sounded proud of his accomplishments, as though he was reciting a long Bible verse instead of voicing remorse for past crimes.

This vile man is a menace to innocent people—to society as a whole, Perry couldn't help but think.

When all the information had been covered, Perry sat back in his chair and crossed his arms over his chest. His clients were unaware that he had more insight into the chain of events than they could possibly imagine.

Forming his next words carefully, he asked for clarification on those parts of the story that didn't quite match what Tony Caprio had confessed to Caroline. "Lorenzo, your cousin worked for Mr. DeLuca, and through him

you accumulated a large gambling debt to Mr. DeLuca; however, you didn't have the available cash to pay the debt by the deadline. Is that correct?" Perry asked.

"Yes," Lorenzo answered, looking very much ashamed of himself.

"All right. Tony, your cousin, was aware of your pregnant wife's approaching delivery date, and told Mr. DeLuca about the expected twins. On his own volition—and without your knowledge— Mr. DeLuca instructed some members of his employ to abduct one of your babies. He wanted a grandson, and arranged to have the baby taken to his daughter, Juliana. Am I still correctly stating the situation?" Perry inquired.

Both Juliana and Lorenzo nodded.

"Good. Now, Juliana. The Giordano baby was brought to you, but on your way home, your husband had an accident. You were both knocked unconscious and taken by ambulance to the emergency room. When you awoke, there was no mention of a baby being transported from the scene. You met briefly with your father after you were discharged, and he was upset that you had 'lost' the baby. However, he told you he would take care of it. In your mind, you assumed he would track down the baby and return it to you. After that, you would have adopted the baby legally, or at least that was your thinking, correct?" he asked again.

Juliana lowered her head and nodded. "But I didn't know the baby was kidnapped. Like I told Lorenzo, I thought Papa had gotten him from an orphanage. He always knew how to cut through red tape and get things done," she replied, now visibly becoming upset again.

Perry smiled, "I understand, Juliana." He took a sip of water. "I think I have the whole picture, now. I'm going to need a little time to review my notes and to formulate solid legal counsel. In the meantime, I would suggest that you contact me immediately if either of you is called for questioning by local or federal law enforcement officers. Meanwhile, I'd

like to hold on to the tape recording and have it copied and transcribed...with your permission, of course."

Juliana started to object, but Lorenzo touched her arm as if to silence her.

Lorenzo responded, "Do you plan to release the tape to anyone?"

Perry shook his head. "No, this tape is not my property—it's yours. If you prefer to take it with you, I understand." Perry held the tape out to Lorenzo.

"No, that's all right. You keep it here with your notes. How long will it be before we hear from you?" Lorenzo inquired.

"Can you two be back here tomorrow afternoon...say, one o'clock? I think I can have my research completed by that time," Perry said.

"Yes," Juliana eagerly replied, and Lorenzo agreed.

"Fine. Until tomorrow at one o'clock, then," Perry said as he led them out of the conference room and to the lobby door.

* * * * * *

Caroline sat staring at the two urns in front of her on the kitchen table, where they had remained since she returned from the mortician's office. She had meticulously wiped the separate gold name plates free of fingerprints before she attached them to the urns' wooden bases, making certain she had the right names with the right ashes.

For the last three hours, she had talked, laughed, cried, and cycled through those same emotions more than once. She had spoken every stray thought that crossed her mind concerning the two men who had loved her unconditionally. Finally, she sat quietly, drained and exhausted.

When Perry entered the house, Caroline didn't move from her spot. Lightheartedly, he commented, "I see we have house guests," but his comment didn't evoke a similar response from Caroline.

As he shed his coat and scarf, Perry realized his humor didn't fit the somber occasion. He poured himself a glass of orange juice and joined Caroline at the table.

Caroline finally broke the silence, telling Perry about her last few hours alone. "I think I finally released a lot of my bottled-up feelings today," she said in a flat voice.

"I'm glad. Maybe you can put your mind at ease now that there's no more pressure about DNA or positive identifications," Perry responded. "I expect you're in the clear now that the police have released the bodies, and we've provided them with an alibi for Tuesday evening."

"But it's **not** over, Perry," she said emphatically. "I'll never get my mind right until the deaths of John and Mike have been avenged," she said through clenched teeth. "I don't even know if anyone is still after me. But, it's definitely **not** over."

As he set the empty juice glass down in front of him, he reached across the table to take Caroline's hand.

"I believe we have the means and the knowledge to wrap this up, Caroline. Let me fill you in on today's meeting with Lorenzo Giordano and Juliana DeLuca Moretti," he said comfortingly.

"You were only supposed to help me get through **this** awful part," Caroline said as she glanced at the urns. "You're not obligated to do anything else, Perry."

"Nothing would make me happier than for unspeakable revenge to fall on the person responsible for all this carnage. And I think when you hear

what I've learned today—the rest of the story, that is—you'll understand why I'm almost as passionate about this as you are."

* * * * * *

Time was running out. Considering the physical recovery the Viper had made since his mild heart attack, there was no good reason for Lorenzo to maintain his heavy sedation. However, there were pros and cons for keeping the Viper knocked out. The pros far outweighed the cons, with the biggest "pro" being that the Viper would disclose Lorenzo helped to plan his own baby's abduction and covered up his wife's death.

* * * * * *

It was already close to 5 o'clock, and Lucinda had regained some of her memories and was talking more without making herself hoarse. Even though she still wore the big sunglasses, her eyes were finally more accustomed to the ambient lighting in the room.

Juliana had been by her mother's side ever since she had returned from the attorney's office with Lorenzo. In between short conversations about how things had changed during the last two years, Lucinda would occasionally express apprehension about her husband's angry intent to harm her. Even though Juliana would remind her that Vincenzo was sedated, it was obvious that Lucinda wanted him to never wake up.

* * * * * *

Miss Elmore and the Giordano children arrived shortly after noon that same day, bringing with them several suitcases and packed boxes of the children's toys and necessities. As promised, Lorenzo had prearranged for a crib and toddler bed to be delivered, plus a similar nursery arrangement of changing table and rocking chair for use in the opposite guest wing of the DeLuca mansion. The nanny had an adjoining room to the one the children were to share.

On occasional breaks from her mother's room, Juliana visited the children, just to make sure they were settled in. Remembering what she had heard from Lorenzo and from her father's tape, she felt a strong bond to Ricky, the brother of the baby she had 'lost' so shortly after he was delivered to her. Every chance Juliana got, she would pick Ricky up and hold him, even rock him if the nanny would allow it. It was evident that Juliana wanted another chance to bond with a newborn.

Juliana also found Sophia delightful, with beautiful plump cheeks and a captivating smile. She giggled often, and rarely cried. Sophia had the personality of a little comedian, always wanting her playmate to laugh as she did. Just looking into the little girl's twinkling eyes made Juliana's heart melt.

The closeness she was feeling to the Giordano family seemed natural and unforced. She had never felt so comfortable in a family situation before. She hoped in time, Lorenzo would feel the same way. She admired him so very much. And he was a charming, handsome man. That didn't hurt at all.

* * * * * *

It didn't take long after dinner for Juliana to find Lorenzo in the sunroom, sitting on the same divan where the two had taken to having their serious conversations. He already had two fingers of scotch poured in the crystal glass and offered to make her a drink as she entered the room. She accepted a cocktail.

"So, how did you feel about the meeting with the attorney today, Juliana?" Lorenzo asked as he swirled his scotch around in the glass.

"I thought he was very nice, but I couldn't read him very well. What do you think he plans to do?" she asked.

"We're his clients, so we're his first priority. If he has to take evidence to the police to save us from prosecution, that will put your father at risk, of course. If your mother wants to charge him with attempted murder for pushing her down the stairs, that would be up to her. There are a number of crimes your father confessed to in that recording," Lorenzo mused. "How do you feel about what might happen to him if this goes any further?"

Juliana took a sip of her cocktail. "Honestly, I'm torn. He's my father, and he's always been good to me. But apparently he's evil, too. Otherwise, he wouldn't have just killed Diego to get rid of him. I thought he paid him money to leave, which is bad enough. But he killed him, and that's a hard thing to forgive. And to think he took your baby…and your poor wife couldn't deal with it…and now she's dead, too. It scares me to think Papa somehow made that happen, but I believe he must have. If he's that evil, I hope he never wakes up. Mama's in agony, afraid that he will," she said, now crying and upset.

"Your father is in a precarious state right now. It's possible he could have another heart attack, even more serious than the first. You know that's a possibility for a man his age and in his condition," Lorenzo said, matter-of-factly, even though he knew he was exaggerating.

"If he had a fatal heart attack, I would consider it God's will. I can't judge him—he's my Papa—but Mama's scared to death he's going to put her back in a coma or kill her. Either way, she'll have no life left in her. If she continues to recover and he's alert again, she'll always be looking over her shoulder, fearing the worst, even if he doesn't try anything again. I wouldn't want to have her life if that's the way it had to be." Juliana finished her cocktail and set the glass on a coaster atop a marble table.

"I understand that completely. I guess whatever happens will be God's will, then," Lorenzo said as he got up to refill his scotch.

* * * * *

That evening when everyone else was in bed, Lorenzo decided to stay up late so he could check on Vincenzo without interruption. He came into the darkened room and flipped on the lamp next to the hospital bed. Sitting in the Viper's favorite chair made him feel powerful. He stared at Vincenzo who had not moved since the light had been turned on in his face.

"Vincenzo, can you hear me," Lorenzo whispered. "You should be in a sort of twilight sleep right now. I adjusted the flow of your meds earlier, so I'll wait for you to wake up."

Lorenzo leaned back in the chair and thought about what had to be done. He needed to set Lucinda free, and he had the opportunity to do it. He needed to allow Juliana to have a life of her own, and he had the power to do that, too. He needed to eliminate the only person left who knew Lorenzo had been a party to a kidnapping and cover-up of his wife's death—and God only knows what's happened to Genevieve. He had to clear the slate for the DeLuca women and for himself. Otherwise, there would be more murder, more injustice, and prison—Oh, God—Lorenzo knew he wouldn't make it in prison if he was implicated. He knew what power he wielded and he **had** to use it.

"Ummm," Vincenzo murmured.

"Vincenzo, can you hear me?" he asked again. This time it appeared Vincenzo was trying to open his eyes.

"Whaaa…" Vincenzo was still dazed. His speech was slurred. "Wherrree am I?" he asked.

"Remember you had a heart attack, Vincenzo. Remember you told me everything you knew about my baby's whereabouts, about Tony and Carlo, Diego and even your wife? Remember?" Lorenzo asked playfully.

"No...I didn't say any-thing." The Viper was trying to go back to sleep.

Slapping him hard on the face, Lorenzo said, "Of course you did, and I have it on tape. Juliana's already heard it, and we went to see a lawyer today. I think you might be living the rest of your life in prison unless I decide to help you."

The Viper tried to focus on Lorenzo's face, but he was seeing double. "I...I...don't un-der-stand," he said slowly.

"You don't have to understand anything. All you have to do is go back to sleep and leave the rest to me. Is that agreeable to you?" Lorenzo smiled.

The Viper's eyes were still heavy, and he nodded. "Let me sleep a little longer," he managed to say clearly.

"That was my plan, Vincenzo. That was the plan all along," Lorenzo said.

Walking across the room to retrieve his medical bag, Lorenzo thought about what he was going to do. *You'll be no better than him if you do this!* But for once, Lorenzo felt the power. He had to relieve the world of this devil.

From the bag, he withdrew a syringe of liquid Potassium Chloride and walked to Vincenzo's bedside. As he injected the overdose, he knew that within minutes the Viper's heart spasms would be out of control, and his heart would just stop working. It would result in Sudden Cardiac Death.

Even if an autopsy was performed, there would be no elevated blood levels of potassium that could be attributable to anything but what the damaged muscle tissue released into his blood stream, which would be considered normal under the circumstances.

Lorenzo wrapped the empty syringe in a wad of tissue and returned it to his bag. He planned to dispose of it at the hospital where the Viper would be taken by ambulance once his condition was noticed—provided of course, his condition was noticed sooner rather than later. He could drop the needle in the contaminated syringe box that was handy in almost every ER or hospital room. If that wasn't an option, he could always go by his office and dispose of it in one of their exam room depositories. Regardless, it wouldn't be a problem.

All he had to do was wait. He'd slip into his bedroom and retire for the night, he decided. Let someone else find the Viper in the throes of a fatal heart attack.

CHAPTER 40

Tuesday, December 13, 1994

The DeLuca's attending nurse burst through Lorenzo's bedroom door without knocking. She was alarmed, and her voice was shaky as she shook his shoulders. With his back to the door and feigning sleep, Lorenzo had expected her—or someone—to make a dramatic entry into his bedroom during the night.

"Doctor, Doctor! Come quick! I think Mr. DeLuca is dead!" she spoke loudly as she shook his shoulder.

"What?" Lorenzo said, as he turned to face her, pretending he hadn't heard her clearly.

"Mr. DeLuca! I went in to check on him at 2:00 a.m. and his monitor showed a flat line. Please hurry, Doctor!" she said as she stood there anxiously.

"Go get Mrs. Moretti. I'll meet you in the den as soon as I get dressed," he commanded, running his fingers through his hair. The nurse raced out his door.

Finally. Put on your best doctor face, Lorenzo. The show is about to begin.

* * * * * *

No more than an hour later, Lorenzo comforted a sobbing Juliana as they stood in the DeLuca mansion's foyer, watching the EMTs carefully roll the

lifeless body out of the house. The corpse of Vincenzo DeLuca was covered from head to toe with a thick white sheet. The Viper would soon be on his way to the morgue.

"I can't believe it. Last night I was saying awful things about Papa. It's as if God is punishing me by making those things come true," Juliana sniveled as she watched the morbid parade pass her by.

"This is not your doing, Juliana. Remember, we talked about 'God's will' last night? You can't control the life or death of another person through wishing. You have to understand, it was your father's time to go. He knew how much you loved him. Don't ever think differently."

She stared at the back of the ambulance as the EMTs shut the rear doors to the vehicle. As she stood there, Lorenzo put his arm around her shoulder in a comforting gesture as the vehicle pulled away from the house. She leaned into his body, feeling his warmth and the security of his embrace.

* * * * * *

When the office called Perry at home, he had already finished his continental breakfast and was gulping down the last few drops of coffee. It was barely past 8 o'clock, and his first scheduled meeting was set for noon. He had called a staff meeting to re-introduce Caroline to the office employees—this time as his 'love interest.' They were both nervous, but the meeting was necessary, and they were ready for it to be behind them.

"When did this happen?" Perry said into the phone as Caroline entered the room. She paused momentarily, wondering if there had been another murder. They were so common lately.

"Yes, of course. If they believe they can be finished by 1 o'clock, we'll see them then or as soon as they can make it. Thanks," Perry said as he hung up the phone.

He looked at Caroline with a surprised expression. "So, now the plot thickens. Vincenzo DeLuca had a massive heart attack during the night. He didn't survive. Our clients may be a few minutes late to our meeting, considering they're working with the coroner and others this morning." He took a deep breath. "Perhaps you and I need to rethink our future plans. Our strategy is still good, but we may need to revise our tactics."

Caroline nodded. "Okay. I don't think it changes that much, but I'm all ears."

"I have to remind you, Caroline. Once we start this, there's no turning back. We are both committed for however long it takes to finish it…even if it takes years. Are you *absolutely* certain you can make that commitment?"

"Absolutely," she said without hesitation.

Perry smiled at Caroline's determined face. "Good, then let's fine-tune our plans. We don't have long."

* * * * * *

At noon, Perry and Caroline walked hand in hand into the law office's large conference room. Perry was beaming, just as any excited man would in the presence of his beloved. Caroline smiled timidly to the crowd as she approached the head of the table to stand by Perry's side.

"Hello, everyone! I'm excited to welcome Caroline back into our midst. As you know, she had to take several days off to handle some very tragic personal matters. However, she is back now and ready to face the future with us." Some employees smiled, others started to clap, and Caroline nodded her head slightly to acknowledge their welcome.

Perry continued, "One thing we would both like to clarify is this: You may hear or read news that implies Caroline and I are partners in a very

personal relationship. We'd like to provide you with the truth, so that there are no doubts when and if you are privy to such information." The employees were attentive, expecting to hear Perry's vehement denial.

"It's true. We have had a personal relationship for some time, but we both believed that it would be in our best interests not to reveal that relationship to anyone." Some members of the audience gasped as Perry continued. "We have had a little fun at your expense, I'm afraid, by trying to give the impression that we cared very little for each other while working together. In fact, it was and still is quite the opposite." Perry glanced briefly at Caroline who smiled back at him.

"Caroline and I plan to be married sometime next year. Meanwhile, she continues to be a permanent resident at my home."

Perry stopped and surveyed the audience's reaction. Most were stunned, mouths open slightly, trying to comprehend what they had just been told. Others were smirking, trying to figure out how the old man had snagged such a young, vulnerable fiancé. A few were openly happy, thinking Caroline could finally be content with someone like Perry Norton to take care of her.

"One other thing Caroline has asked me to convey. She will immediately drop her former married name in favor of her maiden name. From today forward, please refer to Caroline as 'Caroline Lewis.' She has yet to decide if she will retain her maiden name after our marriage, but I don't take that as an insult," he chuckled. "So many independent-minded, strong women do that nowadays, and Caroline is certainly that kind of woman," he laughed again as Caroline continued her timid act.

"So, we hope you are happy for us, and are thankful we don't have to keep up our charade here in the office," Perry laughed, as he pulled Caroline to him and kissed her on the cheek.

The audience erupted in applause, with a few employees coming forward to congratulate the couple on their upcoming nuptials. Most, however, found their way back to their appointed workstations or offices, all silently wondering how long such a marriage could possibly last.

* * * * * *

It was almost 1:30 p.m. when Lorenzo and Juliana were ushered into the conference room already occupied by Caroline and Perry.

"Please forgive us for being so late. We had paperwork to complete and so many arrangements had to be made. It's been hectic since the early hours of the morning," Lorenzo stated, acting as though he were out of breath.

Juliana sat down next to Lorenzo, immediately reaching for his arm as if she needed stability. Both Perry and Caroline noticed the semblance of affection, but neither commented.

Perry began with the introductions, "I'd like to introduce you to my paralegal, Caroline Lewis, who also happens to be my fiancé. Caroline, this is Dr. Lorenzo Giordano and Mrs. Juliana Moretti." Caroline mumbled her hellos, as Lorenzo and Juliana responded in kind.

"We are both very sorry for the loss of your father, Juliana. I realize he had recently suffered a mild heart attack, but I was surprised to hear he had passed. Our condolences," Perry said as Caroline nodded in agreement.

"Thank you both," Juliana said robotically.

Lorenzo wanted to make certain there was no misunderstanding about Mr. DeLuca's death. "Yes, as you know, sometimes a mild heart attack is just a warning signal. Even though Mr. DeLuca had been resting

comfortably and making some progress, apparently the first cardiac event did more damage to his heart than first diagnosed at the hospital. It was unexpected and sudden."

"I'm sure," Perry commented. "If there is anything I can help you with regarding the estate or any part of the probate process, feel free to contact me," he said as he looked kindly to Juliana.

"Now, shall we get on with today's meeting? I'm sure you are both tired and anxious to get out of offices and meetings so you can catch your breath. So, we'll be brief," Perry stated as he motioned to Caroline to disperse documents.

Caroline slid copies of the transcribed recording of Vincenzo's "deathbed confession" across the table to Lorenzo and Juliana. Each picked up a copy and read it once more.

Perry was eager to present his proposal. "Yesterday when you were here, I heard this tape and immediately wondered how you, Juliana, would fare if this recording were presented to the police. It might have appeared that you were betraying your family. I wasn't sure you would have been completely sold on that idea. Even if burying the tape meant you might have been implicated somehow in your own husband's death—for example, you *asked* your father to get rid of Diego—I still believe you would have been hesitant to 'rat' on your father.

"Which makes the timing of Vincenzo DeLuca's death a blessing in disguise for you both. Forgive me, but now that your father is no longer subject to trial and punishment, it should be easier for you to do the right thing. In this case, I believe we should arrange a meeting with the Sheriff and the FBI Unit Section Chief and play them the tape. They will ask you the same questions I did, and perhaps a few more, but we can prepare for that. Coming forward voluntarily and explaining everything you know—and don't know—will help the law enforcement officials close their

investigations that are currently plaguing them. This tape clarifies at least three open cases that I am aware of, maybe more." Perry finished by leaning back in his chair and crossing his arms on his chest.

Lorenzo wasn't smiling, and neither was Juliana. In fact, they both seemed nervous and disturbed. "Do you really think that's necessary?" Lorenzo asked.

"What did you expect me to be able to do for you, Lorenzo?" Perry furrowed his brow. "You have information that was a 'deathbed confession,' to use your terms. It was recorded without the knowledge of Mr. DeLuca. You brought it to me and wanted advice because you believe your abducted baby was the one Juliana had in her car when they wrecked. You seem to be ignoring the other crimes that Mr. DeLuca confessed to that are actively being investigated right now by the very people who have recently talked to both of you.

"My advice is to turn the tape over to the authorities and have your attorney there, too. If they ask questions that are out of line, that's when the attorney steps in. If they try to arrest you for accessory to kidnapping, murder, aiding and abetting a criminal, obstruction of justice, or any number of things, that's where the attorney takes over. My advice to you is to get out in front of this and do not be perceived as trying to hide anything," Perry was becoming agitated and it showed.

Juliana looked scared now. She had heard too many charges that sounded threatening, and she was too young to go to jail. She looked at Lorenzo as if he had all the answers.

Lorenzo finally said, "All right. But not today. Juliana and I have both been through enough for one day. If you feel strongly that the police need the tape's contents to solve cases they're working on now, go ahead and let them have copies of the transcript. But Juliana and I have several commitments to fulfill before we can meet with anyone else. We're

trying to plan a funeral, you know. And with Mrs. DeLuca gaining consciousness, it's going to be even more trying."

Perry stopped shuffling papers. Looking straight at Lorenzo, he said, "I thought Mrs. DeLuca was in a coma and had been for several years. Is she awake now that her husband is dead?"

Juliana volunteered, "Yes, she's been trying to wake up for a few days. Lorenzo made that happen. He's performed a miracle for us. Mama's still weak and frail, but she seems to have most of her memories back. She'll have to have physical therapy to get mobile again. Right, Lorenzo?"

"That's right. She's making good progress. We're thankful that her long-term nurse was a stickler for exercising Mrs. DeLuca's limbs on a daily basis. Because of that, she hasn't lost as much muscle tone as most comatose patients do. She's very fortunate to have had that advantage." Lorenzo smiled.

"Wonderful news for you, Juliana," Perry smiled. "It's quite a coincidence that you get your mother back but lose your father, all within days of each other."

"There are so many adjustments ahead, Perry. But with Lorenzo's help, we'll manage. He has been a blessing to our family in so many ways," she said as she stared warmly into Lorenzo's eyes.

Awkwardly, Perry broke the spell. "Well, then. I'll get in touch with Sheriff Harvey and FBI Chief McNeal to let them know the transcript is on the way. Once they have the text, I may have to explain how I came to have it in my possession, but you two will have to provide the details attached to the confessions, just as you did here with me yesterday. The officers may want to rush the meeting so they can close their cases, so be prepared to be pressured. If they call you directly, just tell them that the meeting has to be coordinated through me."

Lorenzo agreed. It was apparent that Juliana concurred with anything Lorenzo said or suggested.

"Great. Caroline, would you please see that the transcripts of Mr. DeLuca's recording are forwarded immediately to the appropriate law enforcement officials? Let them know that Dr. Giordano and Mrs. Moretti will be available for personal interviews immediately after the funeral of Mr. DeLuca has taken place—most likely next week."

Caroline nodded and wrote down the instructions on her notepad. "Got it," she responded.

As if Caroline's response had been a formal dismissal, Lorenzo and Juliana stood. As they gathered their things, Caroline caught Juliana's eye. They smiled at each other as Caroline stood and made her way around the table to Juliana's side.

"I'm very sorry about your father, but it certainly is a blessing to hear about your mother. You know what they say, 'when one door closes, another door opens,'" Caroline said comfortingly.

Juliana unexpectedly hugged Caroline. "Thank you. I really mean it. I think Perry is blessed to have you in his life, too." As she released Caroline, Juliana sniffed and reached for a tissue. For some reason, Caroline felt a sudden attachment to Juliana. She could see how Lorenzo might feel the same way toward this sorrowful waif.

Sacrificial Sins

CHAPTER 41

Friday, December 16, 1994

The past few days had been hectic for the DeLuca family. So many decisions had to be made in so little time, but Lorenzo was more than willing to take charge. Juliana had already become emotionally dependent on him, which had been his unspoken goal.

Neither Juliana nor Lucinda objected to cremation of Vincenzo's remains, so that had to be arranged. A memorial service also had to be planned, and it was easy to persuade the two DeLuca women to make it small and private.

The memorial service took place on Friday, with a small gathering of thirty or so friends and family members, including a few of Vincenzo's top "family"employees. Naturally, the butler attended and a handful of the household staff; however, considering Vincenzo's considerable number of followers, the invited group was extremely small. The service was well organized but brief.

Lucinda had been able to attend, only because Lorenzo had insisted that a wheelchair would make the trip feasible. She allowed him to navigate her chair throughout the entire event, leaving Juliana free to shake hands and accept condolences on behalf of the family.

During the service Lucinda never spoke, only nodded to the attendees if they addressed her. Lorenzo was there to explain that she had only recently recovered enough to physically attend, but that her voice was

still strained. Everyone accepted the good doctor's explanation and moved on to Juliana to express their sympathies.

The service went smoothly, as anticipated. Shortly thereafter, Lucinda was back in her bed and Juliana was at her bedside. Mother and daughter silently grieved—and perhaps, rejoiced—that there was no longer a silent threat hanging over Lucinda's newfound life.

* * * * * *

Unable to attend the memorial service, Caroline and Perry stood at the mansion's front door with casserole in tow. Caroline rang the bell while Perry tried not to drop the unpleasantly hot dish covered in aluminum foil.

The butler opened the door, saw the casserole, and took it from Perry as he ushered the guests into the foyer. The hot dish didn't seem to affect the butler's hands, and Perry watched in amazement as the butler firmly grasped the casserole and never flinched.

Juliana appeared in the foyer before the butler had a chance to announce the guests. "I heard the doorbell. I'm so glad you're here," she said as she embraced Caroline. "Thank you for coming," she continued as she held out her hand to Perry.

"We're so sorry we couldn't make it to the service. I hope you understand. But we brought you some food for later. It's Perry's favorite, and we wanted to share it with you," Caroline said softly. "It's his mother's recipe for manicotti, and it's scrumptious."

"You're so thoughtful. Thank you so much. We'll have it for dinner tonight. I know Lorenzo will enjoy it," she responded, as if Lorenzo were now a permanent resident of the household.

Caroline could sense that Juliana was struggling with whether or not to invite them to stay. "Juliana, we need to run, but we just wanted to let you know we're here if you need us, and not just as your legal team," She touched Juliana's arm tenderly.

"Right now, I need a friend. I hope you and I can make that happen, Caroline. I'm looking forward to getting all this chaos behind me and having a normal life again, whatever that is," Juliana smiled.

Caroline smiled broadly. "I'd like that. Let's make it happen. Now go back to what you were doing before we interrupted you. Stay strong and have faith that the future ahead is bright," she said as she initiated the goodbye embrace with her new friend. Perry, feeling awkward, merely stood back as the ladies began their bonding process.

* * * * * *

"I would have liked to have met Juliana's mother," Caroline mused as she and Perry drove away from the DeLuca home.

"There will be plenty of time for that," Perry said as he maneuvered the Bentley smoothly through Southampton. "The way I see it, you and I are about to become recurring visitors at the DeLuca residence. And, they may become frequent visitors at our home, too. I've been thinking that we should start redecorating the house a little more toward your taste."

"Sure, let's go spend some of your money," Caroline laughed and patted his arm.

"You are going to make an excellent partner, Caroline. You already show a healthy knack for spending my money," he chuckled as he grinned and steered the car toward the nearest upscale shopping area.

* * * * * *

Later that evening, after a delicious dinner of Caroline's and Perry's manicotti—plus sides and salads prepared by the DeLuca chef—Juliana and Lorenzo made their way back to the sunroom for their evening cocktail. This had now become their routine. The room gave them privacy and an air of coziness that seemed to suit them both.

Juliana sat next to Lorenzo, only inches apart from each other. "You know, I really do like Caroline. She seems very genuine. I hope we can become good friends. It's always been hard for me to form close relationships with other women. Usually, they are jealous of my comfortable life or are just petty over the least little things. I don't think Caroline is that kind of person."

"She seems nice enough, but she seems a little young for Perry. I wonder what the attraction is," Lorenzo commented absently.

"A lot of women need mature men in their lives. She's probably ready for someone like Perry to be an equal partner. You never know. But if it makes them both happy, I'm all for it." She took another long drink of her cocktail.

"True. I know Cathy never liked taking the backseat to my career, even though I suppose I never really acknowledged that she felt that way. Trying to be successful and provide for your family can be a great goal, but with success sometimes comes absence. I'm not sure I was that great of a husband to her. I wish I could go back and change a few things. I know if I had it to do over, I would make some big changes. Maybe someday I'll have that chance with someone else." Lorenzo finished his drink and rose from the divan to get a refill.

Juliana watched him carefully. In an attempt to make him feel better, she spoke her mind. "I think you'd make a wonderful husband, Lorenzo. Any

woman would be stupid to pass you up. You're just going through a major emotional adjustment right now. Don't sell yourself short."

He turned his head to face her as he stood with drink in hand. "You're too kind, Juliana. But I've made my share of mistakes, and some of them I don't think I'll ever be able to forgive myself for. You don't understand how tortured I really am." He swallowed his refill with a big gulp, as he made his way back to the divan.

"Lorenzo, I understand. Believe me, I do. You're describing me...exactly. I can empathize. If you knew the true me, you'd probably never speak to me again."

"That's funny, because I was just thinking that myself. If you knew what I've been a part of, you'd hate me," he replied as he sat down next to her. He immediately bent over and held his head in his hands, wondering if he should try to cry to make Juliana more sympathetic.

Juliana rubbed his back. "I guarantee you, there's nothing you could say that would ever make me feel that way."

With his elbows still propped on his knees, Lorenzo glanced around at Juliana. "Maybe we need to be honest with each other, Juliana. I admit that I'm attracted to you, and I want to have you in my life. But I won't move forward unless I *know* you accept me for who I am and what I've done."

Juliana raised her hand and placed her palm over her lips in an expression of amazement. "Oh, Lorenzo. I can't tell you how happy you've just made me. I feel the same way about you. If we need to bare our souls to each other for a chance to be together, I'll gladly do it. I will be completely honest with you. Will you do that with me?"

Lorenzo silently hoped he was making the right decision. "I'll try. Maybe I need another drink first."

*** ***

Sheriff Harvey and FBI Chief McNeal had been going over the DeLuca "confession" in such detail, they were tired of picking it apart.

"Don't you think this statement is a little disjointed? There's no one talking but DeLuca, and I get that. But it's almost like there's no transition between separate confessions. It's like he's reading a prepared statement or a grocery list. I don't know…something just seems a little off," McNeal commented.

"You have to admit, if it's a deathbed confession, maybe he felt like he should be in a hurry. But it's not like Giordano is a priest or anything. Why confess to him?" Sheriff Harvey wondered. "Do you suppose Dr. Giordano had anything to do with DeLuca's death? Maybe the doctor forced him to say these things right before he did something to kill him?"

McNeal studied the paper again. "I don't know. Could be. Could be any number of reasons this confession so conveniently turned up. I guess we'll have to wait 'til Monday to find out. Perry Norton asked us to come to his office at 1:00 p.m. to meet with Giordano and DeLuca's daughter. Are you up to it, sheriff?"

"Wouldn't miss it," Sheriff Harvey said with a mischievous smile.

*** ***

Juliana quietly cried as she listened to what Lorenzo had to say. Clearly, it was hard for him to admit that he had willingly allowed her father to abduct his newborn son. She had watched him rant and cry and recognized the shame in his eyes. She felt sorry for him and totally understood how a man like Lorenzo could succumb to the threats of a man like her father.

"Juliana, I thought there was no other way. Tony told me that your father expected me to make the kidnapping go easily. If I didn't, I risked the safety of my entire family. He said I could either cooperate, or they'd eventually take the baby anyway. All this because I was weak, gambled, and got in over my head. I didn't have the cash, and they used it against me. I blame Tony as much as your father."

"My father was a very powerful man. I know that. He had ways of making people do what he wanted, and I always knew that, too. I never wanted to admit that to myself, because it meant I should feel guilty about my lifestyle," she acknowledged.

"But to sacrifice my own child..." he retorted, still weeping as he spoke.

"It was a child you had not bonded with—it could have been any baby. Please, Lorenzo..."

"But look what this stupid plan did to my wife! She was just as innocent as the baby," he sobbed.

"You don't know what happened to your wife...do you?" Juliana hesitantly asked.

Lorenzo tightly closed his eyes. "Yes, I do know. She killed herself right in front of me, and I panicked. I loaded her body in her car and drove to see your father. He 'took care' of disposing of her body. He took her car, too, and told me to make sure everyone believed she just left on her own accord. Juliana, I'm so sorry I lied to you about that. Please forgive me, but I didn't want you to blame me or your father, either." Lorenzo continued to choke back his emotions.

"Oh, dear God. Lorenzo, you weren't thinking right, and then you got yourself in deeper. Please forgive yourself, Lorenzo. Please!" Juliana pleaded.

"I can't forgive myself unless you forgive me, too. I never realized how weak and selfish I was until I got myself tangled up with your father," he dramatically said.

"I forgive you, if you forgive me for what I did. Deep down, I knew the baby couldn't have come from an orphanage. Papa wasn't the kind of man to try to do the right thing. If he wanted something, he took it. I figured he had done that with the baby—just taken one away from someone. I didn't care. I just wanted my own baby," she said as she lowered her head. "I'm sorry for that, I truly am," she whispered.

"You didn't know, Juliana. I still blame your father for trying to play God. He meddled in too many lives, and he caused too many people to suffer. I'm glad he's dead, if I'm being honest," Lorenzo admitted.

Juliana bowed her head as if she were praying. She uttered exactly what Lorenzo wanted her to say, "I'm glad he's dead, too."

He went to her and embraced her tightly. "Juliana, there's one thing I want you to promise me. You can never tell anyone else what you said about where the baby came from. Everyone should think you thought the baby came from an orphanage. Never let anyone else know you had the slightest suspicion that your father had taken a baby illegally for you. Never."

"Okay. I promise. Not even Mama. But I'm worried about you. How are we going to face the police on Monday?" she asked with a hint of fear in her voice.

"I'll be doing all the talking, and I have an idea about that. If you want to hear it, we'll discuss it. But it might be best if you hear it for the first time when we're in Perry's office."

"I don't like surprises. Tell me now," she demanded, preparing herself for something she was afraid she didn't want to hear.

Sacrificial Sins

CHAPTER 42

Monday, December 19, 1994

Thirty minutes before their scheduled meeting with FBI Chief McNeal and Sheriff Harvey, Perry and his clients sat solemnly around the conference room table at his law office. Caroline was nowhere in sight, believing it was better if she postponed meeting with any policemen until she was certain Mike's murder case was officially behind her.

"Are you sure you want to do this, Lorenzo?" Perry asked his client. "There's no guaranteed positive outcome, you understand."

"I don't think there's any way to skirt it. If there's a chance I can start over and put all this behind me, I think this is the only way," the doctor answered. Juliana sat by his side, crying silently and clutching Lorenzo's handkerchief.

"All right. That's the approach we'll take," Perry sighed as he scribbled frantically on his legal pad.

* * * * * *

The small conference room became crowded when Sheriff Harvey and FBI Chief McNeal joined the group. Papers were spread across the table, courtesy of McNeal, who brought every open FBI case file he could collect that had ever been linked to Vincenzo DeLuca. He was anxious to get the meeting underway, hoping that the doctor and the daughter could shed light on the unsolved crimes.

Perry kicked off the session by providing a brief summary of his first meeting with his clients. He explained that Vincenzo DeLuca had been lucid the day following his heart attack and asked Lorenzo (his attending

physician at the time) to hear something he had to say. Expecting it to be instructions regarding his estate, Lorenzo used his pocket dictation equipment to record it to ensure Vincenzo's orders were understood correctly and fully. Once the doctor started the recording, he realized his patient was making a criminal confession instead of instructions about his assets. Soon after, Mr. DeLuca became agitated, and sedation was administered to calm him. Two days later, Mr. DeLuca succumbed to a massive heart attack.

Both the sheriff and McNeal nodded after Perry's summation, indicating their understanding of the situation and creation of the tape.

"The sheriff and I were hoping you could shed some light on the contents of the tape," McNeal said, looking back and forth between Juliana and Lorenzo.

Perry interrupted before either of his clients had a chance to respond. "Yes, we realize that. And that is precisely why I asked to have the meeting here in my law offices. Dr. Giordano believes he may have some insight into some of these crimes. As you may be aware, his cousin, Tony Caprio, worked directly for Mr. DeLuca. Also, his missing wife's body was recently found at the New Jersey crime scene that you are currently investigating.

"Mr. DeLuca's daughter, Mrs. Moretti, has also been recently widowed with the discovery of her husband's body at the same crime scene. She, too, may have similar insights into the illicit activities of her father. Combined, I believe the information they can provide may lead you to solving the open investigations you so eagerly wish to close."

"Sounds like there's a 'but' coming at the end of that," McNeal grinned, anticipating Perry's next sentence.

"Of course, my clients need assurance that they will not be arrested or charged with any crime from which the information provided could

directly or indirectly implicate them. In other words, in exchange for total immunity from prosecution, they will assist you in any way possible to solve your open investigations."

The sheriff and FBI Chief McNeal stared each other down, neither making a comment to Perry. Finally, McNeal asked, "Could you give us a minute, counselor? And, we may need to use your phone."

Perry nodded, and escorted Lorenzo and Juliana out of the conference room and into the hallway, closing the conference room door behind him.

The three stood anxiously several feet away from the closed door. "This is a long shot, you know. I realize you were the only one asking for immunity, Lorenzo; but, it occurred to me we should include Juliana in the initial request. We can always negotiate if they deny us the first time. It's harder to ask for more when an agreement has already been made. But, we'll worry about that after they've made their decision," Perry explained.

His clients solemnly nodded, agreeing that Perry had done the right thing.

Minutes later, the conference room door opened and McNeal stepped out in the hallway, gesturing for the group to return to the room. Perry led his clients back to their seats. They sat quietly, waiting for McNeal to reveal the verdict.

"We have little to go on, here. I would suspect that whatever information your clients can provide may be hearsay or inadmissible in court, should there ever be a trial of other guilty parties." He paused for effect, noting that Lorenzo was shallowly breathing. It seemed as though he had been holding his breath while McNeal spoke.

"However, we believe we have little else to go on now that Mr. DeLuca is deceased, as are some direct members of his crew. Other witnesses may not be brave enough to approach us or would be unwilling to cooperate for whatever reason.

"Considering your willingness and the potential for providing essential information into the crimes that we believe were committed by or on behalf of Mr. DeLuca, we will provide immunity for both your clients. That immunity will be conditional upon their full and complete cooperation into any of the cases you see here in these files." McNeal pushed a stack of files toward Perry. "Mr. Norton, you may take an inventory of these cases which we are investigating that will require your clients' cooperation."

Perry nodded and pulled the files in front of him.

McNeal continued, "Further, neither of you may leave the country—for any reason—during the period that the government requires your assistance. You will both be required to surrender your passports to the government during the assistance period or until such time as the government releases them to you once again.

"If either of you is arrested for *any* criminal act during the period you are assisting the government, your immunity agreement may or may not be revoked by the Department of Justice, at their discretion.

"At some point during these investigations, you may be called upon to testify in a court of law. You will be there willingly, and will answer all questions truthfully under oath. If you believe your life is in danger because of such testimony, you may be required to join the Witness Protection Program managed by the Federal Government.

"When your assistance is no longer required, and the government believes they have all the information that you could completely and honestly reveal, you will receive a document releasing you from requirements of further assistance and verifying your immunity from these specific crimes. Your passports will be returned at that time, unless the Department of Justice or the Department of State can show just cause why they should be retained for a longer period.

"Are you agreeable to these terms?" McNeal asked as he looked sternly at Lorenzo and Juliana.

"Yes," they each said, simultaneously. There was no hesitation.

"Wonderful. Mr. Norton will be receiving documentation of our agreement, and you will each be required to sign. Read it very carefully. If there are any terms stated that you don't agree with, the deal is off. Once the agreement is signed, it is effective immediately. We will be arranging interviews and information sessions as soon as possible. Agreed?"

Everyone nodded, even Perry.

Everyone was satisfied with the outcome—except Perry.

* * * * * *

Caroline waited impatiently in Perry's kitchen, expecting him home at any time. He should have been finished with the Giordano meeting an hour earlier, or so she thought. She paced around between the kitchen and the den, eventually tiring herself and plopping down on the long couch. She picked up a magazine and flipped rapidly through the pages. Finally, she poured herself a glass of chardonnay, anticipating a calming effect that she wished she could immediately feel.

Perry opened the back door and stepped inside, pulling off his coat and scarf as he walked briskly into the kitchen. Caroline looked up with wide eyes. "Well?"

"I'd like a glass of that wine, too, if you don't mind," he said as he sat down at the kitchen table. He looked weary.

Caroline set a chilled glass of Chardonnay in front of Perry. He looked like he needed it.

"Caroline, I suppose I have good news and bad news. The good news is Lorenzo and Juliana were both granted immunity from prosecution in exchange for assisting the FBI with investigation and closure of the DeLuca cases—several of them. It will take a while for that to be completed. The bad news is that this throws a kink in *our* plan. It will be a long time before we're able to execute it without federal interruption or intervention. Can you be patient enough to ride this out?" he asked.

Caroline smiled. "I've got the rest of my life. It's you I'm worried about."

"Don't be concerned about me, dear. I have lots of years left," he countered.

"Well, then. I think we should plan a Valentine's Day wedding, and maybe Lorenzo will agree to be your best man. I'm pretty certain Juliana would agree to be my maid of honor," Caroline giggled.

"You're a witch, Caroline Lewis. I think that's why I like you so much. Shame I wasted all those months at work not really knowing the real 'you.' You're a very special woman," he grinned.

"Thank you very much, and you're a real bastard...which I knew from day one," she laughed, playfully providing insult for insult with her new fiancé.

CHAPTER 43

3 ½ YEARS LATER

June-July, 1998

Juliana Giordano had been summoned by Caroline Norton to meet her downtown for lunch and to help select an appropriate gift for her godson, Teddy Brantley. As had been her custom, Caroline regularly sent gifts to the thriving toddler on special occasions and whenever the mood struck her.

In a few days, Caroline would be secretly celebrating what would have been John Sanderson's fortieth birthday, which was the real reason she wanted to give Teddy a special gift this year.

"I'd really like to meet the Brantleys some time," Juliana said to her lunch date. "If they're that special to you, I'm sure Lorenzo and I would love them."

"You know, that would be really great. Teddy is about Ricky's age, and I think they'd hit it off. Sophia loves everybody, so that wouldn't be a problem, either," Caroline said as she speared her fresh salad.

"Maybe we could do that sometime. Have they been to New York recently?" Juliana asked as she bit into a slice of melon.

"No, they don't have a lot of money to spare. I go to Tennessee every chance I get to check in on them. It's been hard to do it regularly since I've been in law school."

Juliana nodded, "How's school going, anyway. I don't see you much anymore since you're always studying or working."

Caroline wiped her mouth with the black linen napkin. "It's going well. I should graduate in December. Perry thinks I should join the firm as a junior attorney when I pass the bar. That will be an uncomfortable transition, probably. I've been their 'go-to' paralegal for so long. I can't imagine anyone would want to take direction from *me*," she laughed. "It was a hard enough adjustment after I became a 'Norton.' It's taken a while for me to prove myself to some of those nay-sayers. I think they secretly took bets on how long Perry and I would make it."

"I wouldn't doubt it. People didn't understand the connection Lorenzo and I had after we lost our spouses. People actually commented that we had Papa kill them off so we could get together! Imagine!"

Caroline shook her head in amazement.

"I'm glad all that's behind us and the FBI guy finally solved his cases. I was so afraid we'd have to go to trial at some point, and we didn't want to have to join witness protection. But you know, the biggest surprise of all was the FBI mole. I had no idea he was an undercover agent. If it hadn't been for him, some of those loose ends might have never been completely resolved. With his inside information plus what Lorenzo and I provided, all their special cases are now closed." Juliana paused to take a sip of Perrier.

"I wish they could have found Lorenzo's kidnapped baby, but the FBI said they ran into a brick wall. It's considered a cold case now." Juliana looked disappointed, but started to smile again as she continued with good news. "Lorenzo and I have our passports back, and we're free to travel. That's a wonderful feeling. I'd really like to take a trip or something and maybe even take Mama and the kids," Juliana declared.

"How is Lucinda? I haven't heard much about her lately. Now that the estate has been settled—and we were glad to find your father had put everything in your name instead of his—I suppose you're keeping your mother's lifestyle up?"

"Oh, yeah. But Mama had her own money, anyway. She came from a rich family, the Bellinis. They're all rolling in dough they made from an import company. But I asked Mama to stay in the Southampton house with me and Lorenzo so she could be near her new grandkids. She loves them so much, and they make her happy. They make me happy, too. I only wish Lorenzo and I could have one of our own, you know?" Juliana replied as she imagined what a beautiful baby she and Lorenzo would make.

"Yeah, I guess. Parenting wasn't in the cards for me, I suppose. Perry certainly doesn't want a baby at his age, so I'll have to be satisfied splurging on my godson. Which reminds me, we need to get going if we're gonna hit all the good stores before they close," Caroline remarked as she motioned for the waiter to bring her the check.

* * * * * *

When the phone rang, Caroline answered at her desk in the law office.

"Caroline, it's Juliana. Guess what I just heard?" she teased.

"What?" Caroline said, still reading through the file in front of her.

"There's going to be a new cruise geared just for kids! Cartoon characters will be on board— people dressed up like cartoon characters, I mean—to cater to the children. The adults will be able to do their own thing while the kids are off on planned adventures. It sounds like paradise to me, since we haven't been anywhere since we got married. I thought maybe this would be the perfect opportunity for you to bring your godson and

the Brantleys. We'd really love to meet them. If money's a problem for them, I can help out," Juliana said excitedly.

"Money's not an issue. I can handle that, but when is this cruise? I'm already prepping for finals next week."

"Don't worry. It's not until July. It's selling out quick, though. The boat leaves from Florida somewhere, so we'll have to coordinate travel plans. Talk to Perry and see what he says. If you guys are up to a little excursion, it'd be a wonderful break for all of us. And I really hope the Brantleys can make it, too. I'd really like to meet this special little godson," Juliana said before she hung up the phone.

Caroline's mind started working in high gear. Perhaps now would be the perfect time for a trip with the Giordanos. She could probably convince Perry that they needed this break, and a cruise might be the perfect way to travel.

* * * * * *

Once Caroline had a chance to sit down with Perry to relay what Juliana had proposed, he was clearly interested in the cruise.

She called Stella Brantley to see what she thought of the idea and was pleasantly surprised at how quickly she agreed.

"Oh, Caroline! That sounds ideal! Doug will agree, too, just leave that to me. It's time for Teddy to socialize with other children his age. Ever since he came along, I couldn't bear to leave him to go back to work. He definitely needs to interact more with other kids," Stella happily responded. "But, I feel really bad about you footing the bill for all of us. This has to be a really expensive trip."

"Not a problem, Stella. You know that John gave me enough money to splurge on Teddy. He wanted to be a part of Teddy's life, even though he

wasn't able to see it for himself. He and Doug always had a special bond, and John was so happy when he heard about the baby," she said, skirting the truth that she had sworn never to reveal to Stella.

"Well, if you're sure. I can't wait to tell Doug! It shouldn't be a problem for him to schedule his vacation for July. He almost always takes off around that time, anyway. This year, it'll be a more exciting vacation for us all, thanks to you...and John," Stella answered.

* * * * * *

As promised, Juliana made all the travel arrangements for the entire group. She had gotten Stella's phone number from Juliana, and the two had formed a long-distance friendship even before they officially met at the port in Tampa.

The cruise ship was brand new, having made its inaugural voyage the week before. The Giordanos had booked a large stateroom with plenty of room for two additional child-size cots. Its private balcony was situated on the port side of the ship. Juliana was afraid for the children to play on the balcony unless they were supervised, but Lorenzo told her the only people who ever fell off a cruise ship were the ones that intentionally jumped.

The Nortons and the Brantleys had similar rooms, located a few doors down from each other but on the starboard side of the ship, opposite from the Giordanos. Their balconies were private, as well. Stella had hoped that their room would be next door to the Norton's, but that particular room had already been booked.

According to Juliana's schedule, the families were to have breakfast together each day before dropping off the children at the onboard day camp. The adults would spend their next few hours doing whatever they wanted as separate couples. By lunch, they would regroup and spend the remainder of the day together. Juliana had planned everything out, and

the Nortons and Brantleys thought she had done a superb job of creating an acceptable itinerary.

By the end of day one of the four day adventure, they all agreed the cruise was amazingly peaceful and very relaxing. The children were fascinated with the life-sized cartoon characters that catered to their every whim. The adults were getting along very well, basking in the tropical sunlight as they sailed toward the Mexican coast. Everyone agreed that this vacation was exactly what they had needed.

* * * * * *

After two days of nothing but relaxation, the adults were ready to party. Juliana tracked down the Activities Director and discovered that an adult-only party was on the ship's agenda beginning at ten o'clock that evening on the Lido Deck. It was a casual affair and would feature a band with dancing under the stars. Light hors d'oeuvres would be served, along with plenty of liquor and wine.

There was nothing to be concerned about regarding the children. They would be entertained at a group sleepover hosted by their favorite cartoon characters in the same area as the day camp was located.

The Activities Director and the cruise line had thought of everything. There was something for everyone on this unique adventure.

* * * * * *

Before they went to dinner, the group had pictures made together, then as separate couples, for their memory books. It was apparent to the photographer that these couples were very good friends. He would later remember that they all seemed extremely happy.

At dinner that evening, the three couples sat at the Captain's table. Lorenzo had been drinking single malt scotch during the entire trip, but

tonight he appeared to be drinking more heavily than the previous two evenings. After a while, he began to slur his words, and Juliana was visibly embarrassed by him. He knocked over a water glass that had barely missed her lap and started pontificating about politics, a discussion no one wanted to join. Finally, he got up from the table, nearly tripping on the chair leg, and announced, "Pardon me, folks. I need to take a piss."

Humiliated, Juliana started to rise from her seat to follow her drunken husband. Caroline grabbed her hand and whispered, "Don't. He'll be fine." Juliana sat down again, trying to overcome her sudden disgust for Lorenzo's behavior.

Lorenzo's abrupt exit from the table had garnered the attention of an elderly woman seated a few tables over. She had been seated with her back to the Captain's table; however, when Lorenzo stumbled out, the lady turned her head and peered over her glasses toward the Captain's table. She eyed Juliana with an air of superiority, as if she labeled her "idiot" for associating with the drunken man. Juliana noticed the woman's stare, and hung her head shamefully. The lady turned her attention back to the conversation at her own table, ignoring the Captain's table through the rest of dinner.

When Lorenzo didn't return within fifteen minutes, Juliana excused herself to go look for her husband. Having already finished their meals, the Nortons and Brantleys volunteered to help her locate Lorenzo, but Juliana declined their help. She believed he was probably sleeping off his scotch in their stateroom. If that wasn't the case, she'd let them know and then she'd request their help.

The Brantleys and the Nortons returned to their rooms, awaiting word from Juliana about Lorenzo's status. They weren't betting that the Giordanos would be attending the evening party with them.

* * * * * *

"Lorenzo, for God's sake! What in the hell are you doing? You've embarrassed us all. No one will ever want to socialize with us again. Can't you control your drinking? What's gotten into you?" Juliana yelled. Her husband had been snoring on top of their stateroom bed, pants unzipped and shirt out. She hoped he had made it to the bathroom before he got on the bed.

"Huh? Leave me alone, Juliana. It's been a long time since I've had this much to drink, and I want to enjoy every damned minute of the buzz."

"I hope you enjoy the hangover you're going to have tomorrow," she said as she stormed out.

* * * * * *

Juliana knocked on the Nortons' stateroom door, hoping she was still in their good graces despite Lorenzo's actions.

"Come on in, Juliana," Caroline said as she opened the door to her friend. "Did you find Lorenzo?" she asked.

"Yeah, he's lying on top of the bed in our room. He said he wants to enjoy his drunken buzz, so I left him there to wallow in it."

Caroline chuckled as Perry emerged from the bathroom. "Ladies, talking about me behind my back?" he grinned.

"No, but Lorenzo is probably out for the night. Would you guys still like to go to the party? I don't mind being a fifth wheel," Juliana offered.

"You know what? I think I'd like to spend some time with Teddy, if the Brantleys don't mind. Maybe we should gather the kids and go down to the play area—spend some quality time with the little ones. I don't

particularly feel like drinking anymore, I've had plenty to eat, and I've always been a terrible dancer. What do you say?" Caroline inquired.

Perry nodded his agreement. Juliana shrugged her shoulders and said, "Why not!"

Caroline smiled. "Good. Let me call the Brantleys and see what they have to say. If they want to stay in, maybe they'll let Perry and me take Teddy with us."

* * * * * *

By nine o'clock, the group—minus Lorenzo—sat watching three young children race around a slide as they played tag. It was amazing how the ship had been designed with children in mind. Even this late in the evening, the lighting was so well placed that it seemed like daytime. There was playground equipment, sand boxes, hopscotch areas, and all sorts of entertainment just for kids. Whoever had this grand idea was a genius, or so they thought as they watched their favorite toddlers enjoy their own slice of paradise.

Teddy approached his Aunt Caroline and playfully squirted her with a water pistol he had in his oversized pocket. "It's my own fault," she declared as she laughed with Teddy. "I bought that toy for him before we boarded the boat. I just didn't know he had a license to carry!" she laughed. Teddy giggled, and turned to squirt the rest of the loaded water directly on Ricky's shirt.

"Oh, no! Teddy, don't get Ricky wet!" Caroline shouted as Teddy laughed even harder. Ricky thought it was funny, too. Sophia was glad she had avoided the water altogether. Stella and Doug laughed as Caroline realized a water gun was not the best toy choice for an unpredictable child.

"Now what do we do, huh? I'm damp, Ricky's wet, but you're bone dry, little man. That's not fair, is it?" Caroline teased as she playfully chided her godson. "I think you two boys should take your shirts off and play in the sand. No more water guns for you, mister! Moms, what do you say? It's still awfully hot out here tonight. Shirtless sand box time for the boys?"

"Yeah. It's all right for Teddy to play without his shirt. He does it back home a lot," Stella said.

"I'd rather he not have on a wet shirt, so… okay. Ricky, come to Mama and let me get your shirt off," Juliana said.

* * * * * *

Lorenzo felt like an ass. He knew he'd acted inappropriately. To make matters worse, he did it publically. He regretted it, but *what's done is done*, he thought.

He had taken a long, cold shower after Juliana left the room. He had some coffee and tried to get himself in good enough condition to meet the group at the party. He hoped he could find them somewhere near the Lido deck and make amends. He still felt a little bit of a buzz, but it was manageable to a long-time drinker like him. All he had to do was apologize, and all would be forgiven.

* * * * * *

The children were screaming with delight when Uncle Perry tried to play hopscotch with them. They made fun of him, telling him he was too old and too slow. Perry acted as though he were offended, then surprised them with a growl and a sprint in their direction, sending them running in escape. They were having a blast, and Perry seemed to be having the most fun.

"Daddy!" Sophia yelled, and sprinted away from the group toward an approaching shadow. When he was closer, Lorenzo stooped down and caught his daughter as she leaped into his arms. He carried her back to the play area.

"Feeling better, old man?" Perry asked as Lorenzo approached him.

"Yeah, and guys…I'm sorry about that. I guess I overdid it with the scotch today. In the heat and all, I was a prime candidate to be a drunken jerk. I apologize," he said as he tried to hug Juliana. She stepped away from him, obviously not accepting his apology.

Doug smiled at Lorenzo and said, "Hey, it's not a problem. We've all been there, man." Stella smiled uncomfortably, wondering what she should say, if anything. She chose to stay quiet.

"Thanks, guys. Now what are we playing? Hide and Seek? Cowboys and Indians?" Lorenzo asked the children. Only Sophia was interested in playing with Lorenzo. The boys had discovered the sand box again.

At that moment, Lorenzo looked closely at the two boys as they played side by side. For a moment, he thought the Brantley boy was Ricky. Their heads had similar shapes, and they even had the same build. Both had long waists and long legs. He could tell they were both going to be tall like….him. He stepped closer, and as Teddy leaned forward to pick up a sand shovel, his shorts slipped down below his waistline. Then he saw it. It was right there in the center of the Brantley boy's back. The Giordano birthmark. The little red diamond-shaped birthmark.

Lorenzo stood straight up, then turned to look at Stella and Doug. His gaze went straight to Caroline who smirked a little as she formed a menacing smile. Lorenzo turned abruptly and stepped in the sand box with the toddlers. He picked up Teddy and held him at arm's length, looking him straight in the face.

425

"What are you doing, Lorenzo?" Doug demanded to know, as Stella ran toward her son. She took him from Lorenzo's arms and carried him protectively back to her seat. By now Teddy was becoming upset, wondering what had just happened. Ricky was still playing in the sand box, but turned to look at Teddy as he started to whimper in Stella's lap.

"I ... for a minute there ... I... I don't know. I think I thought your boy was Ricky," he stuttered. Juliana moved toward him, but he held out his hand in a 'stop' gesture. "I'm fine. I was just confused. I'm going back to the room, I think," Lorenzo muttered. "I'm sorry."

As Lorenzo started to turn away, Caroline made a risky move. She ran after Lorenzo and stopped him in an area the group could see but not hear. She said quietly, "I know what you're thinking.

I will explain everything tonight. Meet me in my room at midnight, but don't say anything to anyone else. Perry won't be there—I'll arrange it. Don't tell Juliana, or I swear you'll never know what happened to your son." Peripherally, she saw Juliana approaching.

"Follow my lead, Lorenzo," she said quietly, then started again more loudly. "Lorenzo, you have to do something about your uncontrolled drinking. I know it's hard, but you almost scared Teddy to death back there. If you need help, there are several programs that I know about that will gladly help you," she declared.

Juliana stalled a few feet from them, then slowly approached them. "You should listen to Caroline, Lorenzo. She knows what she's talking about. Ever since we've been together, you've been drinking too much. One day it's gonna interfere with your work like it's starting to interfere with our marriage. Then you'll have nothing left." Juliana marched back to the playground area, leaving Caroline and Lorenzo alone again.

"Midnight. Be there," Caroline warned as she left a stunned Lorenzo standing in the shadows.

* * * * * *

Lorenzo was exactly on time. At the stroke of midnight, he lightly tapped on Caroline's stateroom door. When she opened the door, Lorenzo's expression was unreadable. He looked like a little boy about to be reprimanded by his father. Then again, maybe that was a guilty look. It didn't matter either way to Caroline.

"Where's Perry?" he asked as he entered the room, looking around quickly.

"I told you I'd take care of that. He's playing cards with Doug Brantley a few doors down. He won't be back here for another hour, so we have plenty of time for a private chat."

Wasting no time, Lorenzo asked, "Is the Brantley boy my son?" His eyes looked angry and hopeful at the same time.

"What if he is? What would you do about it?" Caroline teased.

"I never thought I'd see him again. I thought he was lost to me. I don't know what I should do," he answered.

"Let's have a quick drink out on the balcony. It's such a nice night, and the sound of the ocean is soothing to me. I have a story to tell you, and I think you'll be interested in hearing it." She picked up a glass and a bottle of scotch—the kind Lorenzo usually drank. She wouldn't be joining him in his drink.

She led the way through the sliding door and pointed to a chair where Lorenzo was to sit. She dropped the glass, breaking off a big chunk of its side, as she juggled the bottle trying not to drop it. "Great, Caroline. You're a klutz," she said aloud. "Sorry, Lorenzo," she said as she picked up the broken pieces of glass. "Hold this bottle 'til I get back with another glass."

She slipped back inside her stateroom and within a few seconds, she returned to the balcony. Holding a fresh glass inconspicuously laced with chloral hydrate, more commonly known as a "mickey," she took the bottle from Lorenzo's hand and poured him a generous serving of scotch. When she handed it to him, he swallowed it at once and held out the glass for another serving.

"Are you sure you want more?" Caroline asked as she sparingly poured more scotch in his glass. "You need to be alert when I tell you what I know," she said.

As he gulped down the second scotch, Caroline began. "My name is really Caroline Sanderson. My ex-husband, John, found your baby in Juliana's wrecked car and took the infant to the Brantley's to raise. Are you following me, Lorenzo?" she asked as his eyes appeared to be getting droopy.

"Listen to me, Lorenzo! Teddy Brantley *is* your son, but you'll never see him again. Because of you—directly or indirectly— my ex-husband is dead, my brother is dead, your own cousin and wife are both dead, and Juliana's mother almost lost her life. You're no better than DeLuca and you know it. You are *scum*, you worthless motherfucker, and you're gonna pay dearly for all you've done. You think you got off scot-free by helping the FBI. You're wrong, you bastard. Dead wrong," she told him.

He was struggling to understand. He didn't usually get this drunk this quickly. *She must have drugged me!* He thought she said he'd killed someone, but he didn't kill anybody but the Viper. "Did you say Teddy is my son?" he asked groggily.

"Yes, you asshole. And you'll never live to see him or Ricky grow up."

"Wh..hat?" Lorenzo said as he started to stand. Just as he made it up to lean forward on the rail, Perry emerged from the stateroom and joined them on the balcony.

"Did you and Caroline have a good talk, Lorenzo?" Perry asked.

"I thought you were..." Lorenzo started before he began to slump down.

Perry caught him and pulled Lorenzo up where he could lean across the balcony rail. "Caroline, dear, could you help me here, please?" he asked as Caroline made her way to the other side of Lorenzo.

"Let's see if we can make him comfortable, shall we?" Perry said. Caroline smiled.

Perry said, "All right, on the count of three: one...two...THREE."

They looked at each other as Lorenzo tumbled over the side of the railing. After a few seconds, a loud splash could be heard, but the black water revealed nothing but bubbles and waves.

Seconds later, Perry tossed the contaminated drink glass into the dark ocean as the ship sailed on.

* * * * *

The snooty older lady from the dining room was standing in the hallway when Perry and Caroline emerged from their stateroom. They were headed to one of the all-night lounges for a late drink when she appeared.

Always the gentleman, Perry said, "Good evening," as they came within a few feet of her.

"Good evening, counselor. May I join you two for a nightcap? I'm buying," she said and smiled broadly.

"Why, of course, Genevieve. We have wonderful news to share with you about your 'late' son-in-law," Perry chuckled. Caroline gave her a quick kiss on the cheek and grinned happily.

"By the way, how's that new husband of yours? FBI Chief McNeal?" Perry asked teasingly.

"He is wonderful, thank you, darling. And very grateful that you were so kind to help me while I was hiding in that awful Witness Protection Program. If it hadn't been for you two, I'd have gone crazy. Caroline, you've been a blessing, sharing pictures of my three grandchildren with me. It's been such a joy to watch the children playing on this cruise, although it's been hard to stay out of Lorenzo's line of sight most of the time. At least now that won't be a problem anymore, thanks to you," Genevieve Parker said as she hugged Caroline again.

Caroline walked arm in arm with Genevieve, while Perry followed closely behind. They had so much to talk about, and even more to celebrate.

EPILOGUE

Many Years Later

It was a grand day for the families of Theodore Edward Brantley and Enrico Salvatore Giordano. They sat patiently in the audience as the commencement ceremony at Columbia Law School continued, listening to the speeches of well-known faculty members and their guest speaker, a Supreme Court Judge. Theodore Brantley was the class valedictorian, and the salutatorian, missing the valedictory position by just a hair, was Ricky Giordano. The families couldn't have been more proud.

Caroline glanced at the beaming faces of the family members that surrounded her. She couldn't help but think about all the events that had taken place throughout the years and how they had culminated into this important moment in the lives of the Giordano twins.

Sitting next to her was Perry Norton, who had once been thought of as her husband. In reality, Caroline and Perry had changed her name legally to Norton when he adopted her.

An official marriage never took place. The 'fake' marriage was performed in front of a large audience, but the officiator was a friend of Perry's from his childhood. He wasn't an ordained minister, and no marriage license had ever been issued. Nor was the 'marriage' ever consummated. Both Perry and Caroline felt toward each other as parent and child. Perry grew to love Caroline as the daughter he never had and supported her as such.

Perry had managed to convince Officers Hopkins and Davis that Caroline was not aware of her 'brother's' situation and had been with him the entire time the crime at the motel was taking place. After that scare, especially when they so urgently prepared their fake alibi about dropping

off the ice cream, he realized Caroline was strong in her own right and could think on her feet. He believed she would make an excellent trial attorney. He urged her to pursue a law degree and pass the bar, and now she was a full partner at Walker, Harrington, Norton, Stone & Norton. She had surpassed his expectations in her successful career. He couldn't be prouder of his adopted daughter.

On the other side of Perry Norton sat his wife of almost twenty years, Lucinda DeLuca Norton. Perry and Lucinda had fallen in love during the early 1990's and planned to marry right before the terrible accident that Vincenzo DeLuca had caused. During the period after Vincenzo's death, Perry had made frequent visits to the DeLuca home under the pretense of handling the estate. He spoke with Juliana regularly, of course, but always made time to go chat with her mother. She was the only person—besides Genevieve Parker—who knew the truth about his relationship with Caroline. They waited patiently and secretly until the day all the DeLuca crimes were officially solved and Lorenzo Giordano was no longer a problem.

Doug and Stella Brantley sat on the opposite side of Caroline, their benefactor (through her ex-husband's endowment) and to whom they were forever grateful for partially paying for their son's expensive but valuable education at Columbia. The other benefactor, Genevieve Parker, was apparently just a very generous friend of the Norton family. Stella never understood fully why Genevieve felt so compelled to help support Teddy in his pursuit of education, but she was grateful, nonetheless. Genevieve, as a part of her pact with Perry and Caroline, agreed never to divulge her family relationship to Teddy or to Stella, who still believed Teddy was her biological child. The arrangement worked well for everyone.

After the tragic accidental death and unsolved disappearance of Lorenzo on the 1998 cruise, Juliana depended more and more on Caroline and Perry to help her through the red tape of probate and estate handling. Of

course, Lucinda encouraged Juliana to maintain a relationship with the Nortons, advising her that she needed to be around people who cared about her. As a result, the Nortons were frequently in and out of the DeLuca/Giordano house for years to come.

Ever since their first vacation together, the boys had become fast friends. Juliana and Caroline made special efforts to keep them close throughout their childhoods, making trips to Tennessee or inviting the Brantleys to New York for extended stays. By the time the boys finished high school in their respective states, they had emphatically planned to become college roommates, regardless of what school they had to attend to make it happen. Luckily, both boys were smart enough to go wherever they wanted. When they chose Columbia, everyone was happy. Caroline had already informed the Brantleys that Teddy's education expense was a gift from John and Genevieve. Of course, money had never been an issue when it came to the Giordano children.

Sophia had blossomed into a lovely young woman. Now in her mid-twenties, she caught the eye of almost every eligible bachelor in New York. However, much to Juliana's surprise, Sophia had a head for business. Juliana had struggled for years attempting to keep the DeLuca legitimate businesses alive. While attending New York University's School of Business, Sophia started dabbling in the family business matters. Attempting to help her stepmother keep their business afloat, Sophia had initiated several corporate structural changes to help them maintain a steady income flow while decreasing their tax liabilities. Once she had a handle on that particular issue, she began to view the business segments as an enterprise that needed updating. Before she graduated from college, she became the President and Chief Executive Officer of DeLuca Enterprises. Now that graduation was behind her, she focused totally on business, projecting a whopping 200% growth within the next five years.

And of course, Genevieve Parker McNeal sat beside her husband, Alex McNeal. She often thought about the night she was abducted from the

Waldorf. What a terrifying night that had been. If the FBI informant hadn't been in the woods watching the construction site with night vision goggles, Genevieve might well have ended up at the bottom of the well with her daughter. God rest Cathy's tormented soul.

It was amazing how brave Gino Pucci had been that night. He managed to overtake her abductor as the man was dragging Genevieve from the car. After Gino knocked out the assailant, he pulled the man into the well where a dead Genevieve was meant to go. She stood there, petrified and speechless, while Gino explained how he would help her. He told her to get back in the car, and he would drive her to the FBI. She told him she knew Alexander McNeal, and Gino promised to take her to him. When she opened the front passenger door, she saw her Chanel purse lying there. Gino told her he would get her new identification if she would forfeit her purse to the cause. He said it would help lead the police to the bodies in the well. When she agreed, he carefully placed it on the parking lot area immediately in front of the old office building. He went inside the building, and when he came out, the building was on fire. They made a hasty departure from the site as the smoke curled upward to the sky. Before she knew it, she was crying in the arms of her future husband.

Yes, the family had conquered it all: death, murder, kidnapping, lies, more lies, unfairness, and finally justice. They stood the test of time and proved the old saying to be true: "Only the strong survive."

* * * * * *

The entire Giordano-Norton-Brantley-McNeal group gathered at the Southampton estate as soon as the boys' commencement ceremonies had concluded. For a short while, the two new law school graduates had been noticeably absent from the middle of the festivities. They were missing out on the bar-b-qued ribs, pork, and chicken, not to mention swimming in the Olympic sized pool that had become the entertainment focal point of Ricky and Sophia during their teenage years.

When the two young men graced the family with their full attention, they smiled wickedly as they proceeded to the temporary stage that had been erected for the celebration. Ricky stepped up first, reaching out to give Teddy a hand as he stepped up.

"Could I have your attention, please?" Ricky asked the crowd. "Silence."

"I just want to thank you all for being here, honoring me and Teddy like this. It's been rough sometimes, but it was worth it to be standing here today." The audience clapped as Ricky and Teddy smiled at them.

"Today is a great day for another reason," Ricky started. "Today my sister, Sophia, asked me to officially become a part of the family business, and I have accepted her offer effective immediately. As of today, you're looking at the Executive Vice President and Chief Operating Officer of DeLuca Enterprises."

The crowd erupted in a loud round of applause. Ricky took a theatrical bow before starting to speak again.

"And as my first act as Executive Vice President and COO, I would now like to extend an offer of employment to Teddy Brantley to be DeLuca Enterprises' new Vice President and Chief General Counsel. What do you say, Teddy?" he asked as he shook Teddy's hand. Both young men were grinning from ear to ear.

The crowd erupted in a second loud round of applause and cheers. Ricky and Teddy beamed with satisfaction and happiness before the entire family.

"I say yes, of course!" More applause. The graduates raised their clasped hands in unison, high above their heads. When the crowd's roar died down, Teddy continued.

"But I also want to say this to you, Ricky, and all your family. I have never had a brother—or sister, for that matter. As an only child, I never knew

what I was missing until we became childhood friends. I've never felt attached to anyone like I have with you and Sophia...sorry, Mom," he chuckled, as he glanced toward Stella and winked. "So, I want to thank you for being the brother I never had, and I'm grateful to you and your whole family for giving me this awesome opportunity. I won't disappoint you," he said as he emotionally embraced Ricky.

Teddy pointed to specific members of the crowd before he stepped down from the stage. "Mom, Dad, you're the greatest. I love you both with all my heart." Teddy choked back his emotions as Stella beamed with adoration. Doug dabbed at the tears rolling down his cheeks.

"Aunt Caroline, I love you. You're my inspiration. Thank you for always looking out for me. I wouldn't be here today if it weren't for you," Teddy said with tears now pooling in his eyes.

"Oh, yes you would, darling boy. Indeed you would," Caroline whispered as she blew her godson a kiss, unsuccessfully trying to hold back her own tears of pride.

ACKNOWLEDGEMENTS

To all my dear friends and family who took the time to help me with this book, I am eternally grateful:

Brenda Malone, your editing advice and suggestions were spot-on! Your input made the book so much more reader-friendly. I sincerely thank you for your efforts and valuable insight.

Lisa Ferris, I know how hard it is for you to take time from your busy schedule to read a draft manuscript, but you did it for your dear old Mother! Thank you, darling daughter, for your feedback, encouragement and support.

Sandi Crowell, as President and founder of my non-existent fan club, you deserve special recognition. Your encouragement and positive inspiration have kept me going even when I didn't think I could write another word. You are an amazing friend and an excellent cheerleader! *"TO THE BEACH!"*

Glenda McNeal, it was a real treat to receive your positive feedback on the first draft manuscript of this book. Thank you from the bottom of my heart for taking time to review *Sacrificial Sins* and for our everlasting friendship. Even though we are sisters through marriage, you are so much more to me than that!

Chuck Creasy, what an honor to have you design the cover of *Sacrificial Sins!* I can never thank you enough for your superb artistic contribution of this original watercolor masterpiece. I hope everyone who reads this book will visit fineartamerica.com to view and purchase their own Chuck Creasy original masterpiece!

Sacrificial Sins

My sincere appreciation goes to all the other supporters and reviewers who have contributed to the final creation of this book:

Joe & Rosemary Finch   **Daniel Baker**

Faye Martin Crews   **Jennifer Carr**

Keith Gaines   **Marnie Creasy**

And a special thank you to all the exceptional members of the **<u>Mary Gaines Books</u> <u>FaceBook Group</u>** who continually provide me with inspiration and encouragement.

You guys are the *BEST*!

Sacrificial Sins

I dedicate the following passage to my biggest fan, my best friend, and the love of my life, **Samuel Gaines:**

"If you live to be a hundred,

    I want to live to be a hundred minus one day,

        So, I never have to live without you."

— *Winnie the Pooh* - A. A. Milne

ABOUT THE AUTHOR

Sacrificial Sins is the second work of fiction in the "Sins Volumes" written by Mary Elizabeth Gaines.

Her first novel, *Buried Sins,* is a standalone mystery set during the 1950s in her hometown of Shelbyville, Tennessee.

Sacrificial Sins is the prequel to her forthcoming third novel, *Twin Sins,* which is expected to be completed by winter, 2018.

Mary lives in Knoxville, Tennessee with her husband Sam. She enjoys spending as much time as possible with their children and grandchildren, as well as playing with the family dogs, Amos and Gypsy. Mary is an avid reader, a music enthusiast, and she loves vacationing at the beach. She is retired from her management career as a government contractor employee in Oak Ridge.

For more information about Mary and her novels, visit her website at marygainesbooks.com or join her Facebook group, *Mary Gaines Books.*

CPSIA information can be obtained
at www.ICGtesting.com
Printed in the USA
BVHW070832240523
664715BV00005B/50